Praise for

THE
SHROUD
CONSPIRACY

"*The Shroud Conspiracy* is an absolutely brilliant thriller! This riveting, intrigue-filled mystery is like nothing you've read before. Once you start, you won't be able to put it down."

—Brad Thor, #1 *New York Times* bestselling
author of *Foreign Agent*

"Marvelously written and detailed, so exquisitely paced, so vibrantly entertaining that it leads me to ask, 'So when's the movie being made?'"

—Greg Gutfeld of FOX News's *The Five*

"A fast-paced story, with some great twists, it is a page-turner from beginning to end! John Heubusch jumps onto the writing stage with a huge first book. Move over, Dan Brown, you have some competition. . . . A great read!"

—Scott McEwen, coauthor of *American Sniper*

"Indiana Jones meets *The Da Vinci Code*. Definitely one of the most intensely exciting thrillers you'll read all year."

—Ted Bell, bestselling author of *Patriot*

"Faith, science, and human frailty are all knit together in John Heubusch's new thriller, *The Shroud Conspiracy*. Bouncing from Mumbai to Rome, and Geneva to the Eastern Shore, this is a novel you cannot put down and won't want to miss."

—Michael Duffy, coauthor of *The Presidents Club*

"Thrilling for its plausibility in today's technology-driven world . . . this book demands a sequel!"

—*Library Journal*

"An action-packed thriller with enough twists and turns to keep fans of Dan Brown or Brad Meltzer happy, enough science to keep the skeptics appeased, and enough ethical quandaries to keep the philosophers among us well engaged."

—Steve Forbes

"Intense and intriguing."

—Booklist

JOHN D.
HEUBUSCH

THE
SHROUD
CONSPIRACY

A NOVEL

HOWARD BOOKS
AN IMPRINT OF SIMON & SCHUSTER, INC.

New York London Toronto Sydney New Delhi

Howard Books
An Imprint of Simon & Schuster, Inc.
1230 Avenue of the Americas
New York, NY 10020

First Howard Books paperback edition February 2018

HOWARD and colophon are trademarks of Simon & Schuster, Inc.

For information about special discounts for bulk purchases, please contact Simon & Schuster Special Sales at 1-866-506-1949 or business@simonandschuster.com.

The Simon & Schuster Speakers Bureau can bring authors to your live event. For more information, or to book an event, contact the Simon & Schuster Speakers Bureau at 1-866-248-3049 or visit our website at www.simonspeakers.com.

Manufactured in the United States of America

10   9   8   7   6   5   4   3   2   1

Library of Congress Cataloging-in-Publication Data is available.

ISBN 978-1-5011-5570-3
ISBN 978-1-5011-5692-2 (pbk)
ISBN 978-1-5011-5571-0 (ebook)

To the love of my life.
To my mad and beautiful and soulful Sicilian.
Marcella, Sciatu miu.

Peter got up and ran to the tomb. Bending over,
he saw the strips of linen lying by themselves,
and he went away, wondering to himself what had happened.

LUKE 24:12

THE
SHROUD
CONSPIRACY

PART 1

PART 1

CHAPTER 1

Rome, Italy—The Vatican
February 2014

Father Parenti had a problem with swearing, and this morning in the Vatican's sanctum sanctorum of sacred books was no different.

"Porco diavolo!" he muttered to himself, cursing the devil. Then he furtively looked around to see if anyone was within earshot.

The little Catholic priest had fallen onto the ancient floorboards and knocked himself near unconscious when a makeshift shelf he'd napped on collapsed under his weight. A stabbing pain that ran from the small of his back to the base of his neck was so intense that he struggled to breathe. He lay amid a sprawled heap of priceless books. Once his perch had tumbled, three massive rows of shelves in line with it had fallen like dominoes and spilled forth an even greater avalanche of tomes that now lay in the aisle between the stacks. He was in agony, half-buried by splintered shelving and mounds of medieval volumes, some with pages irreparably torn. A musty smell, freed from hundreds of newly awakened texts that had been undisturbed for centuries, wafted into the surrounding corridors.

"Porco diavolo!" he swore again as he gasped for breath and attempted to get up.

"Porco diavolo?" A voice boomed the question from behind a bookcase that still stood thirty feet from the wreckage. "This is the end of it! The end of it, Father Parenti! The second time this year!"

Parenti looked up from the cold library floor toward the wraith-like figure in priest's vestments that glared down at him in disgust. He closed his eyes and prayed for a miracle, knowing there was going to be real trouble this time. Of all the librarians to stumble upon this disaster, it just had to be the prefect himself.

Six feet five inches tall and all of 140 pounds, Father Antonio Barsanti had been a Brother of the Charitable Order for forty-two years and prefect of the Vatican's library for ten of those. But the attitude he displayed toward his flock of beleaguered researchers had proven to be anything but charitable, Parenti thought.

"I think I've hurt something. I'm sure it's my spine," he groaned, desperate to gain sympathy from the dark silhouette that towered above him.

"Rise up, *gobbo*," the prefect demanded as he leaned in only inches from Parenti's nose. The smell of his cheap cologne and a trace of Communion wine on his breath enveloped them both, and Parenti could only cringe.

He could tell by Barsanti's choice of words that his punishment was sure to exceed the crime. He was, indeed, *il padre gobbo*—the hunchback priest. But this was the first time the prefect had hurled the epithet that had been only whispered by others since Parenti left the seminary years ago. He cast his gaze slightly over the prefect's shoulder and focused his eyes on a distant square of brilliant light for inspiration. It was one of the magnificent stained-glass windows near the library's ceiling, one he had studied a thousand times before. The glass bore the image of the Third Station of the Cross, that of Jesus falling for the first time as he ascended Calvary toward crucifixion. Parenti considered for a moment the similarity to his own predicament and began to gather his strength.

He turned his head defiantly from the prefect and flailed his arms to free himself from the mountain of books. Parenti could tell that Barsanti watched in amusement as he struggled in vain to wriggle off the books that surrounded his misshapen back. He was like an overturned tortoise, stuck on his shell. After several futile attempts, he was yanked by his throat and felt himself being elevated from the back of his nooselike collar and pulled into a kneeling position by the prefect's sinewy hands. He knew what was coming next and dared not look up. He had been warned about naps on the job before, and his swearing only doubled the trouble.

"You will gather several archivists to help repair this, Parenti. You will personally inspect every shelf. Every book. Every page!" Barsanti said, his voice chilly and imperious. "And when you are done, you will meet me in Cardinal Ponti's study for reprisal. You will beg for forgiveness, *gobbo*. It will not be granted. And before evening vespers, the Papal Palace will be only a memory to you."

Parenti raised his head and watched in terrified silence as the lanky priest turned and slowly faded into the dark distance. Then Parenti slumped to the floor, quietly considered his predicament, and cursed his luck. Rubbing the remnants of sleep from his eyes, he looked around him. *What a beautiful, miserable prison*, he thought. *At least I will finally be rid of it.*

Flanked at its entrance by the pope's colorfully festooned Swiss Guard, the Vatican Library held more than fifty miles of shelves, stacked in narrow rows thirty feet high, that he navigated like a mouse in a maze. From floor to ceiling, they formed an endless, twisting puzzle filled with priceless knowledge beneath a canopy of splendid frescoes that rivaled those in the nearby Sistine Chapel.

Parenti would often roam the stacks on lonely research errands and crane his deformed neck as best he could toward the glorious heights, sometimes losing his way in the labyrinth below the biblical scenes that peered down at him from above. Of the many divine spectacles painted resplendently across the ceiling from wall to wall, he had chosen three favorites. There was the terrible sight of Joseph, thrown by his family into the hands of the Ishmaelites. He had the audacity to dream and was sold into slavery by his brothers for twenty pieces of silver. In this, the dwarflike priest saw his past. There was also Daniel's miraculous taming of the lions. He stood arms akimbo as they bowed before him. In this, Parenti hoped to see his future. But the one that delighted him most, the creation of Eve, was nearly lost in the shadows of the northern corner of the ceiling. Fresh from Adam's rib, Eve stood naked before him with a wanton expression on her face that had the power to transfix the wayward priest for hours.

Here, in the massive library built for the Court of Rome five centuries before, he had wasted away. Accessible only via an obscure winding staircase that led to its home in the Tower of Winds, it was a comfortless place. For eight long years, Parenti had been an apprentice archivist, an indentured servant, buried in endless research tasks for clerics, cardinals, and religious scholars he would likely never meet. By his estimation, his present backlog of assignments would take more than a year to complete. He was surrounded by his silent companions: more than five million books and a half million manuscripts bought, borrowed, and even stolen by the Church for its collection over a span of a thousand years. In the adjacent secret archives, countless more papal manuscripts were stored under lock and key. They were off-limits to all except those personally granted special access by the pontiff himself. The archives towered above him like ancient sentries of knowledge and contained a collection, indeed *the* collection, of some of the rarest documents known, and unknown, to man.

There were nearly nine hundred priests fortunate enough to work in the Vatican, but only a select few earned the privilege of working among this extraordinary collection. The library's holdings had made it a center of the revival of classical culture that became the Renaissance. Hundreds of thousands of priceless originals and first printings were there. Among them, the entire collection of pristine-condition Greek and Latin classics, ancient Roman, and Chinese manuscripts rarely seen in the modern day; the earliest known versions of the Gospels ever discovered, dating to within a century of the life of Jesus; and the entire collection of the Gnostic "Lost Gospels," including the Gospel of Judas ordered burned by Bishop Irenaeus in AD 191.

There were also the more "modern" texts. All the known edicts of the emperor Genghis Khan; the manuscripts from the trials of the Knights Templar in 1308; every record in existence from the Spanish Inquisition; the documents of the excommunication of Martin Luther in 1521; a letter from Mary, Queen of Scots, addressed to Pope Sixtus, written the night before she was beheaded; the love letters of Henry VIII, along with the papers that annulled his marriage to Catherine of Aragon; hundreds of rare letters that contained Michelangelo's writings and drawings known only to the Vatican; and a collection of unknown writings by Voltaire. More recently, enormous, locked cabinets had been installed to house voluminous records of the Holocaust that included exchanges of letters between Pope Pius XI and Adolf Hitler himself.

Given that his crooked stoop placed him at only four feet eight inches tall, Parenti knew there was little justification for his assignment by Cardinal Ponti to the cavernous Papal Library filled with such magnificent works. Between his height and crippled form, he could barely reach his fingers above the fourth of the twenty ornately hand-carved shelves that seemed to approach the heavens. Balancing safely on the hundreds of ancient wooden ladders that stretched to the ceiling required fervent prayer. His fear of heights made every laborious trip for a book in the upper regions of the shelves a torturous endeavor. Often, when on a particularly difficult retrieval assignment for a book in the higher reaches, he would nervously wobble and cling to the ladder for hours, warily ascending and descending the rungs and cursing every frightening inch of the perilous heights.

His imprisonment in the library had been determined when he made the terrible mistake of boasting to the cardinal that he had an appreciation for books. He bragged that as a child in various orphanages in Sicily, he had even taught himself to read. Within a day of his rhetorical strut, he had been placed under the stewardship of Prefect Barsanti. Parenti knew with certainty there were others in the Vatican court with far better qualifications to serve in an archivist role. It was obviously a job for only the most studious of priests. But while no one of authority had ever confessed it, he was certain that His Eminence had made the assignment for another, unspoken reason. A secret library, far from the public spaces of the Vatican where only a handful could venture, was as good a place as any to hide the spectacle of a decrepit, hunchbacked priest. Here was a crypt where he could live out the remainder of his years as entombed as the ancient books around him.

This was not the life he had imagined. Born the seventh son of a seventh son, Parenti's family—and the entire Sicilian village of Nicolosi, nestled on Mount Etna, where he was born—had near mythological expectations of him. According to ancient belief, such a son was to be endowed with supernatural powers of healing and the gift of prophecy. Tragically, what no one could foresee for the Parenti child at the age of six was the onset of a severe form of Scheuermann's kyphosis, a pathological curvature of the spine. One of the cruelest deformities, his spinal hump stemmed from a rigidity of the thoracic vertebrae causing a severe bowing of his upper back. It was so disfiguring that the simple act of breathing was often painful. Before the age of eight, the handsome boy, once the source of great promise for Nunzio and Maria Parenti, found himself branded *il gobbo*—"the hunchback"—of the rural mountainous village. His destitute parents had been warned by a local priest that the deformity of their seventh son was a sign of disfavor from God. Others deemed it a curse on the entire village.

By the time Parenti was ten, his persecution had become unbearable. Shunned by others and often pelted with stones like a stray dog on the treacherous walk home from school, he was forced to end his education. The only kindness he could remember from this sad time had come from a young girl his age named Pepina. A neighbor from down the street, she had taken pity on the boy and often stole away with him to a nearby meadow to recount what had been taught in school each day. There, they would spend hours reciting poetry and practicing storytelling until the sun would cruelly set. When her parents discovered the friendship, an eruption normally reserved for the ancient Etna volcano spewed forth.

For the young Luca Parenti, it was off to the first of several dismal orphanages scattered across the rural island. They would raise him until a monastery in Palermo mercifully took him in at the age of eighteen. These had been lonely times for the disfigured boy, with painful memories so haunting that he would never return to see the family who had abandoned him or the kind Pepina again. While the Church, and eventually the Vatican, had provided refuge to the crippled priest for years, the menial tasks he was often relegated to had created a lifetime of boredom, trouble, and even mishaps like the debacle he had just created.

Near exhaustion from the repair work, Parenti glanced at the handful of volumes that remained to be stacked. It had taken a team of resentful librarians seven hours of heavy lifting to replace the broken shelving and return the books to precise order. They left together, having chatted about their evening plans while Parenti glumly finished the work in his customary solitude. Each time he bent over to retrieve a book, he craned his head upward. As he did, pain coursed through his spine like molten lava. The scene that stared down on him from above offered no solace. The sole fresco from which he routinely averted his gaze, it pictured the fabled battle for heaven. Frightened by the sight of the war between God's angels and Lucifer's fallen "Watchers," he increased his pace. He was desperate to be finished with the ordeal.

He contorted his back to reach a book containing the voluminous writings of Pope Alexander VI. Then he noticed a small, triangular-shaped protrusion under the base of a bookcase. It appeared to be the corner of an errant book that had slid under a bottom shelf during the calamity. He reached his fingers into the sliver of space between the floor and the shelf and gently pulled on the tome. It wouldn't budge. He leaned over once more and tugged at the volume impatiently. Again, it would not move.

"Porco diavolo!" he said. His eyes instantly darted up and down the aisle to check for others who might be lurking nearby.

Wherever the book had come from, he thought, it was safe to say it had not simply fallen there when the accident occurred. That was impossible, given how tightly it was wedged beneath the shelf. He dropped to his knees and craned his neck as best his crooked spine would allow and peered into the crevice, where he presumed the book could have been lodged for centuries. He was deeply weary in both body and spirit and decided the easiest solution would be to shove the book back into its centuries-old resting place. *What do I care? Soon, I am to be humiliated before His Eminence and exiled to a remote parish in Hungary or Albania to serve out my years. Let that tyrant Barsanti deal with it another day.* He pushed with all his might, but the book would not budge.

Defeated, he rose from his knees to gather the other books to be shelved. Then he hesitated and bent over the volume once more. He closed his eyes and examined the cover again, this time with just the touch of his childlike fingers. What his years in the Papal Library had taught him with certainty was that the stubborn book did not belong anywhere near this section of texts. It had the feel of a truly ancient book—indeed, a much older codex. Stranger, it was missing the protective vellum that covered nearly every volume in the library.

He sat down once more and braced his feet against the bottom of the bookcase. He strained to arch his pitiful back and pulled on both sides of the book as hard as he could. To his amazement, the volume finally broke free with a loud snap. He clung to it fiercely and was propelled backward until his head slammed squarely against a shelf behind him.

"Porco diavolo!" he cried out from the sharp pain. This time he didn't care if the pope himself could hear him from the Papal Apartments nearby.

After he paused for several seconds to let the dizziness fade, he sat up and steadied himself. A bump the width of his thumb had already grown on the back of his head. He ignored the pain and grasped the rescued codex to stare at its cover. *Truly ancient*, he thought. As he held it up and turned it from side to side to examine it in the dim light, he was surprised when a tattered cloth fluttered from the book and fell directly into his lap. He picked it up and studied it carefully.

The size of a kerchief, it was spotted and worn and had been folded several times over and pressed between the pages of the codex. When Parenti turned the fabric over, his eyes grew wide with amazement. The sublime, frontal image of a face, beaten and bruised but seemingly tranquil, appeared in stark relief against the fragile cloth. His heart jumped and then began to race at the sight. If there was even the slightest possibility the cloth, which looked to be as old as the codex itself, was what he suspected it might be, his fortune was sure to change for the better. He had the potential to change his miserable life, but he had to hide and protect his find no matter the cost. He looked about to ensure no one was watching, carefully folded his fragile prize into squares, and slipped it into his vestment pocket; he could study it later, safe from the prying eyes of others.

As he turned his attention back to the book, he could see that a worn leather cord with a tassel crudely bound its cover together. The crumbled edges of the pages opposite the delicate binding were familiar to him. *Definitely papyrus*, he thought, which dated the work to the third century AD at the latest.

Curious, he ran his fingers across the smooth, titleless cover that appeared to be ancient animal skin. He paused, took a long breath, and wondered what rare work he held. Then he removed the leather fastener tied to the binding and opened the book that would change the world forever.

CHAPTER 2

Washington, DC
March 2014

Jon Bondurant surveyed the bright, sunlit auditorium. Only two weeks into spring semester at Georgetown University and already one-third of the worn, wooden seats in the theater-style classroom in Smith Hall were empty. *The herd's thinned*, he thought. He hadn't lectured before a college class in years, but he could tell the deadline for "drop/add"—when wavering students had to opt in or out of the class for a grade—was near. Father Pat Cleary, an old colleague from Princeton sitting in the back of the room, had been after him for months to guest lecture for his popular course on world religions at the prestigious school, and Bondurant had finally acquiesced. The priest, a courageous Jesuit, insisted his students hear from all viewpoints, including those opposite his own.

Cleary had just introduced him as the "most misguided but influential atheist" he knew, and Bondurant smiled at the backhanded compliment. He gazed out the giant Palladian windows facing the Potomac River, which wound its way through Washington, DC, and watched the slowly moving stream of people trickle down M Street and through the narrow cobblestone lanes of the quaint village of Georgetown below. The crowded streets were filled with students ducking into noisy pubs on a warm Friday afternoon, a few of them no doubt Cleary's missing students getting an early start on the weekend.

From his vantage point, he could also see that he had a real problem. For some reason, his battered Jaguar, parked several blocks down the hill on the corner of 31st Street, had begun to draw a small crowd. He quickly checked his jeans pockets and realized his car keys were nowhere to be found. He sighed and squinted in the direction of the commotion. Bystanders peered into his car window and then doubled over laughing at what they saw. He had done it again. He had locked his car with the keys in it and with the engine still on. He had been late for the lecture already, and it was clear the car would either run out of gas or overheat before he could return.

He cursed his luck, turned his attention from the debacle, and sized up the class. Little had changed in the higher echelons of academia since his much-publicized firing from Princeton years before. A few of the undergrads before him might have real promise in the field of cultural anthropology, but they had a long way to go. The confident ones would challenge his authority with irreverent questions. He enjoyed the challenges and preferred those students over the ones simply marking a requirement off their schedule. The third group comprised earnest students he considered to be on the bubble. Like a long line of their predecessors, they would study for an insane number of hours, achieve respectable grades, and enter prestigious graduate schools up and down the East Coast. There, he was certain they would blow through even more of their parents' money before they discovered they weren't cut out for anthropology after all. Some things never changed, he mused.

Yet right in the center was one of the reasons he'd accepted Cleary's invitation to appear. Sometimes one showed, sometimes not. This one was acceptable enough, a thin blonde who wore a tight denim miniskirt. Her long, shapely legs aimed at him at eye level, like a double-barreled shotgun, from the fifth row up. He had no clue who she was, but it didn't matter. He could see she had already eyed him. Tonight, like many other nights, it was not a matter of what he would do to fight the emptiness he felt, but with whom.

Although he was forty years old, he still attracted his share of female adulation. Physically, it all worked. Just over six feet tall, he had inherited his father's lean frame. An NCAA swimmer and diver at Stanford, he had square, broad shoulders and traces of the distinctive Latin look passed down from his striking Argentine mother, now long since gone. His thick, graying black hair and blue eyes, along with the pronounced chiseling of his brow and high-set cheekbones, created an appealing collision of masculine and feminine features capable of drawing stares like the one he was getting from the fifth row. From a distance, he was a catch. Up close, when a woman tried to get to know him better, was another story. He looked up from the notes on his desk at the students scattered before him and broke the silence.

"Father Cleary tells me you have ventured into the topic of religious relics. Congratulations. Let's begin, shall we?" He circled around in front of the desk.

He spoke with an unmistakable tone of authority in his voice, one that commanded their attention. "Whether we're dealing with the ancient Zoroastrians or modern, misguided Christians, like many gathered here today," he said in a low voice so as to send a few students snickering "the faiths are all the same." He took a seat behind the worn desk and rocked back and forth on the rear two legs of the chair. "And let's not forget the Islamic, Jewish, Buddhist, and Hindi. The propensity for religions worldwide to claim authenticity for their ancient relics as having miraculous qualities, as something more than mere symbols of their faith, runs rampant through the ages.

"These relics," he continued, "served a useful purpose for Christianity in particular. In medieval Europe, they were big business. This was an era of superstition, when the practice of magic and miracle-related relics were commonplace. The world was flooded with 'bogus bones.' It was a time when the Black Death had descended on the continent. The Church was preoccupied. It did virtually nothing to stem the flood of false icons. Christians, often to save themselves, made pilgrimages to the shrines of holy people where relics were on display. That meant not only the promise of the forgiveness of sin for the pilgrims but also vital commerce for burgeoning cities. Indeed, relics nourished the faithful and filled the coffers. But in the end, they were then what they are today—merely props for the ignorant."

Father Cleary, seated in the back, wore an amused sort of smile on his face but kept silent.

But for a student in the third row, it was apparently too much.

"Don't you think calling them 'props' is a bit much?" he shot out. "Epstein's study on religious relics found their use prevalent across the world's most popular religions. How can a billion Buddhists worshipping the healing ashes of their Masters all be wrong?"

"Well, if it's numbers we're counting," Bondurant responded with an exaggerated drawl, "I have my money on the Christians and the bones of their saints. They outnumber your Buddhists by two to one, my friend."

Bondurant continued. "Would it surprise you to know that the world's poorest countries are also the most religious? A vast number of the billions of people we're talking about, whether they're the two billion Christians, the one and a half billion believers of Islam, or the billion Buddhists you've defended, are functionally illiterate. Can they *all* be right? They live and die believing in diametrically opposite beliefs, in a world of many gods, conflicting dogmas, and disparate conceptions of the afterlife. They are as susceptible to the mythology of artifacts and rituals of faith today as their ancestors were a thousand years ago."

A brunette wearing mirrored aviator glasses and a red beret looked up from her iPad for the first time that afternoon.

"Dr. Bondurant, given we are dealing with the divine, which is beyond man's understanding, maybe even yours," she said as she smiled, "are you willing to concede, even as an atheist, that at least some of the relics held forth by the world's religions may have unexplained healing attributes and have actually helped the blind man see or the crippled man walk? History is full of witnesses to miracles."

"Spoken like a true Christian," Bondurant said. "You are Christian, correct?"

"Since birth."

"All right, then," he pushed back. "Since you asked, let's zero in on Christianity for a few minutes, and when we're done, you tell me if the blind man sees."

Two Lands' End catalog–worthy preppies ceased their texting and looked up with interest.

"How many here are familiar with the Veil of Veronica?" Bondurant asked as he scanned the room.

Only two hands rose.

He pointed to the one of the two who had braved sitting in the front row. "You're it. What's your name?"

"Tom Kelso," the student said somewhat sheepishly. "I think it has something to do with the Crucifixion of Christ. There's something about a veil given to Jesus. I believe it's depicted on one of the Stations of the Cross."

"Close, Mr. Kelso." Bondurant rose from his chair, walked around to the front of his desk, and sat on it.

The blonde in the miniskirt quietly snapped a photo of him with her phone and nervously looked away. If she thought he hadn't noticed, she was wrong. And that's when he knew for sure he had found another hapless victim. Sleep with her for two, three nights running, he figured. Give her nothing to latch on to. Then ignore her for days until she got the message. He knew there would be some guilt from how he'd treat her, as there had been with the others, but there wasn't a chance she would ever get to know him. *How could she?* he thought. He was still a mystery to himself. He refocused his mind on the lecture.

"The Veil of Veronica, also known as the Sudarium or the Volto Santo, meaning 'Holy Face,' is a Catholic relic, a cloth that is said to bear the actual likeness of the face of Jesus Christ. This makes it, boys and girls, a first-class relic, an item directly associated with Jesus's life. Also first class would be a physical part of a saint, such as a bone or a strand of hair."

He turned to his laptop computer, which rested on the stool in front of him.

"I need one of you next to the windows to pull the shades and kill the lights," he said.

As the fluorescent lights overhead went dark, an image of what appeared to be a crude painting of a bearded face on a small cloth appeared on the large screen behind him.

"This is a first-class relic?" one student asked as he leaned toward the screen. "No fair. It's just a painting on a napkin."

"Painting or not," Bondurant admonished as he pointed to the image, "this cloth—the 'Veil of Veronica'—is said to have touched the face of Jesus Christ. In fact, its appearance is said to be, by miracle, the actual image of Jesus's face. And as far as relics go, you don't get more first class than that."

"Well," another student suggested, "if this is first class, whatever comes in as second or third is definitely suspect."

"In the second-class relic category," Bondurant said, pressing forward, "is something—anything—owned by or associated with a saint, like a shirt, a crucifix, a book, or, interestingly, instruments of torture used against a martyr. The latest estimates put the number of saints at between twenty and thirty thousand, so imagine the number of second-class relics that are claimed to be associated with them. Third-class—well, they are absurd. You don't want to hear about them."

"Might as well," the blonde in the denim miniskirt called out confidently.

"Okay," he said. "Welcome. Did you drive to class today?"

"Yes," she replied, worried she was going to get more than she bargained for by chiming in.

"Throw me your car keys."

Reaching into her purse, she flung them forward. He held them aloft for the class to see.

"If these keys, or even the—it's a Porsche, is it?" he asked.

"It is," she said.

"Well, if these keys or the Porsche she apparently drives ever come in contact with the veil you see here—let's say she ran it over—or if they ever touch the bone of a saint, they would be considered a third-class relic."

"How about you? You seem old enough to have lived with the saints," another said. "Wouldn't that make you a third-class relic, Dr. Bondurant?"

The room tittered.

"Astute. Now back to the veil," he said. Having secured his ride home, he slid her keys onto the desk behind him and prepared to turn toward the screen again. She crossed her legs, threw him a ready look, and smiled.

"According to Church legend," he said, "Saint Veronica approached Jesus during the Passion, the agony of bearing the Cross up Mount Calvary. Miraculously, when she wiped clean the face of Christ with her veil, this image of the savior's face was left indelibly on the cloth. A miracle!

"Now," he continued, pointing again to the bold image on the screen, "it has been believed for twenty centuries that this veil has the power to cure blindness, quench thirst, and, like Christ, raise the dead. Since the fourteenth century, the veil has been one of the most venerated relics of the Church, has it not, Father Cleary?"

"To this day, my misguided friend," the priest replied.

"Who here has ever been to Jerusalem?" Bondurant asked.

No hands went up.

"Well, I recommend it. Among the hundreds of souvenir booths you will wade through on Via Dolorosa—the 'Way of Grief,' where hawkers sell crucifixes and other Passion tchotchkes—you will find a small church known as the Chapel of the Holy Face. That is the supposed site of the miracle that brought us the image of Jesus Christ's face on Veronica's Veil.

"The New Testament is exhaustive on the Passion of Christ and his bearing of the Cross up Calvary, and yet there is not a single mention of Veronica's Veil in any of the Gospels," Bondurant said. "And then the veil is lost to history for over a thousand years, until it miraculously appears somewhere in the twelfth or thirteenth centuries in St. Peter's in Rome.

"Here the plot thickens," he said, and grinned.

"In the year 1600, the veil mysteriously disappears. Then, like the loaves and fishes of the Gospels, a multitude of veils appear out of thin air," he said as he rubbed his hands together. "Another miracle, one presumes? Today, there are at least six Veronica's Veils, all claiming to be the original. All of these veils are venerated by the Church as miraculous originals. And each of them bears an entirely different image of Jesus's face."

He advanced the slides . . . click . . . click . . . click . . . click . . . click . . . to reveal several more images of Christ's face on cloth, each cruder than the one before, and all radically different.

"They can be found in chapels and monasteries spread across the European continent. From St. Peter's in Rome—"

Click.

"—to the Hofburg Palace in Vienna—"

Click.

"—to the Monastery of the Holy Face in Spain. The last time the Church allowed an inspection of one of the veils was over a hundred years ago, and the report of the image seen on the veil fell somewhat short of miraculous. To quote from the summary of the report: 'Two brown spots on faded material connected to each other.' Looks like a Rorschach test, doesn't it?"

Kelso in the front row interrupted.

"Are there any documented miracles tied to the veils?" he asked with a trace of hope in his voice.

"Documented scientifically? None," Bondurant replied. "Not a one. Now, someone ask me about the True Cross."

"Is this a trick question?" a bearded hiker type with a ponytail offered from the back.

"That depends on your point of view," Bondurant replied.

"Okay, I'll bite. What about the True Cross?" the hiker asked.

"It's false," Bondurant deadpanned.

Click.

A small piece of wood and a broken piece of a stone tablet next to it appeared on the screen.

"Of course, we are talking about the cross upon which Jesus Christ was supposedly crucified," Bondurant said. "Found by Saint Helena, mother of Constantine the Great, who traveled to Palestine during the fourth century in search of relics. Pieces of the True Cross can now be found preserved in literally hundreds of churches across Europe. This particular piece, along with a piece of tablet that has half of INRI—meaning 'Jesus of Nazareth, King of the Jews'—inscribed on it, can be found in the ancient Basilica of Santa Croce in Rome."

"Why is this so far-fetched?" a pretty redhead with glasses to match asked from the side.

"Well, like I said, there are so many churches that claim to possess a piece of the True Cross that during the Middle Ages, the famous theologian John Calvin estimated that if all these pieces of wood claiming to be from the Cross were gathered together, one could build an entire ship. My recollection from the story of the Gospels is that it was Jesus Christ your savior alone, admittedly with some help from Simon of Cyrene along the way, who carried the Cross up Calvary.

"Now, good Catholics," he asked, his cynicism on display for all to see, "what is this?"

Click.

A rusty, twisted spike appeared on the screen.

"It's obviously an old nail of some kind," someone replied from the back.

"Not just any nail," Bondurant protested. "This is reportedly one of the three or four nails the Church believes was used in the Crucifixion of Jesus. It rests in that same basilica in Rome along with a piece of the True Cross. Having supposedly pierced the body of Jesus, you won't find a relic more first class than this."

"So what's the problem?" a student with a deep Boston accent asked.

"The problem," Bondurant said, "is that at last count there are thirty or more of these Holy Nails on display in churches from Venice to Nuremberg to Prague. My recollection of the Gospels is that while Jesus was said to be a carpenter, the Roman soldiers did not help him build a house up on Calvary. They say they nailed him to a cross."

Bondurant punched quickly now through his slides in staccato fashion.

Click.

"Here we have one of several dozen Crowns of Thorns placed upon the head of Jesus before the Crucifixion," he said. "Your reading of the New Testament will reveal that there was only one such crown. It is one of the most venerated relics in the history of Christianity. Despite enormous scientific effort, none of the many in existence have ever been authenticated."

Click.

"Here we have the Iron Crown of Lombardy and the Bridle of

Constantine, said to be made from yet more Holy Nails from the Crucifixion."

Click.

"Here we supposedly have the Holy Lance, the spear used to pierce the side of Jesus when he was on the Cross to ensure that he was dead."

Click.

"Here we have the supposed Holy Sponge, the one described in the Bible as having been dipped in vinegar and offered to Jesus on the Cross. How many of you have kept a sponge around for more than a few months?"

Click.

"Not to beat a dead horse, but here we have the supposed Column of Flagellation," he said, "the post Jesus was strapped to during the Flagellation, his torture. This is kept in the Basilica of St. Praxedes in Rome."

Click.

"Now here before us come the supposed Gifts of the Magi to baby Jesus, on display at St. Paul's Monastery on Mount Athos in Greece."

Click.

"These are the supposed clothes of the baby Jesus in Dubrovnik's Cathedral in Croatia."

Click.

"And this unrecognizable object is"—he paused and winced—"well, a number of churches in Europe have claimed at one time or another to possess—at the same time, mind you—the Holy Prepuce: the foreskin from Jesus's circumcision."

The blonde put down her soda and leaned forward in her seat. "Oh, for God's sake," she moaned.

"For God's sake, indeed," Bondurant whispered.

"Which brings us to the most remarkable and controversial religious relic in the history of mankind." He moved to stand directly beside the screen for effect.

Click.

"The Holy Shroud," he said with false reverence.

An outline of a body stared down from the screen and glowed in the dim light like a phantom. It was the startling, lifelike, and sublime image purported to be of the body of Jesus Christ, the son of God. Some of the students shifted uncomfortably in their seats.

"For those of you who are wondering whether this will be covered on the midterm," he said, "Father Cleary tells me the answer's yes."

The sound of laptops and notebooks opening filled the room. Every student leaned in and peered at the screen.

"What you are looking at is a negative image of a photograph of the Shroud of Turin—the Sindon—taken in 1898 by amateur photographer Secondo Pia. 'Sindon' is a word derived from the New Testament. It refers to a fine linen cloth used to wrap the dead. Since the fourteenth century, it's been more commonly known as a shroud. The shroud before you is the most studied and controversial religious artifact in the world," Bondurant said, this time with real reverence. "In fact, the study of this relic alone has gained so much attention in the last century that a branch of science—sindonology—has been named for it."

He continued. "According to believers, the Shroud is the burial cloth that was wrapped around the body of Jesus of Nazareth as he was laid to rest in his tomb. It is referenced in all four Gospels—Matthew, Mark, Luke, and John.

"Look closely," he said. "The remarkable image you see in the midsection of the linen cloth, at center, is purported to be the face of the Son of God. While the Catholic Church has never officially accepted or rejected the Shroud as the actual burial cloth of Christ, numerous popes have taken its authenticity for granted. In 1958, Pope Pius XII gave his blessing to the image of the face shown here as that of Jesus Christ. You will find this face engraved on medals and jewelry throughout the Christian world. Some of you may wear it now. For over four hundred years, this burial shroud has been kept in the Royal Chapel of the Cathedral of St. John the Baptist in Turin. Millions of visitors, including Pope John Paul II and your Pope Augustine, have made pilgrimages to Turin to see firsthand what their predecessors deemed to be the true image of the face of Jesus Christ."

"Dr. Bondurant," said Kelso from the front row, "I'm sure at this point you are going to explain why you believe it's a forgery. But I have to say that the image, the face shown here, looks a lot like Christ."

"Yes," Bondurant said. "Your own preconceived notion of Christ. That's exactly what the medieval artist who forged it wanted you to believe. But believe me when I tell you there are no definitive records in existence referencing the Shroud before the fourteenth century. None. Today, there are seven different churches spread from Italy to France, all which claim to have a piece of the Shroud.

"Now," he said as he paced back and forth, "how is that possible? I could not put it better than Calvin, the French theologian, a favorite of Father Cleary's whom I'm sure you will study. In his *Treatise on Relics* in 1543, he said, and I quote: 'How is it possible that those sacred historians, who carefully related all the miracles that took place at Christ's death, should have omitted to mention one so remarkable as the likeness of the body of our Lord remaining on its wrapping sheet?'

"Calvin also wrote," Bondurant continued, "that anyone who peddled the Shroud as being authentic should be 'convicted of falsehood and deceit.'"

He moved back toward his chair quietly, folded his arms, and gazed out at the students sitting in rapt attention as they studied the glowing ghostlike image.

A full minute went by before the silence was broken. The student with the beret removed it, tossed her hair back, and spoke.

"Dr. Bondurant, this looks as real as it gets," she said. "Like it was painted by an angel or something."

"Yes," he responded. "I have to confess that it does. What is its true origin? We know that it was first put on display in the small French village of Lirey in the year 1356. Some claim it is actually the work of Leonardo da Vinci. That would make it a masterpiece, wouldn't it?"

"You mean to say this could be a painting?" a student asked.

"Possibly," he responded. "Some historians also say that it is the work of a talented but admitted forger and murderer. Church documents from the year 1390 tell us that a memo was written from Bishop Pierre d'Arcis to Antipope Clement VII proclaiming that the Shroud was a forgery and that the artist had confessed."

"What do you believe?" Kelso asked.

"For me," Bondurant responded dryly, "it's not a matter of belief. It's not a matter of faith. Or better put, I guess you could say I put my faith where it belongs—in science. You may know me as an author, but my first love is science. I know that over thirty years ago, a team of experts was allowed to examine the Shroud up close. They were able to take with them small samples of linen cut from the Shroud. And the radiocarbon dating tests they performed on those samples stated conclusively that the Shroud's fabrication lies somewhere between the years 1260 and 1390."

"That's too bad," a student noted. "It is just magnificent."

"Yes," Bondurant replied as he stared intently into the image of the face that beamed down on him. "A magnificent fake."

CHAPTER 3

Rome, Italy—The Vatican
March 2014

Domenika Jozef spoke with her usual confidence but with precisely the amount of measured respect required of a senior adviser in disagreement with the pope.

"Holy Father, I believe this is a grave mistake," she said as she tried to mask her frustration. She folded her hands on the table and stared up at the massive crystal chandeliers in the pontiff's spectacular study. Every wall was adorned with priceless paintings as old as the Renaissance itself. She tried to ignore the icy stare of the red-cassocked cardinal beside the Holy Father.

"Ms. Jozef, as was explained to you earlier this morning," Cardinal Ponti interrupted brusquely, "His Holiness has reached a decision on this matter, and the time has come to—"

"Your Eminence, I realize that as secretary to His Holiness, your view carries great weight," she interrupted. "But when this advice was proffered to the Holy Father following your meeting of the cardinals last week, there was not a single adviser present who has experience in public relations. I have advised the Vatican on policy matters of extraordinary sensitivity to the media for several years now and have never—"

"Ms. Jozef!" Cardinal Ponti's voice elevated in volume even more quickly than he rose from the ornate golden chair he had been sitting in. "Your guidance on this matter has been appreciated, but the Holy Father has spoken," he said with a certain finality. *"Meus Deus, is mulier exertus meus patientia!"*

My God, this woman tries my patience, Domenika quickly translated in silence. Obviously Ponti had forgotten she was fluent in eight languages, including Latin and ancient Aramaic.

Pope Augustine sighed heavily and closed his weary eyes for a moment. He clasped his large, aging hands together, revealing the famous golden Fisherman's Ring, which signified his succession from Saint Peter, founder of the Church and a fisherman by trade. The pope leaned forward slowly and rested against the massive antique mahogany table that appeared to be as old as Rome itself.

"Domenika," he said as his rich voice filled the resplendent room, "this is not a decision that I have made lightly. I have considered the question for several days and have given the matter much prayer. This path is unconventional, I confess. But I believe the gift brought to us by the grace of God in the heroic hands of Padre Parenti must be handled this way."

Domenika detected from Father Parenti's expression that the priest could not believe his ears. She watched as the little priest glued his eyes to the gilded portraits of previous pontiffs that surrounded them in order to avoid the furious bulging eyes of Father Barsanti. The prefect, afflicted with Graves' disease, which produced his buglike eyes, could barely contain his disgust at Parenti's good fortune.

He had cringed when the Holy Father mentioned the little priest by name.

The pope grasped the ancient codex on the table in front of him, locked eyes with Parenti, and held the codex to his heart.

"There has never been a gift of greater salvation for so many," he proclaimed, making the sign of the cross with the book he now held with outstretched arms. "But first, the world must be readied."

It was not an exaggeration, Domenika thought. It would always be a mystery why the codex had been discovered by the pitiful priest. If not for his accident, it could have rested in obscurity for centuries. Still, she had to wonder if the hand of God was in his find. It was too random and too astonishing that out of all the obscure books in the library not touched by human hands in hundreds of years, this one was discovered. *Miraculous*, she thought.

In the eyes of Vatican experts, the contents of the book itself were more valuable than any holy relic ever discovered. The title of the sixty-four pages of delicate papyrus in ancient Greek text was etched in gold leaf with the mind-numbing words *Revelation of the Shroud*. Domenika had been assured it was the only book of its kind in existence. Dated to the year AD 49, its contents had been translated from Greek and studied meticulously by the pope's most trusted historians since its discovery by Parenti weeks earlier. After their intense examination, there was no question the book the pontiff held before them proved beyond all doubt the authenticity of the burial cloth, the Holy Shroud of Jesus Christ. With the Shroud's legitimacy now confirmed through the *Revelation of the Shroud*, a remarkable text and the first of its kind, the famous burial cloth in Turin took its place as the earliest and most credible historical evidence in existence detailing the last, tortured hours of Jesus Christ.

"Every precious page of this document, every word set forth here, provides all believers with a renewed foundation of faith, a bridge between the spiritual and the worldly greater than mankind has ever known," the pope pronounced, his aged hands visibly shaking as he held the book before them.

The Shroud of Turin, the burial cloth referenced by the Gospel of Mark, had been revered by previous popes and the faithful as the most sacred of relics since it was first discovered and gifted to the Catholic Church in the late fourteenth century. It had been kept under constant guard in the Royal Chapel of the Cathedral of St. John the Baptist in Turin, Italy, for over six hundred years. Although derided as a fake by scientific experts and nonbelievers for decades, it had served as a source of inspiration to countless Christians for centuries. A simple herringbone twill cloth that measured fourteen feet three inches long by three feet seven inches wide, it revealed from top to bottom a faint, mysteriously lifelike image of a naked man bearing the markings of a body that had suffered a brutal death. Indeed, not just any death but a crucifixion that involved the precise torture and agony—the Passion—experienced by Jesus of Nazareth as documented in the Scriptures. The Shroud was said to be true evidence of the ultimate sacrifice of God's Son sent to absolve the sin of all men, and a reminder of the eventual death and resurrection of mankind.

The purported documentation of the authenticity of Jesus's burial cloth as contained in the *Revelation of the Shroud* was comprehensive and complete. As written, it provided an unmistakable guide to the artifact that had been resting in Turin for centuries. Much of it read like an ancient coroner's report. There was the revelation that the cloth had first been secreted by Thaddeus Jude to Edessa, one of the first Christian communities established along the Silk Road between the Tigris and Euphrates Rivers. There were the extensive writings, page after page that described the burial cloth in detail that only the most intrusive inspection of the Shroud itself could reveal. There was the exact match between the text and the actual measurements of the relic's length and width recorded in the modern day. A detailed description of the markings that appeared on the cloth, from the small cuts surrounding the image's forehead, presumably formed by a crown of thorns, to the puncture wounds clearly visible on the wrists and feet, revealed the certain signs of a brutal and bloody crucifixion. Remarkably enough, the text also revealed a page of testimony that appeared to be taken directly from Joseph of Arimathea. In the account, he described his meticulous wrapping of the body of Jesus in "large strips of linen cloth" before he laid him to rest in his tomb in Jerusalem.

There were also extraordinary illustrations containing crude but accurate similarities to the markings on the Shroud. Sketches of a body in repose were included with indicators pointing to gouges in the torso. These matched perfectly with the Shroud's present image that bore the signs of the lancing of Christ's side when, according to the Bible, a Roman soldier's spear had been used to hasten his death. References to the numerous wounds across the back and legs of the image were included, denoting the marks associated with a Roman flagrum, a tasseled, whiplike instrument of torture. And dark, vein-like streaks that appeared up and down the image's arms were illustrated, referencing what looked to be a pattern of blood trickling from punctured wrists.

Importantly, there was also a date, extremely rare for a text of this age: the title page was clearly inscribed at the bottom with the inscription "8 Claudius." This provided a reference to the ancient

Coptic "year of indication" denoting the eighth year of rule of the Roman emperor Claudius, who reigned between AD 41 and AD 54. It placed the writing of the *Revelation of the Shroud* at precisely AD 49, approximately fifteen years following historical estimates of the death of Jesus Christ.

The sole piece of inquiry that the pope's experts had yet to resolve in their meticulous examination of the codex was the location of an item that appeared to belong in the tie'pi, the Greek word for "pocket." Apparently, a small compartment had been carefully sewn into the inside cover of the codex marked only by two words—*hagios kalumma*, which meant "holy veil." Yet no such veil was found inside the pouch when the pope's experts examined it. Domenika had been told that this lost piece of the codex had preoccupied the pope for days. Was it the true "Veronica's Veil," the very cloth that had touched the face of Christ, that had been preserved inside the sacred book? She knew that several churches throughout Europe claimed to possess the venerated relic. That was evidence enough to her that the real veil had likely vanished centuries ago.

"Father Parenti, our hero, our discoverer!" the pope exclaimed as he set the codex on the table before them and delicately opened its cover to reveal the empty pocket where the veil likely once rested. The pontiff shook his head.

"I presume you found no other items related to our magnificent codex during your mishap? No other such things?"

Parenti closed his eyes tight and only shook his head to signal an emphatic no.

"Speak up! Speak up!" Barsanti cried out. The prefect quickly stood up. "You are to address the Holy Father with abject veneration!"

Domenika looked down at the little priest, who sat motionless, able only to shake his head in the negative again. All the while, Parenti seemed to fidget with something buried deep inside his pants. The prefect appeared ready to leap across the table to strike and even strip-search the little priest for his insolence, but she could see the pope would have none of it. The pontiff raised his hand to silence the red-faced Barsanti, whose every ounce of blood appeared ready to burst forth from his ballooning eyes.

"Not even a scrap of material of any kind that might have fallen free? And not a clue as to where to find this missing veil?" the pope asked once more.

Parenti took a long, deep breath, one Domenika thought might be his last, given how anxious he appeared to be.

"Not a scrap," Parenti managed to croak from somewhere deep inside his tiny chest.

Even without the holy veil, the historical and religious significance of Father Parenti's accidental discovery of the codex were certain to stun the world. The revelation of the text's existence would reinforce the faith of billions of Christians. Historians would rejoice over the first actual eyewitness account of the life and death of Jesus. Skeptics hung up on the hearsay nature of the Gospels would have to reexamine their bias, and many would convert.

For Domenika, a devout cradle Catholic, the find was monumental. The news of its discovery could be the miracle she needed to obliterate from the public consciousness what had become known inside the walls of the Vatican as The Nightmare. The horrific and public narrative of child sexual abusers among its priestly order had cast a dark and growing shadow over the Catholic Church for a decade. Thousands of criminal and civil suits filed in courtrooms around the world had bankrupted parishes from Los Angeles to Warsaw.

Front-page images of priests and bishops in handcuffs continued to tear at the very fabric of the Church, resulting in a near standstill of new vocations and a huge exodus of parishioners. While no revelation, document, relic, or miracle would ever completely eliminate the devastating consequences of the Church's tolerance and cover-up of pedophilia, a miracle of this nature could at least divert the relentless attention to the issue. She prayed that the story of the discovery and authenticity of the Shroud, and the certain universal adoption of it as the most holy of Christian relics on earth, would provide a real cause for Christian celebration and a sorely needed facelift for the Church and its mission worldwide.

Even the Vatican understood the political implications. It had a long tradition of changing the subject rather than facing hard questions. Unfortunately for the Church, this strategy had lost its potency as the scandal's depth and scope expanded. Its diminished coffers proved the Church needed a shiny new miracle immediately. Domenika was both devout and professional enough to recognize the opportunity. For her, the past five years of managing damage control for the Vatican over the pedophilia scandal had been heartbreaking. It had shaken her confidence in Church leadership and, after a great deal of soul searching, her own faith as well. Now, with the discovery of the ancient codex, the Church had a once-in-a-thousand-lifetimes opportunity it could ill afford to waste.

Which was why she was so distraught with the Holy Father's decision to withhold the news of the text's existence. She had spent the past two weeks devising a worldwide media plan to announce what Pope Augustine had termed the "Glorious Discovery." Her team of highly vetted, confidential professionals had created a high-impact multimedia campaign unlike any effort the Vatican had planned before. However, the pope had rejected the plan and sided with a special committee of cardinals assembled to pray and consider a "divine way forward." She was convinced the "divine way forward" could not be more backward.

"Your Holiness, with your permission," Cardinal Ponti said, "I will summarize our plan for your final blessing."

The Holy Father folded his hands once more as if in prayer and nodded.

"For the time being, the *Revelation of the Shroud* will remain a secret. There shall be no announcements," Ponti said firmly. He glanced coldly at Domenika to prevent any further interruptions. "While there is little question that news of the codex will be released at some time in the future and will provide sustenance to many, the belief of the faithful in Christ's suffering and resurrection has not required such perfect proof for almost two thousand years. The Shroud's authenticity has no relationship with the divine inspiration of the words of Jesus Christ and his teachings. It is our faith, and not the secrets of our library, that serves as the backbone of the Church. Is that not correct, Father Parenti?"

Parenti, who had spent the latter half of the meeting contorting in his chair to hide behind the giant silver candelabra between him and Father Barsanti's glare, sat upright as best he could. "Yes, Your Eminence. It is faith that sustains us all," he said.

Cardinal Ponti continued. "However, there is an opportunity here to end the debate that has had the Church seemingly at war with science over the Shroud for many years," he noted. "Now that we know with absolute certainty the Shroud of Turin is a genuine article, the Church will open it once again to the deepest of scientific scrutiny. Its authenticity will be proven. We will invite from around the world a team of scientists, some representing the most credible skeptics on record, to join us in an unprecedented examination of this most holy relic. We have nothing to lose and much to gain. And with certainty, this is our moment for the disbelievers themselves, using all the modern tools at their disposal, to make our case for us."

The pope beamed and nodded in affirmation.

"Please remind me," the pontiff said, "who is the scientist-scholar you are suggesting should lead the effort?"

"Dr. Jon Bondurant of the Enlightenment Institute in America, Holy Father," the cardinal replied. "He is a leading anthropologist and well-known skeptic in the field of sacred relics, precisely what we are after. I am told that he—"

"Excuse me, Your Eminence," Barsanti interjected in amazement. "Is this not the same man I have had Parenti research at length for you? He has been disgraced, has he not? And he is an avowed atheist counted as an enemy of the Church."

"All the more reason to use him. Truly *use* him," Ponti declared with obvious satisfaction.

Dr. Jon Bondurant. Domenika cringed at the sound of the name. Three years ago she had squared off with him on stage in front of the Cambridge Union Society, the world's oldest and most prestigious debating club. Much to her consternation, she was a last-minute stand-in for Bishop Robert Dorn. Dorn had fallen ill a day before his much-anticipated debate with Bondurant on the topic of the existence of God. She remembered Bondurant looking at her with disdain across the space between them. They had debated for forty minutes, and while their respective podiums were separated by less than five feet, their positions on God and the origin of the universe were light-years apart.

"You mean to stand there and tell me," Bondurant had said to her, "that in all the universe—this ever-expanding, limitless universe, with over a billion potentially habitable planets in our tiny Milky Way alone—that this God of yours has chosen *us*, just us, to watch over? That *we* are the center of *his* world?"

"Yes, that's exactly what I mean," Domenika replied coolly. "And this evidence you refer to that God has created life on other planets— tell me, Dr. Bondurant, in what book do I find that science has demonstrated this?"

She gripped the podium with both hands as if to steer the argument away from the cosmos and onto friendlier, more theological ground. She envied his relaxed poise, although she suspected it was the result of liquid courage from the four shots of scotch she had watched him down just before they took the stage. If he was a drunk, he was a darn good one, she thought. While she vehemently disagreed with his views, she was reluctantly impressed by his confidence and obvious intelligence, both of which appeared to defy the effects of alcohol.

His clumsy flirtation with her beforehand and the statement he made with his two-day-old beard and casual dress at such a formal affair gave her the impression that he was as much a rogue as a genius, but she also knew looks could be deceiving. She was pleased to have held her own during the scheduled hour-long debate, particularly given that she had had so little time to prepare. Schooled at the Vatican for years by some of the pope's most senior theologians, she sensed she had the audience with her. It was her God as creative designer rather than Bondurant's random selection due to the big bang that was winning the day. She expected him to pounce again, and he did.

Bondurant reached into the pockets of his jeans and pulled out a lighter. "I am reminded of our friend Galileo," he said. "Yes; if I remember correctly—and I do—it was the Church that clung to the belief in the face of all evidence against it that it was the sun that revolved around the earth. Having lost that argument, the Church continues to expect us to swallow the concept that while the sun might not revolve around us, a god does. How ridiculously egotistical of mankind, don't you think?"

He fumbled around in the pockets of his sport coat and produced a crushed, nearly empty pack of cigarettes. In an instant he had lit one and started to wave it about like a wand as he prepared to continue.

"Excuse me, Dr. Bondurant," the evening's surprised debate moderator interrupted from the chair centered on risers behind them. The distinguished, gray-haired gentleman was the dean of Cambridge's School of Anthropology and looked completely offended. "This hall has a strict nonsmoking policy, and I must ask you to extinguish that."

"Before or after I extinguish her line of logic?" Bondurant asked. He took a single, deep drag from his cigarette and looked directly into Domenika's eyes. "Honestly, if you'd only had a mind to match that body," he said as he covered his microphone and whispered the insult just loud enough for only her to hear. "Why send a girl to do a man's job?"

"You are a, a—" Domenika stammered, her fury collapsing her words.

"A what, madam?" Bondurant said into the microphone to egg her on.

"A complete fool!" she blurted out. She instantly realized that her gaffe was out of place but reveled in the fact that the audience behind her let out a supportive gasp. Some even began to applaud. Bondurant broke into a broad smile.

• • •

She shuddered as she remembered the embarrassing but winning moment, one she had tried to forget for years. It was only the pontiff's declaration that brought her back to the present.

"Then it shall be," he said as he rose slowly from his chair to signal an end to the meeting.

"*Curse him,*" Barsanti muttered under his breath purposefully loud enough for Domenika to hear as he rose to leave. She could tell he was referring to Parenti, who had hastily departed but obviously gained the favor of the pope.

God help us, Domenika thought as she considered the prospect of working with Jon Bondurant. *God help us all.*

CHAPTER 4

Mumbai, India
April 2014

Dr. Ravi Sehgal slid into his sleek leather chair in the darkened television studio, his back to a collage of digital monitors that displayed news feeds from scenes around the world. Sehgal, now forty-five years old and always dressed impeccably, was slight of build, with a dark complexion and jet-black hair. He was also one of those fortunate few who had a boyish face that made him appear ten years younger than his age.

The buzz of busy reporters who crisscrossed the high-tech set behind him like drones near a hive added to the distraction. Sound engineers whispered to one another as they monitored mixing boards behind glass walls in anticipation of the moment. The studio, black from floor to ceiling, seemed unusually cold, perhaps to manage the room temperature given the bright lights on the set, Sehgal thought. He exhaled slowly. It would require steely focus to ignore the frenzy behind the television camera aimed at him like a gun.

"Please look at only me during the interview, not at the camera, Dr. Sehgal," the news anchor said. She tossed her dark, silky hair behind her shoulder and adjusted the tiny lapel microphone clipped to her red Chanel suit.

I would be pleased to, he thought. Annapurna Shankar was the most famous news personality in India and was as distracting as she was talented. The lead anchor for CNN-IBN TV in Mumbai, she had secured the first interview with Sehgal since the announcement the previous day of his Nobel Prize in Biology. His once quiet life had been a blur of media requests and messages from family and other well-wishers in the last twenty-four hours, many of whom he had not heard from in years. One phone message in particular intrigued him. The well-known American anthropologist Jon Bondurant had left a voice mail insisting they meet about a project he was certain would be dear to Sehgal's heart. Sehgal made a mental note to return the call as soon as the interview was finished.

"Are we all set? Do you need a level?" Anna asked the cameraman as she glanced back in his direction somewhat impatiently. "One . . . two . . . three. One . . . two . . . three," she repeated mechanically.

"Rolling, Anna," the camera operator said.

"Good, then let's get started," she said as she broke into a practiced smile Sehgal presumed she had perfected years ago. She began with an easy question. "Dr. Sehgal, can you tell us what it feels like to be the first Indian scientist in history to capture the Nobel Prize in Biology? You must be thrilled."

"It is a great honor, Anna," he said as he nervously cleared his throat. "When prizes such as these are won, it is very rarely the result of the work of a single person, and that is the case here as well. Many of my colleagues have helped along the way. They deserve a great deal of credit and share in this award." *That came out all right,* he thought. He sat back in his chair more comfortably and relaxed.

"Your modesty is appreciated, Dr. Sehgal. But I'm sure that prizes such as these are awarded only for truly groundbreaking science," she said. He could tell she wanted to move the interview quickly past the usual pleasantries, as it was only a few minutes before their conversation would be packaged for a satellite feed across India and around the world.

"I have studied the Nobel Committee's announcement, and the area of your discovery is fascinating. Could you describe your achievement for our audience in layman's terms?"

"I'll do my best," he said confidently. "For the past twenty years, at Cambridge and MIT and then my own labs, I have focused on advancing an area of science that deals with ancient DNA—or 'aDNA,' as we call it. By 'ancient,' we mean truly ancient, as in strands of life and genetic structures that are millions of years old. A few decades ago, it was the case that biomolecules with important information about ancient plants and animals could be rescued from nature for advanced study, but the decoding processes of the time most often produced very little in the way of valuable information from these specimens. More often than not the ancient DNA was severely degraded from extreme temperatures, water dilution, or contamination from old or newly attached bacteria. It most often proved to be useless for scientific purposes."

"Okay, so far I'm with you," Anna said as she stared intently into his eyes. She had warned him prior to the interview to keep his answers short and nontechnical, and he could see by her look that he had already failed.

"Fast-forward to the development of high-throughput gene

sequencers, the type used in the Human Genome Project," he continued. "My work focused very specifically on chemical processes that, with polymerase chain reaction techniques, or PCR, allow the use of these sequencers to analyze even the smallest amounts of degraded DNA fragments, something we deal with all the time in our study of ancient DNA."

"Now you're losing me, Doctor," she complained.

Sehgal could tell. He had never met a scientist, including himself, who had mastered a sound bite for TV.

"What's important to know at this point, Anna," he said patiently, "is that with this capability in hand it became possible for us to separate the wheat from the chaff. But I am talking about microscopic wheat and microscopic chaff. We developed the ability to confidently differentiate and divide the contaminated DNA from the authentic, ancient DNA, which in turn allows us, after a great deal of effort, to fully and accurately manufacture full DNA sequences very quickly. From there, we can focus on ancient genes of real interest."

"And why is that of value?" she asked.

"Well, with these new tools in place," he continued, certain he had lost her, "it is possible to rapidly sequence entire genome structures for plants and animals when only microscopic bits of their authentic genetic material can be found. This is a tremendous leap forward. It is now possible to fully understand the evolution and composition of the look and feel of plants and animals long ago extinct."

She leaned forward, staring at him with unblinking intensity. "By that, Dr. Sehgal, do you mean extinct creatures as old as dinosaurs, for example?"

"Yes, as old as dinosaurs," Sehgal grinned, happy to see she had regained her footing. "For example, at this point in time, the entire genetic sequence for the ancient woolly mammoth is known."

Her look grew incredulous.

"Are you saying, Doctor," she pressed now more confidently, "and forgive me if this sounds silly, but the world of *Jurassic Park* is here? That you can retrieve the genetic detail to reproduce and clone dinosaurs? That seems impossible."

"Yes, at present it is impossible," he said. "There are really two massive hurdles to reproducing a dinosaur. First, you must have the extinct creature's full genetic code in hand. Today, that's possible." He folded his arms. "But it's another thing entirely to replicate it, to give it life, when there are no living hosts walking the earth that match its own species-specific DNA and that can nurture it into existence. Are you following me?"

"Yes, yes. Please go on." He could see she actually was.

"Today it's the case that if we can locate even the tiniest bit of degraded DNA from an extinct animal, we have the ability to capture its genetic code. Mind you, it's a hugely complex process. Still, we can accurately determine everything from the color of its skin to the length of its feathers, its weight, or the size of its brain. We can determine its appearance and know its composition, but we cannot clone it. At least, not yet. Eventually, with enough DNA material and synthesis, we will."

"Fascinating," she said, shifting gears quickly. "Now if I may, I'd like to turn to an amazing human-interest piece of the story. There is a rumor circulating that you have already decided to donate the entire one-point-four-million-dollar prize to charity. Is this true?"

"Yes, it is," Sehgal said, surprised she had discovered this. He shifted uncomfortably in his chair for the first time during the interview.

"Would you mind telling us who will be the lucky recipient of your generosity and why you chose to support them?" she asked.

"I'm afraid that would take us into a whole other topic," he said. "I'm not sure your audience will want me to jump on my soapbox."

"Let's let them be the judge of that, Dr. Sehgal," she pressed.

He folded his arms again, this time as if preparing to avoid answering the question. She was good enough that he knew he couldn't.

"Well, as I said, I am sure the charitable causes of a scientist are not of any real interest to your viewers," he said reluctantly. "I have been a very lucky man to have so many who have helped me throughout the years. There are many who are not so fortunate."

He paused and wondered where to begin. Suddenly, the camera lens aimed at him appeared to quadruple, to the size of a cannon. His success over the years was due to a lifetime of intense self-discipline and a propensity to look forward, not backward. And now he was in front of a national television audience being asked to bare his soul about the past.

"I grew up on the streets of Calcutta and am a child of Mother Teresa," he said. A sound technician quickly adjusted the equipment to capture his voice, which he had lowered to a whisper. "I have come a very long way in my life, Anna. I am one of the lucky ones."

"I don't think I heard you or understood you, Doctor," she said as she moved forward to the edge of her chair, her knees almost touching his as if to coax him on.

"What I mean to say is that as much progress as the world has made in the fields of science, technology, and medicine, far too many are still left behind in misery. Basic human needs are going unfulfilled all over this planet. Our own nation of India holds one-third of the world's poor, and almost one-half of our people live below the poverty line. A billion more are impoverished around the world. You are a reporter. This is no secret to you."

"Yes," she said, with a hint of defensiveness in her tone. "They are unfortunately an everyday fact of life. There are some who live on the sidewalk right outside these studios."

"I have studied the numbers, Anna. And I believe the magnitude of the problem has now grown beyond our ability to solve it. I mean *mankind's* ability to solve it. Do you understand what I mean?" he said, his voice quavering slightly.

"I'm not sure that I do," she said. "Are you saying that our government cannot handle the care of our poorest members?"

"Governments have proven incapable of responding," he said, with an irrepressible twinge of anger in his voice. "They are filled with bureaucrats who are corrupt or too incompetent to help. Foreign aid is being wasted or stolen. The wealthy hide and secrete their profits in order to avoid taxation. Only a trickle of the wealth of this nation finds its way to the poor."

"That's quite an indictment of the system, isn't it, Doctor?"

"I know this as sure as I sit here," he said defiantly. "Mankind was not meant for this misery. I believe the answer comes from above through Christ our Lord, perhaps guiding our hearts and minds. I am a survivor of the terror of poverty because of the hands of those doing his good work. I am an exception to the rule, but don't have to be. I would like, in my own way, as a scientist, to do something about this misery." He regretted that he had let the interview get so personal, but could not think quickly enough to comfortably change direction.

"So you are speaking from personal experience, Dr. Sehgal," Anna said, urging him forward.

"Well, one memory I have as a child was walking with my father into the Kalighat Temple in Calcutta, known then as the Home of the Pure Heart," he said. "Do you know it?"

She nodded. The TV lights were taking their toll. Beads of sweat had begun to make their way down Sehgal's forehead. He quickly wiped them off with his handkerchief.

"There was a documentary filmed there. It is a famous story. There was no electricity, no lights when they filmed. It was a very dark place in many ways. Yet when the film was developed, the temple was bathed in light. It was said it was a miracle of divine light from Mother Teresa." He smiled sheepishly. "I'm digressing, aren't I?"

"No, please go on, Doctor," she urged.

"It was actually a very modest hospice, a home for the dying established by the Missionaries of Charity. Their Sisters of Mercy will receive my prize money," he revealed.

"So they are the ones?" she asked.

"Yes," he continued, nodding. "Even at the tender age of seven, I knew that my father was dying. Mother Teresa herself took my father in. She was an angel of mercy. She often said that it was a beautiful thing for a person to participate in the suffering of Christ. I can assure you, Anna, that my father participated fully in this suffering during the two months that I held his hand at his bedside before he died. For me it was not a beautiful thing."

"I see," she said softly.

"So," he said as he looked down at his hands, now folded in his lap, "this was a place where many went, not to get medical attention but simply to die with dignity."

"You were orphaned?" she asked.

"In so many words," he said. "My mother had passed years before this. She died from a disease that a mere two hundred rupees' worth of antibiotics could have cured. I was taken in by Mother Teresa with other orphans and the lost children of the streets of Calcutta. I was raised as a Christian. I spent the rest of my childhood in her Nirmala Shishu Bhavan, the Children's Home of the Immaculate Heart. I like to say that *she* was my mother."

"I see." Anna nodded.

"We attended school by day and begged on behalf of the Sisters of Mercy by night," he recounted. "Some were luckier than others. I woke many times in the morning beside other children who would not wake again. There were many illnesses and severe malnourishment. Fortunately for me, some of us who showed great promise to a group of lay Catholics visiting from America were given special treatment. We received clothing and books, even tuition for special tutoring for several years. Eventually, I was able to qualify to attend school and was accepted at the Indian Institute of Technology in Madras. That is where I first began to study science."

"I am sure Mother Teresa would be proud of you, Dr. Sehgal," Anna said. He could tell she was anxious to wrap up before they ran out of time. "One of her once destitute children receives a Nobel Prize thirty-five years after her own."

"I see you know your history," Sehgal said with approval. "I remember the glorious day. I was a university professor at the time Mother Teresa was awarded the Nobel Peace Prize," he mused. "And I hope to be around when she is canonized as a saint as well."

"I am not Catholic, but everyone knows the story of Mother Teresa, Doctor. I understand that sainthood in the Church requires two demonstrated miracles, does it not?" she asked.

"It does," he answered enthusiastically. "One has already been demonstrated. A dying woman with an inoperable tumor fully recovered after a locket bearing Mother Teresa's image was placed on her chest. The tumor was healed, and a team of doctors verified the impossible. So, with this miracle documented a few years following Mother Teresa's death, her beatification by the Church is now complete."

"But a *second* miracle is required for sainthood. And that has not happened as yet. Correct?"

"Technically," he said.

Sehgal suddenly remembered the phone message in his pocket from Jon Bondurant. He intended to return the call immediately.

"But, Anna, you must know, I believe *I* am that miracle."

CHAPTER 5

Rome, Italy
April 2014

There were at least a thousand reasons to despise Father Barsanti, and for Parenti there was no question he and his little friend had so far miraculously survived one more.

It was bad enough Parenti had to work for the prefect in the Papal Library by day. But to have him live down the hall in the same decrepit apartment building on Via Germanico just outside the Vatican was too much. The brown building, a turn-of-the-century structure with nothing remarkable on its façade to denote its presence, sat on a direct line to St. Peter's Square. Consequently, the apartment's dwellers had no choice but to be up and alert each Sunday. It was the day revelers from around the world boisterously made their way past the building to celebrate what for many was a once-in-a-lifetime religious experience.

Parenti's apartment, a small efficiency with room for only a well-worn bed, a shower, a chest of drawers, and a hot plate, was modest even by priests' standards, but he found it comfortable and cozy. Its short distance to Vatican City made his journey home after a long day at work easier on his tired legs, and he was happy to call the spartan quarters home.

He shared the comfy room with a "roommate," a stray dog he had rescued from the streets and named Aldo. He was a tiny, long-haired Chihuahua with large, sad brown eyes and a constant nervous tremor with which Parenti could relate. The dog was always as quiet as a mouse and so small Parenti could secrete him inside his vestment pocket to journey with him to and from work when he chose. The priest considered it a divine gift that he had been able to house-train the teacup-sized pooch with a small litter box hidden on the apartment's balcony just outside his window. Pets, which Barsanti detested, were strictly forbidden in the building. But since the dog usually stayed confined to a miniature travel cage as modest as the apartment that housed it, he had escaped Barsanti's notice. He provided companionship and rested on the little priest's chest at night as he read. The dog carefully watched the priest turn page after page as though he too were enjoying the plot. It was uncanny how the animal sensed Parenti's moods and anticipated his needs. For the first time in the priest's miserable life, he felt he had a friend who loved him unconditionally.

Ready to retire to his bed with book in hand, Parenti reached over for the tiny cage beside the dresser to retrieve Aldo and discovered he was gone. The priest looked around him and shook his head. He could see he had left his apartment door slightly ajar, a crack large enough for even the least adventurous of creatures to scurry through. It was not the first time Aldo had opened the cage door himself, but it was the first time he had ventured outside the apartment.

Parenti rose from his bed and stepped into his red slippers. He first searched his room completely and then made his way quietly into the dimly lit hallway to scan it for any sign of his friend. As he passed by Barsanti's doorway, his heart raced as he considered the consequences of being caught on his late-evening mission.

When he found no trace of the dog near his room, he turned the corner, head down, to search the adjoining hall and bumped directly into the buttocks of Barsanti himself. The prefect, in conversation with two other priests, was in the middle of an animated story, one now ruined by Parenti's interruption. He looked down on the hunchbacked priest with disdain.

"As I was saying, Father Giordano," Barsanti exclaimed, "I was halfway to your apartment when I stumbled over *this*." He held Aldo by his tiny collar and swung him back and forth with delight, clearly enjoying the terror of both dog and owner. "It's a sizable rat, is it not, Father Marino?"

"A rat, or a rodent of some kind," Father Marino posited.

"A rat!" Barsanti exclaimed as he looked first at Parenti and then at the poor dog. "We've enough of them in Rome, have we not?"

"They're quite a nuisance," Father Giordano said. "You know, they've started plagues."

"Do you know this pest, Parenti?" Barsanti asked. "Pets are strictly forbidden in the complex. Do you know where he might have come from?"

Parenti looked down at the floor. "I do not," he said.

"You are certain?" the prefect asked. "Never seen him before?"

"I've not," the little priest said. "I swear I do not know him, but if you want to be rid of him, I will take him off your hands."

"Last chance," Barsanti said. "An owner might claim him now, but then he might be asked to vacate for breaking the rules."

Parenti thought about his cozy apartment and the short walk to work. Aldo stopped his struggle and appeared to wait for Parenti's response. *I am a coward*, thought Parenti.

"I've no such pet," he said. Aldo stared into his eyes, and Parenti felt like he absolved him from his betrayal.

"Then he *is* a rat. Not to be trusted, are they?" Barsanti said once again as he looked at Parenti and happily dangled his catch. "We have a convocation here. Let's decide, then. Feed him to the stray cats outdoors? We'd be doing the community a service."

Parenti stood in glum silence, unable now to claim his helpless friend. He looked away from his pet's gaze, helpless to do anything more than stand miserably by.

"Down the hatch with him, then?" Barsanti asked as he glanced over at the door to the trash chute leading eight stories down.

Parenti turned away from the group, sickened by the drama of the moment.

"Or a swift end to him, here and now?" Barsanti asked. He gripped the dog by the nape of the neck, and set the dog gently down on the floor. He then reared his leg back and in one swift motion kicked the tiny dog like a soccer ball as hard as he could down the hall. With a sickening squeal, the pup's head cracked against a wall like a ripe tomato and splattered blood across the hall.

Parenti fought back the contents of his stomach and put a fist in his mouth to prevent retching. The dog lay lifeless on the floor, and a pool of dark blood spread from his crushed head.

The other priests, shocked by Barsanti's sudden rage and unspeakable violence, said nothing. Parenti was sickened as he watched Barsanti take pleasure in the moment.

"Father Parenti, you have experience with rats, do you not?" he said. "Dispose of this one as quickly as you can." With that, the prefect turned, took his companions by their arms, and headed down the hall toward the stairwell.

Overcome with guilt and grief, Parenti stooped down to gather his poor companion of over two years and cursed himself for his cowardly betrayal. He wrapped the dog gently in his handkerchief, returned quietly to his room, and closed the door behind him. He laid the dog on the bed, took to his knees, unfolded the handkerchief, and began to stroke the creature with his trembling hands. He closed his eyes and prayed for forgiveness in silence for several minutes. Then a far-fetched idea came to him that he knew he had no choice but to try. He had nothing to lose.

He reached for the lower drawer of his dresser and moved several pairs of socks and some underwear aside. He pulled out a plastic bag, and from it, a small, worn piece of ancient cloth. It was the piece of material bearing the blurred but discernible image of a face—the same cloth he had secretly purloined after it slipped from the codex he discovered in the Papal Library weeks before. For that transgression, he was unsure of the punishment. Lying to the pope was probably an eternity of suffering in Malebolge, the eighth circle of hell. But from the homework he had quietly done since the veil's discovery, he strongly suspected he knew exactly what he held. It might not only help Aldo now but also maybe even save him from the fires of hell one day.

His hands began to tremble. He held his breath and listened carefully for anyone outside in the hall. He heard nothing. Then, careful to protect the image on the cloth, he laid it over the dog like a protective blanket, stroked it slowly, and closed his eyes to pray once more.

A minute passed before he felt a tingling sensation in his fingertips.

Impossibly, something had moved beneath his hands. He shuddered from head to toe as the world around him seemed to spin with the movement. The air turned icy cold. When he opened his eyes to look down, the veil appeared to stir. Something was alive beneath the cloth. Would it bite? He considered whether to snatch the rustling bundle and pitch it across the room.

He cautiously lifted the veil's edge. Stunned, he watched as the dog, still bloodied but now fully healed, climbed happily from under the miraculous veil and into the crook of his arm.

"My friend, you have returned!" Parenti cried out, flooded with joy. He brought Aldo close enough to his nose to kiss him. "You *must* forgive me."

Aldo looked back with an expression of great gentleness and compassion. The warmth and depth of the dog's love and forgiveness rendered Parenti weak with relief. He held the dog close to his heart. Aldo wagged his tail and snuggled closer. "What has happened is beyond my wildest dreams. No one must know," Parenti said as he stared at the faded image on the cloth. "Not now, not ever."

CHAPTER 6

St. Michaels, Maryland
April 2014

Bondurant was exhausted. Twenty-four hours of flight time from Mumbai to Baltimore with four stops in between had taken its toll. He gazed out at the lush green lawn that stretched almost fifty yards from the Enlightenment Institute on Perry Cabin Drive all the way to the Miles River. The signs of late spring in St. Michaels, Maryland, flirted with the approaching summer and filled his large window frame. Bright white petals from the dogwood trees outside his office window floated to the ground like snowflakes with the slightest breeze. In the distance he could see an afternoon ferryboat, red and white, full of weekend tourists on its slow trek across the East Bay toward Annapolis.

He took another drag on his cigarette and crushed the butt into the dozen others that lay dead in the ashtray beside him. He cursed the addiction he couldn't shake. He had picked up the habit years earlier as a way to keep others at bay, or lose them entirely with obnoxious smoke in the moments when he wanted to be alone. Now the weakness of addiction had turned on him, and there was little he could do about it.

He reached for the glass of Macallan single malt he had poured, his lone companion on the porch just outside his office. He cradled his scotch in one hand and the contract that had just arrived from the Vatican in the other. Then he kicked open the worn screen door at the rear of the large Victorian farmhouse he had converted to his Institute offices years before. It was a large covered porch that enclosed a half-dozen rocking chairs and an antique dining table. As much debate as food had been served at the table, just the way Bondurant liked it. He glanced over at the horizon to his right and could see the familiar sight of ships' masts that extended just above the distant tree line. There sat the Baltimore clippers moored at the Maritime Museum, a half mile upstream.

He took a sip. After twenty years of drinking the same whisky, he still marveled at its smoothness. It was the same scotch his father used to drink, and Bondurant was certain his own taste for it was one of the few decent traits the old man had left him.

He watched a tired white skipjack from an oyster fleet chug past on the green river, and in trail right behind it, a sleek new sailboat on its way to the bay, filled with revelers likely up for the weekend from nearby Washington, DC. At the bow of the sailboat were three tan twentysomething girls stripped to their bikinis. They laughed, waved their arms, and pointed toward him. He watched as they toasted, their drinks high in the air, and shouted in his direction. He waved back halfheartedly and casually returned the salutes. Between the drone of the boat's motor and their distance from him, he couldn't hear a word they had yelled. He stood absolutely thoughtless for almost ten minutes as they faded from sight around the river's edge.

It was another "Bondurant Moment." Some had suggested his random lapses into oblivion were the classic sign of an absentminded professor. His huge intellect did have a way of crowding out the trivial in favor of more important things, but that was only partly to blame. Other people were less charitable about it and believed his bouts of solitude could be traced to heavy drinking.

But for the few who had known him since boyhood, his eventual success, like his oblivious moments, came as no surprise. With an IQ of 165, he ranked near the "highest genius" category. Raised in Baltimore just across the street from a Catholic church and within sight of a dilapidated horse track, he had grown up as one of two sons of Big Jack Bondurant, a gregarious alcoholic, professional gambler, and absent single parent all in one. He was routinely left alone with his younger brother, three years his junior. They were usually left to fend for themselves without a clue as to their father's whereabouts. Bondurant had home-schooled himself and his sibling in their neglected apartment from the age of ten. He applied for and received a full academic scholarship to Stanford at the age of sixteen. His adoring brother and only "schoolmate" had met a different fate.

"With every blessing comes a curse," his father used to say. Sure enough, he was right. It was only as an adult that he would come to understand it all. He had found his younger brother, then ten and tiny and his only friend, hanging by the neck from the coat rack of their bedroom closet. He could remember his father's shouting and all the crying and the funeral too. He remembered the visits of the priests from across the road. All of it had been a blur.

As he grew older, certain functions of Bondurant's brain became so dominant that they allowed him to concentrate on a level few could ever reach. His ability to focus on detail, coupled with obsessive interest in whatever subject caught his eye, made him a quiet, intellectual phenomenon. He drifted in his self-studies toward a half-dozen diverse academic disciplines, from anatomy to history to anthropology, but given little guidance, he settled on none. He immersed himself in them all, which years later propelled him to the top of his field in ancient forensic anthropology.

He was often socially dysfunctional, and he knew it. Relating to others had seemed like a waste of time, as the child genius had regularly found his thoughts more important than the people around him. Eventually, he'd become strangely paralyzed by an acute shyness, particularly around his father's procession of lady friends, who came and went as they pleased. The more they doted on the handsome but reclusive boy, trying to coax him out of his shell, the more his symptoms flared.

A social worker dragged him to a child psychologist, who diagnosed the problem as "gender selective mutism," saying it stemmed from the complete absence of a mother or more permanent female figure in his life. He had never known his mother and had gotten along fine without her, Bondurant recalled telling the psychologist. At fourteen, he dressed the doctor down, telling him he was clueless, citing chapter and verse from the American Psychiatric Association's *Diagnostic and Statistical Manual of Mental Disorders*. If there really was something wrong with him, it was not to be found in any of the several manuals he had read.

But there *was* no letting people get close or letting them in. He never went there. As he grew older, finished his studies, and entered his profession, his unnatural shyness toward others, including women, subsided some. He felt less awkward around them. And, like his father, he discovered over time that they served a useful purpose, staving off the incessant loneliness he often came to feel. While he sometimes suffered unpredictable bouts of severe withdrawal as an adult, his episodes would come and go. When they came, they were devastating. It was normal for an adolescent to appear extremely shy. Most found it endearing. But as a grown man, a sudden or unexpected fit of acute shyness or detachment in public situations would come off as odd or downright rude.

He had to admit it was probably the strange emptiness he felt inside that had led to his undoing as a professor at Princeton. It was strictly forbidden for faculty to have relationships with their students, which was fine by him. While he craved companionship to fight the loneliness he often felt at night, he was no fan of relationships. Relations, yes. Relationships, no. He had discreetly enjoyed the late-night company of a long line of pretty, smart coeds who, unfortunately, didn't differentiate between the two words the same way he did.

In his last year at the university, he underestimated the wrath of one coed in particular, a twenty-two-year-old senior enrolled in his anthropology course whom he had slept with once. She was stunned to receive a near-failing grade on her midterm. He thought nothing of giving her the D he knew she deserved, but she was furious and threatened to take her grievance to her father. Bondurant, nonplussed, told her she was free to do so. Parents, even alumni, had no pull with grades, he informed her. Unfortunately, he didn't realize she was the daughter of Dean Thomas Armstrong, the head of his department, who was not amused. Bondurant later described the contentious encounter with the dean and his daughter to a colleague as "acts of submission." Before the meeting was over, she had admitted to her father that she'd slept with Bondurant, and Bondurant had submitted his resignation.

Despite the dean's efforts to keep the matter quiet, the campus and local newspaper splashed Bondurant's resignation all over the front page and cited the reason. Like all good scandals, the story zipped around academic circles, which resulted in the catastrophic gutting of his prestigious reputation and professional academic career. Left with no choice, he struck out on his own. He headed south for Maryland, bought a Victorian farmhouse in disrepair on the edge of town in rural St. Michaels, pulled together a handful of some of the most promising graduate students he could find, and formed the Enlightenment Institute: a nonprofit organization named after the famous movement of the eighteenth century that favored human reasoning over blind faith and religious doctrine. Its mission was the promotion of science in the tackling of religious and historical mystery.

While Bondurant's academic career path had been ruined, his reputation as a leading forensic anthropologist able to solve mysteries in the realm of historical discovery was not. The array of projects he and his young team took on during the first several years of the Institute's operations was exciting, enough to keep a mystery writer busy for years. And for Bondurant, it did. For every vexing historical question his Institute took on, he had agreements that allowed him to write companion books detailing his work. His articles for *National Geographic* quickly caught the attention of the biggest publishing houses in New York, which produced one book deal after another. His books, perennially on the *New York Times* bestseller list, had made him a well-known author and lecturer.

His first book, *Still Missing*, delved into the disappearance of Amelia Earhart, the famous aviatrix who was lost at sea during her attempted round-the-world flight in 1937. Hers was one of the last great unsolved mysteries, and several competing theories as to her fate and final resting place had circulated for years. One particularly well-known exploration outfit—ISOA (In Search of Amelia)—had made repeated journeys to the tiny island of Nikumaroro, some 2,100 miles south of Hawaii and directly in line with her planned flight path from New Guinea to Howland Island, where she was to refuel. Convinced the evidence led to a likely crash landing of her plane on a reef at the tip of Nikumaroro, ISOA's attempts to prove the theory were relentless. After ten excursions over several years to the remote area of the island in the South Pacific and an investment of $5 million, ISOA had discovered a handful of promising items, including the heel of a woman's shoe, a compact, and buttons and a zipper from a flight jacket, all of which appeared to be from the Earhart era.

News organizations became increasingly doubtful of ISOA's theory when further evidence ceased to accumulate, but the group's eleventh expedition produced a jackpot—or so they believed. They returned to the United States with great fanfare and the "undeniable" evidence in hand. They staged a press conference in Washington, DC, that proclaimed the discovery of three bone fragments thought to be from the finger of a female of "northern European origin."

The Smithsonian Institution, skeptical of the findings, received permission from ISOA to examine the bones and promptly hired Bondurant. It took his team at the Institute and the Molecular Anthropology Laboratories at Oxford three weeks to resolve the case. With excitement and anticipation building, Bondurant was asked by ISOA whether it would be appropriate to fly Earhart's great-niece to Washington, DC, for a press conference confirming the extraordinary discovery. It was the niece's DNA Bondurant had used to compare to the bone fragments ISOA discovered.

"Not unless she stems from a long line of sea turtles," Bondurant replied. "The mystery remains."

His second book, *Children of the Czar*, dealt with the Enlightenment Institute's intensive examination for *National Geographic* of the remains in graves discovered outside the city of Yekaterinburg, Russia, in 2007. The stakes for the organization and its magazine were high as they prepared to publish a cover story making the remarkable claim that Czar Nicholas's daughter, the Grand Duchess Anastasia, long thought to be dead, was actually alive and living comfortably in a nursing home in, of all places, Cleveland, Ohio. The czar, the last monarch of imperial Russia; his wife, Alexandra; and their children were thought to have been murdered in a basement in Yekaterinburg by Bolsheviks during the revolution in 1918. Rumors had endured for years that one or more of the czar's children, including Prince Alexei and the Grand Duchesses Maria and Anastasia, might have escaped the assassins' bullets. Previous excavations in the nondescript Russian countryside had turned up incontrovertible evidence of the bones of the czar, his wife, and an undetermined number of children.

Bondurant, convinced the collection of burned remains he had been shown was indeed incomplete, traveled to Russia to investigate further. Within forty yards of the original sites he found another makeshift grave, this one containing an additional forty-four bones never before discovered. He meticulously matched the newly discovered bones with photographs of the children and, using fragments of DNA from a bloodstained shirt of their father's that had been preserved in Russia for over a century, the team Bondurant assembled saved *National Geographic* immeasurable grief. Only a day before the magazine's cover story was scheduled to go to print, Bondurant had been able to convincingly conclude that all the czar's children, including the youngest, Anastasia, were shot and brutally stabbed almost a century before.

Bondurant's most recent book, *The Boy King*, dealt with the most extensive and historically important postmortem of the famous Egyptian pharaoh Tutankhamun, better known as King Tut. Previous examinations of the mummy had led many to believe that King Tut had met with a terrible accident or had been the victim of murder at the age of eighteen or nineteen. The evidence supporting this stemmed from a hole found in the back of his head, thought to be the result of a blow from a fall or blunt instrument. Bondurant, having studied volumes of material on King Tut, had his doubts. There were clues to another culprit Bondurant had in mind, a source more benign than murder. In the opportunity of a lifetime, Bondurant was asked to lead a team of scientists to whom the Egyptians gave unlimited access to determine the true cause of King Tut's death.

From previous DNA studies that had revealed the presence of parasites, Bondurant had been convinced King Tut had been the victim of chronic malaria throughout his youth. But it was not until he was able to examine the remains of King Tut himself that he was able to put multiple sets of evidence together and deduce the truth. Given obvious signs of bone disease and a resultant fracture of King Tut's leg, the team determined a bout of malaria had likely severely weakened his immune system to the point that a severe infection had taken his life. The source of the hole in the back of his head was obvious, Bondurant felt. It was too perfectly formed to be the result of a fall or a murderous instrument. Rather, it was evidence of the technique sometimes used by ancient embalmers to reach the brain and liquefy it in preparation for mummification.

His contribution had solidified the scientific community's opinion of him as first-rate.

Now, Bondurant had just signed an agreement that called for him to embark on his next discovery, one such as he had never thought possible. Setting down his glass of scotch, he reached for a pad of paper and scribbled for the first time the title of his next book: *False Shroud.*

CHAPTER 7

Alitalia Flight 643
June 2014

It was dark enough in the first-class cabin for Bondurant to doze, but he couldn't fall asleep. The sleeping pill he had chased with scotch had obviously not worked. Too much on his mind, he thought. Alitalia Flight 643, bound for Milan, had less than five hours of flight time remaining before it landed. Add to that the two-hour train ride to Turin and the loss of six hours for time zone changes from Baltimore, and it was going to be a long day. He envied the peacefully dozing passengers in their comfortable sweat suits in the seats around him. Why was such an easy escape always so difficult for him?

An attractive flight attendant with long legs and brown hair noticed he was the sole passenger still awake and leaned over from behind him. She gently grasped his forearm.

"Can I get you another Macallan, Dr. Bondurant?" she asked softly. Startled at her touch, he shifted quickly in his seat and stared forward silently for a moment before responding.

"Dr. Bondurant?" she asked.

"I'm fine. Just fine, thank you," he said.

He pulled a letter from his dossier and squinted to read it in the darkness. He had read it several times before and had almost committed it to memory. He was still amazed that after two months of tense negotiations, an agreement with the Church had actually been reached. The letter, embossed with the Vatican's seal in gold leaf at the top, was to the point:

Dear Dr. Bondurant:

It is with great satisfaction that I enclose the countersigned agreement setting forth the protocols the research team you have agreed to assemble will use to examine the Shroud of Turin. As you know, while the Catholic Church has officially neither accepted nor rejected the authenticity of the relic as venerated by the faithful over many centuries, the Holy Father believes that further and comprehensive investigation by responsible scientists is warranted to address the mystery. As was stated by his predecessor, the Blessed John Paul II, in 1998: "Since it is not a matter of faith, the Church has no specific competence to pronounce on these questions. She entrusts to scientists the task of continuing to investigate, so that satisfactory answers may be found to the questions connected with this Sheet." The Church's position remains unchanged.

Per our agreement, all of the necessary arrangements have been made to place the relic at your team's disposal at the agreed-upon laboratories in Turin, Italy, for a two-week period commencing June 7, 2014, and ending no later than June 21, 2014, subject to the appropriate oversight and safeguarding of the artifact during this period by the Church officials assigned. Given the breadth of advanced scientific techniques and equipment at your team's ready that were not in existence during previous examinations of the relic, we are hopeful that this research effort

as called for in the agreement, and under your leadership, will produce a
definitive and credible conclusion to what has been a lengthy debate.

Upon your arrival in Turin, please contact Ms. Jozef, the Church's
official administrator for this examination, at the address provided on
the attached. She will make all the necessary arrangements to ensure your
research efforts and requests are promptly considered as you proceed.

In Christ's Name,
Giovanni Orsini
President
Pontifical Academy of Sciences

A letter from heaven, Bondurant mused. But who was Ms. Jozef? He was certain he had heard the name before but couldn't place it. He was positive she had not been involved in the endless conference calls with Vatican officials over the past few weeks. The last thing he felt he needed was the Church injecting someone new into the picture, some potentially bothersome handler just as they were going to finally get down to business.

It didn't matter. He had thirty-eight pages of signed protocols for study of the Shroud. They were more permissive than any previous investigation of the relic in history. So permissive that he wondered if this investigation was the Vatican's attempt to surrender to science after all these years. Before he left for Turin, he had debated with several of his colleagues at the Institute and with his publisher whether Pope Augustine himself had determined the relic was an albatross from the past, that it was time for the Church to step into the twenty-first century with a new approach of openness to scientific scrutiny. That was his theory. How else could one justify the Church's willingness to allow such an invasive examination of its most holy relic?

And what explained the Vatican's willingness to choose him, of all people? He was known as a high-profile, vocal skeptic of the relic's authenticity. He had found himself the target of criticism from the Catholic Church at religious conferences and in opinion pieces written for Christian periodicals. He had even received what some would describe as hate mail from leading Evangelicals because of his outspoken views. At a conference in Brussels the previous year, he had appeared on a panel to debate the theory of intelligent design and had been shouted off the stage. Allowing him full access to the Catholic Church's holiest relic was like handing him the keys to the kingdom. He felt that if the pope wanted to drive a stake into the heart of the Shroud's authenticity, he had picked no surer way to do it. However, Bondurant wondered whether there wasn't something amiss. It was all just too easy. He wondered what the Vatican knew that he didn't. If they somehow had credible evidence that the Shroud of Turin was no medieval fake—and there was a one-in-a-million chance of that—Bondurant knew his entire career would be called into question, and he would have some soul searching and a lot of explaining to do.

Whatever the pontiff's rationale, Bondurant was happy to play along. Two weeks to study the Shroud up close was definitely not enough time, and his team would have to conduct their experiments at a frantic pace around the clock. But, with the right planning and the best talent he could find, it would be enough time to credibly study the relic and collect the samples the Church would permit for further study in sophisticated labs in the weeks ahead.

Bondurant had assembled a team of renowned scientists, each bringing a unique expertise in his or her field to the project. He was certain their collective work would help to redefine "sindonology." He was determined that their conclusions would be beyond reproach and would settle, once and for all, the mystery of the Shroud.

His team stemmed from three fundamentally important disciplines: biological and medical forensics, material historical analysis, and material chemical analysis. Including Bondurant as lead, the group comprised seven scientists, some of whom he had worked with before. To a person, they had jumped at the unprecedented opportunity to join the highest-profile examination of an important religious artifact in many years. Even before the investigation had begun, hundreds of media outlets had covered the Vatican's announcement of its willingness to allow an intense investigation of the Shroud. Chat rooms were buzzing, dozens of related blogs had been started, and more than a million tweets had been recorded concerning the Church's decision. Nearly all of them speculated on what Bondurant's team would find. There was even a betting line in Las Vegas, where odds were running two-to-one in favor of evidence proving the Shroud was a fake.

From the field of biological and medical forensics, a field in which Bondurant was considered preeminent, he had selected two other scientists. For his role, Bondurant would lead the anatomical forensics review. In some respects, he held the role of "coroner," but without a body. His investigation would determine in precise detail the "anatomical correctness" of the *image* of the body presented on the Shroud. Were the body parts as represented on the image natural and in proper proportion to the rest of the body, or were there subtle distortions that would imply the image had been fabricated by something other than human remains? Were the various markings on the image connoting torture and crucifixion indicative of how such trauma would actually appear in these areas of the body? Bondurant's work would represent the closest examination possible of the Shroud's bodily image short of an autopsy.

In the field of image analysis, he had chosen Dr. Haruki Sato, a leader in digital image processing research at Sony Labs. He held thirty-seven patents, making his net worth in excess of $400 million. He was best known for his work using computer image analysis to differentiate shades of color so fine that it was possible to determine whether an image had originally been formed in two or three dimensions. Three-dimensional images, those with "depth" that might have been naturally formed by an object such as a human body, could be made distinguishable from two-dimensional images that had been painted on a surface such as canvas or cloth. Sato had recently been involved in solving several celebrated cases with this technology. Supposed priceless masterpieces had been discovered to be fakes because he'd found highly irregular and computer-generated brushstrokes during microscopic image analysis.

Bondurant had been introduced to the eccentric Sato by a mutual friend just prior to a classic-car auction in Philadelphia. Bondurant was interested in a single car at the auction. He had been stalking it in the market for three years—a 1965 Jaguar XKE 4.2, serial #00001. Unfortunately for him, it had turned out that Sato had flown in on his private jet from Kyoto to purchase the same car and was intent on outbidding all buyers. The two had become fast friends.

To round out the field for the biological and medical forensics team, Bondurant thought he had pulled off a master stroke. While he had never met him before, he had flown round-trip from Baltimore to India over a four-day weekend and succeeded in convincing Dr. Ravi Sehgal, the recent Nobel Prize–winning biologist from India, to join the team.

Sehgal's findings, next to the data gleaned from radiocarbon dating, were likely going to provide more definitive evidence than any other discipline on the authenticity of the Shroud. He had made a worldwide name for himself in the field of ancient DNA analysis, and his presence on the project meant instant credibility. His work was going to be crucial in determining whether the bloodstains purportedly present on the Shroud, and any other microscopic evidence of DNA discovered, were actually real. And if they were real, his examination would be able to pinpoint their source as animal or human and their date of origin, blood type, and composition.

To represent the field of material historical analysis, he had enlisted two acknowledged experts, one in ancient fabrics and the other in soil particle analysis. While the field was little known, it was a certainty that Dr. Jean Boudreau possessed a body of knowledge on textile analysis like no other. In his mid-fifties, quiet, and balding, he was the only grossly overweight Frenchman Bondurant had ever met. He had marveled at Boudreau's obesity until he realized years after first meeting him that Dr. Jean Boudreau was the same Jean Boudreau who had authored the three bestselling French cookbooks of the last decade.

His laboratory in Paris, right across the street from his famous restaurant, held the world's largest collection of ancient fabrics. It was possible for Boudreau to differentiate between region-specific Middle Eastern twill patterns and sewing techniques found in every century leading back to ancient Egypt. If the linen represented as the Shroud of Jesus was found to be of material that originated anywhere but in the Middle East during the first century AD, or if it revealed a sewing pattern not found until the Middle Ages, Boudreau would catch it.

Boudreau was not the only team member from an obscure field of study. Dr. Michael Lessel, of the University of New Mexico, was a world authority on soil particle analysis. He knew dirt like no other.

A bona fide redneck from Alabama with a drawl so deep it deceived many an observer into underestimating his IQ, he was both brilliant and uncannily strong. Pushing seventy-five years old, Lessel was half Bondurant's size, but he had once challenged Bondurant to an arm wrestling contest in a biker bar not far from his home in St. Michaels following an academic conference. After five straight losses, Bondurant had become a laughingstock in front of a swarm of bikers and some rowdy cadets from the US Naval Academy in Annapolis.

Lessel knew that the Shroud, like any other material of its kind and age, very likely contained trace elements of various soils that could be isolated and identified in terms of composition. Using high-resolution devices on microscopic particles of dirt, he was able to determine whether soil samples found on objects were native to a particular region of the world or even a specific locale. If dirt samples taken from the Shroud didn't match the known properties of Middle Eastern soils in the area of Jerusalem, this would be a sure sign that the relic was a fake. Lessel had his suspicions.

Finally, in the field of material chemical analysis, Bondurant had secured his good friend and colleague Dr. Terry O'Neil, one of the world's leading authorities on radiocarbon dating. O'Neil, dean of the University of Oxford's Chemistry Department, had worked with Bondurant on previous investigations of relics, including those involving Amelia Earhart. They'd both gone to Stanford, though almost a generation apart, and had become good friends. O'Neil knew how important this investigation was to Bondurant and his reputation, and Bondurant knew O'Neil would ensure that the data he gathered was beyond reproach.

Using a process developed by scientists at the University of Chicago in the late 1940s, O'Neil had a proven track record of determining the age of any ancient substance by measuring its levels of radioisotopic carbon-14. There were two things that Bondurant and O'Neil were sure of before the investigation began. First, unless the Shroud was from another universe, it was a carbon-bearing substance. And second, given this, it could be dated—not within a year or two, or even a decade, but with O'Neil involved, Bondurant was convinced the origin of the Shroud could be pinpointed to within as few as fifty years. There was no test of the relic's age more important than radiocarbon dating, and Bondurant knew he had the world's greatest authority in O'Neil.

The last scientist to join the team was Dr. Lisa Montrose, an expert in the study of material pigmentation analysis at Duke University. Bondurant knew her by reputation only. Calm and soft-spoken, she was an authority used often by the National Geographic Society when highly complicated analysis was required on the composition of unusual artifacts. She specialized in the area of microfiber analysis using electron microscopes to determine the chemical composition of compounds found on ancient materials. Determining precisely what substance had left the ghostlike image on the Shroud would not be easy, given its age, but it was a certainty she could produce the most definitive results. Had the image of the Shroud been painted on the relic's linen surface using any chemical compound known to man, she would be able to determine the source.

Bondurant stared at the letter from the Vatican one more time. *Worth framing someday*, he thought. He folded it and put it away. Then he looked at his watch. The blue digital numerals at its center slowly blinked a pair of numbers: 11:07.

Eleven years. Seven months.

CHAPTER 8

Geneva, Switzerland
June 2014

Geneva had a reputation for being a peaceful, beautiful city, but the stark and modern two-story cement compound that presented itself when their driver slowly pulled up to the guard gate resembled a bunker from the Cold War era. It was a cheerless place. Rain from an early summer thunderstorm was coming down in sheets, and the steely sky above blanketed the entire world around him in muted shades of gray. The guard who greeted their black limo peered in through the crack of the rear passenger window to identify them by sight, his mood clearly matching the weather.

Dr. François Laurent had one simple goal for the meeting he was about to enter inside the Demanian Church headquarters. He wanted it to end with an agreement so they could launch a plan before it was too late. Of the two men he had gathered, he was fully familiar with one. He had been of service to Hans Meyer, the supreme elder of the Demanian Church, for just over two years. It was two years more than he liked. With any luck, within a year his obligation to Meyer and his absurd cult would end, and he would be able to return to Paris with his family, restart his medical practice, and move on.

The third person who had accompanied him on the dreary ride to the sect's stronghold that morning was Ravi Sehgal. Laurent had greeted him in person for the first time only an hour before at the Geneva airport. The Nobel laureate had a layover on his way to Turin. Their conversation on the rainy car ride to Meyer's fortresslike offices in the Carouge district along the banks of the Rue du Rhône had been promising. Laurent found Sehgal likable, if a bit naive. Laurent had known him by reputation to be somewhat vain, but their string of conference calls during the past week had convinced him that Sehgal and Meyer might have enough common ground in mind to make a deal possible.

Laurent knew that for Sehgal's part, he wanted simply to "save the world." *Laughable*, thought Laurent. Sehgal had spoken of some altruistic dream he had that, with his knowledge of DNA, might conjure up a child with Christlike powers, a scientific "second coming" as it were. Sehgal imagined a child who would grow to adulthood under his care and would learn to rain miracles down on the world and save the poor—especially the children—from their plight.

Laurent knew Meyer's vision of their creation was not nearly as altruistic as Sehgal's. For Meyer, the creation of such a child was all about power. Power for his church, and power for himself. Laurent felt he would be able to control Sehgal during their meeting to reach an agreement, but was not as confident about his sway over Meyer.

"So what are you saying, Dr. Sehgal?" Meyer asked as he looked directly at him.

The Demanian leader was an unappealing middle-aged figure, sullen, with thinning hair and afflicted with a horrendous case of adult acne. On the table in front of him was an Electrolarynx, a small machine the size of a toaster, without which their conversation would be impossible. Meyer had lost his vocal cords from a laryngectomy a decade earlier, an operation made necessary due to throat cancer from smoking several packs a day. His voice, amplified by the microphone pressed to the spot where his larynx had once been, generated words in a sickeningly electronic monotone. They had been negotiating for thirty minutes, and time was growing short. Sehgal's flight to Italy, where he was due to meet with Bondurant, was scheduled to depart in just a few hours. Meyer pressed the microphone pad to the side of his throat and asked again. "I said, so what *are* you saying?"

Sehgal shuddered, the drone of the robotic voice unnerving. "I'm saying that this is going to be a struggle," Sehgal said. "It comes down to how many blood samples I can get my hands on. It's possible that Dr. Bondurant may not be able to secure enough from his agreement with the Vatican to do the job. He'll provide me a shred of the evidence he'll gather, but I may need it all. Every last bit. We won't know until we know."

"I thought this was a slam dunk for you, with your Nobel and all," Meyer said. "You're not backing away from that claim now, are you?"

Sehgal grew red in the face.

"Sometimes I wish I could just bury that prize," Sehgal said. "It's more of a nuisance than anything."

Laurent looked surprised.

"How could you say that?" Laurent asked. "It's over a million dollars. It's fame worldwide."

"It's also very difficult to achieve the results that people want to see," Sehgal said. "Yes, we can sweep DNA clean. Yes, we can work with particulate DNA as never before. But if the DNA is badly contaminated, and has been for thousands of years, we may need all the blood we can find for this to work. I'm telling you it's no mean feat to pull this off."

"You'll do your best to get it all, Doctor," Meyer replied in an expressionless voice. "And if you can't, I won't wait for you. I'll have my people there to obtain every drop by any means necessary. Time is short. Laurent, who did you say is overseeing all this for the Church?"

"I have a source that's identified her," Laurent said. "She's apparently close to the pope."

"Make a note, then," Meyer said. "I want her tailed. Everywhere she goes. If the Church gets cold feet for any reason and they're holding up *my* blood samples, we're just going to need to take them. That's all there is to it."

"I am also going to need to play with the results a little," Sehgal said. "Enough to keep the scientific community at bay for a while."

"What does that mean, Ravi?" Laurent asked. It was not something they had discussed.

"I need you to listen very carefully here," Sehgal said. "Lord only knows what we might find on this Shroud. A speck of dirt? A Roman sentry's blood? The precious blood of Christ our Savior? I don't know. But I do know this. If I make an announcement that Christ's blood is in our midst and there is even the slightest hint that Demanians are involved, we all know where that will lead."

"I know where you're going with this," Meyer said.

"It means the world is going to presume we are near the point of a clone-born Christ. I cannot attempt to do my work with a grand circus surrounding me. I don't think we want millions to believe the impossible is real before we make it real. There will be many who want to stop us. That would be a terrible distraction, I think."

"He has a point, Laurent," Meyer said. "So now what?"

"Create a distraction, if we can. I'm simply going to have to manage the results if need be. I don't want to. I don't like it. But we'll need to throw everyone off the trail and take their attention elsewhere. I'm not sure exactly what I'll say when the time comes, but I have some ideas, starting with leaking a document so that—"

"Fine, fine, fine," Meyer interrupted. "Spare us the details. Now, what is this I hear from Laurent about your insistence on the notion of using a virgin? Are there really any left in this world? This is a joke, right?"

Laurent could see Sehgal wince at Meyer's question. Try as he might, he had not been able to get Meyer to agree with one of Sehgal's more peculiar demands. It was up to Sehgal now to make the case for himself.

"It has obvious biblical precedent. This child will enter the world as he should, under the chastest of circumstances," Sehgal stated flatly. "There is no other way. You want my help? That's my condition." This was the swagger that Laurent had detected before. He had seen very few men stand their ground with the supreme elder. He braced himself for Meyer's response.

"You see some of my chattel, Dr. Sehgal?" Meyer said as he pointed to two attractive women as they passed by the glass-walled conference room they sat in. The women walked down the hallway with eyes cast directly in front of them. A steady stream of women had headed in the same direction for the last half hour. "You know where they are going, I presume?"

"I've been told it's your egg depository," Sehgal said.

"The largest in the world, my friend. We have five of them on three continents. Tell him, Dr. Laurent. Tell him how many are now stored."

"Over a hundred thousand eggs at last count, Hans," Laurent said.

"You need our huge depository of eggs, and we need you, Dr. Sehgal. Now tell him, Laurent," Meyer insisted. "Tell him how many dedicated Demanian women in our ranks have made this possible. Tell him."

"Well over ten thousand, I believe," Laurent said, as if reading from a script he had rehearsed. "They come from all over the world. As you know, Dr. Sehgal, we need such a large number of eggs given the failure rate for cloning insemination."

"All this sacrifice, and a Demanian woman is not good enough for the task, Dr. Sehgal?" Meyer's face began to turn red with fury.

"I have nothing against your women," Sehgal said. "But if I understand Demanian ways, they have all been violated, have they not? There are no technical virgins."

"As is their wont, Doctor," Meyer said as he cranked up the volume on his amplifier to provide the emphasis his voice could not. "Don't proselytize to me. Just who do you propose to use as this Christian virgin surrogate, if indeed you can find one of age in this world? It is a wild-goose chase, and you know it. You will come crawling back to me."

"Leave that to me, Mr. Meyer," Sehgal said. "I am sure there are devout virgins who would jump at the chance when it becomes clear what role they will play."

Laurent felt Sehgal had no idea whom he might find for this special surrogate, but he was impressed with the stubbornness he displayed with Meyer.

"All right, then," Meyer said. He waved his arm in the air as if he had checked a box on an imaginary list before him. "If you insist on the fairy-tale version of virgin birth and all of that, so be it. Like I said, you'll be back for a willing host when you've failed. Let's get to the more important issue our partner, Laurent, says you have raised. What about the child? Who is to care for the child?"

"I will reluctantly agree to joint custody," Sehgal said. "But I want him raised in India, where he can do the most good for as many as possible until at least the age of eighteen. Those are my terms. Take them or leave them."

"I'll leave them!" Meyer said as he spun the volume-control knob on his machine as loud as it would go. His synthesized voice was ear-shattering and vibrated the glass walls around them.

"Fine," Sehgal shouted as he rose from his chair to leave. "Best of luck in your quest, Mr. Meyer."

"Wait, wait," Laurent protested. "We have come this far. We are so close." The end of his obligation to Meyer was within sight, a moment that would not likely come again. He would lock the door to prevent Sehgal from walking out if he had to.

"Easy for you to say, Laurent," Meyer countered. "You have a son. *I* made that possible. Now this man comes here with a plan to deny me mine?"

"He said 'joint custody,' Hans. Joint. Surely you can live with that?" Laurent pleaded.

Meyer folded his arms and paused for what seemed to be an eternity, obviously bitter about the ultimatum. Sehgal rose from his chair and moved toward the door as he prepared to leave. Laurent got up to block his path.

"All right, then," Meyer said reluctantly, the resignation in his voice apparent, even in monotone. "Joint custody."

"Then we have a deal?" Sehgal asked as he turned and moved toward the table to extend his hand.

Laurent looked at Meyer and carefully studied his eyes, the same lifeless ones Laurent had grown weary of after two years. He knew it was at moments like this when the voice machine on the table robbed a listener like Sehgal of being able to detect nuance or true intent. It provided Meyer with a distinct advantage. Laurent was certain Meyer was using the machine to lie through his teeth, but there was nothing Laurent could or wanted to do about it at this point. His commitment to Meyer was nearly complete, and no force in the world could stop where they were headed.

"We have a deal," Meyer said as he smiled. "Now let's remake the world."

CHAPTER 9

Turin, Italy
June 2014

Sehgal was not usually one to remember his dreams when he woke, but during the first night in his hotel room in Turin he had the same strange dream that had been repeated over and over, and this one remained with him.

It always began in a church confessional, one he didn't recognize. He was a young boy, and he kneeled on one side of the booth in the dark. The only light came from a small, worn, yellow plastic screen just inches from his face. On the opposite side of the booth sat his father, in the role of the priest and confessor. The screen between them masked their identities, but he knew from the sound of his father's voice that he was there.

"Bless me, Father, for I have sinned," he rushed to say. "It has been too long since my last confession."

The young Ravi, happy to know his father had returned from the dead, anxiously awaited his blessing. He couldn't wait to end the charade. All he wanted was to go to the other side of the barrier to give his father a hug and be taken home. Instead, his father's voice was stern.

"Ravi, have you examined your conscience? What have you made of yourself today?" his father demanded.

"I have won a prize, Father," Ravi proudly said.

"Yes, Ravi. But this is a place to confess. You are alive, and I am dead. Why am I dead, Ravi?"

Ravi began to cry.

"For this, I am truly sorry, Father."

"What good are you? You know your mother is dead too?"

He desperately tried to touch his father by pressing his small fingers through the holes in the screen between them. It was impossible.

"There are many here with us, Ravi. There will be many more. Now what will you do with your prize?"

"I will create the baby Jesus, Father. I will bring him back to live again."

"And you will save us? All of us, Ravi?"

"Yes, all of you," Ravi cried.

Ravi awoke from his dream unable to move. He felt as though there were another presence in the room, as if someone were watching and pressing the weight of his body deep into the bed. He lay perfectly still and prayed for a dreamless sleep and the light of the morning to come.

CHAPTER 10

Krakow, Poland
June 2014

Domenika had planned to visit with her parents in Krakow for three days on the way to her assignment in Turin, and she was convinced her stay, as usual, had lasted a day too long. She loved her parents dearly, but her visits with them were like stepping into a time machine. Though Domenika had just turned thirty-one, her father had a way of treating her like she was fifteen again. And then there were the constant comparisons to her younger sister, his favorite, who had gone abroad but not returned in years.

"Domenika," he said in frustration, "I've told you and your mother a thousand times that your sister, Joanna, will put you up in New York. You are wasting away inside that museum."

"You are the only person I know who refers to Vatican City as a museum," Domenika replied. "Please. It is the Holy City, the home of our Holy Father." The cuckoo clock on the wall behind them ticked and tocked incessantly, and louder than she remembered as a child. It was as if it were setting a tempo for their conversation.

He slammed his massive fist on the dining room table, rattling the china his wife, Julianna, had so carefully set in place for their Sunday dinner.

"How about listening to *this* father, *your* father, for once, Domenika?" he urged as he reached for his tumbler of vodka. "Your sister is earning thousands of dollars every time those magazines take her picture, and you are every bit the beauty she is."

"*Dosc!* That's it!" Domenika's mother pleaded. "Can we not have peace for just this moment? Her life is at the Vatican, where it should be. And she is leaving for Turin tomorrow. Let us enjoy our meal before she is on her way again."

Domenika turned away from her father and stared out at the scene framed by the large corner window of her family's modest fifth-floor apartment. The rectangle formed a magnificent postcard view of the Grand Square in the ancient Polish city of Krakow. It was her favorite time of day. The summer sun was close to setting over St. Mary's Basilica and lit the city's magical skyline in pale hues of orange and pink. Shadows of nearby buildings had begun to steal their way across the busy outdoor cafés below her. Off in the distance, she could hear cathedral bells toll the eight o'clock hour. The trumpet sound, heard for centuries from the taller of St. Mary's two towers, would be next. She quietly counted and, just as she expected, the famous trumpet blast blared forth precisely at her count of eight. She felt she had timed the lag between the bells of the distant cathedral and the horn of St. Mary's ten thousand times since she was a little girl.

Domenika had grown up in Krakow, and she knew the city as a comfortable village with narrow cobblestone streets and great, wide-open squares. A romantic, candlelit place by night, Krakow was large enough to be endlessly explored but small enough that one rarely lost one's way, even as a child. She seldom passed anyone whose name, or whose cousin, she had not known for years. Domenika smiled and turned toward her father.

"Papa," she said softly as she looked toward a cover of *Cosmopolitan* magazine her mother had framed and placed on the credenza in the apartment's cozy living room, "Joanna is beautiful. She earns the kind of money she does because she likes being a model. I don't have her looks, and I am perfectly happy with my work in Rome."

Domenika had been born at the University Hospital of Krakow, within sight of St. Mary's Basilica. Her father had chosen her name because it meant "belongs to the Lord" and raised her to love God and the Church with her whole heart. Her middle name, Maria, was in honor of the Virgin Mary, and her familial name of "Jozef," meaning "God shall add a son," was viewed by the family as an omen. Unfortunately for her father, the prophecy of a son was never to be realized. Between the two daughters, Domenika bore the brunt of her father's criticism.

From her early years, she was a stellar student and became the first in her family to go to college, and the first woman ever to receive a prestigious scholarship to the Vatican's Gregorian University. The rumor was that the pope had personally chosen her from a pool of thousands of qualified applicants. No doubt she had a first-rate mind. But as the cardinal of St. Mary's Parish for years, the pope had known her since she was a young woman and had been deeply impressed. She was knowledgeable to be sure, but he had seldom heard a child speak so eloquently from the heart and with such courage of conviction for her faith.

She went on to earn master's degrees in theology and communications and graduated at the top of her class. Her academic gifts were surpassed only by her musical ones, and she was invited to play violin with the Rome Symphony Orchestra. After graduation, her professional opportunities were wide-open, and most thought she would pursue a career in music. However, she was intrigued by the internship she had taken with a public relations firm that helped publicize the plight of AIDS victims in Rome. Flush from a successful fund-raising event she had designed and overseen, she accepted an internship with Edelman Italia PR.

Edelman, the largest public relations agency in the world, had been hired by the Vatican years earlier to help manage the multinational media and legal fallout from the child sex-abuse cases exploding in the United States and Europe. Domenika was both fascinated and repelled by the work they did to contain the damage. When she was offered a full-time position on the damage-control team, she found herself torn. She wanted the job but struggled with the terrible acts they wanted to defend. On the one hand, she recognized the need to distance the Church from the human sins of an evil minority. On the other, she found it hard to forgive the pattern of cover-ups and neglect from the Church's hierarchy and its disregard for the victims.

After several weeks of reflection, and some prodding by her mother, she resolved to take the job. Part of her decision stemmed from pride. She was the only woman on a list of a dozen others considered qualified for the post, all of them men. She believed in her heart there was not another who could more capably stand by the Church and defend it, regardless of gender. She threw herself into the role offered to her as deputy communications director of the Vatican Incident Response Team. Cardinal Luca Ponti, charged by the Holy Father to manage the global crisis, had sat through several strategy presentations she had developed on managing the crisis. He too saw what the Holy Father had recognized. He admired her passionate defense not only of the Church but also of the pope's strong support of punishment for those who were guilty of covering up the heinous acts of child abuse in the first place. This, in turn, led to her eventual and unprecedented hiring for the role by the Vatican as a special assistant for public affairs. The position suited her well.

Domenika looked over at her collection of high school track-and-field medals. Next to the picture of Joanna on the cover of a fashion magazine, her mother had placed a picture of Domenika as she was performing a solo at Rome's Oratorio del Gonfalone concert hall. Domenika remembered the moment well. Her mother had taken the photo before she could turn from the lens, which was her natural instinct when cameras were around. While Joanna was certainly a stunning model, many had told Domenika that her father was right. It was often said throughout Krakow that Domenika's beauty outshined her sister's. They talked of her almond-shaped, emerald-green eyes, her sharply sculpted cheekbones, and her noble nose. Her mass of auburn hair glowed in the sunlight like a halo and curled wildly about her shoulders.

Domenika herself didn't see it, which is why her boyfriends were few and far between. She cared little for those who cared only for looks. Looks were temporary things, and the comments about her beauty only embarrassed her. She cared for books, stories, and strange languages that spoke of faraway places, places she would one day visit and write home about. Most of all, Domenika had learned to love God and all of the mystery that surrounded her faith. Catholicism was the very essence of Krakow, the place Saint John Paul II had called home.

"Such a waste," her father said, setting his tumbler back down.

"Oh, and one more thing," Domenika said as she stirred her tea and cast her eyes downward to avoid his glare, "you won't find me living in New York City because I can't stand Americans!"

"And what, Domenika, have they ever done to you?" her father said. "I say God bless them. God bless their President Ronald Reagan. God bless New York City. God bless them all."

"Papa," she replied patiently, "Ronald Reagan is dead. He's been dead for years."

"Well, God bless him anyway; he was a saint even if he wasn't Catholic. Just what is it with you and the Americans? They fought with us against the Germans. They helped bring down the Russians."

Domenika's mother intervened again. She came to the table and pressed a plate of herring and vinegar, her husband's favorite appetizer, against his chest.

"Franka, let the girl speak, will you?" she asked as she unfolded a napkin across his lap.

"Papa, I have visited Joanna twice in New York," Domenika said. "I had my fill of them there. And then there are the usual throngs of exchange students from America who believe they own the streets of Krakow each spring. It's their attitude of entitlement I don't care for."

"Yes, the same attitude that helped us defeat the Nazis, that threw the Russians out, that helped secure our freedom, Domenika," her father said.

"It's arrogance, Father," she said. "They strut about the world with such confidence, as though they own it. If they desire something, they buy it, never mind the price. They know little about a subject? No matter, you will hear their opinion anyway. Life is difficult? They will invent a technology to fix it. Have enough of your family? Get a new one. Tired of one faith on Sunday? Find another more suitable to your liking on Monday. Honestly, I have no use for them."

"Oh, please, Domenika," her mother intoned. "Whatever you do, don't get your father started again."

Domenika watched her mother retreat to the kitchen to avoid what she knew was coming next. *Here comes the storm*, she thought wearily.

"Let me tell you something about faith. Our own Catholic faith," her father said. He hissed the words as his face grew redder and his manner more agitated. "Now, I believe in the Father Almighty, the maker of heaven and earth. I believe in his Jesus Christ, his only be-gotten son—"

"Papa," she stopped him. "I know the Apostle's Creed. We all know the creed. You don't have to recite it here. I know where you are going with this; it's the same place you always go."

"What?" he said in a whisper. "Are you worried that I am going to criticize today's *modern* Church? The same *modern* Church that has convinced my daughter that the shame it has brought upon itself, its fascination with little boys, is something that can be explained away by you or anyone else? It is sinful, Domenika, sinful that *the Church is paying you* to whitewash its sin."

Domenika knew the vodka was fueling his fury as he pushed his point. There was nothing he loathed more than the smugness of the Church about its systemic abuse of innocent children. He was tormented by its refusal to be humble in the face of the grievous charges, and it rankled him to his core that his daughter was a paid shill in its service. As much as he loved his Church, he was infuriated by the way it had disgraced the rules of God. Domenika had heard it many times, and always felt the familiar feeling of letting her father down.

He tapped into her own misgivings about her role in the smoothing over of the tragedy.

"Papa, please believe me. I know that my work for the Church and what you have read in the papers when I have defended it has upset you," she said, fighting the welling of tears in her eyes. "But we must stand by the Church. You have told me that ever since you carried me on your shoulders to St. Mary's. It has made some terrible mistakes, but it needs our devotion now more than ever." She knew her words sounded rehearsed, but she meant them.

Her mother returned to the table with a large, steaming platter of pork and potatoes, only to see her strong-willed daughter on the verge of tears.

"Oh, for goodness' sake, Franka," she said. She looked like she was tempted to drop the dinner platter directly in his lap. "Let the poor girl be."

"Julianna, it's all right. She was just telling me a very sad story about attacks on the Church, and I look forward to her defense."

Domenika decided it was a hopeless cause and changed the subject.

"Mother, you asked me why I have to return to Turin. The reason is that the Holy Father asked me to manage—or, rather, babysit—an obnoxious American and his team of scientists. They are coming from all over the world and are bringing the most advanced scientific equipment with them. Their goal is to prove that the resurrection of Jesus Christ is a lie."

Her father banged his fist on the table once more, this time so hard one of the brass candleholders fell over. It spilled burning hot wax across the tablecloth and onto the top of Domenika's hand. He quickly reached for her but she calmly wiped a napkin across her skin. She shrugged off his concern.

"What are you saying, Domenika? Are these so-called men of science bringing some ridiculous invention with them that they claim will disprove our faith?"

"Papa, they are bringing many devices," she said as she relit the fallen candle with a second one from across the table.

"These crazy Americans! These crazy Americans!" he shouted.

"Papa," she said, laughing for the first time that evening. "What I'm saying is that these scientists have been invited to Turin by the pope himself to examine the Shroud of Christ."

"What is there to examine? It has been in full sight of the world. We took you there after your first Communion when you were ten years old. Do you remember?"

"Of course I do. I will never forget it." Believing the temporary exposition of the Shroud twenty years earlier might be their only opportunity to see the holy relic in their lifetimes, her parents had saved their earnings to take the family on a pilgrimage to Turin. They had traveled by train for hours and stood in line an entire day and night to view the relic and receive a blessing.

"So, what is the problem? Are they coming to buy it? Is it the same man who bought the da Vinci notebook? What's his name?"

"Papa," she replied patiently, "no one is going to buy it. The scientist's name is Jon Bondurant, and he is coming to conduct the tests they will perform on the holy relic. I pity him, because if he knew what I know, he would spare himself the trouble. He is wasting his time and is going to suffer incredible embarrassment."

"What is it you know, Domenika?" her mother asked.

"I cannot tell you. I am under a strict agreement not to discuss it. But I can say to you both that when Dr. Bondurant has finished his task, when all is said and done, it will be a new day for the Church.

A new day of faith for all of us. And I am quite sure it will be utterly humiliating both professionally and personally for the man I consider a thorn in the side of the Church." She couldn't help allowing a smile as she considered the prospect of his eventual tumble from fame.

Her mother looked at her with concern. "This man you're speaking of, this Dr. Bondurant," she said. "It sounds like you have prepared a trap for him, Domenika. Is that the Christian thing to do?"

"He is not a Christian man, Mother," Domenika said. "Not by any means."

"'Love your enemies and pray for those who persecute you,' Domenika," her mother said. "This is what we have taught you."

Domenika turned from her and looked pensively toward the towers of St. Mary's. Her father strained to get up from the table, staggered slightly, and headed toward the kitchen to pour another glass of vodka.

"I will do my best, Mother."

"That is wonderful," her mother said as she reached out and stroked Domenika's hand. "But there is something else troubling you about this, I can tell. What is it?"

Domenika couldn't pinpoint why, but her mother was right. She looked forward to her assignment over the next several weeks with nervous excitement, given the secrets the newly discovered book had revealed. She was about to manage an effort for the Church that was going to electrify the world and restore the faith of millions. Still, she felt a strange premonition of dread that made no sense. She wasn't sure if it was her personal animosity against Bondurant or if it was the vague fear that the hunter could become the hunted. She shook her head at her own fanciful thinking. It was absolutely, without doubt, a risk-free exploration. They had the extraordinary documents to prove it.

She lifted her mother's outstretched hand and pressed it to her own cheek.

"Mother," she whispered. "For the first time in my life, I am afraid and I don't know why."

CHAPTER 11

Turin, Italy
June 2014

"S up, dawg?" a voice shouted over the static on the cell phone.

Sehgal flinched and held the phone away from his ear. He stood on the corner of a busy intersection in historic Turin when he finally connected with his adopted son, who was also his most junior lab assistant, in Mumbai. He still wasn't used to Kishan's oft-used and strange slang.

"Kishan, please. Must you address me that way? Now that I have achieved the Nobel, do you think it could be time for you to stop calling me a canine?" He loved his son, and his son loved him, but Sehgal knew he had spoiled him.

"Don't let that prize go to your head, dawg," Kishan taunted affectionately. "You're the same color as me. You're black. We're all representin'."

Sehgal struggled to hear Kishan over the sound of traffic. Slow-moving red and green trams that created gridlock, and the cars that blared their horns at them mixed with the shouts of street vendors parked nearby.

"As I have said ten thousand times, Kishan, you are not black," Sehgal said with growing irritation.

"What's my name? What's my name, Doc?"

"Kishan. It is Kishan," Sehgal said, exasperated. "I gave it to you."

"And what does my name mean? What's it mean, Doc?"

"All right, all right. It is Hindi for 'black,' but you are not African American, as much as you might admire their colorful language." Others more expert had told Sehgal his son's homegrown slang was a poor imitation of the real thing in America, but Sehgal hadn't the heart to tell him. "You are Indian, Kishan. You are Hindi."

"I'm a dawg. You're a dawg. What can I do for you, my man?"

Sehgal pulled the cell phone from his ear and pressed it to his chest as though to smother the conversation and start over. He had tolerated Kishan's antics since he had rescued and adopted the lovable boy years ago from the footpaths of Dharavi, the largest slum in the suburbs of Mumbai. Sehgal knew the area only too well. Located between the city's two main railways, Dharavi's million inhabitants—growing by hundreds of indigent families per day—occupied tens of thousands of tiny, illegal huts strewn along Mahim Creek. The small river was used by young and old to urinate, defecate, and even bathe. Its low-lying location, once ideal for fruit orchards now long ago abandoned, was twice cursed. Poor drainage ensured it would be routinely devastated by floods during the rainy season each year.

A close colleague visiting Sehgal from Harvard a decade before had convinced him to ride along on a "reality tour" of Dharavi. The tour was conducted by an outfit on the outskirts of the city that catered to tourists looking to get a glimpse of life in the shantytowns rimming the burgeoning city once known as Bombay. Sehgal had been reluctant to go along because he found it absurd that tourists would pay guides to navigate them through some of the poorest and filthiest living conditions on earth. For him, the conditions for the "prisoners" of Dharavi, occupying the largest slum in the world, were brutal reminders of his own miserable life as a child and the hopelessness he had struggled with each day.

On the tour, they had found twelve-year-old Kishan, standing nearly naked. He was alone atop an enormous hill of trash, picking his way through a pile in the blistering sun. Sehgal was struck by the energetic way the child was conducting his search, and by his shouts of glee when he found something salvageable. When Sehgal approached the lad, Kishan smiled at him and asked if he wanted to buy a shoe. Not a pair of shoes, but a single beat-up tennis shoe. When Sehgal said yes, the boy grinned with delight. Joy and anticipation lit his face from the inside out, and his dark brown eyes sparkled with pleasure. There was something so compelling about the spirit of the orphan that Sehgal felt an instant bond.

A self-described "workaholic," Sehgal had been married to his career his entire adult life. But there were aspects of the boy that reminded Sehgal of himself as a child. Sympathy for his plight was only natural. Sehgal too had been rescued from similar circumstances. So with very little effort, he filed to adopt Kishan and succeeded. Until he found the boy, he had had very little use for lasting relationships. Outside of work, he minded Kishan carefully and at close range. He often found the challenges of rearing the boy all alone to be all-consuming and all the family life he could take at any one time. Now, ten years after the adoption, Sehgal felt as close to his son as if he were his biological parent.

The challenges of inserting a scrappy street urchin into a materialistic culture that included a steady dose of American satellite television took its cultural toll on Kishan. This, combined with his incessant playing of one of his prized possessions, a box of old Chris Rock cassette tapes he had found while rummaging in a particularly lucrative pile of debris, helped Kishan to develop his own form of "Hindi Ebonics." It amused his colleagues in the lab, but often drove Sehgal to distraction.

Kishan's jargon was popular with his young coworkers, who encouraged him all the more with appreciative laughter. Sehgal had learned this the hard way a few years earlier when he decided, against his better judgment, to take the excitable eighteen-year-old with him to a conference in Chicago sponsored by the *New England Journal of Medicine*. Sehgal had been invited to present a paper on prehistoric DNA rescue techniques. Kishan had worked tirelessly for him on a project for eight months, and his adopted-son-turned-assistant was thrilled to finally visit America, fulfilling a long-cherished dream of his. Sehgal considered the trip a reward for Kishan's conscientious effort in the lab, but was nervous about his behavior. Once they arrived in Chicago, they got hopelessly lost on the way from O'Hare Airport to the conference at the University of Chicago. Sehgal made the mistake of asking Kishan to roll down his window and ask directions from two young black men stopped in the car beside them at a traffic signal in Englewood on the South Side.

"Wassup, my gangstas?" Kishan shouted. "Can you brothers from another mother tell us how to get to I-90 East?"

Five minutes of high-speed pursuit, twenty city blocks of sheer terror, and a badly damaged rental car later, they were overjoyed to be stopped by the police, who mercifully ended the chase, impounded their car, and likely saved their lives.

"Kishan, please, listen up," Sehgal said as he shouted over the noise of a car alarm that blared behind him. "I have been trying to reach you all day. I need your help with something."

"Talk to me, my brother. Walk and talk. Walk and talk, my man."

"I need you to prepare the lab for some intensive analysis that will commence in two weeks when I return," Sehgal shouted. "Do the usual drill. Test-fire everything. Pay particularly close attention to calibration. And check the storeroom to ensure we have all the reagents required for a full-spectrum analysis."

"You got it, my man. What do we have here? Animal? Vegetable? Mineral? Talk to me."

Sehgal grew further frustrated and paused before he answered.

"Human; human's what we got here, I think, Kishan," he said with a twinge of uncertainty in his voice.

"We talking blood?"

"We talking 'I don't know,' Kishan. There could be blood, hair, skin, tissue. I won't know that until we retrieve the samples."

"How old are you talking, Doc?"

"That's a good question, now, isn't it, Kishan?"

"My man! This is that test on the big Kahuna? The Jesus death rags, right? The one everybody's been talkin' about. King of the Jews, right?"

Sehgal ducked into a quieter alleyway and clucked his tongue in frustration before he answered.

"Kishan. Listen to me carefully. I'm about to get to work here. Just make sure everything is in order for when I return. I want to do a very fast turnaround on these samples. I will personally perform the work."

"You the man. You the man. You da *Nobel* man now, Doc."

"Kishan, one other thing," Sehgal said as he lowered his voice. "There are going to be some crates with some new lab equipment for an unrelated project arriving next week. They will be coming from the Sisters of Mercy. I need you to simply store the crates in the warehouse, but under no circumstances are you to open them. Do you understand me?"

"You mean the nuns that run that convent down the road? What do they have to do with the King of the Jews? I'm just asking."

"Kishan, my son. Repeat after me," Sehgal said. His voice had grown even more irritated.

"Repeat after me."

"There are some crates coming."

"There are some crates coming, Doc."

"I am going to put them in the warehouse *unopened*."

"I am going to put them in the warehouse."

"*UNOPENED*, Kishan!"

"*Unopened*, Doc."

"Thank you, Kishan. I will call you later."

"You my dawg, Doc. You my dawg."

PART 2

CHAPTER 12

Turin, Italy
June 2014

Domenika opened and closed her menu for the fifth time and scanned the cozy, bustling restaurant for any sign of Bondurant. A waiter, carrying a tray filled with a brightly colored mix of orange-and-white shellfish atop a plate of steaming pasta, rushed past, leaving an inviting aroma in his wake.

"This is what I mean about Americans," she complained. "Thirty minutes late! Doesn't he know we have a schedule to keep?"

The tiny restaurant they had chosen as their meeting place, Trattoria Torrecelli, was a local favorite in Turin, off a narrow alleyway connected to Via San Domenico near the bustling city's center. With the noisy lunch crowd overflowing, the maître d' had begun eyeing the table they had occupied a long time without ordering.

Father Parenti fidgeted nervously, trying to cut the tension. He had spent the morning with his dog walking the banks of the Po River, which ran through the sun-washed city. Aldo was his constant companion and generated warm greetings and effusive compliments wherever they went. The two of them wandered the streets like eager sightseers taking in some of the most charming piazzas, museums, and churches outside of Rome. Turin had once served as Italy's first capital, and it was the home of dozens of gardens and orangeries and some of Italy's most prestigious universities. In the center of town stood the Cathedral of St. John the Baptist, the home of the Shroud of Turin.

Parenti's tiny legs, tired from his morning adventures, dangled a few inches above the brightly checkered tile beneath them. He swung them back and forth like a child enjoying a high chair. The glow that had begun when Cardinal Ponti awarded him the role of "project secretary" for the Shroud investigation several weeks before hadn't faded. The priest was happy to be out of the Vatican Library and beyond the reach of Father Barsanti.

"We're done waiting, Father," Domenika declared as she pushed away from the table.

The maître d', who hovered nearby, jumped in to assist. He rushed over to gather their menus and reclaim the table. Parenti, distraught over missing an expected meal, reluctantly began to clamber down from his chair. As he did, a tall man in a dark blue suit and open-neck collar came toward them, dodging the red-and-white checked tables in his path. He was hurriedly making his way from the front of the restaurant.

"Sorry I'm so late," Bondurant said as he raced to set his valise on the table to stop the maître d' from repossessing it. He faced Domenika, who had her back toward him as she bent completely over to reach for her purse on the floor. Her rear, prominently elevated, was pointed directly at him. "Ms. Jozef, I presume?"

She quickly turned and rose, tossed her hair back across her shoulder, and gave Bondurant a chilly look.

"Do you know that we have been waiting here for a half hour?" she said.

"For God's sake!" Bondurant blurted out when he caught a glimpse of her face. He looked as if he had seen a ghost. The diners at the table nearby stopped talking to watch the spectacle. "*You're* Ms. Jozef?"

"Yes, for God's sake, I am." She couldn't help but smirk at the irony of his words and his predicament.

"You're the girl they sent," he choked out.

"To do a man's job?" she said, finishing the insult for him. A sly smile replaced the look of rage on her face. She extended her hand and continued. "I am the Vatican's representative on this project. I believe you were informed of that earlier. And this is my assistant, Father Parenti. Welcome to Turin."

Bondurant glanced at her again for just a moment. She could see blood rush to his face.

"I'm a . . . I'm a . . . I'm a . . ." he stammered.

She watched as Bondurant pressed hard against the corner of the table to steady himself after the news.

"I know you are not a fan of my work," Bondurant said as they sat down. "We are obviously not getting off on the right foot again."

He avoided looking Domenika in the eyes. Clearly troubled, he picked up his menu and stared into it for a long moment and said nothing. Mercifully, a waitress stopped at the table and broke the awkward silence between them.

"*Buon giorno*. Please, for the table some water?" she asked. She was attractive and barely out of her teens, and her attempt at English was endearing.

"Yes, with gas," Parenti offered.

"I'll have the same," Domenika said.

"A Macallan, neat. Double it," Bondurant said.

Domenika looked at her watch. "You do realize it's not yet one o'clock." She could smell the whisky on his breath from across the table. "I'm sorry, sir," the waitress interrupted apologetically as she rested her hand on Bondurant's shoulder. "We have only wine and beer here. I would be happy to—"

"Let's try another restaurant, shall we?" Bondurant said. He began to get up from the table to leave.

"Water for him as well," Domenika said, her voice stern enough that it sent the waitress scurrying away. "Dr. Bondurant, I'm not sure how much you've been drinking or what you're on, but I want you to listen to me for a moment, and I want you to listen very carefully. Are you prepared to do that, or are we in for another debate?"

Bondurant looked away from her and forced a smile. She knew she was in a position to end the most important quest of his life or make it a living hell if she wanted, and there was little he could do about it. "I am prepared, Dominique."

"Domenika," she insisted.

"Domenika," he repeated, apologetically.

When he averted his eyes, she took the opportunity to frankly appraise him. Quirky as he might be, he had a presence about him up close that she hadn't noticed during the Cambridge debacle. She couldn't explain it, but she felt she hadn't seen it in *any* man before. She was both attracted and repelled by the energy he exuded even in distress. Still, she saw how quickly he recovered and was determined to press on while she had the upper hand.

She continued. "You'll recall we inserted a morals clause into the agreement?"

"Page twenty-nine, paragraph four," Parenti interjected, reciting it from memory. "Participants agree to conduct themselves with due regard to public conventions and morals, and agree to refrain from committing any act during the course of the study to degrade themselves in the eyes of society or bring themselves into ridicule."

"I did not interpret that to mean a ban on single malt scotch whisky, *Ms. Jozef*," Bondurant said as his anger started to surface.

"Interpret it as you will, Dr. Bondurant. It is my responsibility to ensure the Church's most sacred relic is in perfectly sober care, and we cannot, we will not, leave it in the hands of a . . . a . . ."

"A complete fool?" he asked.

She smiled. Maybe it was time to give him an inch of space.

"I'm searching for the right word," she said.

"A drunk?" Parenti said, supplying the word for her.

She shot the priest an annoyed look. She wanted Bondurant in his place, but wasn't looking to insult him. "What I meant to say is that our research illustrates there is an issue with alcohol, Doctor."

"Your research?" Bondurant said, incredulous. He seemed to have fully regained his confidence.

The waitress returned with a large bottle of sparkling water and poured it for the three of them.

Parenti hunched over the table and extended his tiny arm to get his water, just out of reach. He rocked forward in his chair to grab the glass but in the process bumped into the table hard enough that he knocked over a delicate decanter of olive oil. Bondurant dove to reach the bottle, but it rolled off the table, exploding on the floor. Beyond the broken shards of glass that lay scattered across the aisle, the contents had splattered widely, making their way to the skirt of an elderly woman sitting at the table beside them. She was clearly startled and, seeing the mess, not amused.

The maître d', who had been standing vigil near their table, threw his arms in the air. *"Bastardi!"* he yelled loud enough for the entire restaurant to hear.

Parenti cupped his face in his hands like an embarrassed child.

Bondurant immediately rose from his seat and, towering at least a foot over the maître d', stiff-armed him to keep him from approaching the table any further.

"I am sorry," Bondurant said, looking menacingly in the man's eyes. "It's *my* fault. I seem to have spilled something here. If you will take care of the floor, I will take care of this nice lady."

Domenika and those dining nearby watched in silence as Bondurant leaned in toward the woman at the neighboring table, whispered briefly in her ear as he reached for his wallet, and pressed a hundred-euro note in her hand. He gently dabbed at her skirt with a napkin, blotting the worst of the oil while she enjoyed the attention of the handsome stranger in front of her friends.

Domenika looked down at her menu and feigned a lack of interest, not wanting to let on that she found his chivalry toward the little priest endearing. She was certain Parenti had actually been sent to Turin as a spy, another set of eyes and ears who would report back daily to the Vatican on the project's findings, but she liked him nonetheless.

When he finished tending to the woman, Bondurant sat down and placed Parenti's water glass where he could reach it. He resumed where they had left off.

"So let's hear about this research again," he said calmly, trying to put the priest at ease.

Domenika thought about stopping to thank him for his kindness, but thought better of it. "As I was saying," she said, determined to reassert control of the conversation, "surely you can understand that the Church would not place its most valuable possession in the hands of someone we cannot fully trust to protect it. There will be no drinking of alcohol during the course of the study. There can be no missteps. I can start this; I can stop it."

"I see," Bondurant said. "And what else does your *research* say? Does it go so far as to reveal the size of my underwear?"

Parenti stared up at the ceiling for a moment as if to recall whether he had studied the topic. He kept silent.

"Let's not be ridiculous," Domenika said.

"Well, you are going to wish it did," Bondurant responded after a while. "I seem to have misplaced my suitcase containing all my clothes."

"Misplaced it? You mean the airline has lost it?" she asked. "We have people who can contact them and ensure its delivery." She began to pull out her cell phone.

"Maybe 'misplaced' is the wrong word," Bondurant said. "I have a notion I left it in the trunk of my car."

"Here in Turin?" she asked.

"No, in Baltimore, at the airport," Bondurant said with a sigh.

Domenika and Parenti looked at each other and broke into laughter. Domenika tried to hold back the outburst for Bondurant's sake but couldn't. It was exactly the kind of absentmindedness they had been warned about. Bondurant had fit the mold described for him to a tee, and for the first time in his presence, she felt firmly in control.

"Does it go so far as to tell you what my findings on the Shroud will reveal before I've even begun? Maybe I shouldn't have bothered to make the trip," he said.

"In fact," Parenti said, "we have some unique material on that.

Contrary to your previous writings and assertions, we are absolutely certain you will determine the Shroud of our Lord Savior is authentic."

"And what gives you such confidence, Father?" Bondurant asked.

"Well, it's obvious. It's the book. As soon as we discovered that—"

Parenti stopped midsentence and swallowed the rest of his words, then bent down and massaged his shin from Domenika's swift kick under the table.

Domenika had started to pity Bondurant, but had no interest in providing him clues the Vatican hadn't authorized and which he didn't deserve.

"What Father Parenti is saying, Dr. Bondurant," Domenika said, "is that the *Lord's* book, the Bible, is very clear on the events of the death and resurrection of Jesus Christ, and the Church has every confidence that your investigation of the Shroud will support it."

"May I ask a more fundamental question, then?" Bondurant said. "It's something that has been gnawing at me for weeks."

"Please do, Dr. Bondurant," she said.

"Why me? Of all the forensic anthropologists in the world, why has the Vatican chosen me to lead this effort? I can't seem to get a straight answer."

"Are you suggesting your interest in the project is waning?" Domenika said with a twinge of hope in her voice.

"No, no, no. Don't get me wrong. It's the opportunity of a lifetime, and I would trade it with no one. But why choose a well-known skeptic of the Church?"

"Put simply, Dr. Bondurant," Domenika said, "you may be a skeptic, but you're the best in your field. We expected you to pull together a team whose findings will be universally accepted by the world, and you have." She had to give him that.

Bondurant looked across the table, shifted in his seat, and stared directly into her eyes for the first time. She could tell he had completely regained his footing, and recognized the look he'd sent. It was one she'd seen from other men she'd had to rebuff before. *Let's not go there,* she thought. *Of all people, not you.* She was also certain as he held his eyes on hers that he knew her explanation was not the entire truth.

"I look forward to working with you," Domenika said. "But I want to repeat, Dr. Bondurant—"

"I know. I know," he said as he cut her short. "You can start it. You can stop it. I heard you," he said.

Domenika could tell the anger that grew in his voice was from the predicament he was in at the hands of a woman.

Bondurant abruptly got up from his chair. "This is going to be a very long two weeks, Ms. Jozef."

"Where are you going?" Parenti asked. "We've not even ordered yet."

"I seem to have lost my appetite, Father," Bondurant said as he looked at Domenika once more. "And I'd like to see the Shroud in its resting place in St. John's Cathedral before it's moved to our labs. I'm sure I'll see you both at the hotel as we get under way this evening."

As the front door of the restaurant closed behind Bondurant, Parenti was the first to speak.

"Do you think we might have been a bit hard on him?" he asked.

"He's a big boy, Father," she replied. "We needed to get this off on the right foot. He *is* one of the best in the world, and for his sake and ours, he needs to act it." She was speaking with bravado, but the look he had given her and what it might mean for the next two weeks was unsettling.

"But he's a good man. Why aren't we telling him, of all people, about the existence of the codex?" Parenti complained as he rubbed his sore ankle.

"The Vatican's orders, not mine," she said. She didn't like being so curt or hiding the existence of the codex either, but knew they had no choice, given the plan.

"It would assist his work and drive the truth," Parenti complained. "It seems unfair. He's turned out to be such a nice fellow, and he's going to be humiliated. I didn't sign up for this."

"Believe me," she said, "I didn't either. It was Cardinal Ponti's plan. His decision."

"Mark my words, Domenika," the priest said as he lowered his voice so no one but she could hear. "I think we are asking for trouble."

The waitress finally returned to their table to take their order. She looked disappointed. "The gentleman, he is gone?" she asked. "He is finished before he has begun?"

"Yes, he is," Domenika said as she watched the once crowded restaurant begin to empty. "Yes, he is."

CHAPTER 13

Turin, Italy
June 2014

Bondurant was pleasantly surprised.

When he arrived, after hours, through an unlocked side door of St. John's Cathedral to get his first look at the Shroud of Turin, he had expected some sort of an official handler and plenty of security to protect the world's most famous religious relic. Preparations were soon to be made to move the Shroud from the cathedral and into Bondurant's hands at a secure laboratory nearby, but you wouldn't know it. Instead, what he found when he made his way through the large, dark cathedral to the Chapel of the Shroud was a lone janitor at work, mopping the elaborate marble floor just in front of where the famous but hidden relic stood.

"You are the American? They told me you would be coming," the aged, balding man said to Bondurant. He had more hair stemming from his bushy eyebrows than the top of his head, and the kindly man had a natural stoop that looked to have been formed from many years of laboring with his mop.

"That's me," Bondurant said. He was pleased that there was no bevy of church officials with whom he'd have to glad-hand while he tried to get a good glimpse of the Shroud. He had seen thousands of photos of the relic over the years, but this was the first time he would actually see the controversial artifact in person. "I don't suppose there is an attraction nearby, one that people wait in line to see?"

The janitor pointed his finger toward a large, gold braided rope that hung from an ornate frame. The frame supported a thick, red velvet curtain nearly thirty feet wide.

"Would you mind giving me a hand?" the janitor asked. "They told me you'd want to see it."

Bondurant was happy to help. He walked over to the braided rope and, joined by his newfound guide, pulled down hard to open the massive velvet wall that hung between him and the Shroud. With each yank of the rope, the royal red fabric parted further, opening in both directions from the center. After about ten good pulls, the curtain was completely open and exposed what looked to be a large brass display case roughly twenty feet long, paneled with glass on both sides. The chapel surrounding the case was dark enough that it was nearly impossible for Bondurant to make out the contents of the rectangular box, although he was certain that with a little light he would find exactly what he'd come to see.

"Got a light?" Bondurant asked his companion.

"We have a light," his guide responded. The janitor slowly shuffled over to the wall on one side of the case and flipped the simple light switch on. A light inside the brass case flickered on and off for a moment, and then went completely dark. A couple good whacks from the janitor's wooden mop handle against the box that held the light switch resolved the problem right away. The image inside the display case was now awash in golden light.

"Sir, behold the Holy Shroud of Turin," the janitor said in a Roman dialect familiar to Bondurant. He spoke with a practiced but clearly exaggerated enthusiasm. With that, he resumed the work with his mop and pushed the sudsy water before him from side to side.

Bondurant smiled as he stood at eye level with the artifact. He was within five feet of the display case and studied the Shroud for about ten seconds.

"It's a fake," Bondurant said. This time he smiled even wider. "It's a painting."

"They said you'd say that," the janitor said.

"Who's 'they'?" Bondurant asked. He walked from one end of the image to the other as he began to study the relic more carefully. What he saw appeared to be a shadow of both sides of a male body, lying prostrate, left behind on a badly burned and damaged linen sheet.

"'They' are the 'royalty,'" his companion responded. "A few cardinals. Several bishops. Made their way up from Rome. They said you'd say that. Overheard them."

Bondurant stared intently at the face of the image. The ghostly visage he could see reminded him greatly of the Jesus so many Christians wore on medallions or had seen depicted in paintings and books throughout the world. It was a handsome face, with strong features.

"Would you like the audio tour?" the janitor asked. "We have it in three languages. Costs just a euro."

"Fine," Bondurant said, curious to know how the Church had packaged and promoted the history of its famous prize. "Are there headsets? Where do I get the device?"

"No headsets. That's for day visitors," his companion said. "I'm afraid you'll have to get it from me."

Bondurant laughed at his newfound friend's entrepreneurial spirit.

"Go ahead, then, friend," Bondurant said as he handed him two euro coins. "I'm all ears."

"Ladies and gentlemen, boys and girls," the janitor said. "Welcome to the world-famous Holy Shroud of Turin, the one and only authentic burial cloth of our Savior, the Lord Jesus Christ." The old man's practiced delivery started off as a tired drone that Bondurant feared might last a long time.

"Wait," Bondurant said. "I want my money back."

"Why's that?"

Bondurant chuckled again. "Because that's not true. You said it's authentic, but you don't know that."

"Neither do you. Listen," the janitor said. "It's a great story. And I need the money. Let me tell it."

"You were at 'Ladies and Gentlemen,' I believe."

"Yes, yes," the janitor said. "The journey of the Shroud is a long one."

"Can I at least get the short version?" Bondurant asked.

His friend looked perturbed but pressed onward.

"Legend has it that Joseph of Arimathea, a disciple of Christ, bought the relic you see here after the Crucifixion of Jesus. It's in all the books: Matthew, Mark, Luke, and John. You can look it up."

"Yes, continue, please."

"Then Saint Peter finds the rags in Jesus's tomb after being alerted by an angel that the cloth was there. We know this to be true because it was all written down several hundred years later when the Bible was first written."

"I see," said Bondurant. "So for about four hundred years, the Shroud is somewhere. But no one knows where. Someone just wrote about it, right?"

"Well, yes, but it's common legend that the Shroud was taken by Thaddeus Jude to Edessa, somewhere in Turkey. We are talking almost two thousand years ago."

"Go on," Bondurant said.

"There, he hid it inside a city wall, where it sat for several hundred years."

"I see. It sat in a wall for over five hundred years. No one messed with it?"

"Right. It is then spirited to Constantinople. Unfortunately, the city was sacked. Burned to the ground. The Venetians found it and stole it."

"Took it where?" Bondurant asked.

"No one knows."

"Right, and then?"

"Fifty years later it shows up in the hands of Geoffroi de Charny, the most chivalrous, pious, and magnificent of all the knights of his time. He was a nephew of a member of the Knights Templar. I don't know what the Knights Templar is, but it's on the recording and apparently it's a big deal."

"Yes, and how did he come to find it?" Bondurant asked.

"No one knows. But we do know he died valiantly in its defense and left it to his wife, Jeanne de Vergy. Although the church first insisted the Shroud was nothing more than forgery, de Vergy placed it in their hands. They brought it here, where it has been on display for over five hundred years."

"Aren't you leaving out a part or two?" Bondurant asked.

"You said the short version."

"Yes, but even the short version has—"

"Fire and water," the janitor said. "Yes, fire and water. It has been nearly lost to fire and water. It was traded at one time for a castle, then moved—"

"To where?"

"No one knows."

"Uh-huh. And from there?"

"No one knows. But we know it traveled from church to church across the continent five hundred years ago and then was lost and found numerous times over many more years. Like I said, it arrived here over five hundred years ago. Now *that* I know with certainty, as the Shroud stands before you and the records are here to prove it. It hasn't left us since."

"Bravo," Bondurant said as he looked intensely into the eyes of the image before him. He was so mesmerized by the composition of the face on the Shroud that he hadn't heard a single word of his new-found friend's last remark. He wished he had. Because as Bondurant turned to address his companion once more, his friend was gone.

CHAPTER 14

Turin, Italy
June 2014

After two days holed up in a windowless conference room at the Hotel Victoria with Bondurant and his team of scientists, reviewing seemingly endless protocols for the study of the Shroud, Domenika and her handful of Vatican colleagues were satisfied they had heard enough about Bondurant's plans. Bondurant was left with only twelve days for his investigation. At the end of the meeting, Bondurant had asked Domenika if she knew how to get to the nearest department store so that he might pick up some clothes. He'd been so focused on the work ahead that he hadn't had a moment to think about his wardrobe. His suitcase still sat in the trunk of his rental car in Baltimore, and the extra clothes he'd packed in his carry-on would last only another day.

Domenika had seen a beautiful pair of Italian shoes in the window of a department store right down the street earlier. She offered to take him there.

Once inside, she stepped off the escalator, pointed him in the right direction, and turned to find the shoes she sought. But Bondurant surprised her by insisting she stay to help him choose a few things, and she reluctantly complied.

For a short while she trailed behind him as he seemed to wander aimlessly about the store. It was the least she could do, she thought. She felt guilty over how she'd treated him during their disastrous encounter a few days earlier at the restaurant and wanted to make amends.

They were surrounded by neatly maintained aisles of fine clothing bearing designer labels shipped straight from Milan, but he was getting nowhere in his quest. She watched in amusement as he made a few fainthearted attempts to select an item that caught his eye, but she could tell he was helpless. After just a few minutes of his directionless roaming, she stepped ahead of him and took the lead. He followed her from aisle to aisle like a child as she browsed. She couldn't help but exact a price for her service, and she decided to have some fun.

"What's the matter?" she asked as she turned around and stared at him. He looked like a lost puppy. "Does your wife do this shopping for you at home?"

"Oh, no. Never been married," Bondurant said.

Not surprising, she thought. While the clothes he'd been wearing were disheveled, she could tell they were expensive and nicely tailored. *Someone* had helped him with his look.

"Your girlfriend, then?" she asked. She was curious to know his story but tried to sound disinterested. She spun him around so that he faced away from her, glanced at the width of his shoulders, and pressed a pinstriped Oxford against them for size. His athletic, swimmer's frame presented an impressive V-shape from his shoulders down to his waist. She reached for another size of the same shirt from a higher shelf. The one she had chosen was several sizes too small.

"No, no girlfriend," he said, sounding aloof. "It's rare they stick around long enough to make it to the shopping stage."

"Oh, and why's that?" Domenika asked nonchalantly. She pressed another shirt to his shoulders, checking once more for size. Her choice was still too small. She could see two female store clerks eyeing them, ready to make their way over to assist. Domenika held up her hand in their direction to stop them in their tracks.

"I suppose it's my preoccupation with work," he said as he laid the shirt she had chosen across his arm, along with a brown polo shirt he had hastily chosen earlier. "At least that's what most of them say."

"I see." She picked up the polo he had selected and gave it a bemused look. "Not your color," she said as she set it aside. "What do the rest of them say?"

"What do you mean, 'the rest of them'?" he asked.

"You said 'most of them' lose you to work," she said. "What about the rest?"

She pulled a deep blue chambray shirt from a table and held it next to his face for a moment to frame it against the color of his eyes. They were magnetic. "That's a keeper," she said, quickly turning away from his gaze.

Bondurant hesitated for a moment before he answered.

"The rest? I don't know. There've been a lot. But I try not to stick around long enough for love to set in with the serious ones," he admitted. "It bores me. They bore me."

"I see," Domenika said. She turned her back toward him, rolled her eyes, and motioned for him to follow. She had enjoyed the innocent flirtation, but he'd proven to be predictable, and it was time to move on. "Let's make our way over to the pants, shall we?"

She held up a pair of black slacks that looked like they would go with the shirt she'd chosen. "Here, try these on," she said.

He slung the slacks over his shoulder and looked about the store for a dressing room. By the look on his face, Domenika sensed he was looking for a graceful end to their conversation as well. She couldn't help herself.

"Humor me, Doctor," she said. "How does someone who does not believe in God ever actually love someone else?"

"What's that supposed to mean? I don't believe you have to believe in God before you can be attracted to another person," he said.

"That's not love. That's sex," she said as she shoved another pair of pants she judged might fit into his arms. He took a step back, and she could tell she'd hit a nerve.

"All right, then," he said. "You define it. Define love."

Domenika took a deep breath, reached for the pile of clothes he held, and set them all down on a table that displayed an assortment of brightly colored ties. *Why not?* she thought. She reached her arms forward, took his face in her hands, and stared directly into his eyes, only inches away. His confidence seemed to vanish instantly.

"I'm sure I might as well be talking to a wall, and I'm not going to debate you *again*, not here in the middle of a store," she said. "But *God* is love, Dr. Bondurant. Love comes *from* God. To know love, to love another, you must first love God with all your heart."

She watched him process her words, carefully calculating each of them. For a brief moment, she thought she might have broken through.

"Now, that's *deep*," he said disparagingly. "How many times have you practiced that?"

She continued to stare directly into his eyes, this time with some remorse. "Three years later and you're still a complete damn fool," she said.

As she squeezed his face tighter to reinforce her words, he grabbed her wrists and slipped them behind her. "Childish insults to convince me how to become a better lover?" he said, staring unflinchingly into her eyes.

She flushed and struggled to remove her hands. He let go, and she rubbed her wrists.

"You bring it out in me," she said, startled at how easily he pushed her buttons. The man was infuriating.

He smiled at her discomfort, but she was surprised to see there was no sign of mocking.

"You bring it out in me as well," he said.

"Are you flirting with me, Dr. Bondurant?"

"No more than you are with me," he said. He smiled and then gestured toward the dressing room he'd spotted.

"Will you accompany me, or must I struggle alone?"

"I'll wait out here," she said. Her face burned.

As she sat outside the curtained fitting rooms and waited for Bondurant to emerge, she seethed. It had been a mistake to offer to help him in the first place, she thought. It went against her better instincts. It had been an even bigger mistake to join him inside the store. She could have simply shown him the front door. And it had definitely been a mistake to carry on about love and God or any other meaningful concept when she knew that they were worlds apart on things that mattered.

Yet she had. She didn't know why; she had to remind herself that in less than two weeks the project would be complete and he'd be gone. *Stick to the plan,* she thought. Soon, he'd find his tail between his legs, having to report to the world that he was wrong and the Shroud was real. He'd have some serious thinking to do, and she would relish a conversation with him after that.

As she looked up from the notes she had prepared to transmit to Rome, she saw Bondurant emerge from behind the curtain of the fitting room with *three* young female clerks now in tow, including the two who had been eyeing them since they first arrived. Shirtless, tan, barefoot, and wearing only the black slacks she had chosen for him, he strode up to her.

"What do you think?" he said. "Will these do?"

She swallowed hard. The man was simply beautiful, and it was almost painful to look at him. The trousers fit as though they'd been custom tailored, and it was all she could do to resist the urge to put her hands back on his face and pull him toward her.

This is ridiculous, she thought. She scorned her girlfriends for their shallow crushes on good-looking men. But he was the whole package. Smart and gorgeous, and he knew it. He'd have to be a moron not to notice how the fawning saleswomen gawked at him. It was as if an alarm had sounded and a small crowd gathered around. She smirked, seeing how easily he grinned back at his admirers.

"Do I pass inspection?" he asked her.

"I guess they'll do," she said as she turned away from him.

"Bellissimo," one of the clerks said. She was clearly enjoying viewing everything about Bondurant, including the pants.

"Magnifico," said another.

An older woman, saying nothing, simply stared as if she were admiring a painting.

"Had enough *love* for one day yet?" Domenika asked, agitated. "How about you put on a shirt and we get out of here?"

Bondurant smiled at her reaction and retreated behind the fitting-room curtain, once more followed by the store clerks. Domenika was left alone. She shook her head.

She cursed herself quietly all the way back to their hotel for volunteering for the silly shopping adventure. She took solace in the fact that they'd be going their separate ways in a matter of days.

When they arrived at the lobby, Bondurant thanked her awkwardly for her help and went directly to his room. Domenika expected several messages from the Vatican and went to the front desk to get them. Soon, she felt a tap on her shoulder and turned. The woman who stood before her was the attractive waitress who had served them at Trattoria Torrecelli the day they arrived. Domenika looked her up and down, surprised.

"Pardon me, signora," the waitress said apologetically. "I am sorry to be disturbing to you."

"Oh, no, that's fine," Domenika said, a little off balance. "Nice to see you again."

"*Sì*, signora. I am in the right place to meet him?" She was dressed impeccably for an evening out and didn't look at all the part of a waitress now.

Domenika looked further confused. "I'm not sure what you mean. What do you mean 'the right place'?"

"He tells me to meet him here, at the hotel. Maybe you know his room?"

"Dr. Bondurant? Is that who you mean?" Domenika asked. "You are supposed to meet him here?"

"*Sì, sì*," she said excitedly. "He say he might be here to find him." Domenika paused and stared at the beautiful girl, certain she was half

Bondurant's age. For some strange reason, she hadn't felt so awkward in years. She bit her bottom lip, almost breaking the skin. There was a reason she rarely opened her heart.

"I'm sorry to tell you I don't know his room number. I haven't seen him all day," she said as she cast her eyes about the lobby as if to search for him.

"*Va bene,*" the waitress said. "Okay."

"Oh, if I do see him, I'll absolutely tell him you're looking for him," Domenika said, now infuriated with herself. She knew the sarcasm would be lost on the pretty brunette. "You can count on it. Just the minute I see him. I'm sure he would just *love* to see you."

The waitress winked appreciatively and turned away. As she turned toward the elevators and drifted from sight, Domenika quickly left the hotel for a walk so she wouldn't have to be there when Bondurant emerged with his date.

It was the first time in years she had felt like a child—indeed, a girl. Just like the one Bondurant had claimed he'd met just a few years before.

CHAPTER 15

Mumbai, India
June 2014

Kishan's scooter had sputtered for almost a half mile, which meant he would soon run out of gas, as he had countless times before on his biweekly trip to Dharavi. The slums of Dharavi, his home until the age of twelve, were best approached from the heavily commercialized Sion-Mahim Road. There he could chain his scooter to a lamppost or guardrail and still stand a decent chance of it being there when he returned with a small bottle of gas to fill it once more and head home.

Today, he would need to walk the rest of the way up the steep and muddy incline, past the slum's occasional small temple and an assortment of tiny makeshift factories. The small huts were filled with gleaming pottery, just baked, and the smell of cheap leather goods destined for sale around the world.

The two plastic bags slung over Kishan's shoulders were heavy, and he made his way carefully along raised wooden planks meant to spare his feet from the sewer water that flowed freely to Mahim Creek.

He'd tried to get used to the stench of the water and rancid waste that lined his route up the road, but he never did.

His bags were filled with locally grown vegetables and fruits, some potatoes, rice, lentils, bottles of water, and even a jar of milk pudding with cashews and raisins for dessert. All of this, plus a few rupees, was destined for someone his adoptive father, Ravi Sehgal, did not know about. It was meant for Kishan's sister, Saanvi.

Saanvi, fourteen years old and pregnant with her first child, bore a remarkable resemblance to her brother, Kishan. Naturally pretty, with long, dark, lustrous hair and eyes near emerald green, she somehow had the grim and hardened look of a woman at least twice her age. The lines of her young face were carved deep by years of survival, pain, and very little joy. A life of poverty could rob the youth of even the most promising and enchanting of girls.

Her husband of one year, Parth, owned a ramshackle leather goods workshop several alleyways from their tin-clad home. It was a house held together by heavy twine, containing a single room that measured twelve by eighteen feet. Parth's tannery stamped out twenty to thirty belts, necklaces, and bracelets each day, plus an occasional purse when Saanvi put her mind to it. Often, extra cash was needed at the end of the month to keep the bill collectors at bay. As difficult as it was to make ends meet, Parth was both a clever and fortunate man. After months of digging beneath their hovel, he had found a way, like so many others, to tap into the city's water and gas lines for free. This was dangerous and illegal, but these savings alone greatly increased the odds that their first newborn might survive.

Many words and many stories had been shared between Kishan and Saanvi since his adoption by Sehgal ten years before. But never— not once—had they discussed how she might be spared her miserable life if only Kishan were to say these words to Sehgal: *"I have a sister. She is in trouble. Can you take her in?"* Saanvi, eight years younger than her brother, had been nowhere in sight on the day Ravi Sehgal had found Kishan selling his wares atop a hill of trash. In fact, Kishan had not seen his sister for a week at the time. And while Kishan could remember the countless times he had the opportunity to talk with his adoptive father about his sister, the words had, strangely, always been out of reach. Kishan convinced himself that asking Ravi to take her in after he had done so much for his adoptive son was a terrible and greedy overreach. It might threaten his own standing and comfortable way of life. Then, as the years slowly passed, Kishan worried Ravi might find him selfish and cruel for hiding her existence for so long. How could he have sentenced her to a miserable life that might have been so vastly improved long ago? Whatever the reason, Kishan found his best and only way to make amends for the state of affairs was to support her as best he could. Much of his own salary, occasional winnings from gambling, and even some of Sehgal's petty cash, if necessary, was used to alleviate her plight. The guilt he felt for her as the child left behind was oftentimes overwhelming. His missions of mercy every other week were the very least he could do.

Kishan pulled aside the rug that served as a makeshift door to their home and peered within. He heard his sister's soothing voice before his eyes could adjust to the darkness inside. It was not until Saanvi's gentle embrace and peck on his cheek that he recognized her familiar profile.

"Sit down, Kishan. Let me take those bags," Saanvi said. "Gifts from the gods, aren't they?"

She always says that, Kishan thought. If only she knew—and perhaps she did—what sacrifices he'd made over the years to help her.

But for her, he was silent. The thought of his cowardice often made him sick.

"How is the baby?" Kishan asked. "Has it moved about some more? Can I feel it?"

"I've not felt it kick for over a week," she said. She sounded a little worried. "But we are fine. Everything is fine. I spoke with the Shaman some days ago. He blessed us both. He says everything is fine."

Kishan shook his head the moment he heard she'd visited a Shaman. He knew Saanvi needed to see a doctor to ensure her firstborn had the care it needed, but it would take a month's salary to make that happen. These were the times he *needed* Ravi. Kishan had his sister sit on the floor. He put his hands on her belly, hoping to feel the child make even the tiniest of kicks. They sat together for twenty minutes, but as they talked, Kishan felt nothing.

Kishan's eyes had fully adjusted to the dark now, only to be assaulted by the smoke. It wafted from the large coffee cans in the corner of the room that served as a jury-rigged stove. As he peered through the smoke, he saw that something had moved near the stove. Kishan realized that Parth had been huddled over the cans in the dark to warm his hands. He'd not bothered to greet his houseguest. Kishan didn't have to wonder why. The last time he had visited his sister, he'd found bruise marks on her arms and her neck. Saanvi claimed she'd had an accident, but Kishan knew better. At sixteen years of age, Parth had a great deal more learning to do.

But where was he to get it? Kishan thought. Kishan had been one of the very fortunate few—in essence a project of Sehgal's. Ravi had ensured the orphan had everything a boy might need: a first-rate prep school, tutors at his beck and call, college tuition, and, most valuable of all, at least a Master's practicum in chemistry and genetics taught to him on a daily basis in labs run by none other than a Nobel Prize winner.

"Has he touched you again? Has he hurt you?" Kishan whispered.

"No, Kishan. Not once. Not since you threatened him," Saanvi said.

"That's good," Kishan said. He glanced over his sister as best he could without making a scene and saw nothing new to be concerned about. "Remember what I said about protecting yourself and the baby. Remember to use it if you must."

Kishan knew that Saanvi was certain of exactly what he meant. She glanced over at the small hole in the tin wall where Kishan had placed a crude knife for self-defense. He hated the idea of leaving his sister after such a short visit, but he'd promised Ravi he would prepare the lab just as instructed for the tests to be run once he returned.

Before he left, he helped Saanvi store the bags of vegetables and fruits in the various cardboard boxes she had assembled to serve as makeshift shelves. Then he opened her hands and slipped into them all of the rupees he could spare. He needed enough to buy a small amount of gas for the ride home, but she would take the rest.

Kishan used to cry each time he left his sister in this way. But all of the trips over the years had hardened him badly. He knew that as long as his sister remained a captive to these slums, he too would be a prisoner of Dharavi.

CHAPTER 16

Turin, Italy
June 2014

It was eight o'clock in the evening in the dimly lit laboratory of the Politecnico di Torino, and for Bondurant the moment of truth had come. The usual volt of "Vatican Vultures," as he called them, was not expected for another two hours. Still annoyed by how they seemed to peer over his shoulder during every moment of the investigation, Bondurant had purposely provided them with an outdated schedule of the day's lab activities. He would apologize profusely when they arrived, after his work was completed.

He tried to ignore the splitting headache of forced sobriety that had hounded him for days. Getting only four or five hours of sleep a night had him exhausted, but the adrenaline that coursed through his veins in anticipation of the moment—the world's first virtual autopsy—had him completely alert.

The famous Shroud of Turin lay before him, waist high, stretched end-to-end on a long, elevated light table like those used by photographers to examine film negatives. For Bondurant's session, like all others so far, the Shroud lay inside a specially equipped "clean room" to ensure that not even microscopic traces of dust or airborne microbes could contaminate the exposed relic. It had been carefully transported there by Church officials protected by armed carabinieri. The Vatican's representatives had painstakingly removed it from its resting place, the vacuum-sealed, bulletproof glass display case in the Cathedral of St. John the Baptist where Bondurant had gotten his first glimpse of the relic.

He slipped on his headset and stepped toward the precious cloth to record the historic examination. Before he could begin, the familiar sound of the air lock on the door of the dimly lit observation room behind him sounded. A large red light flashed, signaling someone had entered. He had lost his privacy just when he wanted it the most, and he turned to see who had intruded on him so unexpectedly.

Domenika stood at the doorway alone and wagged her finger at him, as though she had caught him red-handed. Truthfully, she had. He reluctantly waved her into the clean room to join him, knowing there was little he could do to stop her intrusion. The air lock on the door leading from the observation platform sounded and the green light above it began to glow, signaling the room was sealed. Domenika, wearing a lab overcoat and sterile booties, was now inside. He couldn't help but notice how oblivious she was to her looks, and he felt his heart contract when she came close. Even nearly drowning in the oversized lab garb, like a sterile white bag that completely covered her from head to toe, she was one of the most stunning women he'd ever seen.

"I thought your observation wasn't scheduled to start for a few more hours," she said.

The suspicion in her voice was obvious, and Bondurant relished his ability to irritate her.

"It wasn't," Bondurant said. "Looks like I fooled everyone but you. I presume you'll now ask me to delay until everyone else can make it here to gawk from their usual perches?" he said. He could see her struggle to remain calm.

"No, go ahead," she said. "I read about your machine. I think you're attempting the impossible. If you're going to fall on your face, I figure someone ought to be here to witness it."

"Ye of little faith," he said as he wagged his own finger. He pointed to a nearby stool and asked her to sit. He looked down at his notes on the table beside him, staring at them for more than a minute without comprehending them. He couldn't focus. He looked up at her, and decided to just say it.

"Hey, about the other night, I understand you ran into my date at the hotel—"

Domenika wouldn't let him finish his thought.

"Yes, your pretty waitress," she said. "I hadn't realized you'd already made such fast friends. What is she? Seventeen? Eighteen?"

Bondurant looked up at the ceiling, avoiding Domenika's eyes.

"I just want to say I'm sorry. I should have told you about her," he said.

"Told me?" Domenika said. "What business is that of mine? There's nothing to apologize for."

"That's not what I mean. You were kind to offer your help that evening. I should have—"

"How do you turn this silly contraption on?" Domenika asked.

Bondurant took the hint. The conversation was over. He turned toward the sleek metallic instrument panel beside him and pointed to the small red button in the center of the console.

"Press it," he said.

Her eyes lit up as she reached across him and pushed it. Nothing happened. He looked curiously at the control panel and pressed the master control switch and the button himself several more times. He sat back in his chair, confused.

"I know," she said. "Let's try plugging it in." She pointed to the plug that lay on the floor below the electrical outlet on the wall beside them.

In his haste to get the equipment set up and his observation under way before anyone arrived, he'd forgotten his most basic setup task. He could feel his face turn a bright red. He bent over, quickly jammed the plug into the outlet, and said nothing, hoping to save himself further embarrassment. He nodded to her to try again.

She did, and she looked pleased as the network of miniature cameras and laser projectors he had rigged with meticulous precision above the Shroud began to hum and, in rapid succession, blink to life.

Constructed by Bondurant and two of his ingenious grad students at the Enlightenment Institute, the apparatus could only be described as experimental. It had *usually* performed in tests he'd conducted in the weeks that led up to his trip, but now he needed it to shine. He watched nervously as the expected large, diffuse blob of blue light about the size of a coffin materialized from the projectors and began to form just above the sacred relic. Domenika's face, especially her eyes, glowed in the strange hue. In a few more seconds, the system's high-resolution cameras found their target and zoomed in on the familiar image on the Shroud below. As they reached a focus, the previously diffuse aura of light that floated before them began to slowly concentrate into a more refined, sharper box of light suspended in air.

Then, as if by magic, the light shrank further in size and began to form something magnificent: a hologram in the distinct shape of a human being. The ghostly three-dimensional image of a lifelike body wobbled back and forth, flickered, and disappeared entirely for a moment. Then it reappeared as quickly as it had left, only now it floated on its back. Domenika took a step backward and looked at Bondurant as though she were looking at a ghost. The object came to rest no more than an inch off the light table, as though it had risen from the fabric of the Shroud itself.

"Come forth!" Bondurant said, deliberately echoing Jesus's command when he raised Lazarus from the dead. He looked about quickly to make sure nobody could see or hear him from the glass-paneled observation room next door.

"My God in heaven," Domenika said. "This is impossible. It's sheer genius."

"I know," Bondurant said proudly. "Thank you."

He was now actually glad Domenika had interrupted his special moment, as it was an experience that had to be shared to be believed. He reached for the microphone on the headset that was connected to the recorder in his pocket. He could tell she wanted to say more, but he held his forefinger to his lips to silence her. He looked at the clock on the wall.

"Wednesday, June 11th, 8:03 p.m.," he said. His tone was sterile. "Forensic anthropologic observations of Shroud of Turin. Investigation of Dr. Jon Bondurant. Subject examination through holography."

Even Bondurant was stupefied at what he saw before him. Just as Secondo Pia had brought the figure on the Shroud more fully to life for the world through his photographic negatives a hundred years before, Bondurant had given that same image three-dimensional life through the modern-day technology of holography. While the hologram was only an illusion of light made possible by precision laser projectors and multiple sheets of delicate Mylar-type film, it represented the most lifelike image ever seen of the man who appeared on the Shroud.

Bondurant passed his hand directly through the midsection of the glowing blue-green light before him and adjusted the tint control on the console. He gently reached for Domenika's hand and had her place it alongside the image. He asked her to hold it there. He then returned to the control panel and carefully adjusted the skin color of the levitating apparition to match her own until it looked uncannily human.

"You can move it now," he said as he pointed to her hand.

She hurriedly made the sign of the cross and stared at what was before her.

"Subject is male, approximately five feet seven inches, approximate weight 150 to 160 pounds," Bondurant said into his microphone.

It took him only a moment to conclude that the three-dimensional figure that glowed before them revealed details of the image on the famous Shroud that had never been seen before. *This is actually going to work*, he thought. What once had been a flat, ghostlike figure of a man on cloth now stood out in bold relief and brought Bondurant's goal, an anthropological autopsy of refracted light, within reach.

He knelt and stared intently up at the body bathed in light only inches from his face. He scanned the figure from its head to its toes.

"The image presented appears anatomically correct in all three dimensions," Bondurant said. He tried to mask his surprise. He pulled a small tape measure from his lab coat and leaned slightly over the body of light.

"Hold this for me, will you?" he asked Domenika as he handed her one end of the tape. He measured various elements of the luminous figure from end to end and side to side. "I find the lengths of the extremities, both arms and legs, to be in correct proportion to one another. The same is true for the width of the shoulders and thorax. Individual's muscular and skeletal elements appear to dictate mid- to late thirties in age."

He leaned in and observed the several inches that separated the light table and the apparition that floated before him. He shook his head. "Subject shows markings throughout that appear to be signs of a scourge. Evidence of welts and indentations found on the neck, back, buttocks, and rear of legs."

Domenika dropped to her knees beside Bondurant to see exactly what he was referring to. Then she held her hand to her heart and quietly began to cry. He saw the tears streaming down her face and, helpless, hadn't a clue what to do to console her. He placed a hand on her shoulder and squeezed it gently to comfort her, but felt instantly uncomfortable. He removed his hand quickly. Reluctantly, he left her on her knees, stood up, and peered closely at the hands of the hologram, which rested on its abdomen. Then he turned toward the image's feet. He examined them at close range in silence for several minutes. There appeared to be large indentations in both the wrists and feet of the image. He took a step backward from the figure and folded his arms, deep in thought.

He reached again for his microphone. "Individual was crucified," Bondurant concluded reluctantly.

Opposite him on the other side of the light table, Domenika was whispering the Lord's Prayer.

"Entry holes in the wrists," Bondurant continued, "are approximately two centimeters across and appear to be the result of square-shaped spikes. Judging by the size of the cavities, of which the wound on the left hand is more pronounced, I would estimate a two-centimeter width to be associated with nails approximately twelve to seventeen centimeters long."

He grimaced. "Clever," he said. He looked toward Domenika and pulled her over toward him by the hand. "By all appearances from the holes in his wrists, these spikes were driven directly into Destot's space. Do you know what that is?"

She shook her head slowly but couldn't respond. Bondurant grew concerned by the trancelike state she'd almost reached. He wanted to engage her to keep her present in the moment.

"It's between the carpals and radius, transecting the median nerve. They were trying to avoid major arteries and bone fractures," Bondurant said. "They had no interest in letting this individual bleed to death quickly. The subject was meant to suffer. These are signs of experts executing slow torture."

Another tear ran down her cheek.

Bondurant knew his stoic method of fact-finding was only making matters worse for her.

"Are you sure you want to remain here through the rest of this?" he asked. It had been a long time since he had felt so sympathetic toward anyone. Actually, he wasn't sure he ever had. He tried to brush the feeling from his mind, like an unwanted cobweb. But he found himself genuinely worried about her, and his examination was only half complete.

"Yes, yes. Please finish," she said. "I'll be all right."

He turned from her, stared once again at the holes clearly visible in both of the image's feet, and, given what he surmised, felt slightly disgusted. He reported his findings rapidly to spare Domenika and to speed up the examination.

He looked at the clock on the wall again and grew concerned that Domenika's colleagues might return from their dinner before he was finished.

"One nail. One *large* nail," he said hurriedly. "Both feet were nailed together, one on top of the other, by a single spike, as evidenced by the three-centimeter hole through the intermetatarsal space in the right foot. There is little doubt it punctured the terminal branches of the deep peroneal nerve. A smaller hole, approximately two centimeters in width in the left foot, what would have been the rear foot, received the slimmer, sharp end of the aforementioned spike."

Bondurant stopped for a moment, startled. He noticed that his own chest had started to heave back and forth. He figured his symptoms were caused by normal anxiety, considering the astounding nature of the discovery. It was impossible not to feel empathy for the torturous death the victim before them had obviously suffered. After a moment to catch his breath, he resumed his meticulous examination of the image from the upper thighs to the feet. But something bothered him.

He pulled up a chair, sat on it, leaned in, and looked at the holographic image from the side, slightly confused. He reached into his memory of the Gospels and recalled from Christian folklore that it was the two criminals on either side of Jesus who were shown the "mercy" of having their legs broken by Roman soldiers. According to the Gospels, it was a "favor" to them withheld from Jesus. Unable to use their shattered femurs to push themselves up the length of their crosses while they hung, the thieves would have experienced massive blood loss from the compound fractures and suffered the full weight of their bodies during crucifixion. According to biblical lore, they mercifully died more quickly. The same could not be said for this victim.

"No signs of crucifragium here for the subject, no broken legs to hasten death on what was presumably a wooden cross."

Domenika looked up, distraught. "Why do you insist on calling this miracle you've created before us a mere 'subject'? It is man-made, an object of light, I know. It's the stuff of cameras and film and marvelous machines. But this is the image of Jesus Christ, my Lord and Savior. Surely you must know that by now."

Bondurant was shaken by what he'd seen, but tried to keep his composure. He knew the image before them could be representative of many thousands of men crucified since the practice had first begun, but he wanted no arguments with Domenika, especially now. He had studied dozens of examples of ancient and even rare modern-day, Third-World crucifixions prior to his examination of the Shroud, and he knew the crucified individual before them could be anyone. However, until that very moment, Bondurant had not asked himself the obvious question. Was it possible to concede that he was, indeed, examining a figure so many had come to know as "Jesus"? The similarities between the body of light before him and the Bible's description of the crucified Jesus were remarkable. The consequences for Bondurant if it was true were life-altering. But he canceled out the absurd thought as quickly as it had arrived.

"Given these wounds and the obvious evidence of massive trauma through crucifixion," he reported into the microphone, "cause of death for this individual was most likely exhaustive asphyxia, labored breathing over several hours compounded by probable cardiovascular collapse."

Domenika looked exhausted. She said nothing.

Bondurant rose slowly from his chair and brought his nose to within an inch of the image's sublime face, the one that followers of Christianity the world over believed was that of Jesus Christ.

"Who *are* you?" Bondurant whispered to the image of light before him.

He cleared his throat and stared closely into the face of the image again.

"I find no evidence of insects or birds or animals burrowing their way into the eye sockets, nose, or mouth of the subject. All orifices appear to be intact. Unlike the majority of crucifixions with which I'm familiar, this individual was not left to hang on display for days."

After he carefully examined the left side of the image's chest and found no evidence of any deep or serious puncture wounds, he consulted his notes and walked around to the other side of the light table to examine the opposite side of the image.

Domenika looked up. "I know what you're looking for," she said.

Bondurant didn't answer but looked intently up and down the glowing chest cavity for any sign of a mark or indentation. He was mindful of the biblical story in which a Roman sentry, Longinus, belatedly lanced Jesus's side with a spear to spare him from further misery. Amazingly, a faint line on the chest about the width of a fist, just above where the image's right ventricle would be, appeared before him. In utter disbelief, Bondurant dropped to the floor on both knees and studied the mark carefully with a magnifier for several minutes. Domenika knelt down and joined him at his side.

"Not possible," he said. It was one of few times in his life when Bondurant was completely astonished.

"More than possible," she replied. "Divine."

Bondurant reached over to the control panel, his hand shaking, and tried to adjust the contrast knob to sharpen the outline of the image. It was no use. His eyes began to blur from the lack of sleep, accompanied by an unmistakable lump that began to form in his throat. He closed his eyes and gathered his strength to compose himself.

"Strike that," he said as he opened his eyes once again. "Image appears to reflect a marking of indeterminate origin, right side of chest cavity, below the pectoral muscle. Bears further examination on video capture tomorrow. Day three of investigation."

With that, he quietly turned toward the console and pressed the off button at the bottom of the panel. He watched the crucified image slowly dissolve from view, leaving only their two souls, the mysterious relic, and his newfound questions in the darkness around them.

CHAPTER 17

Turin, Italy
June 2014

Where to? Where to, lovebirds?" the young African cabdriver asked with a broad, toothy grin. He spoke with a French Algerian accent.

"Hotel Victoria, and step on it," Father Parenti said as his face broke into a smile. He began to laugh, and the cabbie joined in the merriment. "I've always wanted to say that. This is my very first cab ride, you know?" the priest said, delighted. Aldo leapt from Parenti's small satchel and scampered quickly from the backseat to the ledge against the rear window of the cab so he could take in the view behind them.

"Félicitations, mon père!" the driver said as he pulled the cab slowly away from the curb into heavy traffic. "A first time for everyone!"

It was day seven of the investigation, and they were blessed with a relaxed Sunday off, their only break in the two-week work schedule. Parenti and Domenika were returning from the Ristorante Barolo, where they had lunched after a long and pleasant walk from Mass. Domenika was in a particularly good mood as well, given that the examination of the Shroud had produced promising results thus far. By all accounts, Rome was pleased. She turned to Parenti and arched her eyebrows.

"I'm curious. What else were you able to find on Bondurant? Did they send the additional report I requested?" she asked.

Parenti had expected the question. He'd read the confidential dossier the Vatican Archives had sent the day before. Their cab was stuck in traffic, and he could tell the ride back to the hotel was going to provide ample time to answer the questions she had put to him earlier. He also had some unexpected news. But just as he opened his mouth to answer her, the cabdriver spoke.

"*Pardonnez-moi*, my friends," the cabbie said. "You are traveling with others?"

"No," Domenika said. She looked around. "What do you mean?"

"There is a car behind us, very close," he said. "The black Mercedes. He's changing lanes with me. Many times."

Both Domenika and the little priest turned to look behind them to see an expensive four-door sedan on their tail. Aldo began to pace back and forth atop the ledge. The driver of the Mercedes wasn't visible in the sun's glare off the car's windshield, and Domenika shrugged her shoulders.

"Not with us," she said.

"My fault, then," the cabbie said. "Silly thinking."

Parenti turned back toward her.

"Where were we? Yes, Bondurant. You know the basics already," he said. "Most of what our researchers have gleaned from the additional documents we have and the interviews of those willing to talk are really just trivial in nature, personal things that I don't think would terribly interest you."

"Don't spare the mundane, Father," she said.

He was glad to see she had taken a genuine interest in Bondurant, although he could tell she would be the last to admit it. Bondurant was by no means perfect. He had his vices. But it had taken only Bondurant's single act of kindness toward the little priest when they had first met for Parenti to be won over. It was a measure of the man's heart toward those less fortunate than himself, and it meant a great deal to the priest. Parenti had no quarrel with playing matchmaker, as unlikely as the prospect of the two of them together might seem. Although she was leaning back in her seat, he could tell that when it came to deeper insight about Bondurant, she was really on the edge of it.

"An addictive personality, to be sure," Parenti said as he shook his head.

"Yes, the drinking. Tell me something I don't know," she said coolly.

"Well, our research reveals it goes beyond that. He is bright, no doubt. Top of his class and all that. But accomplishments have often come too easily to him. You might say he often finds life a bore. Type A, always reaching for something, anything to fascinate him long enough to hold his interest. Then he's off to something new. The addictions, they're merely for passing time, I think. The drinking, the smoking, the conquests, the—"

"The what?" Domenika asked.

"The conquests. The conquests of women. Surely you have noticed this."

"No, actually I've not, Father," she said as she once again feigned disinterest.

"Well, he has certainly noticed you. He's not stopped talking about you since the day we arrived and you swept him off his feet."

"You can't be serious about that, Father," she said dismissively. "When has he even had the time?"

Parenti knew he was exaggerating a little, but he was thrilled with the prospect of Domenika and Bondurant falling for each other. Oddly, they seemed a fit to him. He'd detected the unspoken attraction between them from the moment they came together in Turin, and he was excited for her. Parenti adored Domenika and was particularly fond of her kindnesses toward him, a disfigured and crippled priest. He saw the Vatican as a prison where only aging clergy should be sentenced to live out their time. It was no place for a woman with her spirit and such a promising life ahead of her. He reached into his satchel, retrieved a treat for Aldo, and continued.

"I like him, our Dr. Bondurant, but be on your guard, Domenika," Parenti said. He looked out the window while the cabbie accelerated past one of Turin's lovely gardens. "You know Father Alfeo, the specialist in the modern literature branch?"

"No, I'm sorry. I don't."

"He's a psychologist by training. He reviewed Bondurant's file for me. He used an American expression. Very clever, I must say."

"And what was that?" Domenika asked.

"He says Dr. Bondurant is not interested in 'Mrs. Right.' He wants 'Mrs. Right Now.'" Parenti slapped his knee and began to laugh. "That, only an enchanting woman like you can cure."

Domenika's instant frown brought Parenti's merriment to a halt.

"So, let me paraphrase from Alfeo's report," the priest said as he stared at his papers and avoided Domenika's eyes. He began to tick off the list of character traits the dossier revealed to describe Bondurant: "Highly promiscuous, lacks a capacity for vulnerability or romantic feelings. Callous toward the feelings of women, sees them as objects of comfort, enjoys—"

"Enough!" Domenika protested.

"But there's much more here, Domenika," Parenti said. "Misogynistic, willing to—"

"What *else* is there beyond his difficulty with relationships, Father?"

"An American story," Parenti said. He carefully folded his notes and spoke from memory. "Smart man. Grew up fast, apparently. Self-taught. Impatient. Doesn't suffer fools gladly."

"Anything else?"

"Well, he's rich. I can tell you that. But those who know him well claim he is generous to a fault. He has been known to give his money away to friends, even strangers, faster than he earns it. Greed is one of the vices he's gone without. And then there's that remarkably odd watch. I suppose it says something about him as well."

"What do you mean? What's wrong with his watch?" she asked.

"Haven't you seen it? The one he wears?"

"No. What's so special about it?"

"It doesn't keep time—at least, not time like you and I know it. It tells *his* time, as in how much he has left."

"I don't understand what you mean," Domenika said.

"He explained it to me. He has a patent on it. Developed it himself. It's a countdown clock of sorts. He believes he knows how much time he has left on this earth to the year and the month. I can't tell you exactly how he's calculated it, but he's documented every aspect of his lifestyle—his genetic disposition, his family's health history, his risk factors, cholesterol level, blood pressure, the drinking, the smoking, hours of sleep each night, vitamin supplements. Apparently it's all in a formula that predicts the end."

"The end?"

"His end."

"Now that's just morbid," she said.

"Maybe," Parenti said. "But he says he doesn't lose sleep over it. He said it reminds him every day that time is running out and that he'd better make the most of it."

"And how much time does it say he has left?"

"He wouldn't say. When I asked, he just said 'not enough.'"

"We all might wear jewelry like that, Father, if we believed, as he does, that we have just one life to live."

"*Pardonnez-moi* again, my friends," the cabbie interrupted. "I take it back. We *are* being tailed."

"You're kidding me," Domenika said as she turned to look behind them once again. "Who is it? Is it the police? What would they want with us?"

"This is not police, my friends," the cabbie said. "Do you want me to lose them?"

"Yes, yes, yes! Now this is fun!" Parenti exclaimed. He could tell Aldo sensed real trouble behind them as well. He had jumped from his perch on the rear window ledge back into his satchel and now began a low growl.

"It's certainly *not* fun," Domenika said. She craned her neck to get a good look behind them once more. "Who could possibly have an interest in us?"

"I haven't a clue," Parenti said. "But there's no shortage of strange people in this town who know that we're here and what we're doing. Some are taking bets."

Parenti stared behind them too, but it was still impossible to see who was inside the car just a few feet behind them. He watched as Domenika became visibly nervous.

"Just get us back to the hotel safely, please. That's all we ask," Domenika urged.

There was one more piece of information about Bondurant the priest had learned. It was difficult news to relate, and far more disturbing than anything he had come to learn before. He had debated in his own mind whether to reveal it to Domenika or to anyone, but given the insight he knew it would provide, he decided he had no choice. It had been located by Father Alfeo in a locked file cabinet placed in an obscure private reading room of the Vatican's vast archives that very few were aware of and even fewer were authorized to enter. Parenti looked behind them nervously once more and turned to address the cabbie.

"How much longer to the hotel, do you think?"

"The traffic is bad today, Father," the driver replied. "At least another ten minutes."

"Okay, then. Let's get this over with," the priest said as he turned to face Domenika. He took a deep breath. "I believe there are extenuating circumstances for Dr. Bondurant's history of opposition to faith. Something that might have you see him in a, in a—"

"In what, Father?"

"In a, well, a new light. A different light."

"Father, it's no secret why he's an atheist. He's written books on the subject." She continued to look at the traffic backed up behind them but had momentarily lost sight of their pursuer.

"Yes, yes, indeed he has," Parenti said. "His logical construct to argue against the existence of God as an atheist and as a skeptic is of the classic mold. Evolution, cosmology, and all of that. He's used our doctrine like a punching bag, has he not?"

"It's no secret to me, Father. I've had the misfortune to tangle with him on stage."

"So I've heard. You should know, Domenika," Parenti said as he joined her in minding the scene behind them, "I believe there is a source of anger, even hatred, within him toward the Church and our faith that, to tell you the truth, is justifiable. Things unspeakable. But it explains many things."

The cabbie edged his way onto the widening avenue near their hotel, veered across two lanes of traffic, and slowed the taxi to a crawl to test their pursuers' resolve. He shook his head as the black sedan followed suit and emerged behind them once more.

Parenti hesitated. He didn't know why they were being followed, and wondered whether he should drop it and leave it for another time. But he didn't know when he might have another chance. He tried to decide how to explain what he'd learned, and then he summoned his courage, reached out for Domenika's hands, and took them in his own.

"There are lists," the priest said. A wave of nausea suddenly consumed him. He bit down on his lower lip to repress it. "Some of them quite old, some of them new. I did not know about these lists before, but apparently they contain the names of *the offended*. Father Alfeo has confirmed it." Parenti cast his eyes downward and sat completely silent, now at a loss for words.

"What do you mean by 'the offended,' Father?" She gripped his hands in hers to reclaim his attention.

"They are the names of innocents revealed to us by certain priests, nuns as well, over many years," Parenti said. "The names of countless children violated by some in the clergy. Names, names, names, all of them secretly recorded on lists. From what I can tell, Domenika, there are *thousands*. They are known *only* to the Church through those who have confessed their terrible sins."

Domenika looked at Parenti with a sadness in her eyes that he had never seen before. They had begun to well with tears.

"These people, these monsters," Parenti continued, "were required to document the names of their victims as they came forward over time to seek absolution for their acts. Most of their stories are death-bed confessions. These lists of unfortunate children and the terrible acts committed against them reveal the darkest secrets of the Church."

Parenti watched as Domenika hung on his every word. It was as if his revelation had wound its way toward her and taken on the shape of a large and terrifying snake. Domenika released her hands from the priest's, pushed away, and looked at him as though another revelation was coiled before her, ready to strike.

"Father Parenti, I think I know what you are about to say," she said, her hands now trembling.

At that very moment their taxi pulled up in front of their hotel. The sedan that had followed their every move pulled up beside them and came to a complete halt. As their cabbie leaned from his window to get a look inside the mysterious sedan sitting only inches away, its engine suddenly burst into a roar and sent the car speeding away.

"I'm not sure you do, my child," the priest responded. He paused. "I've confirmed that our friend Dr. Bondurant's younger brother is on the list."

CHAPTER 18

Turin, Italy
June 2014

Eight days into his investigation, and Bondurant was driving his team to make progress at a breakneck pace. He had no choice. He knew some of the most difficult work lay in the days ahead. After that there would be several weeks of painstaking analysis required of over a hundred scientists in five different laboratories spread from Albuquerque to Tokyo before a report on their findings could be released. He was proud of his team's effort since the relic had been transferred to the university's labs a week earlier, but they had fallen behind schedule, and emotions had begun to run high.

And just as Bondurant had expected, it was the pentagonal-swatch removal tests by Dr. Terry O'Neil and his team that had caused the greatest amount of heartburn for Church officials thus far. In fact, a fistfight with the "Vatican Vultures," as Bondurant had dubbed them, had nearly erupted in the lab over the issue, and he was happy to have those arguments behind them.

There was history behind the confrontation. Previous scientific experiments on the Shroud that dated back to 1988 had involved the permanent removal of a tiny swatch of fabric from the cloth—the size of a match head—for the express purpose of destroying it. Destruction of the sample then was a requirement of carbon dating, as it was also for O'Neil's present effort, but no other element of study science had to offer would come closer to validating the precise age of the Shroud than O'Neil's carbon dating work.

Carbon existed in every living thing and was found in hundreds of millions of forms. When living things died, the carbon-14, or C-14, in the organism dissipated at a certain rate over time. Measuring the remaining carbon fraction of a linen sample taken from the Shroud would determine the age of the material. However, as a result, the five swatches the Church had agreed O'Neil's team could remove from the Shroud would be completely destroyed and never replaced.

O'Neil's work was critical, because the C-14 tests performed on material from the Shroud twenty-six years earlier by the Armed Forces DNA Identification Laboratory, the University of Arizona, and the Swiss Federal Institute of Technology had become the subject of intense controversy. Their conclusions had been the subject of widespread dispute. The scientists involved had estimated with 95 percent certainty that the Shroud's origin was in the Middle Ages, not the time of Jesus, thereby proving it was a fake. What they didn't know during their study was they had chosen a fabric sample from an area of the Shroud that was in reality a medieval repair patch.

Testing the wrong area of the Shroud's fabric had been an honest mistake. To avoid it, one needed precise historical documentation of the many repairs made to the fabric over several centuries, knowledge the scientists did not possess at the time. Before the Shroud had been placed on display in Turin, it had been stored in a small chapel in

Chambray, the capital of the Savoy region. There it was nearly consumed in a fire in 1532 when molten silver dripped onto the fabric and burned symmetrical diamond-shaped holes through the layers of the folded linen cloth. Nuns had worked feverishly for months, painstakingly patching the damage with the local fabric of their time. Over 160 years later, further repairs were made to these same medieval patches. Two centuries after that, more repairs were sewn into the cloth beyond the patches first made by the Poor Clare nuns in 1532. And as late as 2002, the Vatican had restored the Shroud even further for public exhibition, removing material backing from it, as well as taking off more than two dozen previous patches.

To avoid the C-14 sampling mistakes of the past, O'Neil was left with a difficult task that involved the removal of five tiny fabric swatches from the burial Shroud in a "pentagonal" pattern across the bodily image presented on the cloth. Their selection would be made so as to ensure the ghostlike image was accurately tested while avoiding entirely the numerous medieval patches. Removal of even the tiniest of samples that involved the head and face of the Shroud's image was strictly off-limits. This left O'Neil to choose sites for the removal of fabric swatches from other critical areas. These spots included an area on the image's clavicle, just below the neck, as well as two other places in parallel locations on the image's thoracic and leg areas. The size of the swatches cut from the cloth was to be no larger than three times the size of the head of a pin, or six millimeters in diameter. This way, O'Neil could get a sufficient amount of carbon-bearing material for his tests. In turn, the Church could ensure that the image of the Shroud, while permanently altered, would not visibly suffer.

The melee that had nearly erupted, one that Bondurant had anticipated might occur long before O'Neil's work had begun, involved the sample retrieval in the thoracic region of the image. O'Neil, Bondurant, and Sehgal had studied this area of the image with great interest, because it was there that the purported blood of Jesus was found to be most prevalent. As the Gospel of John recounted, Christ's demise from crucifixion was followed by the lancing of his side by a Roman soldier who used his spear to ensure Christ's death. While Bondurant's own holographic analysis of the area was still indeterminate as to a precise cause for the wound, a large, brown stain in the abdominal region of the image on the Shroud in this very area strongly implied the presence of blood. The collection of material that contained samples of blood was critical to the investigation because that material was certain to be original to the Shroud, making it suitable for C-14 testing. It was also important to the DNA testing Sehgal would perform to determine the many critical qualities of the blood's source. Was it indeed blood? Was it human? What was the blood type? And this was not to mention the unprecedented treasure trove of traits to be drawn from Dr. Sehgal's DNA analysis of the sample itself, including sex, hair and eye color, body measurements, and remarkably specific facial features. Every Vatican official present during O'Neil's sample taking objected to the removal of any shred of fabric that could contain an ancient droplet of the blood of Jesus Christ. But Bondurant held firm and pointed to the discretion his team was allowed in the protocols that dealt with the pentagonal-swatch scheme. After a late-night, tension-filled call with the Vatican, during which Domenika had stunned Bondurant when she ran some helpful interference, Bondurant and O'Neil were able to ensure that two of the five swatches of cloth gathered from the Shroud contained trace elements of blood. Four of the samples were required for O'Neil's C-14 testing, and the fifth was destined for Sehgal's lab in India.

Now stored in five separate vials contained in a bulletproof briefcase, the samples never left Bondurant's side.

In related and less controversial work, Dr. Jean Boudreau had already carefully removed material half the size of a postage stamp from the lower left-hand corner of the linen fabric composing the Shroud. His delicate process involving material removal had been approved by the Vatican in the research protocols agreed to with Bondurant. It was evident before Boudreau had begun his work that frayed fabric exposed exactly the type of twill pattern necessary for him to determine its antiquity and geographic origin. The precise spot chosen for fabric removal by the Vatican was also the requisite twelve inches away from the bodily image presented on the Shroud. While the sample removed was tiny, it required eighteen hours of observation and the kind of delicate incision normally accorded to brain surgery. The extraction complete, Boudreau and his team were already at work in his lab in Paris preparing to examine the tiny linen sample they'd captured through high-powered microscopes.

Also complete was the ticklish work of Dr. Lisa Montrose, which involved the material pigmentation analysis of the ghostlike image on the Shroud. While she needed only microscopic samples of the residue that formed the humanlike shadow on the fabric, her complicated task involved a retrieval of these tiny samples from at least twelve points across the image, all without disturbing the integrity of the likeness itself. The only element of the bodily image off-limits to her work was in the area purported to be the face of Jesus. As hard as Bondurant had tried to obtain approval of data sampling from the image's facial area, the Vatican would not budge. They feared an accident or other mishap might disturb the most important aspect of the miraculous image. Dr. Montrose's meticulous sample-gathering work lasted for an interminable thirty-six hours under intense oversight by the Vatican's representatives. Fortunately, her team had harvested the requisite number of particles required by the labs at Duke University. They would soon reach conclusions on the chemical process that had occurred to produce the image on the Shroud.

But they were increasingly behind schedule, and Bondurant had begun to grow impatient.

"Listen, Harry, we have just three hours left to get these images complete before we need to dismantle this rig," Bondurant pressed. "Lessel needs to be in here at eleven to begin the soil analysis. He's going to need every bit of this room for his own equipment."

"Jon, I get it, I get it," Dr. Harry Sato shot back from his perch near the ceiling twenty feet above. The Shroud was suspended horizontally like a phantom in the darkness below him. The tension in his voice reflected his precariously shaky roost. He sat on top of temporary scaffolding that bristled with customized lights and lenses and that surrounded the Shroud beneath him like a birdcage. His computer-generated images would provide definitive evidence as to whether the image of Jesus on the Shroud was a natural occurrence or something man-made. Unfortunately, he was far behind schedule.

"The lighting has to be perfect, Jon, or all of this will just be a complete waste of time. Just give me a minute to make a few more adjustments," he said.

With that, he signaled his assistant, who shifted the lens of the main camera, one of a nest of twenty, by another three inches to the left. The image fixed on the monitor needed to fit precisely in line with the crosshairs centered over the face of the Shroud displayed on his screen.

"Jack, move that center spotlight further to the right, and we'll have it," Sato said as he motioned quickly to his assistant with his free hand.

"My right or your right, Harry?"

His assistant used a thin, metal guide to carefully push the small, fiercely hot halogen light across the rod affixed to the scaffolding toward Sato.

"No, no, no, Jack. Your other right. Here."

As soon as Sato leaned across the center beam of the scaffolding to pull the tiny eight-ounce halogen light closer to his perch, disaster struck. The weight he shifted onto the crossbeam stressed the scaffolding's center pole, and the two-inch hollow steel rod holding the eight hundred pounds of scaffolding collapsed with a sickening metallic snap. Sato, and the trusses that supported all his cameras and spotlights, launched into a free fall and hurtled toward the most revered religious relic known to man.

"Watch out!" Jack yelled as he leaned helplessly from his ladder with one arm and swiped with his other toward Sato to catch him in flight. He missed him by a full foot and watched helplessly as Sato dropped like a rock toward the fragile Shroud.

Bondurant's heart sank as he watched the collapse of the scaffolding, its wire rigging enveloping Sato on his way downward.

Incredibly, Domenika had chosen this exact moment to return for her nightly inspection. As she swung the lab's main door open to enter the room and caught sight of the collapse under way, she let out a scream.

As Sato somersaulted toward the holy relic from his perch twenty feet above, he became trapped in a tangle of cables, wires, cameras, and lights, some that were burning hot. Miraculously, the electrical cords that entwined him arrested his fall in a sudden jolt five feet above the center of the Shroud. He stared helplessly down at the image that faced him and let out a moan. Then, in one more violent lurch, he dropped once again toward the Shroud as more wires gave way under his weight. He halted again, suspended less than two feet over the center of the delicate relic.

In all the chaos, one large high-intensity halogen light still under power began to tumble directly toward the Shroud. Sato saw the burning hot fixture as it slithered downward toward the priceless linen like a snake. Were the light to continue inching downward on its course, the Shroud was certain to ignite in a flash from the heat and be lost forever. Sato didn't hesitate. He reached out and grasped the white-hot light with both his hands, pulled it away from the Shroud, and cried out in agony as it burned through his palms to the bone.

The lab grew eerily quiet as the sickening smell of burned flesh began to waft through the room. Out of instinct, Bondurant dove toward one of the scaffolding's four corner support posts, squared his shoulder against it, and began to heave forward with all his might.

"Jon, what are you doing?" Jack yelled out. "You're going to bring the rest of the scaffolding down on the relic!"

Bondurant's face remained the picture of calm. "Jack, Domenika, listen to me. Get to the other corner post on this end and shove it toward the wall with everything you've got."

"You've got to be kidding me," Domenika cried out. "He's right. You'll topple the rest on the Shroud."

"I mean it, both of you. This is our only chance," Bondurant shouted.

Jack jumped down from his ladder and, joined by Domenika, began to shove at the bottom of the support post opposite of Bondurant's, just as he'd said. As they pushed back and forth at the base of the posts, Sato and the nest of equipment he was tangled in began to swing back and forth in an arc like a ball on the end of a string.

"C'mon. This is it. Heave it, heave it, heave it!" Bondurant cried out.

As they dug in together, all three pushed against the steel posts over and over with everything they had. The scaffolding rocked back and forth several times until its supports violently sheared from the bolts that grounded them to the floor and broke free. Suddenly, the entire framework lurched forward until it collapsed like a wounded spider on the laboratory floor, five feet away from the Shroud.

As Bondurant had calculated, Sato and his whole contraption of cameras and lights swung clear of the Shroud by inches during their descent to the floor. Sato let out a moan when he hit the ground and momentarily blacked out. Meanwhile, the Shroud lay before them on the examination table undisturbed and completely intact.

"Domenika," Bondurant said as he collapsed from exhaustion in the darkened lab. He was certain the climax of his life's work had come to a disastrous end. "Must this go in your nightly report?"

CHAPTER 19

Mumbai, India
June 2014

Kishan turned the pilfered key in the lock and then slowly swung Ravi's office door open. In the unlikely event a lab technician or a janitor was still at work somewhere in the building late that night, he would need to stay hidden. It was forbidden for him to be there after hours. His heart was pounding so hard he could hear it beat. He stopped for a moment and stood still to listen. Then he turned to look in every direction before he entered to make sure the nearby offices, each with windows where he would be visible, were completely deserted. Ravi's large office, silent and darkened since he'd left for Turin, contained a small metal box in the lower right-hand drawer of his desk. It held the money Kishan needed.

He had performed this heist many times before, but carefully enough that he felt the small amounts he had stolen from the company's petty cash box would not draw attention. Lately, he had stolen enough to know it was possible he could draw some suspicion. He crept his way, catlike, across the office in the dark toward his father's desk and prayed Ravi had been as careless as usual and left the desk unlocked. That would make things a lot easier. Kishan reached for the handle of the bottom drawer, tugged at it slightly, and breathed a quiet sigh of relief when it began to glide slowly open. *Jackpot!*

He grabbed the box by its handle and placed it delicately on Ravi's desk. He unlatched it and squinted in the darkness to see how much cash was inside. He needed only 1,600 rupees, just over twenty dollars, to pay the mechanic who had repaired his scooter, as well as the usual amount to help his sister, Saanvi, survive. It wasn't the total amount of cash in the box that was important to Kishan, but rather the size of the bills. Stealing too much would reveal an obvious theft that his father or an accountant might notice, enough to set off a bothersome investigation inside the labs. Taking just what helped him get by as well as helped his sister had worked before, and so far he had avoided an embarrassing manhunt in which he knew he would be among the primary suspects.

He peered into the box, lifted the first few bills up by their corners, and smiled. Right on top were a few fresh one-hundred-rupee notes, and beneath them a large stack of thousands. As he sifted through the money, he began to count out the 1,600 he needed, but stopped midway. He noticed a small piece of paper near the top of the stack. It looked like a note. He strained to read the writing in the dark but determined quickly it was his father's unusual script, bold but nearly illegible. He pulled the note from the stack of bills and held it up near the light of a small desk clock that glowed in the dark.

"Kishan:"—the note read—"Thou shalt not steal. What you take you must return. I have counted this <u>and</u> am counting on you. Love, Ravi."

Kishan immediately turned and looked around him in a panic as though his father stood right behind him. He quickly counted out the amount he needed, shoved it into his jacket pocket, and peered into each of the darkened corners of the room. He saw no one, breathed easier, and plopped himself down in his father's chair behind the desk. He was filled with both rage and embarrassment. He kicked the desk in front of him hard enough that the center drawer, the one that was *always* locked, popped open slightly. Surprised, he leaned over and pulled the drawer slowly toward him to get a glimpse at the treasure Ravi had kept under lock and key for as long as Kishan could remember. He sifted through its contents and found inside only an unremarkable assortment of pens, paper clips, rubber bands, a few coins, and several notepads. But just as he was about to close the drawer, he noticed something strange: a small red button mounted halfway up the side. It was impossible to resist. He pushed it.

He first heard a latch open, followed by what sounded like a coin hitting a tile floor. Kishan grabbed the illuminated clock from the desk to light the floor below him. A small metal key caught his eye. He looked toward the closet door across the office, the one he was certain only his father had ever entered. It was nothing but a simple key, but if it were to open the door, Kishan felt sure it would reveal his father's deepest secrets.

No one but Ravi enjoyed access to the closet. Ravi's secretary and others in the office referred to it as the "Forbidden Zone" or the "Bomb Shelter." Some had jokingly speculated it was the true resting place for Mahatma Gandhi. Others said it was a portal to the famous Lost Temples of India. Whatever lay inside the closet, Kishan was certain that if he disobeyed his father's explicit instructions to stay out of it, he would face the most severe punishment. It was even possible his father would disown him. Kishan quickly calculated in his mind the distance between Mumbai and Turin. He knew his father did not plan to return for several more days.

His curiosity got the best of him. He quietly crept across the office with key in hand and stopped at the closet door to take a deep breath. The moment of indecision ended. There was no way he could resist the urge to find out what was behind the mysterious door. He inserted the key into the lock, closed his eyes, and turned the key ever so gently to the right. The moment he did, the closet door sprung open as if on a spring, revealing a space as dark as ink. He felt around for a light switch inside the closet and found one with his palm, but stopped short before he flipped it on, afraid of the light that would set his father's office aglow. He stepped inside the closet, shut the door behind him, and hit the switch.

The first thing that struck Kishan when his eyes adjusted to the light was the size of the room he had entered. It was no mere closet. The room, windowless, faced the interior of the building and was deceptively large, nearly the size of Ravi's office itself. The second thing that struck Kishan was the altar.

In the center of an array of shelves before him was a modest red velvet pad on the floor—presumably to kneel on—in front of what could only be described as a shrine. In its center were two large candles and a photograph of Pope Augustine giving a blessing to Ravi in the pope's offices in the Vatican. Right beside the photo was a large black-and-white picture of Mother Teresa in what appeared to be a hospital, surrounded by children.

To his right, Kishan caught sight of a large collection of framed photos on the wall, none of which he could place. One, encased in a cheap and worn plastic frame, was a tattered photo of a mother and father holding the hands of a small boy who stood between them.

Kishan wasn't sure, but he thought it might be the only photo Ravi had of his parents before they had both died so young. They almost looked like children themselves. He had never seen another picture of them.

Arrayed in a square in the center of the wall was another collection of photos Kishan hadn't seen before. They were photos of trips he and his father had taken over the years. His favorite was one of the two of them in their seats at a Chicago Cubs game, taken during their trip to America. Both of them were smiling broadly. Kishan recognized every moment when each of the pictures had been snapped. On a small table below the photos were a stack of his school report cards, ones his father had obviously felt should be safely stored.

On the opposite wall, centered in the middle, was a heavily decorated diploma encased with an 18-karat gold medal bearing the image of Alfred Nobel. Kishan had been shown the prize by his father once before, but after that it had disappeared. He was tempted to touch it, but he thought better of it and left it alone. Then he turned back toward the wall with the door he had entered through and gasped.

As he approached the sight, his stomach turned. It was a collage of death: a collection of at least a hundred Polaroid photographs of dead, mutilated children was strewn across the wall, pinned there haphazardly with thumbtacks in no apparent order. He could barely bring himself to look at the photos of the unfortunate children. Some with eyes completely missing, others in various stages of decomposition, and many more malnourished—they had obviously starved to death. Kishan turned his head away in disgust. He didn't need someone to tell him where these victims were likely found. He had been rescued by Ravi from this world. They were the product of the slums of Mumbai, the poverty of Calcutta, and countless other cities and rural regions of India from Pradesh to West Bengal. Kishan tried to imagine why his father would collect and display such horrible images. He'd always sensed his father's frustration. While Sehgal had made it in this world and Kishan had been spared a life of misery, there were so many others like him who had met with senseless death by poverty. Kishan was certain the photos were kept as painful reminders of the work Ravi had left to do.

He wanted to leave the forbidden room as soon as he could but first turned toward the only other small table in the room. He was shocked to see a pistol lying there. His father was passionately opposed to firearms, and yet here was a particularly lethal-looking gun. Next to the gun was a stack of books, some magazines, and dozens of brochures. Kishan picked up one of the books, leafed loosely through it, and then turned to the pile of magazines and articles nearby to scan their contents. This was strange, he thought. He stuffed one of the pamphlets into his jacket pocket and made his way quickly toward the door. He turned off the light, closed the door behind him, and wondered what could possibly possess his father to hide a gun and take an interest in something as strange as the Demanian Church.

CHAPTER 20

Turin, Italy
June 2014

Bondurant was certain there was no time to lose. Even though one of his best friends and most qualified scientists he knew lay semiconscious in the hospital from his accident the night before, it was critical to examine the photo imagery Harry Sato had gathered before the accident that almost destroyed the Shroud. It was one of the few puzzle pieces Bondurant could put quickly into place to answer an important question about the Shroud without having to wait weeks for answers.

Fortunately for Bondurant, the vast majority of the evidence he needed from Sato's work had already been neatly packaged by Sato's team on a hard drive, and the drive was now in a computer at Bondurant's fingertips. Bondurant would have preferred to have Sato right at his side to interpret the findings, but that was impossible now. He had received a lot of on-the-job training from Sato about how to interpret the results of photo imagery, and he felt he could adequately manage a rough interpretation of the evidence on his own.

But, just as with the holographic examination of the Shroud he'd conducted a few days before, Bondurant had Domenika in the examination room. This time she'd been an invited guest. He wanted her there so that she could view the evidence at the same time he did. Bondurant felt particularly certain that Sato's computer-aided photo imagery might cast particular doubt on the authenticity of the Shroud, and if that were to happen, he wanted Domenika present to see it.

At this point, even Bondurant had been surprised at his own findings drawn from holographic presentations of the Shroud. There was no question his study of the ghostly image that had arisen from the lab table several nights before pointed in one clear direction: the Shroud of Turin could indeed be the burial cloth of a crucified man. Now Sato's results could help confirm or deny that finding, and it would only require a few minutes of study to determine the truth.

As Bondurant calibrated the massive projectors that would beam the high-resolution image of the Shroud upon a giant screen, as large as that of a movie theater, Domenika settled into her chair at the control desk. Bondurant pushed a button, and the entire examination room faded to black and left the control board as the only source of dim light in the room. "You're sure you're plugged in this time?" Domenika teased.

Bondurant winced.

"Yes," he said somewhat sheepishly. After a few taps on his keyboard, a massive image of the face of the Shroud was projected on the screen.

"Good, then," Domenika said. "I see you've chosen the face of our Savior to start with."

"Yes, I have," Bondurant said. "It's the face on the relic that so many Christians identify as that of Jesus Christ. I figure let's get right to the heart of the matter."

"Fine," Domenika said. "The image is certainly sharp. And large. I've never seen the face of our Lord in such magnificent detail before."

"Harry's equipment is worth many millions of dollars. The image has never been as clearly and sharply seen as this," Bondurant said. "Now I'm going to center on the image's right cheek, just below the eye, and I'm going to magnify it one thousand times."

He zoomed in to the shade of the image's face. Black and white lines, most of them haphazard as to their direction, appeared before them.

"Huh," Bondurant said.

"'Huh'? What does 'huh' mean?"

"It means 'huh,'" Bondurant said. "Just 'huh.' You've said it before."

"Yes, but when I say 'huh,'" Domenika said, "it usually means I'm a little surprised. What does 'huh' mean to you?"

"It means I'm a little surprised."

Domenika shook her head.

"You know, sometimes you just—"

Bondurant cut her off.

"Let's go to ten thousand times now," Bondurant said. He typed another command into the keyboard.

Now the image before them revealed the same lines as before, only when Bondurant moved the image from place to place across the screen, every line magnified. The lines looked random in nature, and did not seem to follow any particular pattern or direction.

"What the . . . ?" Bondurant said in amazement. He then stared in silence at the screen.

"Jon, you're driving me nuts," Domenika said. "What's 'what the'? Is that good or bad? It's bad, isn't it?"

"It depends on your point of view," Bondurant said. "For me right now, it's bad. For you, it's good."

"What do you mean?" Domenika said. "C'mon. Act like a scientist. What is 'what the' in scientific terms?"

Bondurant moved his cursor so that he could capture as much of the image of the face on the Shroud as possible at such high resolution before he responded.

"'What the' means my mind just can't grasp what my eyes clearly see," Bondurant said. "I was expecting something totally different."

"What were you expecting?" Domenika asked.

"Paint strokes, actually," Bondurant said. "There's always been the speculation that the famous Shroud of Turin was actually the work of an artist with a lot of imagination, a bolt of linen cloth, and a fine paintbrush. But this is not the work of an artist."

"How can you tell?"

"These are not brushstrokes," Bondurant said. "There's no uniformity whatsoever in the lines that configure the image we see. And they are not patterns conjured up by a machine. The randomness of the lines is just too great."

"So what are you saying, Jon?" she asked.

Bondurant moved the magnification down to 100X.

"I'm saying that the evidence so far is telling me we are looking at an image that was formed naturally, and not by man," Bondurant said.

Domenika drew her chair as close as possible to Bondurant's and simply smiled. Bondurant went through the same procedure as they looked at over a dozen other areas of the Shroud with the same magnifying tool. On each occasion, he found the same result. No evidence of medieval artistry or more modern-day technique appeared to create any point on the image of the Shroud. The evidence simply wasn't there.

Bondurant took a break and stared up at the giant screen. He couldn't believe what he'd seen. Domenika reached over for the computer mouse he'd been using. She double-clicked on an icon for a folder Bondurant had ignored all morning. Before he could look down to see what folder she was opening, she'd already been able to open the image on the screen. It was a photo, and Bondurant could see that the folder she'd opened was entitled "For Bondurant, As Requested." He leapt to reach for the computer mouse, but it was too late. Domenika held it firmly in her hands.

On the screen before them was a giant photograph of Domenika appearing positively radiant in one of the gardens outside the lab. She wore a pair of faded jeans and a casual white cotton shirt. The photo captured her striking beauty and had obviously been taken with her unawares, most likely through a telephoto lens from afar.

"What the . . . ?" Domenika said.

Bondurant could only look down at his lap. He glanced sideways and saw that Domenika was studying the stolen image of herself in a private moment. She wasn't smiling.

"I guess it's my turn now," Bondurant said. "What does 'what the' mean to you?" He still couldn't bring himself to look at her.

"I guess 'what the' means," Domenika said, "that if you wanted a photo of me, you only needed to ask, Jon."

Bondurant summoned the courage to look at the one and only woman who seemed to have the ability to tie him in knots. He was mystified as to why.

"I guess, well, I guess I don't know," Bondurant said. "Perhaps I thought that asking for a photo of you might affect our professional relationship. I don't know." At this point, he felt no more than twelve years old.

"Huh," Domenika said. There was a long pause.

"Now I need to ask," Bondurant said, "what does 'huh' mean to you?"

"It means 'I like you too,' Jon, I guess, regardless of our professional relationship. I hope you enjoy the photo. Maybe one day you'll share one of yours with me?"

Bondurant smiled. He couldn't believe Domenika had let him off the hook so easily, and he was thankful.

"Of course, I love, I mean, I mean, I'd love to, you know what I mean, I'd love to share a photo with you. That would be great."

"Jon," Domenika said. "What does what we've seen here today in these photos mean to you? The ones of *the Shroud*, I mean."

"We have a lot more tests to run, Domenika. A lot more," Bondurant said. "I didn't think it was possible, but so far the evidence points to an authentic Shroud."

"Huh," Domenika said, a smile on her face.

"Huh," Bondurant said as he stared at the photo of Domenika on the screen. His smile grew just as wide as hers.

CHAPTER 21

Turin, Italy
June 2014

I hate hospitals. I just hate them," Bondurant said as he peered through the green-tinted glass window of the Intensive Care Unit in the Amedeo di Savoia Hospital in Turin. "I start feeling ill as soon as I walk through the door."

The lime-green cinderblock walls that surrounded them and the glaring neon lights above were just the first measures Bondurant took of the hospital they were in. The smell of bleach permeated the halls.

"Are you saying hospitals make you sick, Doctor?" Domenika asked.

"Let me tell you something about hospitals. Everything about them—the sick people, the odors, the noise—it makes me feel like there must be something wrong with *me*, but I just don't know it yet," Bondurant said. "Whenever I step inside one, I start to think that I might have cancer and don't know it, or that a heart attack is just around the corner."

"They remind you that you're mortal?" Domenika asked.

"Yes, exactly."

She looked down at Bondurant's wrist. "Like your watch," she said.

Bondurant quickly pulled the sleeve of his jacket over his watch to hide it. How did she know about it? "Well, that's a little different. That—"

"Jon, you are an interesting study," she chided as she pressed her nose lightly against the glass once again. She stared at Haruki Sato, who lay in a semiconscious state in a room on the other side of the window.

She had called him by his first name again, and Bondurant liked the sound of it. He took the opportunity to study her while her eyes were fixed intently on his friend. He had yet to figure out why he cared about her impressions of him or her feelings, but he did.

Two days had passed, and Domenika had yet to inform the Vatican of the accident that had come within inches of destroying its treasured Shroud. *I can start this; I can stop it* was the refrain he'd heard over and over in his head since the disaster. He was stunned she hadn't called Rome that night and killed both the project and his reputation on the spot. He was worried about tempting fate, but his curiosity over her sudden change of heart toward him and his work had him vexed. He had to ask.

"Domenika, tell me something. I'm sure you must feel bad about Harry. We all do."

"Of course," she said.

"But I know you don't know him well enough to want to do him a favor, even a little one. And I know *I* have not been on your most-admired list since we met. It's no secret you've been opposed to this investigation from the beginning. So what I can't understand is why you've given me such a pass."

"You mean, why have I looked the other way?" she asked, her voice rising.

"Well, I—"

"You mean, why have I put my own career and reputation on the line by ignoring my obligation to protect the Church?" Her voice had jumped an octave.

"It's just that—"

"Especially where it concerns the near loss of the Church's most sacred relic on earth?"

There was no disguising her anger, and Bondurant was instantly sorry he'd raised the subject. He had visions of her changing her mind then and there.

Her voice suddenly softened. "Jon, let's just say I gave it a lot of thought. In the end, I think the Church owed you one. More than one. It owes you a lot, and—"

She stopped herself short, and Bondurant could tell she was hesitant to continue.

"Let's just say doing nothing was the right thing to do," Domenika said.

Bondurant was perplexed. Not a word of her explanation made any sense. The Church owed him nothing, and he was left with a puzzle even larger than the one he'd been thinking about for days. He decided not to press it. What mattered most was that the Shroud was safe and his work would continue, thanks to her. It was an unexpected gift he would not soon forget. He would repay it someday if he could. He focused once more on his friend on the other side of the glass.

"You know what's going to give me nightmares for a very, very long time?" Bondurant said. "The sight of Harry when he is fully conscious and finds he's lost both hands," he said. "He was an inventor. His hands were his life. That's going to haunt me forever."

Domenika grimaced at the sight of Sato. Motionless, he faded in and out of a drug-induced sleep. He hadn't yet turned his head or noticed his visitors behind the glass. Both arms lay limp at his side, covered with bandages that extended to his elbows. The doctors at Amedeo di Savoia had hoped they would be able to save Harry's hands, or at least portions of what remained, so that he would enjoy some semblance of use. But, unfortunately, the immense heat generated by the halogen lamp he had heroically smothered was so intense, it was as if he had caught a bolt of lightning in both hands.

"Some are called, Jon," Domenika said softly.

"What does that mean?" Bondurant asked. This was no time to prepare for another sermon he didn't want to hear.

"It means that some are called in service to the Lord in ways they may never expect. Dr. Sato gave of himself to protect the very image of Jesus Christ, our Lord. There are few higher callings I can think of than that."

"Maybe that's the case in your mind, Domenika," Bondurant said. "I know what you want to believe. But we don't yet know whose image is on that Shroud. Only that it does not seem man-made."

"You saw it yourself. The image is miraculous," she pressed.

He didn't say anything for a moment. "Tell that to Harry, who will likely never take his kids by the hand again."

"Oh, do we have to start with this again?"

She frustrated him to no end. How such an intelligent woman could be taken in by dogma not even a child would accept was beyond him.

"I suspect—"

Domenika wouldn't let him finish. "I suspect you will be singing a different tune when this is all over, Doctor," she said.

The reversion to addressing him now as "Doctor" rather than "Jon" did not escape him either.

"What I mean, Domenika, is that—"

Bondurant stopped himself short. Sato had slowly turned his head and noticed them at the window for the first time. His legs began to stir. Bondurant could tell Sato recognized them through the glass. Sato motioned Bondurant to his bedside with a slight movement of his forehead and eyes, as if to say "Come here."

The signs that met Bondurant at the entry door to the ICU could not be more clear:

ENTRY BY PERSONS OTHER THAN HOSPITAL PERSONNEL STRICTLY FORBIDDEN.

Bondurant turned to Domenika.

"Keep an eye out," he whispered.

"What? Are you kidding me? You can't go in there," she said as she grabbed him by the sleeve.

Bondurant turned and peered down the quiet, dimly lit hallway littered with empty gurneys and an assortment of wheelchairs. He saw only a single nurse preoccupied with paperwork at the brightly lit receiving desk at least a hundred feet away.

"Shh," he whispered, placing his forefinger to his lips.

Before she could protest further, Bondurant was free of her grasp and slipping deftly through the door.

He approached Sato's bedside. Sato motioned with his eyebrows, as if to ask Bondurant to come in closer. Bondurant saw that Sato had over a dozen tubes and wires running to and from his body.

"Jon," Sato whispered hoarsely as tears welled up in his eyes. "I am so sorry."

"Harry, please. I am the one who's sorry. I got you into this mess in the first place. I'll never forgive myself. Never."

"How badly was the relic harmed?" Sato asked, straining to speak.

Bondurant smiled. "Not a scratch on it. You saved it, Harry."

"I have a few of my own, though, huh?" Sato said as he forced a smile and looked down at the bandages that enveloped both his hands. "I have been fading in and out for a few hours, Jon. They told me before they put me under that there was no chance of saving them. But that little priest, the one with the hump. He says he disagrees."

"Father Parenti? He's been here to see you?"

"Yes, snuck in just like you." Sato's breathing was labored. "At first, he scared the heck out of me. I thought he was here for the last rites."

Bondurant laughed.

"But we prayed together. Never done that before. He had an old cloth he put on me for a minute. He says it will save my hands and maybe even me as well," Sato said. "He called it a 'laying on of hands.' We both laughed about it. I'll take any cure he's got."

Bondurant reached out and stroked Sato's forehead. He pushed back a lock of hair that had fallen in front of his eyes.

"Jon?" Sato whispered. "Listen to me."

Domenika began to tap lightly on the window. Jon turned and saw a panicked look on her face. Someone was coming.

Bondurant took a knee, leaned in, and placed his ear close to Sato's lips so that he would not have to strain to speak.

"Some are called," Sato said, almost inaudibly.

Bondurant froze in place. He couldn't believe his ears. "Harry, what did you just say?" he asked as he bent over him to completely block Domenika's view.

"I said 'some are called,' Jon." Sato's eyes closed momentarily as if to gather the strength to remain conscious for a few more moments. "When I was hanging there, as terrified as I was, I had a moment of real clarity. An epiphany."

"You mean like one of those 'whole life passes before you' moments?" Bondurant said sympathetically.

"Yes," Sato said. "One of the electrical cords had gotten itself wrapped around my neck so tight, I started to choke and lose it. Jon, I mean *really* lose it."

Domenika began to tap harder on the glass, a real sense of urgency now showing on her face.

"Jon, I have heard," Sato said as he began to wheeze slightly, "that at that very moment when it is almost done for you, some see the face of Jesus."

"Yes, so I've heard," Bondurant said reassuringly.

"Well," Sato said as his breathing strained from the pain, "I was staring right at the face of Jesus, Jon. Literally. He was not a foot from my face. I am not a religious man. And I said a prayer that I would live to see my kids. And, Jon?" Sato began to drift off.

"Yes, Harry?"

Sato looked up one last time as he tried to finish his sentence before he succumbed to sleep once more.

"The Shroud of Jesus Christ is real."

At that moment, two hospital orderlies burst into the room and ordered Bondurant to leave.

"Just what do you mean, Harry?" Bondurant said. "I've seen your photos. Is that your professional opinion? Do you know what you're saying?"

Sato could not answer. He had fallen back into a deep, morphine-induced sleep.

"You can read the sign? You can read the sign?" one of the order-lies shouted as he tugged Bondurant from the room and toward the elevator. "You too, miss. This way."

As soon as they were clear of the elevator and the orderlies, who had unceremoniously shoved them out onto the first floor and toward the exit, Domenika turned to Bondurant.

"What was that all about? What did he say?" Domenika asked as her eyes grew wide with curiosity.

Bondurant hesitated before responding.

"Did you know your Father Parenti was here before us?" he asked.

"No, he didn't tell me."

Bondurant searched for what to say next about Sato's parting words. He dared not repeat them to Domenika. If Sato, whom he trusted implicitly as a scientist, was hazily casting about odd notions from a drug-filled dream, that was one thing. But if Harry, his life-long friend and a known agnostic, had undergone a near-deathbed conversion to Christianity, that was something different and alto-gether important.

"Harry? He said he was sorry," was all Bondurant could bring himself to say. "That's about all I got from him. The rest, well, it was the morphine talking, I'm sure. It just had to be."

CHAPTER 22

Turin, Italy
June 2014

When Bondurant entered the break room four doors down the hall from where the Shroud rested safely on its examination table, he encountered complete silence. Usually this was a lively place for banter and casual conversation, but now, aside from the hum of the snack and soda machines against one wall, the place was eerily quiet. What made the room unusually uncomfortable was that two of the most prestigious scientists in their fields sat across a small table from each other and glared.

Bondurant didn't like the look of the scene, most especially the obvious tension between the two men. He also didn't appreciate being woken from the nap he had planned for the only three-hour break he had that evening.

"I'm told that each of you wanted to talk about the samples we've collected off the Shroud," Bondurant said.

It was four o'clock in the morning. Only three days of study on the Shroud were left. He yawned, rubbed his eyes, and placed an aluminum briefcase on the table between his two colleagues. It contained the five small samples of the Shroud, each in its vacuum-sealed bottle. He opened the briefcase between them.

Both O'Neil and Sehgal immediately dove toward the bottled samples like crabs scrambling for a prized prawn. The shoving and elbowing almost sent the briefcase tumbling toward the floor. Bondurant slammed the case nearly shut with both O'Neil and Sehgal's hands trapped inside. As he pressed down on the case, both of the combatants pulled their arms out.

"He started it," O'Neil cried out.

"No, *he* started it," Sehgal said.

"Gentlemen, if that's what you are, these sample containers are fixed inside the case," Bondurant said. "Try as you might, there's no yanking them out."

O'Neil and Sehgal both studied their forearms to determine whether they'd been bruised.

"Just what is going on, Terry? Ravi?" Bondurant said as calmly as he could on one hour of sleep.

"I'll tell you what's going on, Jon," O'Neil said. He was twice the size of Sehgal, and the thunder in his voice was meant to prove it. "This 'blood merchant' here is attempting to turn our entire test protocol on its head. All along he's insisted he can characterize the DNA off the Shroud with a single droplet of blood. Now he wants more. He wants all the blood we have off the Shroud."

Bondurant was sleep deprived, but he was awake enough to understand the consequences of what O'Neil had said.

"Ravi, is Terry accurately representing your point of view?" Bondurant asked. "You've always insisted that, given the molecular structures you deal with, you needed only a speck, way less than a drop of the subject's blood to get us all the data we need. What's changed your mind?"

"I've not changed my mind," Sehgal said. "I think you must have misheard me at the start. Indeed, my work is at a molecular level. But there is a chance that if I come away with just a single droplet of blood, there might be contaminants that would render the sample useless. I am trying to be safe, that's all."

"Correct me if I'm wrong," O'Neil said, "but wasn't the entire reason you won the Nobel Prize in this area because you figured out how to decontaminate DNA at the microscopic level in the first place? Why would you be worried about that now?"

Bondurant stared at Sehgal with some trepidation. He didn't believe he'd ever "misheard" Sehgal, and he was absolutely certain Sehgal had said that a single droplet of blood from the Shroud would suffice for the all-important DNA work they were counting on from his tests. Something had changed Sehgal's mind about the amount of blood he needed off the Shroud, and Bondurant wanted to figure it out.

"We are working on the very leading edge of biology and chemistry, Dr. O'Neil, and there are always factors we need to consider as we work. I have said from the beginning that we would need every bit of bloodstained material we could get to ensure we provide the best data possible," Sehgal said.

Now, that's a lie, Bondurant thought. Sehgal had said when he was first asked to join the Shroud team that he would need only a few molecules of blood.

"Ravi," Bondurant said, "you know that if we cede the only two blood samples we have to you, it will cut the number of samples we have to test using carbon dating, right?"

"I do," Sehgal said.

"Jon," O'Neil said. "Ravi's mind may have changed in the middle of all this, but mine certainly hasn't. I've said from the start that if you want ninety-five percent certainty on the age of this Shroud, I need all four samples promised. Anything less than that, and the age of the Shroud is going to be called into question. There goes your whole project. It's as simple as that."

"And if I don't get both blood samples I need, there goes your project as well," Sehgal said.

"What do you mean by that, Ravi?" Bondurant asked. He was becoming really agitated. This was getting out of control.

"I mean I'm off the team," Sehgal said as he folded his arms.

"So it's take your marbles and your Nobel and go home, is that it, Ravi?" O'Neil said.

"That's about right," Sehgal said.

Bondurant couldn't afford to let it end this way.

"Ravi, let's take a step back, can we?" Bondurant asked. "I'd like to sleep on this for what? Another hour? I have the lead on this project, and while I'm tempted to flip a coin, I have to decide what's best in the way of scientific process and outcome. Ravi, I hope you don't do us the terrible disservice of walking. It's a threat I don't take lightly, given what an honor it is to have your mind on this team."

With that, Sehgal shook both O'Neil's and Bondurant's hands and left the room.

"Now you tell me what that was all about," O'Neil said. "I know a bait and switch when I see one, Jon."

"I know, Terry, something's not adding up," Bondurant said. "My gut's telling me this is his once-in-a-lifetime chance to make a mark where the Shroud is concerned, and I'm beginning to wonder if there is more here than Ravi is letting on. If he's as good as that Nobel Prize says he is, he doesn't need all this blood. Something else is up his sleeve, and I'm going to need to figure it out."

"So what are you going to do, Jon?" O'Neil asked. "How are you going to rule?"

"Oh, I'm ruling in your favor, Terry," Bondurant said. "That's never been in question. What's in question now is just who Ravi Sehgal is working for besides me, and why."

CHAPTER 23

Turin, Italy
June 2014

They waited outside the hospital in the dark for the cab he'd called almost twenty minutes earlier, but it never showed. It was a warm summer evening, the stars were out, and Bondurant figured it was about a half hour's walk to the university labs, long enough for him and Domenika to clear their heads. The trek ahead of them was well lit and took them through a historic and romantic part of town. But the unplanned walk also provided something that had eluded Bondurant for days—time away from the project alone with the most vexing woman he'd ever met.

The past week had been physically draining for him and his entire research team. He'd spent one exhausting eighteen-hour day after another, meticulously organizing dozens of tests involving the recording of thousands of bits of data and evidence. Then there was the constant management of more than a half dozen "world-renowned" scientists from several different disciplines, all with egos as large as their reputations would suggest. Throw in the permanent maiming of one of his closest friends and add to it the near total destruction of the priceless relic he had the responsibility to safeguard, and Bondurant had seen little rest.

"Jon, let's reset," Domenika said as she removed her high-heeled shoes and bounded on her bare feet across the cobblestone street to catch up with him. "Before we go further, I want to talk to you about something. It has nothing to do with the Shroud."

Bondurant was game to talk about anything but work at the moment. "Sure. What's on your mind?" He shifted his suitcase—the locked case that held the samples of the Shroud—to his left hand, and with his right he lit up a cigarette and took a long, satisfying drag.

"Do you mind?" she asked as she waved away the smoke that wafted in front of them as they walked.

"I'm sorry," he said. "Does this bother you?" He wanted to be polite but had no desire to put it out for her. He needed to relax, and a cigarette would help.

"Greatly," she said. Domenika reached down, gently grasped his wrist, and pointed to the watch he devised that had so impressed Parenti. She tried to get a glimpse of the numbers on its face, but Bondurant pulled it away quickly. "I bet you're a whiz at math. You know your habit is subtracting years, not adding them, right?" she said.

"So the good father has briefed you further, I see," Bondurant said. He knew the habit was indefensible, and an argument for smoking would get him as far with her as his love of scotch. He often smoked simply to keep people at bay so he could be alone with his thoughts, but this walk was definitely an exception. He took one last satisfying drag and flicked the glowing cigarette toward the curb without complaint.

The early summer night air was chilly, and he could see she had crossed her arms as they walked along the ancient, tree-lined street. He slipped off his new sport coat and draped it around her bare shoulders. She smiled and nodded appreciatively as the jacket enveloped her. The nearly full moon that rose behind them lit their path and cast long, shadowy silhouettes before them. They turned the corner onto Via Pianezza. The street, normally a hive of traffic and pedestrians during the day, was deserted at night.

"What I want to know," Domenika said playfully as she glanced at a pair of shoes in a shop window they passed by, "is whether it was your preoccupation with science that led you to atheism, or your atheism that preoccupied you with science."

Not this again, he thought. He had enjoyed some small talk with her in the lab during the last few days. She had proven herself a lot smarter than he wanted to admit, and she had a wicked wit about her as well. But he was also wary of another debate over faith to set them back again. He knew that what could start out as a civil discussion with her on just about any religious topic usually fast turned into heated argument. He wanted to avoid another of those at all costs.

"That's an interesting question," he said as he set down his briefcase. It cushioned the tiny fragments of the Shroud samples inside. He bent over to pick up a small rock from the side of the road. "But I'd like to ask *you* a question first. I have a stone in my hand right now."

"Jon, it was just a simple question—"

"Yes, and I'll answer it with a simple question as well. Do I have a stone in my hand or not?" he insisted.

"Well, yes. Of course you do. You just said you did."

"And what evidence do you have that I am holding it in my hand?"

"The fact that you told me you are." She playfully grabbed for his wrist to wrest the stone from him, but he was too quick for her. He hid his hand behind his back.

"Did you see me pick it up?"

"No, but I saw you bend over, so I presume you did."

"Okay, so let me ask you again. Do I have a stone in my hand?" he persisted.

"Yes. You said you did, so I believe you."

"Oh, I see. You *believe* me. But do you *know* I have it in my hand?"

"No, I don't," she said, now agitated. "I'm taking your word for it. I believe you. Maybe that's a mistake," she said.

He could see she regretted asking the question at all.

"Maybe it was a mistake," he said. Bondurant opened his hands. They were both empty.

"And your point is?"

Bondurant could sense another ugly argument before them. He stopped short and looked up at the stars that glimmered in the night sky. He thought for a moment and then looked toward her. "What drove me to science and what drove me to atheism were really the same thing, Domenika. A need to *know*, not to believe."

She stepped back and swept her hand skyward, as if to draw an imaginary line across the heavens.

"Are you willing to agree that man cannot know everything about this universe? That there are some things that are beyond our ability to know or understand?"

He shrugged.

"Things like where we came from. We can never know—"

"No, I don't believe that. Domenika, I know where we came from. We're all just bits of material, descendants of stars that exploded billions of years ago."

Domenika frowned and held a rock in her own hand. She placed it in his. "Oh, you *believe* that. But do you know it?"

Bondurant let out a laugh and a long sigh. She was incorrigible. He reared his arm back and threw the rock toward a traffic sign at the intersection ahead. He missed it completely.

"Domenika, let me ask you this," Bondurant said. She was the one evangelist he had met who was worth saving from herself. "You are ascribing meaning to your life based on a biblical story, right? A story from a long time ago. It is powerful and wonderful and inspiring, I admit. But what evidence do you have beyond a tale from a hundred generations before you that your own resurrection is even remotely possible? You're smarter than that, I know it. Does it seem right to live your whole life by some voodoo that others who lived primitively thousands of years ago once believed?"

She kept her calm, and they resumed walking.

"Why have you come here?" she asked as they approached the Via Pianezza Bridge, which was shrouded in pale yellow light from the streetlamps arching overhead. The ancient bridge towered over the Po River, flowing noisily below. "You have believed for many years that the Shroud is a fake, and now you *need* to know for sure?"

"No. I've *known* it's a fake. All of the evidence gathered before I arrived in Turin suggests that's the case."

"But now?"

He hesitated. What he'd seen so far was compelling, but it wasn't strong evidence. In weaker moments, he'd been tempted to believe, but his rational side knew he needed to trust in his scientific training.

"I'll follow the evidence. I think the Shroud was made by natural means. But at this point, there's no reason to assume we will find that that Shroud had anything to do with the historical figure of Jesus

Christ. It's you and your backward Church that need to know the truth, and I will confirm it one way or the other."

"I see," Domenika said. "But are you willing to agree that science may never be able to grasp the divine?"

"Now you want me to believe in miracles?" he asked.

"What I want you to consider is that the image you are studying on the Shroud is of divine origin. That it was made by someone not solely human, and that it was produced by a life force that neither you nor science are equipped to comprehend."

"And where have you seen this life force before? Can you prove it?" he asked.

"I can," she said. "I know it when I am playing the violin and lose myself in time and space. It's God's grace playing through me. I know it when I look upon a masterpiece and marvel at what guided the artist's hand. I have seen it in great works of literature, and even the marvel of your machines and what you would call scientific discovery."

"Domenika, I don't want to have to break it to you, but—"

Out of nowhere, something hit the back of Bondurant's head and knocked him to his knees. Pain blinded him, and it took him a moment to see clearly. He was bleeding. He reached up and felt a gash at the back of his head. What had hit him? He wasn't sure, but he grasped the briefcase with both hands and rolled sideways to avoid another blow. Lying back, he saw a brick sail toward him, this time headed directly for the left side of his face. He swung the armored briefcase into its path and managed to block the blow.

Bondurant heard Domenika cry out for help. He rolled over again and tried to gain his footing. Another brick landed just in front of him, and he jumped back. He turned and saw someone no more than ten feet away, wearing a hood and a red ski mask, dressed all in black.

His hands were empty, his store of bricks now spent. Bondurant staggered toward him. He towered over the assailant.

"Domenika, get behind me," Bondurant said.

She ignored him and dashed toward a piece of broken brick that lay in the roadway. She picked it up and heaved it as hard as she could toward the hooded figure. She missed by several feet.

"You throw like a girl," was all Bondurant could think to say as he prepared to charge the attacker. He could see the assailant had edged far too close to Domenika for comfort.

"That would be a mistake, Doctor," said the hooded figure. He had a deep voice, and the accent was unmistakably Middle Eastern.

"Do I know you?" Bondurant asked. His vision was blurry and blood dripped down his neck, but he was ready to charge.

"Give me the case," the voice said, pulling a large dagger from under his jacket. It glinted brilliantly in the moonlight. Bondurant took a step backward. As he did, the shadowy, catlike figure sprang from his fighting stance and leapt toward Domenika. He was on her in an instant.

Domenika screamed and tried to fight him off, but he overpowered her, wielding the knife with ease. He grasped her from behind and yanked her by her hair. He leveled the razorlike blade directly against her exposed throat.

"Give me the case," the assailant demanded.

"Don't do that," Bondurant warned.

"She will die, Doctor, I assure you," the figure shouted. He stroked her delicate neck with the blade, taunting Bondurant.

Bondurant hesitated for a moment and then reluctantly extended his arm with the briefcase. He wasn't eager to hand it over in exchange for Domenika. He knew the most valuable evidence he'd ever gathered was inside the case, and if he lost it, his investigation would come to an end. But Domenika was in real danger, and he knew he had no choice.

"He's bluffing, Jon, don't do it," Domenika cried out. Barefoot, she dug her heels firmly into the pavement and pushed backward as hard as she could against her captor.

"I swear I'll kill her," the hooded figure warned again.

"Not if I can help it," Bondurant said. He heaved the briefcase hard, directly toward him. It sailed toward the attacker, who dropped his knife to grab it. He reached up to catch the case, but was pushed off balance by Domenika's thrust against his chest. As he stumbled slightly backward, he fumbled the catch and watched helplessly as the briefcase hurtled in an arc over his head. It sailed past the bridge railing on its way toward the rushing Po River below.

"You idiot!" the figure shouted out. His back to the railing, he craned his neck to look behind him, gauging the distance to the water below. Then, lowering himself into a crouch, he sprang into a perfect acrobatic backflip over the railing and plummeted in silence to the darkness below.

"Jon, what were you thinking?" Domenika cried out. "Your whole life was in that case!"

Bondurant cut her short. "Shh," he whispered. He listened intently. "One . . . two . . . three," he counted aloud.

On "three," they heard a faint splash, the sound of their attacker plunging into the cold rapids below. Bondurant calculated the distance to the water. Then he climbed up onto the bridge railing, kicked off his shoes, balanced himself, and looked down. "It's 144 feet," he said. "I've done 150 before. Call the police."

With that, he leapt off the bridge and into the darkness below. In the brief time he had before he hit the water, he thought about the three things he knew for sure. First, his briefcase would float. It was designed to. It held the most important pieces of evidence for his investigation, and no one—and no river—was going to take that away from him. Second, although his head was aching from the blow, he had not yet met the man who could outswim him in a current. And third, as a collegiate diver, he knew how to enter water from great heights. He had taken some bad spills before. Striking the river with anything less than perfect positioning would be like hitting cement. He bent his knees slightly to better absorb the impact and locked his arms at his sides to prevent his shoulders from being dislocated. But Bondurant knew his entry into the water was going to be violent no matter how smart he was about how to strike it. He'd begun to count the moment he leapt from the rail.

"One . . . two . . . three . . . *four?*" When he reached the count of four, all he could think was *Oh, no.*

He'd miscalculated. At four seconds, he had traveled *256* feet, not the 144 he'd figured before. He broke the surface of the water at the brutal speed of 128 miles per hour. The pain and the shock absorbed from his feet to his hips were almost enough to knock him unconscious. He plunged twenty-five feet down into the cold and murky depths until his feet touched the muddy bottom. He kicked off the bottom with all his strength and knew immediately that he'd probably bruised his Achilles tendons when he'd hit the surface. He was in agony, and the extent of his other injuries remained to be seen, but he shot up like a torpedo and broke the surface of the frigid water. He was quickly swept up in the swift current.

He had a lot of catching up to do. In the bright moonlight, he could make out the figure of a man flailing in the wide river, moving toward a shiny object thirty yards away. Bondurant's metallic brief-case floated downstream ahead of the attacker, who had predictably dislocated one or both of his shoulders when he'd collided with the water only seconds before.

Despite his injuries and the ice-cold water, Bondurant's train-ing took over, and he glided easily through the water. He began to gain ground on both of his targets quickly. He figured he had about twenty seconds before he reached his assailant. His adrenaline kicked in, and he freestyled his way forward in an all-out sprint. He breathed hard, closed in fast, and hit his attacker broadside like a shark. He scissor-kicked with his legs and lunged out of the water as high into the air as he could. As he did, he reared his arm back and punched the man's masked face with all his might. His was sure his blow had bro-ken facial bones the moment he struck. He punched again and again in quick succession, pummeling his attacker with his fist until all resistance was gone. Then he twisted the man into a headlock. With his catch in the crook of his arm, Bondurant began to tug him rescue-style toward the riverbank fifty yards away. But between the resistance from his captive's dead weight and the fast-moving current that carried them both downstream, Bondurant had little to show for his effort. Meanwhile, his briefcase only drifted farther from sight.

As he held the assailant in a viselike grip, Bondurant knew that at his pace and exhaustion level, the riverbank was going to be tough to reach. But he had no choice. He took a deep breath and yanked the man in the crook of his arm toward the nearest part of the shore. The assailant inhaled river water, choked, and struggled furiously for his life.

Suddenly and unexpectedly, Bondurant's work was done for him. A massive rock that jutted from the center of the river appeared out of the black directly in their path. Driven by the speed of the swift current, the attacker's head slammed hard against the face of the rock and was instantly crushed. Bondurant released him and let the limp and lifeless body of his faceless attacker tumble away in the stream.

Bondurant then surfaced again, swimming hard in an all-out pursuit of his briefcase. After another exhausting, minute-long dash, he finally caught up to it. He seized the sturdy handle of the case and began to sidestroke his way toward the riverbank, prize in hand. For the first time, he felt the frigidity of the rushing river surround his entire body. His arms and legs were numb, practically to the point of paralysis, as he dragged, then slipped, then dragged himself again onto the muddy hillside and up an embankment that led back to the bridge almost a mile away. His heels felt as though they were on fire, but he must have only bruised rather than torn the tendons in his feet. Still, merely walking would be a lesson in torture for a while.

Bondurant stopped to catch his breath. As he did, he began to see the flash of blue lights from several police cars as they reached the center of the bridge span. There he also saw a solitary figure framed in the light of the moon behind her. It was Domenika, who peered out into the uncertainty of the darkness ahead for them both.

CHAPTER 24

Turin, Italy
June 2014

Bondurant stared down at the filthy, checkered tile floor of the interrogation room at the Polizia Locale substation in Turin and shivered. A large air-conditioning vent in the ceiling blew cold air over the spot where he was handcuffed to a steel table bolted to the floor. He was unable to move away from what felt like an arctic blast from above, though he knew his bodily tremors were the precursor to hypothermia. His adventure in the Po River two hours before had soaked him to the bone. The puddle of river water that welled beneath his bare feet had grown larger as the useless interrogation dragged on.

"Listen, I am freezing to death here. If you would just get me a blanket or something, I'll even cop to the Sacco and Vanzetti murders if you'd like," Bondurant said. He jerked his handcuffs hard against the metal loop that fastened them to the table to accentuate his point.

After several more minutes of banter that went nowhere, Turin's chief commissioner of the local police, Senor Botta, entered the room. He gestured to his deputy inspector, who'd been questioning Bondurant, to remove the handcuffs. Bondurant could tell the inspector, Senor Vitali, was unhappy. Botta had burst into the interrogation cell from the room next door when it was obvious his deputy had failed. Vitali had gotten nowhere in his attempt to glean something useful from Bondurant in the case of the dead man the polizia had just fished from the river. Freed from his shackles, Bondurant quickly took the opportunity to slide to the opposite end of the table, away from the cold wind tunnel he'd been trapped under before. Another inspector, this one a woman, hurried into the room and brought with her a large woolen blanket that Bondurant wrapped about his shoulders. Vitali was keen on relaying to his superior the one bit of useful information he thought he'd been able to get Bondurant to spill.

"We finally have some names," Vitali said. "He's now just given two. I don't know them from Turin. A Senor Sacco and a Senor Vanzetti."

Bondurant bit his tongue so he didn't laugh out loud. He watched the commissioner do his best to contain his own laughter as well.

"Vitali, go now," the commissioner said. "Find everything you can for me on this Sacco, this Vanzetti. Then get in touch with Senor Bianchi at the morgue. Soon we will all need to pay him a visit."

Vitali was quickly out the door in pursuit of his assignment. It was now three a.m., and Bondurant was thankful someone with some smarts had taken charge.

"Commissioner Botta, I know my history," the young inspector who had brought Bondurant his blanket chimed in. "Sacco and Vanzetti were Italian anarchists who were executed almost one hundred years ago. They killed two guards during a robbery in America. But there was some doubt as to the real killers, I think—"

"A gold star for you, Daniela," the commissioner said. "The rest of the investigative team in the observation room and I have a bet. How long will it take my ambitious deputy to figure that out on his own? My bet is at least a day."

The young guard could only smile and shake her head.

"Senor Bondurant, my name is Commissioner Botta. We—"

"Before we get started," Bondurant interrupted, "where is Domenika? Is she all right?"

"Safe and sound, two doors down," Botta said. "You need not worry about her. She's been very helpful. We've spoken with the Vatican. We know who you are and why you are here. "What we don't know is your relationship to the dead man, the one lying in the morgue downstairs."

"It's just as I've told your deputy," Bondurant said. "I honestly don't know him. He tried to steal some important evidence we've gathered for our project here in Turin, and the next thing I know, I'm in the river fighting for my briefcase and my life."

"We know the contents of your briefcase, Senor Bondurant," Botta said. "What we can't understand is why this man would have an interest in stealing it. These bits of material you are carrying around are certainly from an important relic, but they have no value beyond your intended use, is that correct?"

"That's right," Bondurant said. "They are scraps of material. They're all meant to be destroyed as part of our experiments. Perhaps an antiquities dealer might have an interest, but they're all generally meek types. I've not heard of one hiring ninja warriors like this guy to steal, jump off bridges, risk their lives—those mundane sorts of things."

"Uh-huh. Tell me, then, Senor Bondurant," Botta said. "I heard you from the other side of that wall before, but I want to hear it again. How did this 'ninja warrior' meet his death? You said it was an accident."

"You could call it that, I guess," Bondurant said. "A fortunate accident. If that rock didn't come from out of nowhere to kill him, I've no doubt that I would have done it myself. Maybe I shouldn't put it that way, but it's a fact."

"Maybe you shouldn't, but I get your point," Botta said. "You were the last person to see this man alive. That's not good for you, especially in a city where we have very few homicides and even fewer suspects."

"Have you had your coroner examine the body?" Bondurant asked.

"Of course."

"Then you know the suspect you are looking for is dark, about fifteen feet tall, and weighs, oh, I don't know, about ten tons?"

"You're referring to the river rock you've said our ninja friend met with on his way down the Po," the commissioner said.

"That's the one."

"Yes; fortunately for you, our divers found plenty of skin tissue on the outcropping of that rock that matches the victim or suspect or whatever it is we want to call him."

"Good, then," Bondurant said. He stood up stiffly. His heels screamed. "Domenika and I can go now, right?"

"Yes," Botta said. "But we will want you to stay in town for a day or so in case we have the need for further questioning. However, there is a small matter—a formality, really. We are trying to learn the identity of your ninja friend. We are going to need to make a trip to the morgue for that."

Bondurant's face went pale. He knew the scene would be grue-some, as well as a useless exercise.

"You mean you are going to want me to examine the body to try to identify the man?" Bondurant asked.

"Yes, yes. I can't release you without that," Botta said. "It is proce-dure, and you must do your best. Both you and Ms. Jozef, I'm afraid. Each of you got a look at him."

Botta opened the interrogation room door and motioned for Bon-durant to follow. Domenika was waiting just steps down the dimly lit hallway, shadowed by the young inspector who had brought him a blanket. As soon as Domenika saw Bondurant, she raced over to him and wrapped her arms around him. Bondurant was just as glad to see her. They said nothing to each other. Eventually, Domenika pulled away.

Botta led the other three to the elevator at the end of the hall and pushed the down button. Just as the elevator doors were closing, Bon-durant heard fast-moving footsteps headed their way. Out of the dim light of the hall, Inspector Vitali, Botta's deputy, appeared, making his way into the elevator as fast as he could. He made it through the doors, out of breath, just before they closed.

"I think we have a lead on this man Sacco," Vitali said, anxious to reveal his news. "He is known to us and could be important to the case. We're not certain. But no Vanzetti has turned up."

Bondurant could tell Vitali was hot to impress his boss and just as eager to get Bondurant back into the interrogation room.

"Excellent," Botta said, barely able to disguise his embarrassment for his deputy. "This man Vanzetti—he could be the key to this case, I'm sure."

"What in heaven's name are you talking about?" Domenika asked. "These men lived a century ago. How could they possibly—"

"There have been some developments, many developments," Bondurant interjected before Botta could speak up. "Inspector Vitali is pursuing a very unique angle to the case. It's promising."

Bondurant watched the contortions in Vitali's face as they went from excitement to confusion to suspicion in a single moment.

Before Vitali could continue with his theory on the case, the elevator doors mercifully opened on the floor of the city morgue. The morgue was a large, white sterile room with several metal tables affixed to the floor. Alongside them was an entire wall of stainless-steel drawers. Bondurant presumed that behind one of them was the refrigerated remains of the suspect in question. The party was greeted by a balding, bespectacled man whom Bondurant thought looked the part. His glasses were so thick that Bondurant wondered how he had any vision at all.

"Welcome. I am Dr. Vincenzo Bianchi, the coroner here," the man said. "And you are here to view the subject, the one who has drowned in the river?"

"We are, Vincenzo," Botta said. "A simple identification check is all we're here for. If you could point us to the body, we'd appreciate it."

Dr. Bianchi sauntered over to the long row of drawers that contained the corpses presently in his charge. Bondurant could see the coroner needed to use his hand to count the number of drawers they passed, given how poor his sight was. When Bianchi reached the drawer marked "39" he stopped. Without a word, he turned and pulled hard on the drawer in a sweeping theatrical motion. It sped out quickly and sounded like a thunderclap when it came to a sudden halt. With as much fanfare as the coroner could muster, he yanked the clean white top sheet from the body before them. To a person, including Commissioner Botta, they let out a gasp.

What they saw in front of them was the body of an obese, naked woman who, by Bondurant's estimate, weighed nearly four hundred pounds. She was split directly in half, from head to midsection. Both Domenika and Inspector Vitali took several steps backward, and Vitali began to dry heave at the sight. Commissioner Botta simply shook his head, as though he was not surprised. Bondurant grimaced. He had seen autopsies before, but none that looked like this. It looked to him like a difficult autopsy left only partially complete.

The coroner, having now moved within a few inches of the cadaver, squinted behind his thick spectacles and noticed his mistake.

"Porko miseria!" he cried out in one loud blast as he shoved the drawer closed and sent the massive mound of flesh careening back into its refrigerated home. "My mistake. My mistake. It is here that we want," he said.

With a great deal less fanfare than his first attempt, he stepped one space backward to Drawer 40. This time he was careful to show the corpse more respect. He slowly slid the drawer open and simultaneously unveiled the body before them. A broad smile lit up his face.

Much to everyone's confusion, and Commissioner Botta's strong consternation, another wrong body lay before them again. Bondurant's fists began to tighten, and his real anger at their predicament met its limit. The time for hide-and-seek with cadavers was over.

"All right, that's it," Bondurant said. He grabbed the manifest the coroner had been working from to determine whether he could find the right drawer himself. He stared down at the paper to find the newest entry on the page, as he presumed no other bodies had arrived after the suspect they sought. It was then that he noticed the coroner's mistake. The cadaver they sought was laid in

Drawer 63, not Drawer 39. The coroner had read from his manifest upside down.

Bondurant led the group to Drawer 63 and nodded to the commissioner, who slowly slid it open. Even though he knew that they had located the right resting place for the suspect this time, Bondurant still believed the exercise was a complete waste of time. Neither he nor Domenika had gotten a worthwhile glimpse of the hooded figure, whether on the bridge or in the river. But if this was a formality that would release them from police custody, he was happy to oblige. Bondurant had only two days left to complete his work. According to the agreement he'd signed with the Vatican, his time would soon run out.

As the commissioner slowly pulled the sheet from the victim's face, even the hardened Bondurant had a difficult time setting his eyes on what he saw. Half of the man's skull was gone.

"I don't recognize him," Domenika said. She left Bondurant's side and rushed toward the exit door. Commissioner Botta, Inspector Vitali, and Dr. Bianchi all stared at Bondurant's face to see if it registered any sign of recognition of the man.

"There's plainly not enough here to recognize anyone," Bondurant said. "I'm sorry I can't help you. I wish I could." He turned away from the bloody mess and closed his eyes.

With that, the coroner began to pull the sheet over what remained of the corpse's head. But before he could finish the task, Bondurant turned and stayed his hand.

"What is it?" Botta asked. "You said yourself you can't possibly recognize this," he said.

Bondurant moved closer to the corpse. "Have you got some sterile gloves?"

The coroner pulled a pair from his lab coat and handed them over. Bondurant covered only his right hand. His interest was in the area of the cadaver's neck. A large fold of skin, once part of the victim's neck, was bent over and out of place. It rested almost on the cadaver's shoulder. Bondurant reached in, tugged on the fold of skin, turned it right side up, and, like a piece from a puzzle, placed it back where it belonged across the victim's neck. Dried blood covered the entire patch of skin Bondurant had set back in place.

"A cloth and some water?" Bondurant said to the coroner. Within a minute he had what he needed. With a wet cloth now in hand, he scrubbed and wiped the area of skin that was his concern. As he did so, the once-bloodstained skin was wiped clean, revealing a remarkable clue.

A strange tattoo, in the form of a symbol and about the size of a coin, stood out in jet-black ink.

Bondurant thought he had seen the symbol somewhere before, but couldn't place it. He made a mental image of it as best he could and turned to leave.

"You know this symbol?" Botta asked. "I've not seen it before."

"I don't know," Bondurant responded in earnest. "I have to do some research before I can be sure. Let's compare notes."

Before they left police headquarters, Bondurant called Parenti and described the unusual mark in the hope the priest would be able to provide a clue as to who was so bent on stealing the fragments of the Shroud. Bondurant was as clueless as ever as to who was so intent on halting his progress to seek the truth of the Shroud, but he was also as determined as ever to find out.

CHAPTER 25

Turin, Italy
June 2014

Y ou're late," Father Parenti admonished them. Aldo, who had been napping beneath a chair, skittered and slipped his way excitedly across the ornate marble floor of the library to greet them. Domenika bent down and scooped up the little fellow, stroking his head while his tail wagged in appreciation.

Parenti stood atop a wooden chair on one end of a long, leather-topped table in the main reading room of the Royal Library of Turin. He was dwarfed by several disorganized stacks of rare and ancient books he had collected in ten hours of frantic research. Several towers of texts toppled into one another. The glorious library, which resembled a cavernous wooden cathedral of vintage books and manuscripts that rose with stained glass windows stories high, was closed for the evening and deserted. The ancient and magnificent structure was shrouded in darkness save for the glow of four small reading lamps that cast strange shadows about the room. It had served as the work space where Parenti had labored late into the night. He had the permission of the library to remain after hours in trade for a loan of manuscripts missing from the House of Savoy—manuscripts the Vatican had hoarded for years.

"Late for good reason, Father," Bondurant said as he collapsed into a chair at the table.

Domenika sat down right beside him, Aldo still in her arms. She looked exhausted as well.

"This has been two days from hell," Bondurant said.

He had not exaggerated. The Polizia Locale had finally relented and set them free with the proviso that more questions would come. More important for Bondurant, after the intercession of the Vatican arranged by Domenika, they had been released from questioning *with* his briefcase and all its artifacts intact.

As if the grilling over his role in the death of the masked stranger weren't enough, Bondurant had spent time earlier the previous morning in a bitter, unexpected dispute between Dr. O'Neil and Ravi Sehgal over Sehgal's sudden new requirements to continue participation in the investigation. When their meeting had ended and the argument was over, Bondurant, as the project manager, had decided in O'Neil's favor. But his victory came with a price. He had angered and alienated Sehgal, whom he was counting on to add immense scientific credibility to the project's findings.

"All right, Doctor," the priest said as he held a rolled-up newspaper in his hand and waved it about like a conductor's baton. He stood in front of the piles of books arranged like orchestra players before him. "Let me make sure I have your description of the tattoo correct so that I'm not wasting our time. You were very brief on the phone."

"Yes, yes. Go ahead," Bondurant said, near the point of nodding off.

"Okay, then. You said the symbol you saw in the form of a tattoo appeared as a sort of pretzeled square with a right-facing swastika. Correct?"

"That's right," Bondurant said. He rubbed his bloodshot eyes and concentrated as best he could. "Another way to describe it would be a swastika inside an interlocking cube."

Parenti produced a pen from his pocket and held it forth.

"Draw it for me, Doctor. As best you can."

Domenika leaned in and looked over Bondurant's shoulder. Aldo scampered up into Bondurant's lap to watch. Bondurant sketched the symbol he had glimpsed for only a second or two.

"Okay," he said confidently. "Something like this."

All three stared intently at the drawing he had produced from memory. The symbol was both elegant and devious. It appeared to form an infinitely connecting path of geometric shapes, containing within its core the disturbing image of a swastika.

"Yes! That's it! That's it!" Parenti cried out. "Now I know what you're thinking, Doctor."

"What am I thinking, Father?" Bondurant asked, eyes closed.

"You're thinking the obvious. You're thinking it's some modern-day variant of the infamous swastika. The kind employed by the, what do you call them? The—"

"Skinheads," Domenika offered as she suppressed a yawn.

"Yes, the skinheads. Well, then, Doctor, you would be wrong."

"Who said 'skinheads'?" Bondurant protested as he looked over at Domenika. "I didn't say 'skinheads.'"

"Or perhaps you are thinking this image has its roots in the early 1930s," Parenti said as he pointed with his newspaper baton to a stack of tall books on the Third Reich. "An early forefather symbol, as it were, of the Nazi Party, or perhaps the, the—"

"Gestapo!" Domenika said.

"Yes, the Gestapo!" Parenti said as he slammed his baton on the table for emphasis. "But again, Doctor, you would be dead wrong."

"*I* would be dead wrong, Father?" Bondurant complained.

Parenti continued. "Or perhaps you have taken a measure of the other books around you on this table, Doctor. Perhaps you will have taken notice of the fact that the majority of books I have pored over suggest the culture of origin is actually—"

"Egyptian!" Domenika said as she stared at the stack of Egyptology volumes in front of her.

"Again, you would be completely foolish to suggest that, Doctor," Parenti said with a laugh. "Quite near the brink of stupidity."

"Okay, okay," Bondurant said. "How many more guesses do I get before she makes me out to be a complete idiot, Father?"

Parenti was clearly enjoying lording his information over them.

"One last question, Doctor. What do I hold in my hand?"

"Oh, he's good at this game, Father," Domenika said dryly.

Bondurant hesitated, presuming a trick. Domenika lit up with the answer.

"It's a—"

Bondurant reached over quickly and cupped his hand over Domenika's mouth.

"It's just a newspaper, Father," he said.

"Close enough, Doctor," Parenti said as he unrolled the paper on the table before them. "It's last Tuesday's *New York Times*. Here I've been all day on a wild-goose chase reviewing symbols of every ancient cult imaginable stemming back two thousand years. And where do I find it? Where do I find it? Last Tuesday's *New York Times*."

Parenti carefully opened the front section and turned to the third page.

Bondurant couldn't believe his eyes.

"*Incredible!*" Bondurant said as he stared at a drawing identical to the symbol he had just sketched.

"What is it, Jon?" Domenika asked.

"I should have figured this out. I should have put two and two together."

"So you know of these people, Doctor?" Parenti asked.

"Yes. They are well-known in the field of religious studies, but their symbol is not. And believe me, these people are completely nuts."

The headline from the *Times* appeared at the top of the fold on page A-3 in broad, bold type:

DEMANIANS MOVE ILLEGAL
CLONING EXPERIMENTS OFFSHORE

Bondurant scanned the story quickly and placed his finger on the last paragraph of the piece. He read it several times before he looked up. He had a troubled look on his face.

"What is it, Jon? Come on. What is it?" Domenika pleaded.

"It's a big problem," he said as he stared down at the article once more.

"Domenika," Father Parenti intoned. "Don't you see, these people are—"

"Crazy," Bondurant said emphatically, with a tinge of fear in his voice. "I mean just C-R-A-Z-Y."

Domenika looked frustrated. "I'm sorry. I'm just not getting this," she said.

Bondurant sat back in his seat and shook his head.

"The good news is that Dr. Laurent might have left the Demanians," he said. "The bad news is that no one can find him."

"Explanation, please, Jon," Domenika begged.

"Long story," he said. "Demanism is a 'UFO religion' of sorts, or better put, a cult. They believe that life on earth is the result of aliens from another planet. They're atheists, but not my kind. They don't believe in a God, but they do believe in aliens. The sect was founded in the '60s by a Frenchman who adopted the name of 'Déman.' There are tens of thousands of Demanians scattered around the world."

"So what does that have to do with us?" she asked.

"You have to know something about their origin," Bondurant said as he set Aldo on the table and got up from his chair to pace. "Demanians believe not only that a species of extraterrestrials—the 'Sevarin'—created life on earth, but that the religions in existence today are really the result of prophets sent by the Sevarin to instruct mankind on their behalf. According to them, Moses, Buddha, and, Domenika, even your Jesus Christ were such prophets sent to inform and guide us all to a peaceful future."

"Oh, *please*," Domenika protested.

"Yes, I agree. They're crazy. But—and my apologies to you both—no more loony than just about every other organized religion I've studied."

"Here we go again," Domenika deadpanned. "Prepare yourself, Father."

"No, no. I'll stick to the Demanians," Bondurant said as he paced nervously in a circle around the table, the dog now following in his wake. "This particular religion has all the usual trappings involved in the absurd origin of just about every faith. Its founder claims to have been beamed into a spacecraft, where he joined a Last Supper of sorts with everyone from Jesus to Buddha to Muhammad. Like many sects, while they're just plain absurd—these are the 'crop circle' guys—but they're considered harmless and have been ignored for decades."

"Then why the worried look, Jon?" Domenika asked as she pushed the stack of books on the Third Reich away from her.

"Because, like the headline says, they are also *the cloning people*, Domenika," he said as he picked up the news article before him. "Here's the deal. At the root of their religion is a belief in eternal life."

"That's no different than Christianity, Jon," Domenika objected.

"Yes, but these people don't buy the kind of resurrection that you do. They believe that mankind is destined to live forever through human cloning. Throw in some nanotechnology—the rapid, guided self-assembly of cellular 'machines'—and the transfer of one's personality into a clone, and mankind can be made to live forever. Scientific resurrection. For infinity. Remember their symbol? It's an infinite loop as well."

"I'm not fully getting it. How's that possible?" she asked.

"The idea is you extract a small sample of someone's DNA when they have developed the wisdom, personality, and memories that you would like to see last forever. You preserve the sample. On the day of the person's death, you remove cells to be used for future cloning."

"But human cloning is impossible," Parenti objected.

"Some would beg to differ, Father," Bondurant said. "Mankind has perfected the cloning of several animals, some with genetic makeups similar to humans. The list is long, and growing by the day. From frogs to cats to dogs to pigs and horses and sheep. Monkeys, wolves, cattle, and deer have all been added to the list in the last few years."

"All animals," Parenti said.

"Humans could be next," Bondurant said. "Even *ancient* ones. Scientists have replicated genome sequences of humans from as far back as the dawn of man. There's little difference in what we can understand genetically about a caveman and someone walking the earth today."

"It's illegal. Human cloning has to be illegal," Parenti said with certainty.

"Not exactly, Father," he responded. "Experimentation on human cloning might be discouraged in many countries, but the UN has never been able to pass more than a nonbinding resolution to ban it."

"The Vatican has opposed it, I am sure," Domenika said as she looked toward Father Parenti for reassurance.

"They have," Bondurant continued. "But their neighbors in the Middle and Far East are a real issue. There are no anti-cloning laws there, which has made the region a magnet for secret human cloning research. And these Demanians have been a real problem lately. They have the goal of mass cloning of humans in mind. Their leader is Hans Meyer, the German industrialist who claimed to have created the first human clone, a daughter named 'Eve,' a few years ago. While most believe it was a hoax, there are many who also now believe we are close to the point where a breakthrough on human cloning is near."

"This is all interesting, Jon, but what does it have to do with why we were attacked last night?" Domenika asked.

"It was likely for the same reason we barely escaped with our lives intact the other day," Parenti said. "Our cab ride back to the hotel became a high-speed pursuit. It had to be the Demanians tailing us."

"High-speed pursuit?" Bondurant asked. "Domenika, you never said anything about a high-speed pursuit."

"Perhaps Father Parenti's side of the cab saw more action than mine," Domenika said as the priest did his best to hide his sheepish look. "But now I know why we were tailed. And no doubt it must have been these Demanians."

"Anyway," Bondurant said, "Meyer and these Demanians, as crazy as they might be, are not without important supporters. Some of them are reputable scientists who have helped to finance and form a genetic engineering company, GenenClone. It's here in this story. It's run by Dr. François Laurent, and it's the same company this story says was just banned from the United States. Meyer has had some wild ideas that would make your hair stand on end."

"Such as?" Parenti asked.

"Such as the cloning of Adolf Hitler in order to bring him back from the dead so he can face war trials at Nuremberg. Sound like a good idea? Or how about his solution to suicide bombers in the Middle East: He thinks we can prevent these attacks by the mere *threat* of cloning. The idea is that these bombers, knowing they can be cloned and returned to life on this planet after their suicidal crimes to face their punishment, will see such attacks as futile."

"That's ridiculous. He's mad!" Parenti exclaimed.

"Quite right, Father," he said. "And his chief scientist mentioned here, Laurent, is a piece of work. His interest in human cloning has a tragic origin. He's an obstetrician and a synthetic biologist. One of the best. He lost an infant son to an accident in childbirth and vowed to bring him back, no matter what the cost. And now this, I'm afraid."

"This?" Domenika asked.

Bondurant stopped his pacing, grabbed his armored briefcase, and set it on the table. Aldo leapt back onto the table to inspect it. Bondurant entered the combination on both latches and opened it up before them. Inside sat four miniature glass vials, all neatly and separately cushioned, each containing a single tiny fragment of the Holy Shroud.

"Domenika," Bondurant said with real urgency, "we need to reach out to Ravi Sehgal the moment he touches down in India with that blood sample he's carrying, and we need to warn him to protect it at all costs."

"Ravi? Why Ravi?" she asked.

"Do you believe in Jesus Christ, Domenika?" Bondurant asked with grave seriousness.

"Yes, of course I do," she said. He could tell she was amazed he had asked the question.

"Do you believe he shed his blood for all mankind?"

"Yes, with all my heart," she replied.

Bondurant lowered his voice to a whisper, reached out his hands, and held her by her shoulders. He looked directly into her eyes.

"Domenika, I think these men, Meyer and this Laurent who has gone missing, are out to get what they believe is the blood of Jesus Christ. As much of it as they can."

"With the purpose—" Domenika clasped her hands over her

mouth and stopped short of saying the unthinkable. He could see that her legs grew weak, forcing her to take a chair.

"Of cloning—" Parenti could not bring himself to say it either. Aldo dove into his lap as if for comfort.

"All right," Bondurant said. "I'll say it. A 'second coming.' The scientific resurrection of Jesus Christ himself."

CHAPTER 26

Turin, Italy
June 2014

Hey, Sis. Hope I didn't wake you."

It was two o'clock in the morning in Turin, and Domenika's sister was calling from New York, where it was only eight p.m. As usual, Joanna hadn't a clue what time it was anywhere in the world except for wherever she was.

"No, no. Joanna, that's all right," Domenika said with as much liveliness as she could muster, given she'd been woken from a troubled sleep. She had the hotel room's thick drapes drawn tight, and the only light was from her cell phone, a green luminescence in the dark.

"Nika"—only her sister ever called her that—"I am going out tonight with that football player from the Giants. You know, the cute one. The one who sent the picture of his rear from my phone—the one I met at Table 50?"

"Yes, yes," Domenika said, now certain the call could have waited until daylight. The absurd photo Domenika had received the previous week had been followed a minute later by a text message asking

Domenika to drop what she was doing and fly to New York for the weekend to meet one of his teammates.

"He has a friend, Nika," Joanna said. She sounded giddy. "He wants to meet you. I told him we were twins. You know, we almost are."

"Tell him that Nika already has her hands full with an American over here."

"Yes, yes, yes! Tell me. How is your American boyfriend treating you? The curious one."

"*Boyfriend?* Who said he was my boyfriend?" Domenika protested. "It's purely professional."

"Nika, stop. It's me. You went on and on about your date with him the last time we talked."

Domenika sighed. "I didn't say 'date,' or 'curious' either."

"It sounded like a date."

"Joanna, it was *not* a date. It was lunch. It's all over."

"Over you? Already? He *is* curious."

"No, what I mean is that—" Domenika stopped herself short. A week earlier she couldn't have imagined defending Bondurant to anyone. But so much had happened since then, and she'd learned a lot that somewhat explained the man she had once despised. "What I mean is that he's complicated, Jo. He's a wonderful enigma, all mixed up inside. He's like a loner who's afraid of being alone, you know?"

"Sounds like a head case to me."

"Maybe so. But he's smart, and charming, and kind. The sad thing is there's just not a thing involving faith that we agree with."

"Who used to tell me that opposites attract, Nika?"

"No, I mean it. I don't think we agree on anything. At least the important things."

"Ah, I wouldn't worry too much about that. He sounds like Papa."

Good observation, Domenika thought. Especially from more than four thousand miles away.

"Papa would love this man, Sis," Domenika said. "Right up to the part where he claims there is no God. No Jesus Christ."

"*Oh*, that's not good, Nika. Handsome?"

"Would you believe gorgeous? And—" She stopped herself again, surprised she had just described him that way.

"Then what are you waiting for? Have some fun."

"Oh, we are having fun, all right. Two nights ago he was willing to throw his career off a bridge to save my life. And a few nights before that he saved someone else." She knew her sister would never fully appreciate any of this, and it was too long of a story to tell.

"Wonderful—sounds like a lifeguard," Joanna said. "What is his name again? Have you ever Googled him?"

"Why would I want to do that?" She had, but it was a long time ago, before they had debated at Cambridge, which now seemed like a thousand years ago.

"Seriously now, what's his name?"

"Bondurant. Jon Bondurant. Dr. Jon Bondurant."

"Okay, hold on." Joanna put her on speakerphone.

"No, Joanna, really. Don't."

Almost a minute passed. She closed her eyes, pulled her blanket all the way to her chin, and wondered again why she had bothered to answer the phone.

"Wow! Do you know how many hits you get for your doctor boyfriend, Nika?"

"I can't say that I do," she said. She tried to sound as disinterested as possible.

"1,386,200."

"Mmmmm. Not surprising," Domenika said. "He's a well-known author. You'll probably find that most of the articles—"

"Religion. Religious studies. Comparative Religion. It just goes on and on. I thought you said he wasn't religious. That's *all* he cares about."

"No, I said he doesn't believe in Jesus Christ."

"Well, he certainly believes in his teachings. He's a saint, like you," Joanna said.

"What do you mean?" Domenika asked. She rose up and sat on the edge of her bed, still drowsy.

"I mean it says right here 'Bondurant's Donations Top Community's Charitable List.' It's from a paper called the *Star Democrat*. It says he's donated over a million dollars from the sales of his books to local charities. Looks like he has a soft spot for abused children. And there's a center he's adopted for them as well."

A slight pain shot through Domenika's stomach, the same one she'd been feeling since she had learned the news of Bondurant's past from Parenti days before. She wanted to talk with someone, anyone, to soothe her soul over it, but it was not something she could share with anyone.

"Well, what I said," Domenika said softly, "was that he didn't believe in Jesus. I didn't say he didn't believe in his teachings." *Did that come out right?* she wondered.

"Suit yourself," her sister said, ready to drop the subject. "I think you like a guy who walks the walk."

"I know, I know. Hey, listen—"

"No, you listen, Nika," her sister said. "Do me a favor, will you? It won't be easy but it will be worth it, I promise."

"What is it? What favor?"

"You're headed back to Rome in a few days, right? That's what Mamma says."

"Yes, our work here is complete," Domenika replied.

"Perfect," Joanna said. "Don't take his calls when you get home. See how bad he really wants you. Make him come to you."

"Don't take his calls? You've got this all wrong, Joanna. I don't expect a single one."

"That's not what my sixth sense tell me, Nika. Remember, don't take his calls. You need to test this guy out. Make him come to you. Trust me, he'll want you even more."

Buzzzzz.

"Gotta run, Nika. He's downstairs. Hang on to that doctor but play hard to get. Seems like you got a good one. Love you."

Before Domenika could protest, her sister hung up.

Now fully awake, Domenika knew she would be up for hours. She got up from her bed and, using her cell phone as a flashlight, went over to the desk where her laptop sat and turned it on.

CHAPTER 27

Turin, Italy
June 2014

Domenika sat across from Bondurant in a quaint outdoor restaurant not far from the Cathedral of St. John. Their table was next to one of many tall plumes of white jasmine in full bloom that left a scent of perfume throughout the leafy green terra-cotta terrace. The lights of the city had just begun to twinkle as the day slowly receded into night. The Alps in the distance, draped in purple and orange, seemed painted against the skyline to frame the perfect scene. The setting was breathtaking. Domenika felt she could stay there all night.

"You know you really didn't have to do this, Jon," Domenika said. Their meal was finished, and the server had just removed the last of their plates. "It's your last night in Turin, and I'm sure you have better things to do before your flight."

Domenika was actually thrilled Bondurant had summoned the courage to ask her to dinner before they went their separate ways in the morning. But she also knew him to be a klutz when it came to real relationships. She had no idea whether she would hear from him again beyond the business at hand concerning the Shroud.

"Here," Bondurant said as he poured Domenika another glass of merlot from the decanter. A third bottle sat in a holder beside them. "Let's have another toast. This one to your success," he said.

"Success? In what way? That we have proven we possess the burial cloth of Christ?"

"Sure, if that's what you want," Bondurant offered.

Domenika stopped for a moment to think about it. She also noticed that the excellent wine they'd enjoyed had set her head slightly abuzz, a feeling she'd not had in ages.

"It seems to me that would turn your whole life upside down, Jon," she said. "Surely that's not what you really mean."

"Domenika, no matter where the evidence leads us on the Shroud, I assure you my life's already been turned upside down by you," Bondurant said.

Domenika only blushed. She had never expected him to be so forward.

"In vino, veritas," Bondurant said. "I know I need not translate it for you."

"In wine, the truth," Domenika said. They toasted each other once again, and Bondurant began to fill the decanter with their third bottle of wine.

"In the end, it's only the truth that matters, right?" Bondurant said.

"I can hardly believe my ears," Domenika said. "Everything is on the line for you here. Your reputation. Your credibility. Yet you act like you take it so lightly."

"Not so, really," Bondurant said. "I care very much about what we'll learn here. I still think I might be right about what I've said about the Shroud all along. But it's not like your faith, Domenika. It's not the end of all things if I'm wrong."

"I see," Domenika said. "My life is built on faith. If I doubt my faith or lose my faith, I have nothing left to stand on or to live for. Is that it?"

"It's a little different for me," Bondurant said. "I stand on the truth and go where it leads me. But if I deny the truth or ignore the truth, then I too am lost."

Domenika took a large sip of wine. She reached for her purse and pulled out an envelope. She handed it across the table to Bondurant.

"What's this?" Bondurant asked.

"Just something I thought you might like to take home with you," Domenika said. She looked on as he opened the envelope.

Bondurant's eyes grew wide as he took out a photograph. It was a picture Bondurant had never seen before, one that must have been taken by a Vatican photographer during a break in the past two weeks. It was a photo of both Bondurant and Domenika, caught in a casual moment together between work sessions. Both of them were smiling. Domenika could tell Bondurant was pleased.

"I don't know what to say, Domenika," he said.

"Then don't say it," she said. "You've already got one of me on my own. I thought maybe you'd like one of us together."

"That's how I'd like to remember us, Domenika," he said.

"Remember us?" Domenika asked. "So that's how you want to leave it? We'll remember each other?"

"No, no, no. What I meant was that—"

Domenika cut him off by placing a hand over his mouth. Then she slid her chair next to his and put her hands in his.

And then, against all good professional judgment, she kissed him.

CHAPTER 28

Turin, Italy
June 2014

ome. Come into the church," Domenika said. She playfully waved her hand back and forth before Bondurant's eyes as if she were attempting to hypnotize him.

She took him by the hand and urged him up the worn marble steps of the Duomo di Torino, the Cathedral of St. John the Baptist, where the Shroud had been safely returned now that Bondurant's team had completed their work. It would be weeks before all the results were analyzed, but their work in Turin was done. It was one o'clock in the morning, and Bondurant, certain that the well-lit cathedral had been closed for several hours, laughed at the futility of her quest. The piazza in front of the famed cathedral was completely deserted except for the shadows of the trees, slightly swaying in the glow of the streetlamps that surrounded the square.

"You're determined to drag me into the light one way or another, angel," he replied, reluctantly letting go of her hand as he took a seat on the timeworn steps facing the deserted piazza. Only a couple of pigeons zealously pecking away at a scrap of bread a few steps below joined them so late at night. The city of Turin was sound asleep.

Domenika tried the brass handles on the cathedral's enormous rear wooden doors, only to find them locked tight. She rapped on them in earnest, sending a loud echo across the piazza.

"Shh. Quiet. We've already spent one night with the police," he pleaded.

She was clearly drunk, and he was not far from it. With the work of the investigation complete, he was free to break her prohibition, and his first taste of scotch in two weeks had brought about its intended effect. Bondurant was feeling high. The nearly three bottles of wine they'd shared over dinner had loosened up Domenika as well. She gave up on the church doors and sat down beside him. Then she fully reclined against the smooth steps, which were still slightly warm from the day's hot summer sun.

Bondurant followed her gaze up at the stars framed in part by the cathedral's imposing spire. His head spun slightly, and he looked instead at Domenika's long, shapely athletic legs stretched out beside him.

"You called me an angel. That's silly. You don't believe in angels, Jon," she said as she looked up at the heavens. She let out a loud hiccup and began to giggle softly. "So much for your angel," she murmured.

"I meant 'angel' in another sense, Domenika. As in the fifth level."

"What do you mean by that?" she asked, turning toward him curiously. She slurred one of her words a little, which he thought was cute. "Is this another story from one of your silly books?"

He wondered whether it was wise to explain what he meant when both of them were a long way from thinking clearly and she'd probably remember little. But the slight hint of orange blossoms from her perfume and the smell of wine on her breath as she exhaled lightly was an intoxicating mix for him. He turned toward her and, quietly, so she wouldn't take notice, inhaled.

"Maybe I'd better not get into it right now," he said as he turned away to stargaze again as well. "Maybe another time, when we—"

Hiccup. She laughed quietly at herself again and held her hands to her mouth. He noticed for the first time just how small and delicate they were.

"No, please. Please, Jon. Tell me all about your angels," she said as she kicked off her heels. One of them tumbled down a few steps and sent the pigeons into flight.

"The last woman I made the mistake of explaining this to slapped me so hard I felt it for hours," he said. "She didn't appreciate where I placed her on the scale."

"I haven't slapped a man in hours, maybe days," she pouted. "Now you've got me curious."

"Just remember, you're the one who insisted," he warned as he reclined next to her, close enough to feel the warmth of her bare shoulder. She didn't move an inch. The stars above him seemed to drift.

Hiccup. "Class is in session, Professor."

"All women, aesthetically speaking, can be placed in one category or another on a scale of beauty, from one to five," he said.

"*All* women?" she asked dreamily.

"Well, not all women. By my calculation, there are a lot who don't make it to the first rung. It's at this point in the story where you are free to slap. This is your chance."

"I'm listening," she said. She yawned and rubbed her tanned bare feet together.

"All right, bear with me. The first level, the first rung on the ladder of beauty, is 'cute.' You know cute. Everybody does," he said.

"I do?"

"Sure. A cute girl was probably a tomboy when she was young. She almost always has short hair. Eyes are her striking feature. Not much makeup. Always petite. She is the girl you can't wait to bring home to meet your family. She looks good in a baseball cap. She's smart, funny. Likes sports. She's one of the guys. Your best friend or your brothers all have a crush on her but won't say it. She's adorable, and your mother wants you to marry her before she gets away."

"I like 'cute.' Go on." *Hiccup.*

"All girls do. Cute's not threatening to other women. Old-school, think Audrey Hepburn."

"I just love her."

"Now, the next level up the scale is 'pretty.' Pretty usually has long, lustrous hair. Pretty knows how to dress. She knows clothes. She's mastered the art of makeup. She's well put together. You like when she stands next to you because she somehow makes *you* look better. She's smooth. She looks good in every light, without trying. She's photogenic. Never takes a bad picture. When you see her, you *have* to do a double take. You're still thinking about her five minutes after she walks by. Modern-day, she's an Angelina Jolie type."

"You're sure there are *three* more levels?" Domenika asked.

"Just wait. The third level of beauty *is* 'beautiful.' This one's a big step up. Several rungs up the ladder. She looks stunning 24/7. She could wear a burlap bag and still be a knockout anywhere she goes. She could wake up in your bed completely hungover, having slept in her own vomit, and *still* look like a million bucks. When this woman walks into a room, you don't just look. You stare. Everybody does.

You're forced to. And women are looking at her as much as men. Magazine looks. A Sophia Loren. A 'cover girl.'"

"I know one of those," Domenika said wistfully. "What could be more beautiful than that?" *Hiccup.*

"Then there's the fourth level. It's 'gorgeous.' There's a dividing line between 'beautiful' and 'gorgeous' that's almost imperceptible, but it's there. And it's all about sex. Gorgeous is beautiful with major-league sex appeal. It's beauty that's inviting you to be bad. It's Marilyn Monroe. Gorgeous says 'I got it. Try to get it.' Beauty is something you want to look at. Gorgeous is something you want to do something with."

Domenika shifted onto her side, directly facing him. No more than three inches separated them. She closed her eyes.

"And the fifth level?" she whispered.

"Reserved for a handful of women. For good reason. Level five is 'angelic.' And just as the word implies, it's a woman that looks like she's not of this earth. Perfection. Untouchable. She walks into a room and it goes quiet. She takes the air out of it. Time stops. Beauty so stunning it's sad because it is so rarified, like it's in danger of extinction. It's a reminder. Everything in this life, including beauty, is temporal. That's why statues are sculpted to preserve it. It cannot be touched or had or loved. At least by no mortal. Someone like Princess Grace. Grace Kelly. That's 'angelic.'"

He turned toward Domenika. She looked to be sleeping. He took advantage of the moment and studied her face for almost a minute.

Hiccup.

"Then why have you called me an angel, Jon?" she asked as she opened her eyes. "I'm no angel."

"Yes, you are," he said, turning away. He could not look directly at her with what he was about to say. He summoned the courage to make himself vulnerable with a woman for the first time ever. "You leave me breathless every time I see you." *There, I said it, for better or worse,* he thought.

With that, Domenika leaned in, pulled him toward her, and kissed him longingly, more softly and warmly than he thought possible. Their bodies touched for the first time, and her fingers moved delicately down his shirt to his waist. He always closed his eyes when he kissed, but he kept them open for a moment as if to see for himself it was really happening. She felt small in his arms.

"Jon, you said they cannot be touched, or had, or loved," she said in his ear, close enough that he could feel her lips as she whispered.

He kissed her again and caressed her cheek. Then he turned away once again before he answered, unable to look at her.

"I did say that, didn't I," he said. "All I can say is that I know you have turned me inside out, and I know that I just love the thought of you sometimes."

"Oh, my. I've always wanted someone to love the *thought* of me," she said, and then giggled.

"That's not what I meant. It's just that you're the closest I've ever come to filling the hole."

"Now you're just being fresh."

He grimaced at how he had phrased it. "That's not what I meant. I meant the hole inside me. It's a little less dark when you are around. I don't know how you do it, but you've bewitched me somehow," he said.

She shifted her hips and crossed her leg over his, pulling him hard against her. Inebriated or not, Bondurant couldn't help but remember where they were. Yet Domenika was tipsy enough that she seemed to be encouraging his advances. Bondurant was no expert on where sex between consenting adults on cathedral grounds fit in the grand hierarchy of sins in the Catholic faith. But he figured it must be high up the ladder of mortal sins, ones that required serious contrition and confession to a priest.

Bondurant didn't want to be responsible for sending Domenika into a confessional to seek forgiveness for something he knew she would *never* ordinarily do. He pulled away from her embrace and stood up. He offered his hand, and while she tried to pull him down again toward her at first, she gently relented, stood, and wrapped her arm around his waist as they descended the cathedral steps.

They walked toward their hotel, a few minutes away. Each of them was as quiet as the night. They said nothing as they walked. Bondurant didn't have a clue what Domenika was thinking as they strode along, but as he led her back to their hotel his own mind raced with a dilemma. He wanted nothing more than to spend the night with her if she genuinely wanted to be with him. But the question of how much of her sudden affection toward him came from the heart as opposed to the wine loomed large for him, and he couldn't quite believe it did. He had been in countless similar situations with women in the past and hadn't hesitated even once to take advantage. Yet now, when he finally found himself head over heels for a woman for the first time in his life, he had no idea what his next move would be.

They half stumbled together out of the elevator on her floor at the hotel. He watched as she fumbled for the room key in her purse. Domenika had clearly forgotten how to swipe the card so the door would open. Bondurant reached over and took the key card from her.

After a few attempts by him, the door light blinked and the suite opened up before them. Before he could stop at the entrance, Domenika took him by the hand and led him through the low-lit room straight to her bed. Bondurant relaxed, laid his head on a pillow, and stared up at Domenika, who looked down on him from only inches away. She smiled at him and softly caressed his cheek. He turned onto his side and motioned for her to lie down beside him. When he reached out for her arms, she gently pushed his away. Domenika sat on the side of the bed as if to think for a moment, and then stood up to make her way to the bathroom. Bondurant closed his eyes and imagined what might come next.

When Domenika came out of the bathroom, she walked over to the bed and turned off the light on the nightstand. Bondurant could see by the faint glow of the clock beside them that she wore only a T-shirt. She slid under the covers and invited Bondurant to do the same. She leaned over and kissed him softly and then finally broke the silence that had lasted since they embraced at the church.

"I have three secrets. Would you like to hear them?" Domenika asked in a whisper.

"I don't care. Tell me a hundred," Bondurant said. He loved the sound of her voice, especially in the dark.

"Listen carefully. The first you may discard, okay? The second you must live with. You have to promise. And the third—well, the third is up to you to change, if you'd like," she said. She rubbed her nose lightly against his and then stole a kiss.

"What's the first?" he asked.

"My hiccups are gone. I think I lost them when we first kissed back at the cathedral." He laughed, and she took his hand softly in hers.

"Okay. That one I'm supposed to discard. What's the second?" he asked as he intertwined his fingers with hers.

"That I am falling for you, and at the same time I cannot stand you. Does that make sense, Jon?"

"Domenika—"

"No, please, Jon. You don't have to say anything. Don't," she implored as she held his hand to her cheek. "Like I said, it's something you must live with."

Bondurant turned away from her and felt guilty that he hadn't committed more deeply to her back at the cathedral, given what she'd said. He gathered the courage to look back at her, this time directly into her eyes. It was then that he felt a sudden rush of anxiety.

"Domenika, I don't think I want to know the third secret."

"It's too late. I've decided," Domenika said. She removed his hand from her cheek and slowly moved it up her exposed thigh so that his fingers gently grazed the space between her legs. Then she rested her head on his pillow and closed her eyes.

"The third is that I am a virgin, Jon," she whispered readily. "I swear it. And, as I said, this you can change tonight."

CHAPTER 29

Rome, Italy
June 2014

Tweet, tweet, tweet . . . Tweet, tweet, tweet . . . Tweet, tweet, tweet. Domenika didn't even have to look at her phone. She knew whose name would appear on her caller ID. After three days of ignoring Bondurant's calls from the United States, she thought he would get the message and leave her alone. But he didn't.

Tweet, tweet, tweet . . . Tweet, tweet, tweet . . . Tweet, tweet, tweet. Bondurant had called at least five times a day, but Domenika just could not bring herself to take his call. At least not yet.

There was the silly promise she had made to her sister to test him out. Was Bondurant smitten enough to journey all the way to Rome to sweep her off her feet? Not likely, she thought. He'd wasted days trying to call her when he could have been on and off a plane by now.

More important, it was what had happened in their last hours together. The way he'd simply left. He hadn't even waited around to say good-bye, to say thanks. No parting words. Just up and left while she slept after what they'd done. She knew Bondurant was a pro at this game of one-night stands, if that's what it was, but she clearly was not. She wasn't ready to face him after the way he'd treated her, the way he'd used her.

Tweet, tweet, tweet . . . Tweet, tweet, tweet . . . Tweet, tweet, tweet.

The past few days, she'd simply turned off her phone to stop the incessant tweeting.

Tweet, tweet, tweet . . . Tweet, tweet, tweet . . . Tweet, tweet, tweet.

She reached over and turned it off now. She had nothing to say to the man.

CHAPTER 30

St. Michaels, Maryland
July 2014

Bondurant sat alone in the teleconference center at the Enlighten-ment Institute a few minutes before nine on a Saturday morning. The marine layer typical of midsummer wrapped around the Chesa-peake Bay shoreline and swallowed the Institute's Victorian home at the end of Perry Cabin Drive in a light fog.

Looks like D-Day, Bondurant thought. He'd not yet had breakfast but had made enough coffee to last the morning. Its welcome scent had permeated just about every room on the first floor, including the one he was in. He turned from the massive window that faced the bay and stared at a bank of flat-panel monitors that formed a video wall in front of him. The screens sat arrayed from floor to ceiling. They would light up one at a time as the videoconference partici-pants logged in. He had made arrangements so that his team could conference in from around the world, a few as far away as India and Japan.

He had taken an early swim off the dock by his trailer, trying to relax, but he was still as edgy as he had been for days. Spread before him was a stack of confidential reports, all written by the handful of scientists who had worked alongside him in Turin just two weeks before.

He yawned and rubbed his eyes. For over a week now, he had found it tough to sleep, and the reasons increased by the hour. There was the Vatican, of course. It had leaned on him hard to publish. Few scientific studies in his lifetime would likely draw as much interest as the outcome of his investigation. Given the stakes, Bondurant found the Vatican was relatively calm, but they were putting him under pressure to come to his conclusion soon. There was also the national and international media that had stalked him for weeks, hoping to find leaks that would indicate whether the Shroud was real or not. TV satellite trucks had hunkered down at the Institute and near his trailer overlooking the river. They bristled with activity at the slightest sign that an announcement might be forthcoming. There were the editors from an assortment of publishing houses in New York vying for book contracts for him. And, if that wasn't enough, there was the stunning piece of confidential and contradictory evidence turned up by Sehgal that turned the totality of findings gathered by the rest of the team upside down. The purpose of the Saturday morning call was to get to the bottom of it.

And there was Domenika, of course. She had seen none of the preliminary reports Bondurant's team of experts had shared with one another, but he had placed her on the videoconference call list, and she had registered to be on the call. She may have ignored his personal calls since Turin, but, feelings aside, it was critical to officially reveal where their conclusions were headed, particularly given the strange news Sehgal had brought forward. He figured that she believed the outcome was certain to go in the Vatican's favor and wasn't waiting for the report to be printed before moving ahead to develop a plan for releasing the good news of his team's findings. That was a problem. He was concerned about her getting out ahead of the actual evidence, not all of which she had seen.

But his thoughts of Domenika that morning were only partly about ancient relics and media releases for the Church. Instead, they had everything to do with his feelings since he had so quietly slid from her hotel room in Turin just weeks before. In his mind, the irony was thick. He now longed to see the woman he had insulted when they'd first met. What he wouldn't give to see her again in person so he could tell her the truth about how he felt.

The truth was that he had fallen in love with her. He had kicked himself every day since their last evening together for not telling her outright.

I don't know. I just love the thought of you, he thought he remembered saying.

Are you kidding me? he asked as he mocked himself over and over. *Is that what you said?* He cringed every time he remembered what he'd said to her and what he'd left unsaid. No other woman had ever made him feel this way.

Bong.

The chime that signaled the first participant had joined the videoconference sounded. The automated voice introduced the first caller. "Now joining the conference: Domenika Jozef."

And there she was, on screen 3, beamed in from Rome with a positively radiant look on her face. It was the first time Bondurant had talked to her or seen her since they had left Turin.

"God, I miss you," Bondurant let out involuntarily. He couldn't help himself.

"Oh, Jon," she said and smiled. It was midafternoon in her apartment in Rome, and he could see the jagged skyline of the city in the window behind her.

She looked a little apprehensive, which Bondurant figured was tied to her having ignored his calls. "What's up with that ashtray on your desk? It's empty."

Bondurant grinned broadly. "I haven't smoked since you asked me to quit that night in Turin." He looked at his watch. It had added ten years, blinking "21:08." She deserved the credit, he felt.

"And the scotch?" Domenika asked.

"Drew the line there," he said. He slowly reached over and slid the bottle of Macallan on his desk several inches out of camera range.

"Well, I did you *some* good, then," she said. He could tell she liked having such a powerful effect on him.

"Domenika, I know you must be busy because you've not been returning my calls, but I really need you to listen to me for just a minute," Bondurant said. He had been rehearsing for days what he wanted to say to her and was anxious to get it out.

Domenika looked away from the monitor for a few seconds as if to avoid what he might say next.

"There is something I've wanted to tell you since Turin," Bondurant said. "It's something I *need* you to know. I know I'm going to look ridiculous for saying it on a videoconference call, but—"

"Jon," Domenika interjected, "there's something I've wanted to talk with you about as well, but I don't think I was ready yet. At least until now. It's why I've been avoiding you. But maybe now's not the time either," she said.

"No, Domenika," Bondurant said. "Please. What is it?"

"It's about our last night together," Domenika said. "But I—I—I just don't want to go about a sensitive conversation like this the wrong way. It's very—well, it's very important to me."

Domenika looked uncomfortable as she spoke, and Bondurant could hear real anxiety in her voice. He decided to put his own unease about what he wanted to say aside for the moment to hear her out.

"What is it, Domenika?" Bondurant said. He could tell she was trying to gather the courage to say something obviously important. "You can talk to me about anything."

"All right," she said. "Well, here goes. It's about our last night together, at the hotel."

He knew immediately where she wanted to go with the conversation, as he'd had to deal with a lot of similar phone calls like this before. Only for this one, he didn't have any difficult explaining to do.

"Well, you weren't there when I woke up in the morning," Domenika said. "I kind of thought you would be. A lot of that night still seems pretty hazy to me. The morning after too. When I woke up, you were gone and already on your plane headed home, so we never got to talk in person. I mean, did we . . . well— Jon, is anyone else logged in on this call yet?" she asked.

"No, no. You're the first one on," Bondurant said, now in a minor panic. He knew he had little time before the rest of the team joined the call and his opportunity to express his feelings would be lost. He had plenty to get off his chest with her as well.

"Are you sure?" she asked.

Bong.

"Now joining the conference," said the automated voice.

"Dr. Terry O'Neil." O'Neil appeared on another monitor and took up almost the entire screen.

"Really? Right now, Terry?" Bondurant said.

"What was that, Jon?" O'Neil asked. "Aren't we scheduled for our call?"

"Nothing, nothing. Sorry, Terry," Bondurant said. "We're just getting some technical issues ironed out here. How are you?"

"Excellent. I'm sure you saw from the draft I sent last night that I have some very interesting news for you, right?" O'Neil's excitement as he spoke was unusual for him.

"Yes, I saw your report, Terry. It's unbelievable, really. But I don't want to get into the subject until the rest have the chance to log in."

Bondurant looked at the other monitor and could see Domenika had broken into a smile, pleased with what she had overheard so far.

In the next five minutes, Bondurant's video wall of monitors lit up with one face after another as his team joined the conference call across thirteen time zones. O'Neil, who had completed the radiocarbon dating tests of the Shroud, had joined from London. Ravi Sehgal appeared from Mumbai and scribbled notes while he waited for the call to commence. He was ready to relay his own findings on DNA and blood type. Jean Boudreau was on the line from Paris to discuss the origin of the relic's fabric. Michael Lessel called in from the University of New Mexico. His labs had completed the work on soil-particle analysis. Lisa Montrose from Duke University was ready with her data on material pigmentation. And, finally, there was Harry Sato, who beamed in from Japan, where it was ten p.m.

"First, let me begin by thanking all of you for joining me, especially those of you calling in at some odd hours," Bondurant began. "I'd like to start with a summarization of what I see as the key findings from each of your reports and, if I may, to focus on an area where some of the data is telling us a very contradictory and somewhat disconcerting story from the trend suggested by all the rest. I wish that science were not such a messy process, but no one's ever said that discovery is always neat and tidy. I'm afraid we have that in spades with this investigation as well."

Bondurant glanced at Domenika's screen for a moment and watched as his words produced a quizzical look. The others on the call who had reviewed Ravi Sehgal's striking conclusions nodded in agreement with Bondurant's assessment of where the investigation stood. Domenika, who was not privy to the various drafts from each of the scientists involved, was to receive a final report for the Church from Bondurant only when it was complete. She didn't know about the contradictions he referred to.

"As to the critical indicators on the age and geographic origin of the Shroud, there appears to be uniform agreement," Bondurant said. "And the news is . . . well—how do I put this?—just astounding. I have to say I would never have believed it before today, but data is data, and I am willing to eat my words as readily as the next guy when I have to. Jean, you are reporting that everything you can glean from the fabric sample you collected points to the first century AD, Middle Eastern origin. Is that correct?"

"There is no doubt about it, Jon," Boudreau said as he took off his glasses to rub his eyes. "The sample we took from the Shroud is of a thread pattern specific to the Palestine region, first century. I have at least a dozen other such material samples of this known origin in my lab, and there is no mistaking it. The linen of the Shroud matches the biblical time period and Eastern Mediterranean geographic region, as claimed. We detected no weaving or sewing that would suggest the handiwork of artisans outside the region or time period in question."

Bondurant looked over at screen 3 again and watched Domenika as she listened intently and took notes. She was clearly pleased with what she'd heard.

"Okay, so the fabric's authentic to the time period. I have to say again, I'm stunned. That, in and of itself, is real news. Dr. Lessel, you are reporting as well that the fifteen separate soil samples and other minerals you retrieved off the Shroud are typical of the region surrounding the Jerusalem area. Is that correct?"

"That's correct. First let me be clear about what we found very little of, which is probably more important," Lessel said. "Only about five percent of the particulate matter we found on the relic is specific to regions of the world exclusive to its stated origin, that being the European continent, where the relic's been stored for centuries. That's consistent with what one would expect."

"So," Bondurant noted as he tapped his pencil on the table, "there is no evidence that the fabric contains grave dust of any kind that would sufficiently suggest it is of European origin or traveled to or from any other region beyond the Middle East?"

"None. And, on the flip side, there was ample evidence of the presence of travertine aragonite limestone, which, as you know, is prevalent in the ancient tombs of Jerusalem. Their chemical signatures are a precise match. Similarly, the vast majority of the ancient pollen samples we lifted from the fabric are specific to the Jerusalem area as well."

"Okay," Bondurant said as he nodded his head in assent. "Moving along, we get to Terry O'Neil's radiocarbon dating analysis. Take it away, Terry. The findings are striking, are they not?"

"Yes, they are, Jon," O'Neil said. He leaned back in his chair. "Not really what we were expecting to see, given previous radiocarbon dating results of the relic. As you know, we disintegrated several samples in the tests, fully expecting to date the artifact to roughly eight hundred or maybe a thousand years ago. But that's not what we found at all. The analysis, repeatedly and very definitively, points to an object that is somewhere—remember, this is not an exact science—between nineteen hundred and twenty-one hundred years old. We are ninety-five percent certain it falls within this two-hundred-year range."

"About the biblical time of Jesus," Domenika said for emphasis.

"That's right," O'Neil said. "This process is never going to give you full precision, an exact decade of origin, but I can guarantee you, this is no medieval relic. It's roughly two thousand years old."

Domenika smiled broadly into the camera and stared directly at Bondurant. He averted his eyes from her screen to concentrate.

"Dr. Montrose," Bondurant said, "your review is fascinating as well."

"To tell you the truth, Jon, I had expected from the outset that we were going to discover that this sepia-colored image was just too good to be true. That it had been applied by some medieval brush or instrument, and that a crude chemical compound used as a paint would be relatively easy to detect."

"Not exactly what you found, correct?" Bondurant said.

"On the contrary," Montrose said. "We found no evidence of this. What we also discovered is that the image formed on the Shroud is really no miraculous occurrence. What we see on the Shroud—what forms its human image—is exactly what one would expect to see in the way of residue left on linen material like this from a body in the first hours of decomposition following death."

"Such as?" Bondurant asked.

"Such as residue from the skin stemming from the chemical breakdown of cellular enzymes within the human body postmortem. We call it autolysis."

"Autolysis?" Domenika asked.

"Yes. The microscopic particles we were able to collect originated from the 'off-gassing' of these enzymes from a corpse. We found mixed within them various organic acids—propionic acid and lactic acid, to name just two—that are the result of a corpse moving from Stage One to Stage Two in the decomposition process. Nothing unusual, Jon."

"Dr. Sato, my friend," Bondurant said. "I have your report here as well."

"Yes, Jon," Sato said. "As you know, my computer image analysis could not be brought to a conclusion for various reasons beyond our control. But I want to thank all of you for your well wishes and support, especially you, Father Parenti."

"I'm afraid he couldn't join us, Dr. Sato," Domenika said. "But I'll pass on your kind words."

"Yes, please do. It's a miracle, actually."

Sato held his hands in front of the camera to reveal only small scars on both palms. Bondurant reared back in his seat. He couldn't believe what he was seeing. This couldn't be right. The healing was unexplainable, given how badly burned and disfigured they had been just a few weeks before.

Domenika looked shocked. She quickly made the sign of the cross, no doubt certain a miracle had taken place.

"Can you see the stigmata?" Sato joked. He held both hands close to the camera so that everyone on the call could see the small wounds centered on his palms. There were slight indentations in his flesh similar to what one might experience through crucifixion.

"Jon, you saved my life, and I swear that little priest saved my hands. For that I am grateful," he said. "In any event, with the work we were able to complete and the images that survived the hard-drive crashes related to the accident, I am prepared to report that there is no evidence as far as I can see that the image on the Shroud was forced or formed unnaturally by an artificial process. None at all. In fact, we tried but could not replicate on any material the same effect that appears on the linen."

Bondurant tried to shake off the shock and confusion that had set in when he saw Sato's hands completely intact.

"All right," Bondurant said, trying to force himself to focus. "My turn. Let's turn to the image on the Shroud itself and talk for a moment about the anatomical forensics review. I want to summarize it for you this way: I don't know if the image on this Shroud is that of a person named Jesus Christ, the supposed Savior of mankind. I don't believe any living being is qualified to say that this day or any other day."

Domenika cast both eyes upward.

"But," Bondurant continued, "my interest was in determining whether the image presented on the Shroud is proportional to a human being in every respect, and whether the markings of purported torture as related in the biblical stories present themselves as credible. Essentially, my interest was in knowing whether there were any irregularities in the image that would cause one to believe it is out of form, out of character or scale, anatomically speaking."

"And?" Domenika asked.

"I can state unequivocally that there are no such irregularities. I could find no flaw or distortion whatsoever in the presentation of the major limbs, the size of the image's head, his hands, fingers, hips, shins—every aspect of the subject, every wound is in exact proportion to natural human characteristics and causes."

"The what?" Domenika asked.

"The *subject*," Bondurant said. He paused for emphasis on the word as he tried to avoid her image on the monitor. "The subject was indeed severely beaten. There are wounds present in the feet, hands, face, and forehead. Swelling under one eye is prevalent, and large shocks of hair appear to have been ripped from the scalp. The blood-flow pattern from the hands, feet, and thorax are all in forensic agreement with a body following the torture of crucifixion. It's all there in my report."

Domenika broke into a broad smile.

"Okay, then," Bondurant continued, anxious to get to the troubling part. "I am not sure how many of you have had the chance to review Dr. Sehgal's work, which was completed just a few days ago—that of the DNA analysis on the blood sample extracted from the image itself. Next to the carbon dating analysis, I don't know of another piece of evidence that has the potential to shine greater light on the subject. Dr. Sehgal?"

"Thank you, Jon. It's a pleasure to weigh in," Sehgal said. "I know that I own really only one piece, albeit an important piece, of a larger puzzle here. I am reminded of that as I listen to the extraordinary findings of my distinguished colleagues on the call today. But the DNA analysis we ran on the single blood sample provided leads me to conclude that while the preponderance of evidence you have gathered apparently implies the artifact is of ancient origin from biblical times, it is indeed an ancient fake."

Bondurant watched as Domenika got up from her chair, folded her arms, and began to shake her head in disbelief.

O'Neil was the first to speak up. "Ravi, I have not yet had the chance to read your conclusions," he said. "What evidence do you have to suggest this?"

"Put simply, Dr. O'Neil," Sehgal stated flatly, "the sample we pulled from the Shroud, similar to the sample provided to you, is indeed blood. Of that there is no doubt. We converted the heme, the red blood cells present, into its parent porphyrin, bilirubin, and albumin. Microchemical tests for blood-related proteins were all positive. The iron oxide detected is a natural residue of hemoglobin. So it's blood, all right. But it's blood of animal origin."

Dr. Montrose jumped in. "What do you mean, animal origin?" she asked. She was incredulous. "You were not any more specific than that in your report."

"We've made a determination on that now. It's a goat. The blood on the famous Shroud is that of a goat," Sehgal stated in an emotionless tone.

"A goat?" Domenika cried out. "If you believe the Holy Shroud of our Savior covered the carcass of a goat instead of our Lord, then you are insane, Doctor!"

"As I said at the outset of this call," Bondurant interrupted, trying to calm Domenika and prevent her from further insulting a Nobel Prize–winning biologist, "science is a messy business. Given all the other evidence, Ravi, when I saw this finding in your report, I have to say, I just couldn't believe it either."

"Data is data. Genes are genes, Jon," Sehgal responded dryly, ignoring Domenika's insult. "Knowing the importance of the conclusions of this project to a lot of people, we took special care in our analysis. The blood is indeed old, but it is not badly fragmented nor contaminated, relatively speaking. We performed over a dozen runs on the sample and were able to amplify a clean DNA structure without much difficulty. We are one-hundred-percent certain that the blood on that Shroud is a precise match to the DNA of a male goat. Specifically, a goat stemming from the ancient Bezoar breed prevalent in the mountains of Asia Minor and the Middle East."

"You're serious, Dr. Sehgal?" Dr. Montrose exclaimed.

"As a heart attack, Doctor," Sehgal replied. "I cannot speak for your disciplines. And I am by no means an authority on religious relics, Jon. I am sorry to have to report the facts as they are. Ms. Jozef, I know how important this is to you, and I urge you to come here if you'd like to personally review my findings. In fact, I'm sure the Church will demand it. But I am presuming the game has changed. What was once viewed by scientists as a fake from the medieval era is simply a fake from a much earlier time."

"Ravi," Bondurant persisted, "are you *totally* certain?" Bondurant had a lot at stake. Sehgal's confident conclusion that the Shroud was a fake fit perfectly with the narrative Bondurant had proclaimed publicly for many years, and findings of false relics like this were the norm for him. Bondurant's famous doubts would be proven right again. But he couldn't put his finger on why something about the puzzle piece provided by Sehgal seemed hard to believe.

"The evidence is in my report," Sehgal said. "Disappointing as this will be to many, including me, I am hard-pressed to believe that a human being, and in this case the supposed body of Christ himself, would bleed like a goat as opposed to the Savior he was."

PART 3

PART-3

CHAPTER 31

St. Michaels, Maryland
July 2014

Bondurant awoke briefly to the acrid smell of burning rubber. He wearily pulled the woolen blanket back over his head and chalked it up to a bad dream with special effects. It was three a.m., and his only interest was blocking the light from the streetlamp that beamed into his silver Airstream trailer along the banks of the Miles River, just outside St. Michaels.

His quarters were cramped, and he needed sleep. His last forty-eight hours would compete with his worst days on record. It had all begun with a late-night call two days earlier from Steve Rohl, a science reporter for the *New York Times*. By Rohl's estimation, he was ten minutes from deadline, and as Bondurant remembered it, he got right to the point.

"Jon Bondurant?"

"Yes?" Bondurant said as he set his third scotch of the evening on his kitchen table. He swatted in vain at a moth that had found its way inside the trailer.

"This is Steve Rohl with the *New York Times*. I hope I'm not disturbing you. We're working on a story related to your investigation of the Shroud of Turin. Do you have a moment?"

"Steve, I don't know how you got my cell number," Bondurant said, irritated, as he opened his front door to chase out the moth. Neither the insect nor Rohl were welcome visitors at the moment. He descended the two steps toward the "front forty," the small patch of grass that formed his front lawn. A warm breeze blew from the north, carrying with it the familiar marriage of smells from where salt and fresh water met at the intersection of the Atlantic and the Chesapeake Bay. "But like I've told everyone else in the press, my report's not complete. When it's final, we'll be coordinating a release with the Vatican. If you want, I can make sure you're on the list to get the advisory."

"Yeah, that would be great. Thanks," Rohl said. "But the reason I'm calling is that we have obtained a copy of your draft report and we are planning on running a story tonight on your findings."

"You're kidding me, right?" Bondurant said. He took a seat in one of the plastic lawn chairs on the grass and tried his best not to sound panicked.

"No, Dr. Bondurant, I'm afraid I'm not. I have the document in front of me, and I'm calling to know if you'd like to comment on your report's conclusion that the Shroud is not an authentic religious relic."

"There's no way you have that report, Steve," Bondurant said. He got up from his chair and began to pace in circles around it.

"What page would you like me quote from, Doctor?"

"Page three," Bondurant said, calling his bluff.

"Page three. Executive Summary. Paragraph four. 'Notwithstanding the radiocarbon tests dating the artifact to the first century AD, the presence of goat's blood obtained from material sampling of an area on the relic previously purported to be human blood casts grave doubt on the oft-cited theory that the object served as a burial cloth of a man known as Jesus Christ.'"

Bondurant stopped in his tracks, dumbfounded.

"Would you care to comment on that conclusion, Dr. Bondurant? I presume you wrote it."

"Would you care to tell me who leaked the draft report to you?" Bondurant demanded, trying to regain his composure.

"I'm afraid I can't do that. I'm on deadline and have just a few minutes. We would really like to get your comment on this story before we run with it, given it's your report."

"It's just a *stupid draft report*, Steve!" Bondurant yelled. He grabbed his lawn chair and flung it toward the river twenty yards away. It cleared the picnic table at the edge of the precipice and sailed toward the river ten feet below.

"Doctor, I know you don't want me to quote you on that."

Try bribing him, Bondurant thought in desperation.

"What I'm asking you—actually begging you, Steve—is to hold off on filing your story until our report is final and the Vatican has had a chance to digest it and respond. It's possible there will be changes in our findings, and it would be a real problem for you to report at this point. I'll give you an exclusive interview when we release if that's what it takes."

"I'm afraid I can't do that. Are you sure you don't want to comment?"

"Hold on." Bondurant paused to think for a moment. His eyes focused on the thin trail of light from the moon that had begun to stretch its way across the river toward him. He knew his quote would be seen around the world. "You ready?" Bondurant asked.

"Yes, go right ahead."

"Okay, Here it is. 'Domenika, I'm sorry.'"

"Excuse me, Doctor?"

"Forget it, Steve. Never mind. Have a nice day."

Bondurant ended the call by throwing his cell phone over the bank and into the river, just where his lawn chair had met the same fate seconds before.

Bondurant went inside and stood vigil by his computer for twenty minutes until Rohl's story appeared. He was certain it was the longest twenty minutes of his life. The headline read:

HOLY SHROUD OF TURIN HOLY NO MORE; VENERATED RELIC DEEMED A FAKE

Huge trouble, Bondurant thought.

He was torn. He'd found himself starting to believe it was real, even wanting to believe it. And sure, he'd had his doubts about Sehgal's motives along the way, but given the evidence he'd presented to the team, he couldn't disagree with the conclusion. Sehgal was the world's leading authority on the subject of DNA. If you believed what he presented so compellingly in his findings, which Bondurant reluctantly did, it was a slam-dunk to call the Shroud a fake. But nobody, absolutely nobody, was ready for the headline, and this was definitely not the way the Church wanted any news to break.

A media explosion followed. Within an hour, major wire services around the world followed the *Times* and began to report that modern science had ended the decades-long debate: the Shroud of Turin was in fact an ancient hoax.

Within two hours, almost every major television news organization from CNN to Al Jazeera reported that the mystery of the

Shroud of Turin had been solved: the Catholic Church's most precious relic was a fraud, likely the work of an ancient artist looking for notoriety in his time.

Within five hours, the Vatican, caught flat-footed by the leak, released a statement that expressed its outrage at the unauthorized release of the report. It condemned the report's findings as inaccurate and incomplete and pledged the release of its own report at a time of its choosing, one that would include previously undisclosed historical material that would refute Bondurant's conclusions.

Within twelve hours, media outlets from around the world that sought comment from Bondurant had launched their news vans toward the tiny town of St. Michaels, which had sprouted satellite dishes like massive mushrooms overnight.

Within fifteen hours, Bondurant had reluctantly bought a new cell phone to replace the one he'd tossed. And of all the calls to receive first, he got the one he dreaded most. As soon as he set foot outside the electronics store in a tiny strip mall a short walk from his place, his phone began to ring.

"Jon, you are a traitor!" Domenika's ear-piercing voice was unmistakable as she cried into the phone. She sobbed uncontrollably. "I don't know why we trusted you to work with us. I don't know why *I* ever trusted you."

"Domenika, you have to let me explain," Bondurant said. "Please believe me, this is the last thing I wanted. Someone on the team—I don't know who—must have leaked the draft report. I had nothing to do with it."

He was panicked. There was no way he was going to salvage anything from their fledgling relationship through a long-distance call. He knew that everything he said would only sound defensive and complicit. And yet he was desperate to convince her of his innocence. "I swear on my life I am telling the truth," he said.

"Would you swear on your job?" Domenika asked. She was angrier than he had ever heard her before. "Would you swear on your career?"

"Of course I would, Domenika."

"Great. At least you still have one. Mine's finished. I've been fired, Jon. By the cardinal himself. This whole thing has completely blown up in the Vatican's face, and they are furious."

"Domenika, I'm so sorry. It's completely ridiculous for them to blame you."

"I warned them about you," she said, near hysteria. "I did. But they insisted this ridiculous study was the way to go, even when we have solid evidence to refute Sehgal *and* your report. Oh, they can't say I didn't warn them."

"Warn them? What do you mean 'warn them'?"

"Never mind. Never mind," she said. Her voice began to trail off. "Are you satisfied? I suppose you got from this exactly what you've wanted all along."

"Domenika," he said in desperation. "*What I've wanted all along is you.*"

It was too late. She had hung up and was gone before he could get the words out.

Within twenty-four hours, he had received a certified letter from the offices of Wilson and O'Brien, attorneys at law in Washington, DC, representing the Holy See in Rome. The letter stated that Bondurant was

"in breach of his agreement to share with the Church all findings and all documents related to his investigation prior to public release as well

*as Clause 32 requiring coordination with the Vatican of all public
announcements related thereto."*

It demanded the immediate forfeiture of all material gathered by
his team during the course of its investigation.

Within thirty hours, the hate mail, some with death threats, began
to find its way through to the Enlightenment Institute's Twitter and
e-mail accounts. The messages started as a trickle, then came in tor-
rents, ending only when the center's servers broke down, hacked in
apparent retaliation for his findings. After he had spent over forty
straight hours at his offices and sorted through the mess, he had retreated to his trailer on the Miles River, where he could get away
from the noise and would hopefully be left alone.

That evening, the second time he awoke from a deep sleep in
his trailer, twenty more minutes had passed. He was really hot, and
soaked with sweat. What he had earlier drowsily dismissed as smoke
was in reality an actual inferno about to transform his entire trailer
into a funeral pyre.

Bondurant bolted upright out of bed. The tires under his Airstream must have melted in flames, because the trailer had collapsed
into a twenty-degree tilt. He reached for the wall near his bed to
steady himself and nearly burned his hand on the glowing hot aluminum window frame beside him. Flames five feet high licked the
outside of the trailer and set the interior of the space aglow, bright
red and orange.

He estimated the temperature inside the trailer at over 125 degrees, and it was sure to get hotter. Shoeless, the soles of his feet
began to burn. While flames had not yet breached the inside of the
cabin, smoke had begun to billow inward through cracks in the floor.
He was certain asphyxiation was his biggest threat. He needed air.

The nearest window in his bedroom, cracked from one end to the other due to the heat, was too narrow for his shoulders to fit through and was hopeless as an exit. He also knew that breaking it for precious oxygen would only create a massive, fiery backdraft and certain death. He felt the hairs on his arms begin to singe, grabbed a blanket from his bed, and covered his body as best he could. He worked his way in the dark by memory through the thick smoke on his hands and knees. The path took him from his bedroom in the back of the trailer toward the lone door on the opposite end that led to the outside. Unfortunately, the closer he got to the trailer's only door, the greater the intensity of the fire.

The front door handle glowed red hot. He couldn't touch it. It didn't matter. His only chance for escape was to burst through the doorway at full speed and clear the flames, which had started to envelop the roof of the trailer as well. Paint had begun to bubble on the ceiling above him, and he knew his time was almost up. In one great thrust, he threw all his weight against the door. But when he slammed his shoulder against it, his body recoiled backward like an outfielder who'd hit a centerfield wall. The door hadn't budged an inch. Twice more he gave it everything he had, but it was no use. It must have melted in place.

Now it's time to panic, he thought. He figured he had less than a minute before incineration. He hoped it would happen fast. He dropped to his knees once again, covered by his smoldering blanket, and crawled his way back toward his bedroom. He turned left just before he reached it and squirmed his way into the tiny bathroom. He closed the door to try to block the smoke. He crawled into the small shower stall and fumbled in the darkness for the handle. But instead of a stream of welcome relief, only the cruel sound of hot, hissing air escaped the shower head. The water pump had obviously succumbed to the flames. *I should have known that*, he thought. *I'm not thinking clearly.*

He sat down calmly in the shower stall and looked at his watch. The hands glowed in the dark. 22:04. He laughed to himself and realized that if it had been accurate, it would have shown only thirty seconds left to live. He closed his eyes and relaxed and tried to take himself out of the terror of the moment. *What does one think of in the end?* he asked himself. He was surprised. He thought of his father wearing a clean, white shirt, holding his hand as they crossed the street for ice cream on his eighth birthday, the only one he remembered. He thought of the time he was caught in a freak thunderstorm hitchhiking to class at Stanford. He had stood under an overpass for an hour, smelling the falling rain. And he thought of Domenika and how she looked the day they'd met.

He opened his eyes and pulled himself toward the toilet, which sat at eye level. He dunked his face into the shallow, tepid water at the bottom of the bowl to cool it. *What an undignified way to die*, he thought. He felt the flimsy floor beneath him bend and buckle under his weight, as it had for years, and wondered why he had never gotten around to repairing it. And then, an idea. He wrapped his arms around the bowl, locked his hands together behind it, and pulled the toilet upward with every bit of strength he could find. At first there was a loud *crack*, and then another, and then a loud tearing sound as the base of the toilet sheared itself away from the rotting floorboards below. He heaved the toilet aside and looked down at salvation: a two-and-a-half-foot hole and green grass below. Wildly, he ripped aside the floorboards and plastic pipes surrounding the hole and wriggled his way into the space. Then he dove headfirst onto the ground under the Airstream. He turned on his back and in one swift motion rolled like a barrel through a thick wall of flame on the south side of the trailer and out into the safety of his yard. As he rose and stumbled backward and then turned to look behind him, the entire ceiling of the trailer gave way in a horrid *whoosh* as it ignited everything inside.

But what caught his eye before he ran down the street for help was something he would remember for the rest of his life. Two large steel beams, fixed in the shape of a cross, were braced firmly like a barrier against his trailer's front door.

CHAPTER 32

Rome, Italy
August 2014

I t took several days for Bondurant to get his life in order as he read-ied for his trip to Rome to see Domenika. All of his belongings remained in a heap of ruins that once was his shiny Airstream trailer. His repeated calls to Domenika since the disastrous videoconfer-ence call went unanswered, just as they had when he'd returned from Turin.

Bondurant had lost patience with that game and decided to buy a one-way ticket to Rome to see Domenika, whether she answered his phone calls or not. Bondurant had more socks in his suitcase than he had ideas in his head as to how he might help Domenika get her job back at the Vatican, but he was willing to do whatever it took to prove that he was there to help.

"Fancy meeting you here, Father," Bondurant said, genuinely happy to see Parenti after weeks apart. He clasped the little priest's hands in his and bent over to give him an awkward hug. "Are you sure this is her building?"

"Quite certain. I have met her here before," the priest said as he glanced around them nervously.

"Is there a problem, Father?"

Bondurant looked up and down the busy street for anything odd that might catch Parenti's eye. They were in the picturesque neighborhood of Navona, just south of the Vatican in Rome. It was an unseasonably cool morning, and the crisp air carried the scent of roasted chestnuts from the vendors down the street.

"My friend, there would be great trouble if I were to be seen with you. Barsanti's spies are everywhere," the priest said as he pressed Aldo's head back into his satchel. He darted his eyes about him more dramatically than Bondurant felt was warranted. "Needless to say, you are persona non grata anywhere near the Vatican, Doctor."

"I beg to differ, Father. I am persona non grata all over the Christian world."

"We all bear our crosses, do we not, Dr. Bondurant?" Parenti said with a scowl on his face. "Mine would be the tourist restrooms of St. Peter's Basilica."

"What do you mean by that?" Bondurant asked.

"I was relegated by Barsanti to the role of washroom attendant in St. Peter's. I can assure you, Doctor, it was not a promotion. Can you not smell the urine on me?" Parenti said.

"I am very sorry to hear that, Father."

"Domenika was even less fortunate," Parenti said. He looked sullen. "I'm sure you know she was dismissed."

"She told me. But the Vatican's insane, Father. She had nothing to do with my conclusions, and they know it," Bondurant said.

"Didn't she tell you?" the priest asked.

"Tell me what?"

"She was not terminated because of your conclusions, Doctor. That was out of her hands," Parenti said. "It was the discovery of her neglect to report your accident that nearly took the Shroud. That was her undoing."

Bondurant nearly dropped to his knees on the sidewalk from the weight of the news.

He was sorry about a lot of things that had happened since that unforgettable evening when his report on the Shroud had been leaked to the press. He'd wondered whether it was Sehgal who had leaked the report, and what possible motivation he might have for doing it. It was as if a bomb had dropped and turned the world upside down. The Vatican had been caught completely off guard, and there had been a lot of recriminations and finger pointing. Things were a mess.

He had been forced to take a leave of absence from the Enlightenment Institute. His board of directors suggested that his presence was a distraction and it would be better to let things simmer down. *What an understatement*, he thought. Bondurant had become even more of an international pariah in the Christian world than he had been previously, which made his presence at the unguarded compound a security threat to everyone who worked there. The Institute had suffered through three bomb scares in a single month.

He was sorry too that he had lost his cozy silver Airstream trailer on a prime spot near the Chesapeake. The management of the quiet trailer park he had once called home refused to let him renew the lease on his lot out of fear of another reprisal. The neighbors felt unsafe and wanted him out.

But most of all, he was sorry for Domenika. She was the one

who had suffered the most. His one bit of luck came when Parenti returned his repeated phone calls and arranged their clandestine meeting in Rome. When his leave of absence from the Institute had been made official, he bought the open-ended ticket to Rome. Twenty-four hours later, he found himself in front of Domenika's apartment building with no plan, a few days' worth of clothes, and no clue what to say if he found her. He was taking it one day and, often, even one hour at a time.

"Okay, so which one is her apartment?" Bondurant asked as he looked toward the tall building before them.

"Lord knows, Doctor. Where we're standing is the best I can do."

"Are you kidding me, Father?" Bondurant said, disappointed. "There must be a hundred apartments in this building."

"Come with me," the priest said. He insisted they get off the street and out of the open.

They ascended the long staircase that led to the building's entrance and were greeted by a massive doorman who stood like a statue as he blocked access to the large glass doors behind him.

"Father, how can I help you?" the rotund figure bellowed as he flicked his cigarette butt down the stairway to join the graveyard of others he'd sent to rest there already. "What is your business here?"

"Yes, we're looking for a woman," Bondurant said as they cautiously approached him.

"Aren't we all?" the doorman grunted.

"No, my son," Father Parenti interrupted quickly. "I am here to perform the sacrament of last rites. And I am in a hurry, if you understand what I mean."

The doorman immediately took a step backward, his face now looking ominous.

"And you are?" the doorman said as he nodded at Bondurant. He reached for the pack of cigarettes in his shirt pocket.

"I am . . ." Bondurant said as he stared at Parenti. He paused long enough for the priest to continue the charade.

"He is responsible for preparing the body when the moment arrives, my son," Parenti said as he pointed to Bondurant's suitcase. "Now, if you would be so kind, I have misplaced my address book, and I am in need of her apartment number. Quickly, if you will. Time is of the essence. Her name is—"

"Domenika Jozef," Bondurant said as he got in on the act.

"Domenika Jozef? Domenika Jozef? That is impossible. You are absolutely sure, Father?" the doorman said. He lit up a cigarette and looked at the pair as though they had just stolen something from him.

Over four thousand miles I have flown to see her, Bondurant thought, *and this is how it's going to end? Last rites? Where on earth did that come from?* A worried thought spread across his brain. *For all we know, she danced past the doorman on her way out of here ten minutes ago*, he thought.

"Sir, we are terribly sorry," Bondurant said as he grabbed the suitcase and readied to leave. "It's just that—"

"I am sorry as well," the doorman replied, looking confused. "I have worked this day shift for six months now, and I have not seen Ms. Jozef for over two weeks."

"Pardon us, sir," the priest said as he looked up at him with a sense of urgency in his eyes. "She has been here wasting away as a shut-in. She should not meet her maker alone. That is not a burden you want to live with."

"And such a lovely girl, Father," the doorman said. He stared pensively out toward the street.

"The apartment number, sir?" Parenti insisted.

"Six-three-six, Father. Perhaps I should come with you. You will need assistance. Really, such a beautiful girl."

"*Lebbra*, my son, *lebbra*," the priest said forebodingly as he shook his head.

"In that case, Father," the doorman said. He stepped aside quickly, as if duty bound. "I shall mind the door. God be with you." He reached out and pressed a series of numbers on the entry keypad, and a loud buzz signaled that the door had unlocked.

They entered the lobby and made a direct line straight to the small elevator ahead. Once inside, Bondurant pushed the button for the sixth floor. He turned to Parenti as soon as the doors had closed.

"Last rites? Are you serious? You could have gotten us thrown down those stairs."

"It was the best I could do under the circumstances, Doctor," Parenti said.

"Listen, you're a priest. Where does it say you can lie like that?"

"You're the world-renowned authority on religions."

"Okay, then. What is '*lebbra*'?"

"I believe you know it as leprosy," Parenti said, smiling as the elevator doors opened onto the sixth floor. He pulled Aldo from inside his coat pocket and set him on the ground. The dog immediately bolted down the hallway as if picking up Domenika's scent.

They made their way down the long, dimly lit hallway and stopped at apartment 636, precisely where the dog sat and waited. Without hesitation, Parenti reached out and pushed the doorbell. A melodious chime sounded inside.

"Are you insane, Father?" Bondurant protested in a loud whisper as he grabbed his hand and stepped back from the doorway.

"Can't you see I am not ready? I need a minute. What am I supposed to say?"

"Ridiculous, Doctor. Of course you know what to say." Parenti reached out quickly and pressed the button once more. "You say what they *always* say in the American movies. You say 'I love you.' She says she loves you too. You will kiss. Five, maybe ten seconds. And that is it. That is why you are here, is it not? Very simple."

Bondurant's heart raced. He started to believe his impulsive journey was a huge mistake. And, worse yet, showing up at her doorstep unannounced after weeks of the silent treatment was sure to produce a disaster. He just knew it.

After almost a minute, there was no answer. Not a sound came from inside. Bondurant knew an opening for escape when he saw one. He picked up his suitcase and began to head back to the elevator. He had no idea where he was going or what he would do next, but he needed some time to get some sleep and regroup before he saw her.

"Just a moment, Doctor," Parenti called out. "*Amazing!* The door is unlocked!"

You're kidding me, Bondurant thought. "Father, don't you dare go in there," he shouted from down the hallway. But it was too late. The dog had already scampered inside the home, and the priest, halfway through the door, motioned frantically for Bondurant to come in.

The three of them stood in the entry foyer of Domenika's apartment, perched as still as frightened birds who had cleverly found their way indoors but hadn't a clue what to do next. They looked around at the small, immaculately kept apartment and the kind of stillness that meant not a soul was home. Bondurant thought again what an enormous mistake it was to enter, violating her space. At the same time, he was captivated as he stood surrounded by the nest she had made for herself, filled with the artwork, books, and mementos she obviously cherished. And the smell. He closed his eyes for a moment and imagined her there, welcoming him to her private world for the first time.

On a small coffee table beside the couch by the large bay window he could see several framed photographs. He made his way slowly over to them and, careful not to disturb them, leaned over to see what images she treasured enough to keep. There was one that looked likely to be her parents relaxing on a park bench. Another with Domenika bundled up on a snowy day in Central Park with someone who had to be her sister.

And then two other pictures caught his eye. One captured her and the entire Shroud investigation team in Turin. Surprising that she had kept that one, he thought, after all that had gone wrong. But it was the second photo that was a stunner. It was the same photo Domenika had given him at their farewell dinner that showed the two of them in casual conversation beside the Shroud. Bondurant couldn't believe she had kept a copy of her own. He picked up the framed photo of the two of them and stood completely still with a lump in his throat.

"You must be Jon Bondurant," a sleepy voice said from the doorway to the bedroom, off the living room.

Bondurant was so startled that he dropped the frame on the rug and dislodged the glass. A beautifully striking woman, almost six feet tall, stood before him in the doorway, topless and wearing only a purple thong. For a moment Bondurant mistook the woman for Domenika herself. She stood casually in the doorway to the bedroom. Her figure was perfect. Brunette hair flowed halfway down her back. She took her time and eyed him confidently from head to toe.

"Nice picture, huh?" she said as she yawned and pointed to the picture he had dropped. "She said you were cute. She was right."

"I'm a . . . I'm a . . ." Bondurant stuttered as he bent over to pick up the photo. "You must be her sister, Joanna?"

"Yes. Now you're not going to run and hide from me, are you?" she asked. "She said you were shy."

Bondurant turned beet-red. Domenika had obviously been talking.

"I'm fine," he said.

"And who is your friend, this adorable priest and his little wonder dog?" Joanna asked as she nodded toward Parenti and the dog.

They stood frozen, their eyes transfixed on the half-nude figure she presented, not making a move. Parenti's jaw was hanging open.

"This is a friend of mine and a friend of Domenika's as well, Father Parenti. Father Parenti, say hello to Domenika's sister, Joanna."

The dog leapt in excitement, but Parenti was still speechless.

"Now who's the one with the shyness problem?" Bondurant said, amused.

"Yes, I've heard of you as well," Joanna responded as she reached for a blouse that hung over the hallway closet door. She slipped it on nonchalantly and covered herself. Bondurant recognized it as one of Domenika's, and it fit Joanna perfectly.

"Listen, Joanna, I am really sorry we have barged in on you like this," Bondurant said.

"Barged? Breaking and entering, I'd say," Joanna said. She smiled and glided gracefully toward Bondurant to take a closer look at him.

"I have flown all night to be here, Joanna," Bondurant said. "I've been trying to reach Domenika for over three weeks. I have just *got* to see her."

"That makes two of us, Doctor," Joanna said. "I just arrived last night from New York."

"The doorman downstairs says he has not seen her for a while as well," Parenti said, finally finding his voice. "Has she gone home to your parents?"

"My parents in Krakow have not heard a word from her either. They're worried sick. It's just not like Nika to go off the grid like this. That's why I'm here."

"Any signs of her at all?" Bondurant asked as he looked about the room.

"There were notices I found slipped under the door. One that says they have been holding her mail downstairs but are starting to return it. And here's another saying she's behind on this month's rent. There is something, though. What do either of you know about India?"

"India?" Bondurant said, stunned. "What makes you suggest India?"

"There was this," Joanna said as she turned toward the desk behind her. She unfolded a copy of a flight itinerary and held it out for both of them to see. "A one-way ticket to Mumbai. Jetstar Asia. Ten days ago."

Bondurant studied the travel document for a moment.

"I should have known it! I had a hunch she might have gone there," he said. The only connection he could imagine between Domenika and India was Sehgal. Had she traveled there to settle the bitter dispute she'd had with him over his findings of an ancient goat's DNA? Her job was on the line. That made sense. And Bondurant

remembered Sehgal had challenged her to come to Mumbai to disprove his results. But she was no scientist, and flying all the way to
India was a long way to go just to give him grief.

Suddenly, nausea overtook Bondurant. He was in love, but he'd
known Domenika for just a matter of weeks. Was it possible that
Sehgal had convinced her to go to India for another reason? He'd
been told through the rumor mill that Sehgal had eyes for Domenika,
and that he had even bragged that she'd confided in him she was a
virgin, but Bondurant didn't want to even imagine the possibility of
the two of them together.

"Is she pregnant, Jon? Can I call you Jon?" Joanna asked as she
approached Bondurant to within just a few inches of his face. She
looked him directly in the eyes, the same way Domenika did.

Bondurant stared at her in disbelief. "Pregnant? What makes you
say something so absurd?" he asked.

"Jon, we're sisters. We talk," Joanna said calmly. "No, she didn't
tell me she was pregnant. But she told me you two were together.
She also said she was wasted and that whatever had happened, she
knew it was *without protection* on her part. I thought she said you
were smart."

"This can't be happening," Bondurant said as he turned away from
Joanna again and stared out the window.

"She told me the day she returned to Rome," Joanna said. "And I
can't think of any other reason for her to drop off the face of the earth
weeks after sleeping with you. Maybe she wanted to get as far away
as possible."

Bondurant couldn't believe what he'd just heard.

"Jon, if she's pregnant, you have to believe me—given her faith,
there is no force on earth that would prevent her from having

that child," Joanna said. "And my father? Well, let's just say India is not far enough away to hide from him if she is pregnant and unmarried."

Bondurant turned toward the two of them and said nothing. He had never felt more helpless or confused. He hung his head down for a long minute as though he'd find an answer on the floor.

"You're supposed to be the genius, Doctor," Joanna said as she tugged on his collar, pulled him from his trance and stared at him with an expectant look on her face. Her resemblance to Domenika in both appearance and attitude was uncanny. "What are you going to do now?"

CHAPTER 33

Mumbai, India
August 2014

Who was on the phone, my man?" Kishan sang out from behind his brightly lit cubicle at Sehgal Labs in downtown Mumbai. Mumbai was a city where giant building cranes had sprouted like weeds his entire boyhood. Kishan had lost track of the number of high-rises he could count as he looked out his window toward the horizon that was once old Bombay. Sehgal Labs was a modest but modern six-floor building centrally located in the city's bustling high-tech zone. His work space, cluttered with reference books, motorcycle helmets, a mountain bike with a flat tire, and a large stack of *Maxim* magazines, had the look of a disaster area.

"That was the boss man, Ravi," his friend Danvir shot back jubilantly. "He's stuck in traffic on the Eastern Expressway and won't be back for at least an hour."

"You my man, you my man," Kishan said, delighted at their stroke of good fortune. Traffic jams were now a twenty-four-hour phenomenon in a city where freeways could not be built fast enough to suit the need. He reached toward the boom box sitting precariously atop a giant stack of folders left unfiled and cranked up the volume. 50 Cent's "In Da Club" began to blare.

"There's a man coming here at one thirty," Danvir said, trying to shout above the din and the tall privacy wall that divided their cubicles. "You're supposed to show him to the warehouse."

"What's his name? Who is it?"

"Don't know. Didn't say. We gon' party like it's yo' birthday!"

"I said what's his name?" Kishan hollered as he threw a softball over the divider in Danvir's direction.

"Like I said, the man didn't say. He just said you meet the man, you take the man to the warehouse, you leave the man alone. In that order."

"Now let me ask you this, Mr. Danvir," Kishan shot back as he turned the volume down slightly. "How am I supposed to let *the man* in the warehouse when I don't have a key? You tell me that. The boss man changed the code a month ago after that new equipment was delivered. So let me say again 'I . . . ain't . . . got . . . no . . . key . . . card.'"

Danvir pitched the ball back over the divider toward Kishan in a perfect arc. He hoped to hit one of the half-filled cups or open cans of soda that sat on Kishan's desk.

"He said 'show him to the warehouse,' Kishan. He didn't say buy him a warehouse or build him a warehouse. Maybe he has his own key. I don't know. What I know is that Ravi won the Nobel Prize, so he gets what he wants."

"Yes, my brother, he does. That warehouse is full of what he wants since that prize money came in." He took a small sip of cold coffee and shuddered. "Did you see that load of stuff that came in those crates last month? A new centrifuge? Inverted stereo microscope?

Incubator? Freezer? Laminar flow hood? What's he planning on growing in there?"

"I thought you said he told you not to open those boxes," Danvir said.

"He said 'Do not open.' He did not say 'Do not open and close.'" The ball flew Danvir's way over the wall once more and landed harmlessly behind him.

"You the man."

"Hey, you want to see something strange, dawg?" Kishan called out.

"You on that nasty site again?"

"No, no. Come over here. I've been banging my head over this all morning. It doesn't make sense. No sense at all," Kishan said. He sounded mystified.

"I'm not dragging my tail over there for a porn site," Danvir warned.

"No, seriously. Come over here and check this out." Kishan had dropped the Hindi Ebonics entirely, and Danvir knew from experience that meant he was serious. He got up and walked around to Kishan's work space.

"When are you going to start selling maps so people can find your desk in here?" he said as he kicked aside the take-out trays and coffee cups that lay strewn about the floor near the trash can, the result of a half-dozen missed shots.

"Okay, look at this," Kishan said. He wheeled his chair closer to his computer. "This morning I was browsing on the S-drive and I found a folder for—"

"You're kidding me, right? We're not supposed to be on the S-drive. Ravi strictly forbids it."

"Yeah, I know. But he's not here, and I can't find the file on stromatolites we were looking for all yesterday."

Danvir stood up and looked around for any sign of life to ensure that no one could eavesdrop. A virus had invaded the lab's computers the previous year, and Ravi's instructions on limiting access to the central S-drive was absolute. It was a fireable offense.

"Okay, what is it? Fast," Danvir pleaded as he took a knee next to Kishan.

Arrayed before them on Kishan's desk amid stacks of documents were two large flat-screen monitors. Kishan moved several folder icons back and forth between the screens effortlessly.

"All right. First, I still can't find the stromatolites file. It's not there."

"Yeah, so?" Danvir began to tap the desk nervously.

"But check this out. In Ravi's alpha folder under 'S,' there is a locked zip file. It's unnamed, like someone didn't want it to be searchable, which is strange. But in it, there are a ton of folders, all with the label 'Shroud.' Look here."

"What do you mean it's locked, Kishan? If you don't have the password, how did you open it?"

"My father might have won the Nobel Prize, but his password is his birth date." Kishan pitched his empty coffee cup toward the trash can and missed by a foot. "I love him, but he's not *that* smart."

"Okay, so what's so strange?" Danvir asked, now as curious as he was nervous.

"Look. Here's an entire array of DNA charts labeled 'Shroud Sample.' And look. All of them—there are sixteen—stem from repeat trials derived from a single source—a blood sample. See? They're all identical."

"So what? Sixteen trials from the same source are going to produce sixteen identical results."

"Uh-huh. Now look at the blood type," Kishan instructed.

"'NI.' What's that?" Danvir asked as he leaned over and looked down the row of cubicles once more to ensure that they were alone. "There's no such thing."

"Uh-huh. That's Ravi's shorthand for 'Not Identifiable.' Now let me ask you another question. You ever read the papers or watch TV? I know you watch TV."

"Every day."

"Okay," Kishan demanded, "then why isn't this chart screaming 'baaaaaaah'?"

"What do you mean, 'baaaaaaah'?"

"Baaaaaaah," Kishan said in a low, guttural tone. "Like a goat."

"That's a sheep, fool."

"Sheep, goat—they all sound alike when they're mouthing off," Kishan protested.

"I'm not getting it," Danvir said as he braced himself for yet another of Kishan's know-it-all lectures.

"Okay, let me put it this way. What do pigs say?"

"Oink."

"How about cows?"

"Moo."

"Okay. What do goats with Not Identifiable blood say?"

Danvir cocked his head for a moment and thought about it. His eyes grew wide. "They don't," he said as he banged the desk. "Trick question. It's not possible. There are only three goat blood types. No outliers. The series is—"

"Z-1, Z-2, and Z-1/Z-2," Kishan said, beating him to the answer.

Kishan moved his cursor and double-clicked to open another folder from the lab's central database. This one was labeled "Animal Types" and was located on the screen on the right. A massive list appeared. He scrolled down the alphabetical list until he came to "Goats." As he double-clicked on the link, a list of more than three hundred different breeds of goats appeared. He scrolled down and stopped his cursor at "Goat, Bezoar." He dragged the DNA chart for a Bezoar goat over and double-clicked so that it expanded before them. Then he placed it side by side with the chart labeled "Shroud Sample."

"So like I asked," Kishan murmured as he leaned in carefully to compare the two charts, "do you watch TV?"

"Whhooooaaaaahhhh," Danvir said.

"Uh-huh. What's my pop doing on TV telling everyone the sample from that Shroud is from a goat?" Kishan asked, now totally confused. He leaned back in his chair and put one foot up on the desk. "There's no relation to a goat's blood type—not even close. One 'Unidentified' from the Shroud that looks to be human, but who knows? The other, clearly an animal, this old goat. And compare their spectrums. Not even close. *You couldn't find two DNA profiles more unrelated than this.*"

The two of them sat transfixed and quietly studied the differences in the DNA charts open beside each other, not saying a word. Danvir got up from his chair and peered around the corner of the cubicle one more time to make sure no one was nearby. The offices were still deserted at lunchtime. He was the first to break the silence. "Kishan, are you positive the charts you pulled up on the Shroud are the real deal? Could you have made a mistake?"

"No way. Look here. There's an entire inventory of Shroud items here. Really extensive. All of them in Ravi's subfolder, and all of them locked by password. 'Shroud Collection Regimen' . . . 'Shroud Background' . . . 'Shroud Research' . . . 'Shroud Blood Sample.'"

"This doesn't make sense," Danvir said as he rose. He was confused.

Buzzzzzzzzzzzzzzzzzzzzzzz.

The entry buzzer at the front door of the office sounded and jolted them both. It caused Danvir to leap like a frightened cat from Kishan's work space. He scrambled back to his own desk and put his head down to make himself look busy.

"Kishan, close out that file and get to the front door. That has to be Ravi's guest."

"Why don't you go up there, dawg?" Kishan said, now obviously preoccupied with the mystery and back in his groove.

"He said *you*, my man," Danvir shot back. "He said *you* take the man to the warehouse."

Kishan got up slowly from his desk, grabbed another empty coffee cup, and spiraled it like a football toward Danvir, who caught it expertly as he had a hundred times before. Kishan turned right and sauntered down an aisle of cubicles toward the front of the office. Danvir peeked over the cubicle wall and watched.

As he reached the reception area, Kishan pulled his ID from his pocket and casually swiped it in front of the electronic keypad. Danvir heard the familiar *clunk* of the magnetic lock release, and Kishan swung the door open. An impeccably dressed middle-aged man in a gray suit holding a suitcase stood before him.

"Wassup, my man," Kishan greeted the stranger.

"I believe Dr. Sehgal is expecting me," the man said with a French accent. "My name is Dr. François Laurent."

CHAPTER 34

Mumbai, India
August 2014

Kishan pried open the window and slipped easily through it, as he had a dozen times before. Outside the temperature had reached 110 degrees. Inside the industrial-type warehouse it was a pleasant 72. He knelt on the cold, gray cement floor of the lab's large warehouse and peered carefully from behind a stack of huge cardboard boxes he had purposely arranged there the day before. His plan was to eavesdrop and unravel a mystery. What he saw was beyond anything he had imagined.

Kishan could see an ambulance idling outside the large rear warehouse door. A woman who appeared to be unconscious was wheeled from the vehicle on a gurney by two orderlies. Starched white sheets covered the woman. Her arms were folded over the top sheet and revealed several IV tubes that ran to infusion bags that hung above her. A man wearing pale-blue scrubs trailed behind the gurney with a small dolly that held two stainless-steel gas cylinders, one white, one blue. The woman's face was obscured by an oxygen mask attached to breathing tubes beside her.

A group was gathered around the patient and framed within a semicircle of tables that held an array of lab equipment and a host of hospital supplies. Some of the faces were familiar to Kishan, others not. At one end of the gurney was Ravi, who looked as nervous as Kishan had ever seen him. He paced back and forth as the orderlies dressed in white moved a few small pieces of equipment into place. Ravi briefly stopped his pacing and looked directly at the small tower of boxes Kishan had assembled for his hiding place. Momentarily Kishan's heart leapt to his throat in fear. Had he already been discovered?

Kishan reminded himself it was impossible for Ravi to see him. The day before, he and Danvir had tested the hiding place and determined it was perfectly constructed. There was not even a remote possibility of being discovered. But the stakes were high. If he was exposed like a rat in hiding, he knew it would mean the end of his employment at Sehgal Labs, or even worse, the end of his relationship with his father. Mercifully, Ravi detected nothing beyond large boxes of reagents stacked atop one another. He turned his glance away from Kishan's corner and focused his attention on the patient at hand.

Kishan calmed his breathing and began to identify the others. Centered over the patient was Dr. Laurent. He recognized him from the day he'd first escorted him to the warehouse a week before. Laurent had buried himself in the lab with "confidential" work, off-limits to all. Now he was dressed in light-green hospital scrubs and wore white sterile surgical gloves below the elbow.

Next to Laurent, Kishan could see the figure of a man he could only describe as grotesque. He wore a dark-blue suit and an odd fedora, the kind Kishan had seen in old-time American movies. He had a bulbous nose and a beet-red complexion that stood out in sharp contrast to his starched white collared shirt. In his left hand he carried a small device about the size of a lunch box, which was connected to a cord he held in his right hand.

Kishan had waited in his hiding place for almost an hour to see what secret events would unfold. He was intensely curious as to what work Laurent had been conducting in private since he had arrived. It was only when he heard that his father had canceled all appointments for the day, two of them critical, that he knew the moment had come. That, and the ever-growing mobile hospital setup he had spied Laurent preparing, were sure giveaways the mystery was about to unfold.

Laurent was the first to speak. "Is the patient fully sedated?" he asked as he stepped toward the gurney.

"Yes," an orderly responded. "Fully under."

"This is your *virgin*, Dr. Sehgal?" the hideous figure asked through a microphone tied to the machine that amplified his nightmarish voice. The sound so frightened Kishan that he nearly gasped out loud.

"As I promised," Ravi said. "We've attempted and failed with many others. Most much younger. But certainly none as devout."

"She looks fine to me," Laurent said. "Vitals are excellent. Otherwise in good health? No abnormalities?"

"None," Ravi replied.

"Looks to be early thirties. Perfect candidate," Laurent added as he briefly pulled the mask away from her face.

"Praise be to God," Ravi whispered.

Kishan leaned in toward the boxes he crouched behind and craned his neck to get the best view possible. He watched as Laurent fully pulled back the top sheet to reveal the woman in a hospital gown, her chest heaving slowly up and down with each breath. Otherwise, she was motionless. Laurent pulled her gown above her waist.

"Help me move her down toward this end of the gurney," he said to the orderlies. Within a few seconds, they had slid her carefully into place toward the end of the bed. Her calves now dangled off the edge. Laurent pulled his surgical mask into place.

"What I would give to get myself a piece of this," the strange man gurgled into the machine he held. He stepped forward, tucked the microphone under his arm, and started to stroke the woman's upper thigh with his free hand.

"Get your filthy hands off her, you pig!" Ravi shouted as he grabbed the man by the wrist and pulled him away from the woman.

Laurent was also not amused, and his face clearly showed it. "I'd like both of you to step back," he said. He then nodded to the two orderlies. He sat down on the small stool in front of the bed and placed himself between her legs. "Someone mark the time, please."

Kishan looked on in amazement.

"Careful," Ravi warned. "There's no more where that came from."

"Here we go," Laurent said.

"This is the day which the Lord hath made," Ravi proclaimed.

"Very simple. There we go," Laurent said.

"Rejoice and be glad in it," Ravi called out.

"There. It is done," Laurent said calmly.

Amazed at what he had seen, Kishan slumped to the floor behind the towers of boxes. The action dislodged his cell phone from the holster on his belt as his back slid against the wall behind him. By the time he caught sight of the phone falling to the ground, it was too late. He swept his hand to catch the phone, but he missed. The sound it made when it hit the floor was not loud by any means. But to Kishan, it might as well have been an atomic bomb.

They were on him in an instant.

CHAPTER 35

Mumbai, India
August 2014

There was only one thing Kishan was afraid of more than his father when he was angry, and it was heights. Which is why he was frantic when Ravi dragged him by the nape of his neck to the rooftop of Sehgal Labs. Granted, it was deserted and far from where other employees might eavesdrop. That would save him some embarrassment. But it was six stories up, and it was the dizziness as much as the anticipation of his father's likely tirade that set his head spinning. Ravi had forgiven Kishan's mistakes before, but he knew this time he was in deep trouble. But given what he had just witnessed in the warehouse below, his father had some explaining of his own to do as well.

Kishan had never seen his father so furious. The moment they exited the stairwell, Ravi shoved him from behind and knocked him to the sea of gravel on the roof that had been baking in the blistering afternoon sun. Kishan scrambled to his feet as quickly as he could, only to be knocked back down again with a powerful shove that sent him stumbling backward toward the edge of the roof.

"You're insane, old man," Kishan shouted. "Are you trying to push me off?"

"That's exactly what I ought to do, you hoodlum," Ravi shouted back. His face was contorted with rage, unlike anything Kishan had seen before. His father bent down, scooped up a handful of the hot stones, and flung them at his son as hard as he could. Most of them missed the mark, but several showered against Kishan's bare legs, causing him to dance in pain.

"What did you want me to do?" Kishan cried as he tried to stand his ground and not back any closer to the roof's edge. He felt faint from the emotions of the moment and the stifling heat, which had topped 112 degrees. "There's been something wrong with you since you won that stupid prize," he said. "It's gone to your head."

"Something wrong with *me*?" Ravi said. "Who's the one unable to mind his own business? I begged you to stay out of the warehouse."

"What did you expect? You're hiding things and going plain mad, and you want me to look the other way?"

"There's nothing mad about what you just saw down there," Ravi said. "There's a good reason for it, but you're in no position to understand."

"I'm not just talking about whatever you were doing with that woman downstairs," Kishan said. "That's just the latest. I'm talking about the lies."

"I have never lied to you, Kishan. Never," Ravi said as he stepped closer to him and rested his hand on his shoulder as if to invite some calm between them.

Kishan shrugged him off and stepped dangerously backward another couple of feet.

"Maybe not to me," Kishan said. "I don't know. But tell that to your friend, that Dr. Bondurant, and everybody else you've tricked with that ridiculous story about goat's blood."

Ravi angrily kicked a small pile of pebbles off the roof.

"Enough!" he shouted. "I won't have a lazy orphan—one I took in, mind you—who doesn't know what he's talking about questioning my motives or the quality of my work."

"Is that right?" Kishan shot back, hurt. "Changed your password lately? It doesn't take a Nobel Prize to know goat's blood from human blood. But what do I know? I'm just a lazy orphan."

Kishan could see Ravi was in anguish over the insults they'd both regret.

"My beautiful son, listen to me. I love you," Ravi said. "I always will. But there are reasons for these things you've seen that are beyond your ability to understand. You have to trust me that there is good behind all this. What I have learned in the quest for that prize will bring blessings upon all of the earth's unfortunates." Ravi tried again to rest his hand on his son's shoulder, but Kishan rebuffed him once more. Kishan was hurt and angry and could feel tears beginning to well up in his eyes.

He focused on the horizon of central Mumbai. He couldn't look his father in the face. He had never felt both so close to and so far from his father. He wanted to believe him. He suddenly wanted *not* to know what he knew. He wanted it to be easy and to go back to the way things were. But of all the things he had seen or heard in the last few weeks, it was the photos he could not forget. The strange and horrid pictures of the poor children in his father's secret closet had haunted him for days. He needed to know who they were.

"Why am I not on that wall?" Kishan asked as he wiped tears

from his face and gathered the courage to look at Ravi again. "Why not me?"

"What do you mean, Kishan?"

"I want to know why I was saved, and not the others." He leaned into his father like a child seeking a hug, and Ravi embraced him. They held each other for several seconds.

"The others?" Ravi asked.

"On the wall. The pictures on your wall. I go to bed at night and I see my face in every one of them."

"What are you talking about, Kishan?"

"The room in your office," he said with surprising calm. "Where you keep the pictures. The dead children. And that gun. I don't know why—"

Ravi exploded away from their embrace and shoved Kishan backward once again, pushing him now perilously close to the edge of the roof. As Kishan stumbled and fell to his knees, he grabbed Ravi's legs and drove forward. The edge of the roof was now just inches away.

Knocked flat on his back, Ravi started to wrestle with him but, disoriented, rolled with his son across the painful gravel even closer to the roof's edge. Less than a foot from tragedy, they exchanged one exhausted, useless punch after another.

Soon Kishan knew his strength was spent. He covered his face with his hands and curled into a fetal position, just wanting the fight to end. His head hung slightly off the edge of the roof, facedown, and all he could see was the sickening sight of the parking lot that waited to greet him below.

"You idiot. I told you, didn't I?" Ravi shouted between gasps. He threw another punch. "I told you to stay out of that room."

Kishan continued to cover his face and lay motionless in fear.

"What are you planning to do now?" Kishan asked.

"What I am going to do, *dawg*," Ravi said, nearly breathless, "is save the children. More children like you. Countless more like you. That is, if you will just mind your own business and let me."

Kishan could tell Ravi too was exhausted, as his blows had no force when they struck.

"What I am going to do, dawg," Ravi said wearily, "is fulfill the promise I made to my father. I want to try to help this miserable world through the birth of the Christ Child. That is all. I just mean to do good."

Kishan heard his father sob with every useless punch. Finally, Ravi was completely exhausted. Kishan watched from the corner of his eye as Ravi relented and slowly crouched down next to him. He could feel his father gently run his fingers through his hair, as if to soothe him.

"Kishan, my son—"

But it was too late. Kishan knew he would never find another moment to free himself. He summoned all of his energy and bolted upright to distance himself from both his father's touch and the roof's edge. He scrambled across the loose gravel as fast as he could toward the stairwell door only ten yards away. Mid-stride, he stopped only once to look behind him to catch a final glimpse of an empty man, the father he would never see again.

CHAPTER 36

India
August 2014

"Y ou know," Bondurant said, "if I didn't know any better, I'd think I was being played for a fool."

"I think if you knew any better, you would duck your head. And very quickly!"

Bondurant spun around abruptly in the near darkness to see the oncoming tunnel and ducked his head in less than a second. The ceiling of the tunnel missed decapitating him by a few inches. Had his newfound companion been less familiar with the ninety-two tunnels passed through by the Mandovi Express train from Madgaon to Mumbai, Bondurant was sure to have met his demise many miles before. Many flights to Mumbai from the southern end of the country, including Bondurant's, had been scrapped for "software performance" issues, as best he could tell. So Bondurant found himself headed by rail toward the massive city where it was possible that either Domenika or Sehgal, or both, could be found.

His acquaintance of several hours, Samar Chandrasekar, had

chosen to ride on the roof of the northbound express for the same reasons as Bondurant and dozens of others on their way to Mumbai. There were no empty seats onboard below, and not a square inch was left to stand in the passageways of the entire train. That, and the slight breeze outside on the roof of the train, made the fifteen-hour ride a tolerable 10 degrees cooler than the 100 degrees that threatened to bake the train's passengers inside. Within the steamy cars, a crush of humanity, along with an assortment of colorful belongings from a baby lamb to crates of watermelons on ice, simply tried to survive through the heat of the early evening.

"Thank you, Samar," Bondurant said.

"You are most welcome. The next tunnel is several minutes from here."

Samar Chandrasekar, a stranger to Bondurant, seemed to possess an encyclopedic knowledge of every tunnel and obstacle on the long, twelve-mile-per-hour run from Madgaon to Mumbai. He also spoke excellent English and, as far as Bondurant could tell, had a sympathetic ear. Beyond these useful attributes, Bondurant could tell Samar was just plain good company on what he hoped was not a wild-goose chase launched by the flight itinerary they'd found in Domenika's apartment in Rome two days before.

While finding Domenika was Bondurant's goal, he'd also determined that he was in a race against time to find Sehgal as well. It was time to secure the full truth, and perhaps rescue his own reputation. To be sure, Bondurant's report—though leaked as opposed to officially released—had debunked the myth of the Shroud. Bondurant's reputation as one of the most daring and successful forensic anthropologists in the world was more than intact. Professionally, while the Catholic Church was in an uproar, he had succeeded beyond his wildest dreams.

Yet something very fundamental about Sehgal's findings concerning the famous Shroud study didn't sit right with Bondurant. And the feeling would not only not leave him alone—it had in fact grown stronger the more time passed.

His doubts had begun on the early June morning several months before when he'd had to play referee between Sehgal and O'Neil about splitting the samples from the Shroud. Bondurant *knew* Sehgal had been less than honest about why he needed all the blood they'd collected during the study. His fears that something was amiss grew fast after the findings were leaked. Some of Domenika's last words to him in her fit of rage were about the "solid evidence" she had that Sehgal was wrong. If Sehgal had evidence contrary to what he'd reported to the rest of the team, something that would fundamentally alter important results, then it was critical to make that information public immediately. No scientist of any merit would knowingly allow false information on controversial research to stand, and it was Bondurant's obligation to ensure that his report was beyond reproach.

As to Sehgal's whereabouts in Mumbai, Bondurant had the address: Sehgal Labs, 22484 Lady Jamshetjee Road, Mumbai. He'd been there once before, when he'd traveled to India to press Sehgal to join his team. This time he had no invitation from Sehgal to visit, nor did he feel that he needed one. Sehgal, like Domenika, had been radio silent since the Shroud report had first leaked. He was nowhere to be found. Bondurant had tried to reach him by phone, e-mail, and text to help manage the fallout from the report, but he'd had no luck.

"Duck again, good doctor," Chandrasekar said as the next tunnel approached.

Bondurant ducked his head quickly and held it there until they were through the short tunnel and the night sky became visible again.

Stars had begun to emerge on the dark-blue horizon ahead of them. Bondurant looked around at the darkness that had befallen them. His eyelids were heavy. He yearned for the comfort of sleep. But he knew the journey forward would require real vigilance. He rested his head atop his suitcase and reflected on what he saw in the vague outline of a wooden bridge they had started to cross. From where Bondurant sat, the rickety bridge looked to be just part of a long and treacherous journey that might involve many steep and dangerous ravines ahead.

When Bondurant awoke atop the Mandovi Express, his companion was gone. So too were the many others who had made their way off the top of the train. He'd been left with a gift from the friendly stranger, a small bag of fruit at his side. The brightest light on the concrete platform that seemed to stretch for an eternity announced clearly where he was: "Mumbai Central," it read.

It was nine o'clock in the evening, too late to try to locate Sehgal at his offices, which Bondurant figured were long closed for the day. He grabbed a cab and asked that it take him to a decent hotel as near as possible to the Special Economic Zone, where he knew Sehgal's headquarters were located. Twenty minutes later, as his cab rolled down Sant Savtamali Road toward a Holiday Inn three miles farther down the road, Bondurant spied a modern, six-story building across the highway ahead, still fully lit under the night sky. It looked familiar. It wasn't until they had pulled parallel to the building that Bondurant could clearly make out the electronic sign that adorned the building's top floor—"Sehgal Labs."

"Working this late?" Bondurant asked.

"Pardon me?" the cabbie said.

"Oh, nothing. Just an observation," Bondurant said. "I'll tell you what. How about if we make a U-turn and head toward the parking lot of that building on our right," he said.

"Most gladly, sir," the cabbie said. "Dr. Sehgal, a name to be praised. He is our hero here. A thousand blessings on his name."

"Yes, yes," Bondurant said. "You mean for the honor of the Nobel Prize, I'm sure."

"Of course, yes," the cabbie said as he strained somewhat with his steering wheel to execute a full U-turn. His cab sputtered back into gear and pulled forward as soon as they were on a straight line again. "He has brought great honor to India. Great honor to Mumbai. Great honor to our people."

"He certainly has," Bondurant replied. "Now if my friend would just simply answer his phone or reply with a text, he'd be my hero too."

"You know this man, Dr. Ravi Sehgal?" the cabbie asked as he coaxed his cab into the lab's parking lot and brought it to a stop. "Praise to your name too, sir."

Bondurant leaned out of his window and surveyed all the floors. While nearly every light in the building was on, illuminating every room, it was the sixth floor where he could see there was clear activity. Given that the windows were masked by lightly shaded screens, it was difficult to count the number of people in the conference room, much less make out the identity of each person Bondurant watched from down below. But there was no doubt in Bondurant's mind he had unexpectedly stumbled across an important late-night meeting that might prove helpful in his quest to track down Sehgal. However, he was going to need his cabbie's help.

"How would you like to make an additional thousand rupees tonight?" Bondurant asked of him.

"I would like that very much."

"Okay, then. I need you to be my observer," Bondurant said. "I am going to push the call button here at the front door. I can't see our friends on the top floor of this building, but you can from over there. I need you to call out to me what's happening as I talk to my friends inside. Can you do that?"

"With a thousand rupees in hand, I would be delighted to do this," the cabbie said.

Bondurant paid the fee.

"Now remember, I need you shouting out exactly what you see for me. Is that understood?"

"Perfectly." The cabbie stood less than two feet from Bondurant at the moment but shouted out at the top of his lungs: "THERE ARE SIX, NO, SEVEN PEOPLE IN A CONFERENCE ROOM ON THE SIXTH FLOOR."

Bondurant stood, shocked for a moment as to how many decibels his partner could reach.

"I think that will do it," Bondurant said, his ear aching slightly. He jogged the twenty feet or so to the call button at the front entrance to the lab.

"Okay," Bondurant said. "I'm pressing the call button. What do you see?"

"I SEE TWO, MAYBE THREE PEOPLE REACHING FOR THE PHONE ON THE CONFERENCE ROOM TABLE!"

"Thank you," Bondurant said. He could hear a phone ringing several times. Then someone answered the phone.

"Good evening, Sehgal Labs. I presume you're calling from downstairs. We are closed for the evening. How can I help you?"

"ONE OF THEM, THE FAT LITTLE ONE, HAS ANSWERED THE PHONE!"

"Thank you," Bondurant said. "I realize you're closed. But I am trying to reach someone, and it's very important."

"Yes, and who would that be?" the voice on the other end of the line said.

"Dr. Ravi Sehgal," Bondurant said.

"And may I ask who's here for Dr. Sehgal?"

"This is Dr. Jon Bondurant. I've been trying to reach him for some time."

"EVERYONE HAS STOPPED MOVING ABOUT. THEY LOOK LIKE FROZEN PEOPLE!"

"Excuse me, can I have that name again?" the voice from the sixth floor said.

"Dr. Jon Bondurant. I'm just downstairs. I've come all the way from Rome to see him."

"I see. Please hold for just a moment," the voice said.

"ALL THE LIGHTS ON THE SIXTH FLOOR JUST WENT DARK. THEY LOOK LIKE SHADOW PUPPETS!" the cabbie called out.

"I'm sorry, Dr. Bondurant, but Dr. Sehgal is out of the country right now. We're so sorry you've missed him."

"ONE OF THE SHADOW PUPPETS IS RUNNING OUT OF THE ROOM VERY QUICKLY!"

"I see," said Bondurant. "Do you know when Dr. Sehgal will be returning to India?"

"I'm sorry, I don't have that information," the voice said. "We are closed for the evening."

"ALL OF THE LIGHTS IN THE ENTIRE BUILDING ARE GOING OUT, AND THE SHADOW PUPPETS ARE GONE!"

"If I could just leave a message," Bondurant said. "I'd like to—" But the line was disconnected.

"I HEAR A CAR STARTING UP!" the cabbie yelled.

It was evident from the car doors slamming and the shouts from

the garage that a car was about to emerge from down below. Bondurant raced from the front door of the building over to his cab.

"I'M BETTING E-CLASS MERCEDES," the cabbie cried out.

As if on cue, a large, black E-class Mercedes came roaring up the
garage ramp, sending itself airborne for twenty feet as it accelerated
past within a few yards of them both.

"Great work! All right now, follow that car," Bondurant yelled as
he jumped into the front seat of the cab.

As they lurched from the parking lot and out into the street, Bondurant sensed quickly that something was wrong. The red taillights
of the Mercedes had begun to shrink into tiny dots on the road out
ahead.

"MY CAR WILL NOT GO FASTER THAN THIRTY! MY
CAR WILL NOT GO FASTER THAN THIRTY!" the cabbie
shouted. His car whined terribly loudly, as though it wanted to make
chase but its wheels would sadly not comply.

Bondurant could only place his face in his hands. He knew he'd
likely lost Sehgal for more than one night. He might have lost him
for good. He reached out to console the cabbie, who was clearly upset
that his cab was not up to the chase.

"Don't trouble yourself. We'll be back," Bondurant said. "For now,
let's give your hero his honor and his due."

CHAPTER 37

St. Michaels, Maryland
February 2015

Bondurant was not one to give up easily, but he knew he had hit a dead end. It was late winter, and in the months that had passed since his trip to India he hadn't turned up a clue of either Domenika or Sehgal, beyond the slip Sehgal had pulled late that night. He'd lost count of the number of leads he had chased in his effort to track down Domenika. His leave of absence from the Institute was over, and the quest to find her had become a frustrating full-time job.

She had simply vanished. Her fate remained a mystery to the police in Rome, who'd found no trace of her there or anywhere else in Italy. Bondurant worked with her sister, Joanna, to place Domenika on Interpol's missing persons list. It ensured that her profile went to every major law-enforcement organization in over 150 countries. But not a single sighting of her had occurred since she'd gone missing almost seven months before. One of the organizations he contacted to help during a trip to Geneva was the International Committee of the Red Cross. They had tried to find her through their global locator service, but it turned up nothing as well.

He turned to social media and created a Facebook page, "Finding Domenika," where he posted photos of her and encouraged the site's visitors to help in his search. The mystery of the beautiful missing woman caught the imagination of thousands, who posted to his board. More than ten thousand "friends" from San Francisco to Cairo "liked" the page, but their comments proved worthless.

His most promising trail from the start, but one that had grown cold quickly, was the airline manifest Domenika's sister had discovered in her apartment late the previous summer. It had taken weeks for Interpol to confirm that she had actually boarded Jetstar Asia Flight 1009 to Chhatrapati Shivaji International Airport in Mumbai. Indian immigration authorities had confirmed that she had entered the country under a tourist visa, but there was not a trace of her to be found. Even though Mumbai was a city of more than thirteen million people, he was convinced she'd stand out, given her striking European features. But Mumbai's police force, with more than forty thousand cops, could find no trace of her. They had checked every hotel, hospital, and morgue in the city, but she was not to be found. They stressed to Bondurant after his journey to India that she had only *landed* in Mumbai. India was a large country, with more than a billion people. He might search for a lifetime and find nothing, they warned.

Then, late one February evening, as Bondurant was in his office skimming recent worthless posts on the "Finding Domenika" page, he decided it was time to shut it down. It had been a long-shot idea from the start, and the vast majority of messages posted to the site had been useless, some even frightening. Most who had seen the handful of photos of Domenika were men who just wanted to meet her if she could be found. Beyond the lonely hearts, most of the other messages posted were from those who sent photos and facts of their own about loved ones for whom they too were searching. He found the whole process pitiful and exhausting.

But just as he prepared to shut down the site at the Institute that evening, a strange message arrived. It was from *"ibcnudawg,"* an odd username Bondurant had never seen before. The text box was empty, but in the subject line was a question in bold:

WHEN IS A GOAT NOT A GOAT?

It was the reference to the word "goat" that forced Bondurant to hesitate before he deleted it as spam. Bondurant quickly typed a response:

I GIVE. WHEN IS A GOAT NOT A GOAT?

He expected no reply, but one arrived within seconds:

WHEN IT BLEEDS ON A SHROUD.
CALL ME + 91 22 226 20735.

Bondurant had seen a lot of strange messages on his board, but this one had his undivided attention. He quickly typed the international area code "91 22" into his search bar to find the country of origin for the phone number posted.

MUMBAI, CENTRAL.

Bondurant's heart skipped a beat. He immediately grabbed the phone on his desk to dial the number. The full seven rings that passed before someone finally answered seemed endless.

"What's up, my brother?" the male voice casually answered.

"Excuse me?" Bondurant said, taken aback by the greeting.

"I said, what's up, brother?" the voice repeated.

"I'm sorry. I must have dialed the wrong number. I apologize," Bondurant said, agitated. He began to put down the receiver. He had better things to do than deal with pranks.

"This is no wrong number, my man," came the response. "What's up?"

"Who is this?" Bondurant pressed.

There was an ominous tone in the other man's voice. "Can't tell you that, Doc. But I can tell you this. There's been some things going on here for months you need to know about. And here's another thing. This one's gonna make you wet your pants. You got that?"

"Go ahead," Bondurant said as he laid his tired head on his desk and pressed the button for his speakerphone. "What have I got to lose?"

"Just your reputation, Doc," the voice said confidently.

"What do you mean by that? Who is this?"

"Like I said, Doc, can't tell you that. Hold on. I just hit Send."

Bondurant raised his head off his desk and watched his e-mail inbox intently. Within a few seconds, a new message popped up.

"Okay, I've got it," Bondurant said. He rubbed his eyes and started to stare at the screen.

"Open the first attachment, my man," the voice on the other end of the line said.

"Okay, I'm looking at it. It looks like . . . like a—"

"A DNA composite, Doc. No doubt, my man, you read these in your sleep. But let me break it down for you. What you're looking at is DNA, male, Mediterranean origin. About two thousand years old, more or less."

"Yeah, so what?" Bondurant said. He wondered where the mystery man was headed and whether it was worth staying on the line a few seconds more to humor him. "What makes this sample so special, and where did you get it?"

"Can't tell you that, Doc. Don't work there no more. Lost my job. But let me tell you this, my brother: I have my sources. Now listen up. It's a *human* DNA profile all right, but with an anomaly I've never seen before, and I've seen 'em all. You with me?"

"Yes, I see it. I see what you mean," Bondurant said. It was a human profile, but there was something unusual about the array. "What's this got to do with me? I've got lab assistants who can help you with this during office hours."

"Well, now you ready for da B-O-M-B?" the man whispered.

"Bomb away," Bondurant said. The man's approach was driving him nuts.

"*It is the DNA—the human DNA—hot off your Shroud,*" the man said.

"*This,*" Bondurant said as he raised his head off the desk in anger to mimic the man's slang, "is where *you're* full of it."

"Thought you'd say that, my man," the man said confidently. "And that's why I'm sending you this!"

"And what's this?" Bondurant asked, clearly miffed.

"It's the next attachment you open on your screen, arriving right . . ."

"Now," Bondurant said. "I got it. Wait a second," Bondurant said as he double-clicked on it to reveal an entirely new and different DNA array than the one that had been sent to him only seconds before.

"Okay. So humor me: What's this?" Bondurant asked as he stared at the second DNA profile chart, radically different from the first.

"BAAAA. That's a goat," the voice whispered.

"So what are you saying?" Bondurant asked, growing a little more nervous but intent on playing the mystery through.

"I'm saying I have the evidence, my man. It's goat DNA, but not off your Shroud. There's no goat's blood on that Shroud. I'm a fool for not finding you to tell you this months ago, Doc, and you're a fool all this time for telling the world a lie. That Shroud's no fake, Doc. It's you that's been had, my man."

"This is insane," Bondurant said.

"Woahawhooooeeee," the strange voice said. "That's the boogey-man, and he's telling you there *ain't no goat's blood on that Shroud*," he whispered, even lower.

"Uh-huh," Bondurant said warily, ready to end the call. "I think I'm being had right now."

"Yeah, I figured you'd say that, Doc. Don't believe me. So let me ask you one more question. What's that say at the bottom of both these charts in my possession? Why don't you read it for me, my brother?"

Bondurant scanned to the bottom of the attachments. He stared at the identical watermarks on both slides, and what they displayed started to make him feel ill:

PROPERTY OF SEHGAL LABORATORIES, MUMBAI, INDIA.

"Who is this, and where did you get these?" Bondurant demanded, now concerned that the documents might actually be authentic. He reached for the wastebasket, worried he was about to get sick. If what the man implied was true, there would be extraordinary consequences.

"Can't tell you that, Doc. Don't want no trouble. Don't want no medal. This has been bothering me for too long. I want the truth, and

I want it out. Like Dr. King said, 'The truth shall set you free,'" the voice declared.

"That's the Bible, from John," Bondurant corrected him. His stomach churned again as he stared at the DNA charts in disbelief. The chart labeled "Shroud" was dated June 20 of the previous year, the exact time of his investigation in Turin.

"Okay, then, my man," the voice said. "Like Spike Lee said, 'Do the right thing.' Now I *know* that's Spike Lee, and I *know* that's what I'm doing."

"And what's the right thing?" Bondurant asked. He fixed his gaze on the contrasting DNA profiles. They could not be mistaken for each other. He still couldn't believe what was right before his eyes.

"Tell the world. Tell the world, my man. You have to set the record straight. And you or somebody needs to get over here before it's too late," the man on the other end of the line pleaded. Bondurant could tell the desperation in the voice was real.

"Too late for what?" Bondurant asked.

"Too late to stop this, man! To stop whatever they got going on with this woman they're experimenting with. Man, who knows what happened to her!" he said.

"You're losing me. What are you talking about?"

"I'm talking about this Darth Vader dude with the tube in his neck. I'm talking about that crazy Frenchman," the voice whimpered. "I got to go, my man."

"Wait a minute. What woman? Did you say Frenchman?" Bondurant shouted into the phone.

The line went dead before he could get a response, but there was no dial tone, so he could tell a line was still open. Someone else had been monitoring the call.

"Hello? Hello? Did you say Frenchman? Did you say Frenchman?" Bondurant shouted into the receiver once more.

Then he heard another click, followed by the dial tone a few seconds later, a sure sign the other man's phone was tapped. He didn't move for a few seconds, trying to take in the implications of what the strange voice had said. And then Bondurant vomited every bit of his dinner directly into the trash can he'd shoved between his knees.

When he looked up from the mess, one of his research assistants stood at his office door and grimaced. He reluctantly held out a pink message slip.

"Pardon me, Dr. Bondurant," the intern choked out. A sickened look stretched across his face. "There's a Dr. Terry O'Neil from Oxford on the line."

"I'm a little busy, Bill," Bondurant groaned. "Can you tell him I'll call him back?"

"Doctor," the assistant insisted apologetically. He held out the note but turned his head away from the putrid scene so that he could continue. "He says it's a matter of life and death."

CHAPTER 38

Oxford, England
March 2015

Bondurant tossed the chart onto the table between them and quietly stared out of O'Neil's stately, oak-paneled office at the scene outside. The spires of Christ Church at Oxford were barely visible across the lush, green lawn. Spring was near. A fog had begun to creep in with the drizzle that had arrived earlier that morning. It was a gray afternoon, and like Bondurant's mood, there were no signs of improvement on the horizon. A small but inviting fire burned in the fireplace, popping and crackling a few feet from where they sat. Bondurant broke the uncomfortable silence between them.

"Terry, how long have I known you? Fifteen years?" he asked. "And all that time, I thought I could trust you."

"Maybe you have a problem with trust, Jon," O'Neil snapped back. "You trust the wrong people. I'm not your problem. If I was, I would never have called you."

"Like I wasn't supposed to trust Ravi?" Bondurant said defensively. "When's the last time you didn't trust a Nobel Prize winner?"

"Now, see? There's your problem. Just because a guy wins an award, you think he walks on water."

"An award? Are you kidding me? We're talking about *the Nobel*."

"Nobel, Schnobel!" O'Neil said sarcastically. He prostrated himself before Bondurant as if in worship. "Who cares, Jon? It's just a bunch of old farts in Norway who lock themselves in a room until they think they've found someone whose excrement doesn't stink. Who cares?"

Bondurant had been angry with O'Neil for a couple of days and hadn't been able to shake it. His head had been spinning ever since O'Neil's phone call to confess what he had found out about the Shroud. O'Neil, who had argued loudly during their previous summer experiments that he required *four* samples to achieve the carbon dating accuracy Bondurant demanded, had been less than truthful from the start. He had needed only three. And, in fact, he had *used* only three. What he had done secretly with the fourth sample—the one with precious blood from the Shroud on it—had produced the stunning evidence on the chart that sat on the table between them.

"Okay," Bondurant said, resigned to putting his anger behind for the moment, "so, let's go through this again. What gave you the idea to test the fourth sample for DNA?"

"I never trusted Ravi from the start, Jon. I can't tell you exactly why. I just didn't. You didn't either. Maybe it was all the hype I was reading after he won the prize—how he was going to save the world and all that. Like he was some sort of Messiah. We had two drops of blood from the Shroud between us, and there was no way I was going to let him get them both."

"That's why you insisted on four for your own tests?"

"Yes, but just after Turin, after our videoconference call when Ravi started babbling about goat blood and all that, I went off the grid for that Tutankhamun project I've been working on," O'Neil said. "A couple of hundred miles outside of Cairo, two camels, and no working sat phone. I forgot about it all for a while. We were busy."

"Right. Then what?"

"Last week we had a couple that made their way out from Cambridge with a sat phone that worked. I got ahold of Serge at my lab and had him run a DNA test on the fourth sample immediately. As soon as I got the results, I came home and called you."

"I see."

"Truth be known, Jon, I could have dated the Shroud with two. But three was for good measure, to keep in my hip pocket in case the results were ever questioned. The fourth, the one with blood, well, like I said on the phone. Here are the results. You can read them for yourself."

They both stared down at the DNA results O'Neil had received from the Molecular Anthropology Laboratory at Oxford, one of the most prestigious DNA labs in the world. As he had told Bondurant on the phone, O'Neil had asked the lab to give him a complete genetic breakdown of the blood found on the fourth sample he had secretly kept. Unfortunately for Bondurant, O'Neil's curiosity hadn't peaked until it was too late. Based on Sehgal's evidence, Bondurant had already issued the final report proclaiming to the world that the Shroud was a fake. The chart they were looking at was the same one O'Neil had sent Bondurant after their call earlier that week.

"So, as I told you a few days ago," O'Neil said, "I've had three scientists study this blood DNA profile, each independent of the others. All of them are eminent in their field here at Oxford, and all used the same technique as Sehgal. And not one, not a one, mind you, will tell you the source of this blood was a goat. They report an anomaly in the human DNA they've never seen before. But they know for sure Ravi is not to be trusted on this."

"Thank you, Terry," Bondurant said sarcastically as he flicked his cigarette butt into the fireplace. "Now tell me something I don't know."

"You still haven't told me how you'd already come to this conclusion when we talked earlier," O'Neil said. "You ruined my surprise."

"Coincidence. I don't know. But right before you reached me, I was on the phone with the strangest of characters who called about the same thing," Bondurant said.

"Who? Great minds think alike," O'Neil said.

"I don't know. He wouldn't say. But this 'great mind' was a nervous wreck. He said his conscience was bothering him. That he had to get the truth out. I'm sure he had to be someone at Ravi's lab. Someone close to him. He sent me Ravi's DNA composites. Anyway, I didn't know what to make of it. I didn't know whether to believe him, and then you called with the same news."

Bondurant took a deep breath to compose himself.

"Okay, listen. This is not about you. It's not about me. I will eat all the crow one man can eat for publishing the wrong conclusion when the time comes. I'm going to have to retract our report entirely. Somebody's going to sue, probably the Church. People will be burning our report, and they should."

"You're right."

"Terry, I'm going to have to rethink a lot of things, not the least of which is that the Church has been right all along. I can't believe I am saying this, but *this Shroud is real!*"

Bondurant lowered his head. For the first time in his career, he felt helpless and cornered. A lifetime of stoic disbelief in faith and spirituality had suddenly burst with the realization he might have been wrong about a lot of things. Was Domenika somehow right? Was there some dimension beyond the reach of science, a place he'd refused to admit existed, one would call divine?

O'Neil got up from the table and poured them each a scotch from the decanter on the sideboard next to them.

"Jon," he said as he pushed a full tumbler in front of him, "every once in a while, there are things that happen in this world beyond our comprehension. Maybe this is just one of them."

"Now you're channeling Domenika," Bondurant said, his voice hoarse. "That's exactly what she would say."

"Lovely girl, Jon. Whatever happened to her?"

Bondurant turned toward the window again. "I don't know. If it's a rock, I've looked under it," he said. He could hear the exhaustion in his own voice.

The two of them stared into the glow of the fireplace and sat quietly nursing their drinks until Bondurant broke the silence.

"Listen, Terry," he said. He grew more animated. "There's another problem. And I'm not sure what to make of it." He pulled another chart from his valise and slid it across the table toward O'Neil.

"What have we here?" O'Neil asked curiously.

"It's Ravi's *real* results. It's the true results he got off the Shroud. It was sent to me last week by the fellow at his labs. Take a close look at it."

O'Neil put on his glasses and placed the chart side by side with his own, the one produced in Oxford's labs. He examined the two carefully for over a minute. The longer he stared, the more puzzled he appeared. He reversed their order on the table. He held them together, one on top of the other, in the light streaming in from the window to discern their differences. He looked at Bondurant, confused.

"The two bear no resemblance to each other. Not even close," he said. "What's the joke?"

"Terry, I've been asking myself that same question since you sent me your copy of the DNA results following our call."

"What the devil?" O'Neil said, bemused.

Bondurant pushed the two charts back together, side by side. "Are you absolutely certain the blood sample you tested here at Oxford was one and the same as what came off the Shroud? Are you totally positive?"

"I'd stake my life on it, Jon," O'Neil said solemnly.

"Then," Bondurant said as he quickly downed the rest of his scotch, "the results prove it. There's no match in the DNA composites here. There are *two* different sources of blood on the Shroud of Jesus. Unrelated. Do you get me, Terry? *Unrelated.* And believe me, neither are from a goat."

"But that's not possible."

"I am beginning to believe that anything is possible," Bondurant said as he gathered his papers and got up to leave. "What did you do with any remaining blood sample from the material you had, Terry?"

"I destroyed it, of course. The last thing I wanted was to turn my labs into some kind of tourist trap if people learned it was here."

"Great. You did the right thing. Unfortunately, I don't think I can say the same for Sehgal," Bondurant said as he grabbed his jacket and made his way to the door. "It's all come together," Bondurant said. "He's put his expertise to work. He saved some of his blood sample for another purpose. His higher calling, you might say."

"Jon, where in God's name are you going?" O'Neil called out.

"In God's name? To India, Terry. Back to India."

CHAPTER 39

Mumbai, India
March 2015

Kishan squeezed the brake handle and gunned the throttle of his Vespa at the traffic light on Mutton Street, the busy avenue that sliced like a jagged knife-edge through the markets along the Colaba Causeway in Mumbai. The bike let out a thin plume of white smoke and a groaning, choking sound, as if to ask for mercy from the strain he placed on the motor.

Her name was Chanda. He wanted to impress her. She had given him a strange look when he handed her a helmet at the front door of her family's upscale home, expecting him to arrive for their first date in a car. He had been saving to buy one for years, but he still needed a new job first, and it would be many more paychecks before a car was a possibility.

On this warm evening, Kishan had her right where he wanted her. She sat close behind him on his scooter, her arms wrapped tight around his waist, just as he had fantasized from the first time he had seen her. After months of circling and stalling, he had finally summoned the courage to approach her at her parents' restaurant where she worked, down the street from his apartment. He'd hesitated about asking her out for a long time. She was show-stoppingly cute, with wide, intense eyes and long, lustrous hair always pulled back in a ponytail, and he'd had to work up the courage to meet her. But she'd said yes, and now they were off to explore the ancient "thieves' market" of Chor Bazaar, dotted with shops and cafés strewn along the narrow lanes like pearls on a thousand strands. He smiled from ear to ear. The warmth from her body penetrated the back of his jacket, and he swore to himself he had never been with a prettier girl.

As he edged his way through the halting traffic and into the bustling intersection ahead, he found it gridlocked. He stopped, hung his arms at his side in frustration, and looked into his side-view mirrors to scan the scene behind them. Then he saw something unusual. Pressing through the traffic behind him, creeping slowly about a hundred feet back, was what looked to be an entourage that consisted of two dark, gleaming Land Rovers surrounded by a pack of matching motorcycles. The riders were all wearing identical black uniforms. The small motorcade's attempt to force others aside to part the sea of traffic had created a cacophony of horns and shouts loud enough to rise above the noise of the already-chaotic bazaar.

Who was in the expensive cars close at his rear? Kishan stared intently into his mirror to get a glimpse of the VIPs. But the windshields of the trucks were tinted so that it was impossible to see inside. As the Land Rovers moved within ten feet of his rear, the motorcycle escorts, all of whose jackets bore an odd insignia he had never seen before, pulled forward like a swarm of wasps and encircled his bike. He tried to give them room and slowly inched his scooter along the line of parked cars against the crowded sidewalk to clear a path for them. One of the escorts, who wore a red knit mask under his open-faced helmet like the others, inserted his own bike between Kishan's and the parked cars, which prevented him from edging further away. The shiny bikes that crowded his tiny scooter revved their engines in a thunderous roar. It was impossible to hear anything else above them.

As he looked to his left to press for an escape route, he saw it was too late. The Land Rover in front pulled directly beside him and stopped. The rear window of the car glided down and revealed the profiles of two men obscured in the darkness of the interior. Over the din of the screaming engines, he could barely hear a single voice call out.

"Drop the bike and the girl, and get in the car," it commanded.

Kishan's date began to squeeze his shoulders with a grip that signaled real fear. He thought the voice from inside the car sounded faintly familiar, but the roar that surrounded them was so loud he couldn't be sure. *Whoever these people are, it must be a mistake*, he thought. He found a small opening in front of him behind the car and surged his bike forward several feet to get out of the Land Rover's line of sight. He didn't want any trouble. But the truck found a similar opening beside him and followed suit. The voice from inside the car called out again, this time with more urgency.

"I said drop the bike and lose the girl, Kishan," the voice demanded. "I'm not going to ask again."

The moment he heard his name called out, Kishan's pulse began to race. They knew exactly who they were looking for. He glanced down at his handlebars and thought about hitting the kill switch. He could stop the engine and comply and try to reason with whoever was in the car. He moved his thumb toward the button, but hesitated as he craned his neck to look for any openings in the traffic ahead. The moment he did, the rider on the massive bike beside him extended his leather-booted leg and kicked Kishan hard in the knee. A sharp pain ran down his leg. He struggled to keep his scooter upright. His frightened passenger began to pound on his back and cry out for him to do something, anything. In an instant, Kishan's fear turned to anger as he realized his long-sought date was probably over before it had begun. His first night with her was likely to be his last.

He detected a small sliver of space, maybe two feet wide, that began to open between the trucks ahead of him. It was far too small for a larger bike or the Land Rover to make it through. He hit his throttle hard. His scooter answered quickly and shot through the opening as his mirrors scraped sharply against the sides of the vehicles on either side. He heard horn blasts and the enormous roar of the entourage now stuck behind him, and he quickly darted his eyes about to seek any opening in the oncoming traffic circle. It was a crowded mess of vehicles, carts, and humanity that crisscrossed in a dozen different directions. A moving van that had been blocking a *galis*, a narrow lane packed with street merchants and food carts, had opened up on his right. He hit his horn, pressed it like it was a siren, and accelerated down the restricted alley. He missed one pedestrian after another by inches. Some shouted in panic and darted from his path. He came upon an even smaller lane, for pedestrians only, and barnstormed into it at full throttle. The tiny alley erupted with angry cries as shoppers jumped toward booth keepers hawking rugs, glassware, and copper pots. They all tried to get out of the path of his speeding scooter.

At the end of the long alley, they emerged onto Ambalal Doshi Road just steps from the ornate Taj Mahal Hotel. He didn't see anyone behind him. He headed west as fast as he could, toward the

University of Mumbai. It was a campus he knew well. They could stop and lie low, and he could get his bearings. His date's grip on his jacket had loosened, and he relaxed a little, since they were out of immediate danger. Maybe this date was salvageable after all, he thought.

As they coasted down the hill toward Mahatma Gandhi Road, he began to turn over and over in his mind who his pursuers could be. How could they possibly have an interest in him? He ticked through the list of possibilities. He was behind in his rent, his school loans, and his utilities, but not by much. He had paid his parking tickets. He had a small gambling debt, but it was for less than five thousand rupees, about a hundred dollars. Certainly not enough to be worth the effort for such a chase.

And then it hit him. As he rounded the corner by Elphinstone College, his mind began to race. It was the Shroud. It had to be. It was the only real secret he knew about, and the only thing he had stuck his neck out for in a long time. But what was he supposed to do? Leave the lie alone forever?

As he rolled into the university grounds, his eye caught a commotion across the cricket fields. Fear spread through him. Accelerating along the central footpath of the fields, where cars did not belong, was the motorcade of cycles and trucks he thought he had shaken only minutes ago. They kicked up a huge cloud of dust behind them. They had spotted him and were headed in his direction at high speed.

His date grasped his shoulders again and let out a cry. "Take me home, Kishan! Please take me home!" she begged.

He hit the gas with all the force his throttle could find, but the engine stalled. The swarm of cyclists, who raced slightly ahead of the Land Rovers was less than a half mile away and closing fast. He panicked and hit the kill switch instead of the start button several times before he realized what was wrong. His scooter's battery, which had turned the motor over and over without a start, began to weaken and moan with every attempt.

He pushed the bike with both feet as hard as he could down the incline they faced, popped the clutch, and kick-started the engine. It sputtered, mercifully clicked into gear, and lurched forward. With his pursuers less than a few hundred yards behind, he aimed his scooter toward the direction of Convocation Hall, the largest of the the-aters on campus. He hoped an event was under way that would have hundreds of people gathered and would afford some protection in a crowd.

But the hall was deserted, with the exception of a few cars that made their way out of the large multi-deck parking garage next door. It sat right next to a second, twin garage still under construction, where crews of men were at work on the top floor, cutting steel. With his pursuers now right on his tail and walls that trapped them on both sides, his only way forward lay straight ahead, toward the parking garage. If there was a small opening or exit door just wide enough for a scooter to fit through on the first floor, he reasoned, he might still escape. His engine, close to overheating, whined as he charged into the dimly lit garage entryway and found it deserted. He scanned the lot on the bottom floor with his headlight for any kind of crevice or door that might provide an opening, but saw none.

Left with no choice, he began the dizzying, circular ascent up the ramps of the garage toward the upper levels. Level Two. Level Three. Level Four. They had climbed high enough now to be trapped, and he knew it. He could feel the motorcycles only yards behind them. The trucks' tires squealed with every sharp turn up the ramp and were only a hundred feet farther back. While escape was futile, he remembered the handful of workers he had seen laboring atop the unfinished parking garage next door. He decided to seek what little protection he could out in the open of the top floor, where the construction workers might serve as witnesses to whatever happened next. As he reached the rooftop deck, his scooter burst into the sunlight. The instant he reached the dizzying height, his acrophobia kicked in, and he knew he had made a mistake. Some of the workers across the way on the adjacent roof were busy grinding steel, but a handful stopped what they were doing to watch the commotion of the motorcycles and the trucks racing in hot pursuit of the couple on the scooter that approached them.

Forty feet separated the two six-story garages. As Kishan's bike accelerated toward the opposite roof, he and his date both began to wave frantically to the workers for help. Kishan spotted a large wooden plank ahead of them that served as a makeshift footbridge from one garage to the other. While it had no guardrails and was only a few feet wide, it looked sturdy enough to hold whatever heavy construction material had moved across it before. If he could keep his scooter squarely in the middle of the plank, he could bolt across it to safety on the adjacent rooftop in an instant. He knew the bikes and trucks that pursued were far too large to make it across. It was a high-wire act, to be sure. And he would rather go through fire than risk the height. But he knew that if he hesitated for even a moment, the gang would be upon them.

He aimed his front wheel toward the ramp, gunned his engine, bounded onto the narrow board at high speed, and tried not to look down. His date squeezed his waist and held on tight. A third of the way across, it was clear to him that the sturdy plank would hold their weight. But what he didn't see as he careened forward were the construction workers frantically waving him off. And what he would never know was that the temporary footbridge they traversed had not been used in months. It was badly out of position. The far end of the board he rushed toward extended barely an inch onto the opposite rooftop deck. As soon as his bike reached the center of the bridge, the plank bowed downward mercilessly beneath their weight and pulled the board entirely away from the lip of the building. In one horrid moment, the footbridge flipped sideways and fell away, sending the scooter, Kishan, and the loveliest girl he would never come to know in a tumble toward a pile of construction debris on the ground six floors down.

The workers raced to the edge of the rooftop to peer below. The bikers and the trucks broke off immediately and fled in the opposite direction, toward the down ramp of the garage.

Medics eventually removed the dead bodies of Kishan and his date. She had died instantly, her head and helmet crushed completely in the fall. Kishan's chest was impaled on a length of thick steel rebar. It appeared that he had survived for several minutes after the fall, because he had reached out his hand toward hers and held it in his own.

CHAPTER 40

Outside Mumbai, India
March 2015

Domenika awoke in the dark, surrounded by the Sisters of Mercy at vigil near her bedside. They looked on in silent earnest while she slept, just as they had each evening for months. Their faces, narrowly obscured by their traditional white-and-blue habits, glowed faintly in the light of the candles they held. Domenika glanced over at the clock on her nightstand and could see it was five o'clock in the morning. An hour before the sun would rise. Their helping hands reached out as she strained to roll from her side onto her back to reach a more comfortable position. Late in her pregnancy, she was relieved the time was finally near.

Confined to strict bed rest on the orders of her doctor for her entire pregnancy, she had not ventured outside the walls of the small room in the quiet convent since being transported there by ambulance the previous fall. She was not allowed to move, with the exception of careful trips to the bathroom across the hall, but she had never grown used to the confinement she had to endure for the safety of her baby. She understood the reasons for the extraordinary measures her doctor, Dr. Laurence, had ordered.

He explained to her the graveness of her condition. Placenta previa, where the placenta is abnormally positioned in the uterus, was relatively rare, but it accounted for a significant percentage of miscarriages and stillbirths and placed both her and the baby at high risk. Had her condition gone undetected, she would have been at risk of badly hemorrhaging, creating a blood loss that would both endanger her life and severely threaten the baby with oxygen deprivation. She was told that the slightest wrong movement could end her pregnancy in an instant.

So here she lay. The guarded isolation was a small price to pay for a healthy newborn. But regardless of the remarkable care she had received from the overly attentive sisters while in the primitive convent, and the visits of encouragement from Dr. Laurence, his nurses, and Dr. Sehgal, it was the loneliness that hurt her most.

A strict Catholic, she had saved herself throughout her twenties because it was church teaching, and it was simply the right thing to do. When she entered her thirties, her vow remained, but her reluctance to give herself to a man was based more on a promise to herself to find the right one. Someone for a lifetime. And for Domenika, surrounded at work with good and decent men who had taken their own vows of celibacy through the priesthood, the right ones were few and far between.

Her pregnancy, while obviously unplanned, should have been one of the most joyous times of her life. Instead, she was alone, with no one to share the wonder of pregnancy and birth. She had always imagined her mother and sister giggling over the changes in her body. She'd imagined them picking out names together and shopping for a layette. Her daydreams included her father's gruff excitement as preparations for his grandchild commenced. Never did she imagine she would be in solitary confinement with only the company of strangers. The constant fear of losing the baby hung over her every moment. While she yearned to exercise and walk about the town, the nuns were fiercely protective. In fact, she felt more like a prisoner than a patient.

The convent, located several miles outside Mumbai, adhered to its strict procedures and primitive ways. There was no access to the Internet, no phone or cell service, and no television. She had to resort to old-fashioned letter writing and to Dr. Sehgal's kind offer to post them for her. She poured her heart out to her parents and begged them to forgive her for the accidental pregnancy. She knew they would be disappointed, but it had never crossed her mind they would greet her news with total silence. She was sure her father would never forgive her. And her mother, irate over the circumstances of her pregnancy, had probably renounced her for good. Her sister's silence, while a disappointment, was not surprising. She had changed addresses like they were outfits in the last three years, and it was unlikely her letters had ever been forwarded.

All of these letdowns were one thing. But what was truly a shock to her very soul was the lack of response from Bondurant. She blamed no one but herself. Of all the men to choose to break her vow, Domenika had chosen Bondurant, the very definition of a serial monogamist. What was she to expect? Domenika thought. He was long gone before her hangover had even set in.

Still, she wrote to him. It was a long, heartfelt letter telling him of the pregnancy and confessing her deep and abiding love for him. "I know you didn't choose this, but I take full responsibility for the baby.

I'm not asking you for anything except to give you the option to be in both of our lives. Our daughter or son will know and love you if it is your will. If I have my way, we will be a family," she wrote. It was painful to admit her feelings so freely and to open her heart to potential rejection by a man with his reputation. A man she had only known for weeks. But it didn't matter. She loved him and was convinced he loved her, even if he didn't know it.

Her last words to him on the phone the previous summer had been bitter, and she now wished she could change them. While their two short weeks together had proven they had little in common, she had left Turin unable to get him off her mind. She tried to reason why. She could not have met a man more in contradiction to her beliefs. He had no capacity for faith, and no interest in finding it. He was an *American,* after all, and carried with him an undeserved sense of confidence wherever he went. It grated on her. A "head case," as her sister had claimed? No, but prone to dysfunction? Absolutely. Emotionally disconnected at times? Definitely.

In most ways, he was the veritable square peg, she the round hole. Yet strangely, while she'd had too much wine and could remember almost nothing from her last intimate moments with Bondurant in her hotel room in Turin, she had chosen *him,* of all men, to be her first. For all his flaws, she had found him to stand above and apart from every other man she had ever met. He was smart, and challenged her thinking at every turn. He was kind, honest, and generous and had the courage of his convictions. He had the character of a man but sometimes displayed the vulnerability of a boy. Her attraction to him was so powerful that she had bought a ticket to fly to Baltimore to surprise him a week after they said good-bye to each other in Turin. At the last minute, she found herself unable to board the plane, afraid of how foolish she would look flying halfway around the world to chase him. Now she regretted staying home.

And soon he was to be the father of her child. She was proud of that. She wondered what that meant to him, and why, even given their falling out, he had ignored her letter asking him to come. She could tell from their brief time together that he was taken with her, but knew that was a far cry from wanting to become a father. But still, she'd thought he would understand his responsibility, whether they were ever to be together or not. She wondered if she had misjudged him, just as she had misjudged Ravi Sehgal.

She found herself in India as the guest of the Nobel Laureate, who had called her in Rome after the disastrous conference call to explain his findings. He wanted to make amends. While she knew very little about DNA, she was certain the results he had reported months before concerning the Shroud had to be wrong. The Vatican held the evidence of its authenticity in its codex, yet he had launched a giant myth to dispute that the Shroud was genuine. There *had* to be a reason for him to invent such a lie. She had accepted his invitation to travel to Mumbai to demand an explanation. She traveled there knowing that if she sorted out the mess and brought forward the truth, the job she'd once had in Rome might await her again.

It was at Sehgal's elegant home on the outskirts of the city where she had discovered the truth. There had been a terrible mistake, he said, one he was ashamed to admit to his colleagues. While his explanation was complicated, the erroneous findings were the result of the work of an incompetent lab technician. According to Sehgal, the technician's error had contaminated the blood sample from the Shroud that Sehgal had received. The mistake had been discovered just days after their conference call to discuss the team's findings, and, plainly worried about his reputation, Sehgal was beside himself about what to do. He vowed to her that he was prepared to rerun his tests, correct the record, and provide his findings to Bondurant. Over some calming tea, he begged her to understand.

It turned out that her meeting with Sehgal was her last conscious memory before she awoke in the tiny convent of the Sisters of Mercy. She had been told that she had passed out on Sehgal's living room couch and had been transported, unconscious, to the emergency room for observation, where doctors made the remarkable discovery that she was pregnant. However, given her high-risk factors discovered in routine tests at the hospital, the attending physician had ordered her to immediate bed rest. Sehgal had used his close relationship with the sisters of the convent to make the arrangements necessary for her to convalesce there in their capable hands. She learned all this when she awoke.

Soon, she would learn so much more.

CHAPTER 41

Rome, Italy
March 2015

Bondurant pounded on Parenti's apartment door well past midnight. When the priest finally let him, he burst through the doorway in desperation.

"Where's your bathroom?" Bondurant cried out.

"Right there," Parenti said. He looked disoriented from being awoken. He pointed to the door behind him.

Bondurant dashed toward the tiny bathroom and slammed the door shut.

"That's it?" Parenti said as he rubbed the sleep from his eyes. "I've not seen you in months. You come unannounced in the middle of the night. Not a hello, not a how are you?"

"Hello. How are you?" Bondurant groaned from behind the bathroom door.

The priest poked his head out into the empty hallway. "No pursuers?" he said.

"It's my stomach," Bondurant replied. "I just landed. I'll never eat Indian food again as long as I live. I swear it."

"I see," the priest said.

"I'll be just a minute. You're a lifesaver, Father."

Parenti sat down on his bed and rubbed his eyes. After several minutes had passed, Bondurant emerged. He looked pale and weak. He pulled up the lone chair in the apartment and sat down beside the priest, exhausted.

"Why didn't you call to say you were coming?" Parenti asked.

"Because you don't have a phone," Bondurant said. He looked around the small, sparsely furnished apartment. It resembled a prison cell more than a home. He could tell the priest was still in a sleepy haze. Bondurant had traveled all day from India to talk to him.

"That's true," Parenti said as he smiled, rolled back into the bed, and reached for the covers. "Have a wonderful evening."

Bondurant kicked the side of the bed to rouse the priest and prevent him from falling back to sleep. He caught sight of Aldo in his cage on the floor next to the bed, reached down, opened the latch, and set the dog on the bed. Aldo immediately scampered to Parenti and began to lick his cheek.

"Father," Bondurant said. He hesitated for a moment and looked toward the bathroom, concerned that he might need to make another trip. He took a deep breath to let his stomach settle for another moment. "I'm sorry I had to wake you, but it's for good reason. We need to talk."

The priest slowly turned on his side and propped a pillow under his arm. He cradled the dog in the crook of his arm and looked up at Bondurant. "Continue," he said.

"First, have you heard from Domenika? Anything at all?" Bondurant asked.

"Not a word."

"I haven't either. But I'm certain she's in real trouble now. I've turned Mumbai upside down again for the last two weeks, and there's still no sign of her anywhere."

"When you left Rome to look for her before, we thought her destination might be Mumbai, but there was no evidence of trouble. Why do you think she's there now?"

"Sehgal's still missing too," Bondurant said. "And if what one of Sehgal's people told me over the phone is true, it's possible she's involved."

"Involved? What do you mean, involved?"

"Cloning comes to mind, Father."

Parenti sat upright and his eyes widened. He was now fully awake. "You're saying she's in league with those madmen, those cloning people with the tattoos? Sehgal as well?"

"Sehgal's got what he thinks is the blood of Christ. He fought for as much as he could get. We know that. He lied about the blood's source. And he has the means to reconstruct the DNA," Bondurant said. "If he's fallen in with Laurent and the Demanians, they might be close to an attempted cloning. I can't be sure, and I know it's a long shot. But if he's got Domenika, as a prisoner or even a volunteer, the circle's complete."

"What do you mean by that?" Parenti asked.

"He's got his Virgin Mary," Bondurant stated flatly. He didn't want to believe what he'd said, especially about Domenika's possible complicity, but he'd grown weary of the endless chase for her and was frustrated. He hadn't slept in two days.

"You're wrong about her. She would never be involved in such a thing. Never," Parenti said.

"You're right. At least, I hope you're right. But she's making it awfully hard to find her. Too hard. It's like she's hiding," Bondurant said. He'd never been more frustrated, and as much as he cared about Domenika, he'd grown frustrated with her over time for vanishing without a word. "She disappears. She tells no one. She takes *my* side against the Vatican when they fight against taking blood from the Shroud. It wouldn't surprise me if she and Sehgal—"

"Nonsense, Doctor. You need some rest."

"And there's another problem, Father," Bondurant said. "A big one."

"Bigger than an attempt to clone the Son of God? With Domenika somehow involved? Try me."

"Okay, I will," Bondurant said. "It's a long story, but I've come to find there are two sources of blood on the Shroud. It's definitive. These Demanians, Sehgal, they've no clue who they're trying to clone."

"You're certain of this?"

"Absolutely. They're playing Russian roulette with a droplet of blood. Son of God? Son of Sam? I'm telling you, they just don't know."

Parenti immediately closed his eyes and pressed his hands over his ears. "LA-LA-LA-LA. LA-LA-LA-LA," he chanted.

"What are you doing?" Bondurant asked.

"I don't want to hear it. I don't want to hear it," the priest said. "If I lie down now and fall back to sleep, in the morning when I wake you will be gone, and this will all have been a dream."

"I wish it were so," Bondurant said.

Parenti closed his eyes and folded his arms together, saying nothing. After a minute had passed, he opened his eyes again.

"I know of a book," the priest said.

"Yes?"

"It is in the Vatican Archives. It's a special book. I've not studied it closely before, but I believe I know where it can be found in the shelves. If we can get to it, it will solve the mystery."

"What do you mean?" Bondurant asked.

"It will reveal whether there are any other true relics in existence beyond the Shroud that may bear the blood of Jesus Christ. That way you can compare the sources of blood, Doctor."

Bondurant shook his head in disbelief. "First, there is no such book. I would know it."

"You are insufferable at times," the priest said. "No wonder it took some time for Domenika to fall for you."

"Father, even if I were to believe—"

"*Believe* me, Doctor. *Believe* me. For all of our sakes, believe me. There is such a book. You are faced with a riddle, are you not? One Shroud. But the blood of two persons on it. Which is Christ? Which is not?"

"You want me to match the DNA I have from the Shroud with another relic that *might* be named in a book and *might* possess the blood of Christ. Is that it?"

"Exactly. You must. How else will you know the origin of the DNA these ridiculous Demanians are trying to resurrect? You have no choice."

"On the contrary, I do," Bondurant said as he got up from his chair. "No more wild-goose chases."

"Where are you going?" Parenti asked.

"To find a hotel. Hopefully I'll feel better in the morning and can think more clearly then about a plan." As Bondurant turned toward the door, Parenti grabbed him by his sleeve and tugged him backward. Bondurant was surprised to see the sudden look of desperation on the priest's face.

"Dr. Bondurant, I have a confession to make," Parenti said.

"Here? Now?"

"You're the only one I can trust with this," Parenti said.

"I think you're talking to the wrong man, Father. Isn't this supposed to work the other way around? The priest hears the sinner?"

"Normally, yes. But at this time of night, you will have to do." The priest took a deep breath, and Bondurant could tell there was something seriously wrong.

"You must know that I possess something I acquired—forgive me—stole a long time ago. Before I met you." He got up from his bed and reached for the bottom drawer of his dresser. He produced a small plastic bag, opened it up, took out a worn cloth, and sat back down on the bed. He spread the cloth on his lap.

Bondurant looked at him curiously. "What is this?"

"I need you to assist me in a brief sacrament. I'm sure you've heard of it. It's the 'anointing of the sick.' Very simple."

"Father, you look just fine to me," Bondurant said. "And second, there must be a thousand priests who—"

"Fine?" the priest interrupted. There was a sudden twinge of sadness in his voice. With some effort, he struggled to rise from the bed again and when he finally righted himself, he turned so that Bondurant had a view of his crooked profile. Bondurant could see the priest was bent over more than he remembered, and was in some pain. He could also hear that his breathing was labored, which he had never heard before.

"I am growing old, Doctor. We all do. But this spine I have been blessed with, well, it seems to be growing more twisted by the day. There is a doctor here in Rome who says at this rate my breath will vanish and I will not last the year."

"I see," Bondurant said. He was shaken by the news of his friend's condition, and his mind began to race. How did he want him to help? "Surely there are specialists in the United States who can help. I'll find you one."

"I'm afraid my condition is far beyond the scope of doctors," Parenti said. He sounded resigned. He sat back down on the bed and reached out to take Bondurant's hand. When Bondurant offered it, Parenti put the worn cloth in his palm. "You hold in your hand the veil—*Veronica's Veil*, Doctor. With it, I will be cured."

Bondurant closed his eyes, shook his head, and tossed the worn cloth on the bed. "I'm done with relics, Father."

"You *must* help me. Please," the priest pleaded. Bondurant could see Parenti had begun to choke up. "Try as I might, I cannot do this alone. I have tried lying on it, sleeping on it, rolling on it. It's no use. I'm convinced it cannot be done alone."

"Father, if it were truly Veronica's Veil, it—"

"I know what you're thinking. I've already checked. Unfortunately, it contains not a trace of blood. But I know the veil is a gift of healing from one to another. And there is no one else I can trust to do this."

"So you think this rag you've discovered has the fabled healing powers talked about for centuries, do you?" Bondurant said. He pitied the desperate priest. He wanted to help, but surely Parenti could see how foolhardy this was. He picked the cloth up off the bed and looked at the smeared image.

"It's no fable," Parenti insisted.

Bondurant checked himself. "Yes, and now you're going to tell me you have seen it work wonders, is that right?"

"Yes. It brought someone back from the dead already," he insisted.

"Who?" Bondurant asked skeptically.

"Aldo," he said as he pointed to the dog that looked on attentively from atop a pillow on the bed. He wagged his tail.

"Enough, Father," Bondurant said. He set down the cloth. "Let's get to work in the morning finding you a doctor who can give a second opinion."

"How would you explain your friend Dr. Sato's hands?" Parenti asked.

Bondurant looked up, surprised. He remembered Parenti had made his way to see Sato in the hospital in Turin, but he'd never given it much thought. Still, Sato had thanked the priest for his kindness. And the healing that had occurred in his hands was by any measure extraordinary.

"I had seen the veil work its wonders on Aldo, a poor little animal," Parenti said, "but whether it would work on a human being— that was another question. And it plainly did."

Bondurant stared at the cloth once more and examined it closely. *Fragile, and indeed ancient*, he thought. And, incredibly enough, once he stared at it some more, the image revealed on the cloth looked eerily similar to some elements of the face he had seen on the Shroud. He looked up and saw the pitiful priest in real pain. He decided he had no choice but to humor him before leaving for the night.

"All right, then, what would you like me to do?" he asked.

Parenti smiled. "Help me remove my nightshirt, if you would. And I want to warn you, the sight is not for the faint of heart."

The priest unbuttoned his top and raised his hands high into the air as best he could, while Bondurant lifted his shirt away by the yoke. Parenti was right. Bondurant was not in the least prepared to see the grotesque hump on the entire upper half of the priest's back. It was filled with massive blue-streaked veins that fed its core while it seemingly ate the priest alive.

"Not an inviting sight, I know," Parenti said wryly.

Bondurant averted his eyes for a moment to buy time to gather his nerve to continue. He tried to pretend he was fine, but he feared the priest knew better.

"You need not touch it," Parenti said. "But I need you to stroke it with the veil, if you will, while I pray."

Bondurant quickly reached for the cloth to get the strange ritual over with as soon as possible.

"I'll do this for you once, Father," Bondurant said. "But not again. And I'll make you a deal. If this works, I'll convert. How's that? If it doesn't, you'll let me find you a specialist. Is that a deal?"

"A deal," Parenti said. "Now start rubbing."

Bondurant gingerly placed the cloth on Parenti's parasitic hump and closed his eyes, unable to watch the strange task he was performing. With every stroke, he could feel the undulating bumps of Parenti's deformed spine surrounded by malformed muscles that strained to keep his upper back from caving in altogether. He listened carefully and could hear the priest's breathing slowly relax, but after a minute of rubbing gave up and pulled the cloth away from the futile task.

"What are you doing? What are you doing? Continue," Parenti urged.

"Father, I'm afraid we're getting nowhere. A deal's a deal."

"The deal was that—"

Parenti, instantly caught short of breath, was unable to finish his words. His eyes bulged from their sockets and began to turn pale yellow, and a long, terrifying wheeze came from his lungs.

"Father, are you all right? Are you all right?" Bondurant called out as he took a step backward to take full measure of the priest. He was worried Parenti had begun to enter cardiac arrest.

The priest, unresponsive, began to contort his face and revealed a kind of pain Bondurant had never seen before. A loud snap, almost deafening to the ears, shot forth from the area of the priest's back, followed by another, and then another. Parenti cried out and writhed in agony. He lifted his head toward the ceiling and struggled to straighten himself. As he did, the sound of bones popping and cracking echoed through the room.

Bondurant, dumbfounded, took another step away from Parenti and tripped over the leg of his chair. He fell backward onto the floor, next to the miniature dog, which now howled like a wolf. Bondurant watched in amazement while the priest shuddered uncontrollably, in full seizure. Then, miraculously, his spine and shoulders began to straighten, and the hump on his back slowly began to disappear.

"This cannot be happening. This cannot be happening," Bondurant cried over and over.

Slowly the priest raised himself upward, inch by inch, until he stood completely straight. Bondurant knew the little priest had not done so since he was a child. The pain in Parenti's face was slowly transformed to a look of sheer joy. Bondurant still could not believe his eyes. Aldo leapt joyously into Parenti's arms and licked his face.

"Now, a deal's a deal, Dr. Bondurant," Parenti said, beaming as he caught a huge, deep breath he'd not felt for a lifetime.

Bondurant looked up at Parenti from the floor, speechless.

"Think of it," Parenti said. "And you're converting! Two miracles in a single day!"

CHAPTER 42

Rome, Italy
March 2015

Bondurant had been inside hundreds of places of worship to study religious relics over the years, but there was not a single one he'd entered in search of God. Today was different.

Even as exhausted as he'd been the past few days, he hadn't slept at all the previous night. The adrenaline coursing through his veins since he'd witnessed Parenti's miraculous healing just hours before, in combination with a pint of scotch he'd downed to calm his nerves, had his head abuzz. Church services had finished for the morning when he arrived, and he sat completely alone in a dark corner chapel of the Basilica di Santa Maria Maggiore in central Rome. Surrounding him in the spectacular church were resplendent fifth-century biblical mosaics glorifying the Virgin Mary. Towering above was the fabled cathedral ceiling gilded in gold Columbus had brought back from the new world.

Bondurant's breathing was shallow, and his chest and stomach were in severe pain from an anxiety he had never felt before. He was in a cold sweat, and for the moment his tired eyes were singularly focused on the life-sized statue of Mary placed above the chapel altar in the small alcove where he sat. Given the startling events of the night before and his present shaky condition, he half expected the marble Madonna to come alive and strike up a conversation. For one long, frightening minute, he even thought he saw her lips tremble and move as if to speak. He knew the hallucination was the result of complete exhaustion and his unsettled state, but the same could not be said of the unexplainable events from the night before.

He was absolutely certain there was no scientific or medical explanation possible for what he'd seen happen. Bondurant knew what he'd witnessed was the very definition of miraculous, something he'd known to be impossible his entire life. The veil he'd mocked over the years as one of many worthless religious trinkets possessed properties that somehow defied the laws of physics, biology, physiology, chemistry, and at least a half dozen other sciences. Parenti's transformation had happened right before his very eyes, and he was certain there was no earthly explanation for what had restored the priest's long-deformed body.

He hadn't come to the chapel because he expected answers. A clinic to treat the dull, throbbing pain he felt in his head and chest would have made more sense. But his instincts told him a church was a good place to start. Or, start over. His mind held a list of terrifying questions to ponder. He still believed in a world of true and false. He knew with all his heart and mind that much of religious dogma invented by man served to simply enslave humankind in a prison of its own making. Yet he *had* seen a miracle. How was it possible that much of what he had learned and even taught over many years could be dead wrong? If a miracle that defied the laws of science could happen, was there truth to other miraculous events claimed in the past, and what did this mean for the future? If there was some unseen force or energy in the world that operated above the laws of the universe as we knew them, what was this force, and where did it reside? Was this, by definition, the work of a higher force?

Of all the admonitions from believers about miracles and faith he could remember, it was Domenika's words above all that came hurtling back to him. *Are you willing to agree that science may never be able to grasp the divine?* she had asked. Amazingly, he now thought the answer to be yes. But, sadly, she was not there to witness the mystery of what he had seen or the effect it had left on his soul.

As he considered how it was possible that his very identity and much of his life's work could be turned upside down in an instant, a sudden wave of wonder and then despair began to overwhelm him. He had no choice. He didn't know what else to do. He placed his hands over his face and began to weep quietly.

Trying to make sense of his new world drained him of what little strength he had left. His body had denied him peaceful sleep for days, but he now wanted rest more than ever. Suddenly, a noise nearby caused him to startle and look up. Directly in front of him stood a young altar boy, still a child. His face was the portrait of innocence. It bore a resemblance to Bondurant's younger brother's. In the boy's hands was a tray of new, white votive candles wrapped in ruby red glasses. The boy had begun the process of delicately stacking each glass on an iron altar rack to replace spent candles, ones that had been extinguished with the passage of time. Over a hundred brightly lit candles remained before the boy, placed there, no doubt, by those of faith, who had lit them in honor of another needy soul or wish.

Bondurant stared at the boy's face, glowing in the warm light, and could see he moved with quiet trepidation. The boy went about his task slowly and deliberately, as though the slightest jostling of a votive candle might disturb someone's sacred intention.

"What are you doing?" Bondurant asked as he wiped the tears from his face. That was it, he thought. He needed someone, anyone to talk to.

The startled child turned quickly toward Bondurant's silhouette in the dark and nearly dropped his tray. He recovered bravely. "I am in service to the Lord," the boy whispered, catching his breath. "I'm sorry if I disturbed your prayer."

"I'm afraid I've forgotten how to pray," Bondurant said. "It's been a very long time."

"Oh, it's easy, Jon," the boy responded in earnest. "You just fold your hands like this." He set down his tray and demonstrated. "Then you close your eyes and speak to God. He hears you. And you need only whisper."

"I've not tried to talk to him since I was a boy, when there was great trouble," Bondurant said. "I'm afraid he didn't listen."

"And how old are you now, if I may ask?" the boy said.

"Forty years on, my friend."

The boy paused for a moment. "That's a long time. Here, then. I'll light one of these just for you. I'm sure it will help."

The boy removed a fresh candle from his tray, turned it sideways, and held its wick over the flame of another. Once it was lit, he set it in the center of the rack before him and turned to smile at Bondurant.

Bondurant returned the smile. "Thank you," he said as he leaned back and rested his head against the pew. He closed his eyes and let his body relax for the first time in days. "That's very kind." In a matter of seconds, Bondurant fell into a deep and trancelike sleep. He was soon pulled into a vivid dream.

In his dream, he looked down at his watch. It read only zeroes, and Bondurant felt surrounded by a terrible dread that death was near.

"My time is done," he said as he looked at the boy who was barely visible in the shadows of his dream.

"Look again," he heard the boy murmur.

As he did, Bondurant could see that the numerals on his watch had begun to spin out of control, wildly careening toward infinity.

"Embrace the mystery of God," he could hear the boy whisper. *"It's within you. If you believe in his resurrection, you too will never die."*

"Another miracle?" Bondurant asked as the boy drifted from his sight.

"Yes," the boy responded. *"For you and all mankind."*

When Bondurant awoke from his dream, the boy who had known his name had vanished. Before him was an enormous sea of glowing candles fully illuminating the chapel in brilliant hues of yellow and white. Bondurant knew that for the first time in his life, he had come into the light.

CHAPTER 43

Rome, Italy
March 2015

The late winter weather in Rome was unseasonably warm. The stench inside the Dumpster where Bondurant lay in hiding was so putrid from having baked in the hot Italian sun all day that he had no choice but to risk being arrested. Bondurant squirmed on his back and braced himself against the mound of trash beneath him. He kicked open the container's heavy lid with both feet and gasped for fresh air. The metal cover of his filthy hideout slammed so loudly against its side when it fell open that he was certain it would send every Vatican guard on night watch headed his way. He didn't care. The odor from the decaying mix of rotting food and soiled diapers that enveloped him had grown so sickening he could take it no more.

Parenti had instructed Bondurant to loiter unnoticed inside the Vatican grounds until after the gates had closed at six o'clock. He told Bondurant to hide in the trash bins in the small alleyway just outside the first-floor restrooms of St. Peter's Basilica. Having toiled as the bathroom attendant there for six months, he could assure Bondurant the nearby containers were rarely used. Bondurant made a mental note to reacquaint Parenti with the term "rarely used" as soon as they were reunited. He crouched behind the Dumpsters and looked about for signs of anyone headed in his direction. Surprisingly, no one appeared. It was then that he noticed the large window above him slide slowly open, guided by two childlike hands that lifted mightily against its weight.

At first, only Aldo's tiny face appeared at the windowsill. His paws quickly covered his tiny nose from the stench. Then Bondurant heard a familiar voice.

"Excellent. You are on time," Parenti whispered. "Quickly! Up! Up! Before you are seen!"

Bondurant scaled his way back up the open trash container, stood firmly on its rim, jumped to grasp the ledge a foot above, and pulled his body up to lean inside the open window. His legs dangled in the air as he found himself an inch from Parenti's scowling face.

"You smell like death," the priest said.

"You think?" Bondurant said as he pulled himself completely through the window, bounded to his feet and looked warily down on the container that had been his miserable hiding place for over an hour.

He looked at Parenti standing newly erect, and could see from the priest's smile that he was enjoying his newfound height. While the little priest was still small, five feet tall at best, he exuded a sense of stature Bondurant had not seen in him before. Bondurant, transformed as well since witnessing Parenti's marvelous healing, had second thoughts about his refusal to consider the priest's plans for locating a second source of the true blood of Christ.

"You must put these on, Doctor," the priest said in a low voice as he pulled garments from the small canvas bag he held. "They will help you blend in if, God forbid, we are seen." He held in his outstretched hands a priest's cassock with a gold cross emblazoned across the front.

"You have to be kidding me, Father," Bondurant protested.

"Don't trifle with me, my son," the priest said as he tossed the robe at him. "There is work to be done this night, and we must not be discovered." Parenti picked up Aldo, shoved him into his satchel, turned from Bondurant, and motioned toward the door.

Bondurant reluctantly slipped on the robe and buttoned it from top to bottom. It hung toward the floor. A perfect fit. He turned toward the mirror to see himself robed as a priest ready for the celebration of Mass and laughed to himself. He wondered what Domenika would think of him now.

"Come, come," Parenti whispered, "we have no time to lose."

The journey from the first floor of St. Peter's all the way to the Vatican Library required the negotiation of a long and winding unmarked trail. Very few could navigate the course from memory, Parenti had told him, but the priest reckoned he had made the confusing trip through the dark passages and up the hidden staircases a thousand times. He took Bondurant by the sleeve and slipped into an alcove nearby before they made their ascent. It contained the first of many ancient doors they would pry open or unlock on their way through the complex labyrinth of corridors comprising the hidden nerve center of the Holy City. They climbed several narrow stairways, carefully opened one door after another, and crept like mice along the darkened and deserted pathways. Parenti had warned Bondurant that it would be a disaster if they were spotted.

The priest had lost his permission to enter the library when his position as secretary had been unceremoniously eliminated the previous year. Entry without explicit authorization from the pope was strictly forbidden. For him to be caught inside the Vatican's most secret sanctum, aiding, of all people, a "Judas," the scientist who had betrayed the Vatican's trust, would definitely be grounds for instant defrocking.

Higher and higher they ascended, until they reached the top of a long staircase at the base of the tower, home to the ancient library. The marble entry foyer, deserted by Swiss Guards after hours, held two massive, ornate wooden doors containing a single large keyhole. Parenti dug into his satchel for the worn iron key he had never returned despite admonitions and threats from Father Barsanti. It had faithfully unlocked the doors to the secret library for centuries. Aldo took the opening the priest had given him when the satchel opened, jumped from the bag, and landed lightly on the floor beside them. As Parenti turned the heavy key, several loud *clank*s echoed throughout the marble entryway, and the massive doors swung slowly open. The library sat in total darkness, save the faint blue glow from its stained glass windows, which absorbed the light reflected off the nearby dome of St. Peter's. Aldo, anxious to enter an old haunt, bolted inside.

"That's a problem," Parenti said as soon as the dog vanished from sight.

"What do you mean?" Bondurant asked. "I've never seen you without him. He must know these stacks as well as you."

"Maybe so," the priest whispered. "But the last time I let him slip from my sight for even just a moment, he ended up dead."

"Hours ago I would have questioned your sanity," Bondurant said as he shook his head. "Today, I can believe anything."

Bondurant crept slowly through the entryway with his arms extended to feel his way through the dark. He couldn't see his hands in front of him.

"It's impossible to see in here, Father," he whispered.

"Never you mind. I could do this blindfolded," Parenti responded. Taking several steps into the pitch black, the priest stumbled into a small wooden book cart hidden in the darkness. It toppled over with a loud crash.

"Porco diavolo!" Parenti whispered.

Both Bondurant and Parenti held their collective breath momentarily and listened for any sign of life around them. Parenti quickly pulled a large flashlight from his bag, turned it on, and threw a large beam of bright light across the room.

"So much for blindfolded," Bondurant said dryly.

He followed the priest past countless aisles as they wound and twisted their way in the darkness through the most magnificent collection of books Bondurant had ever seen. All the while he could hear the dog prance ahead of them like a scout in the distance, presumably knowing where they were headed. While he could see only what Parenti's flashlight illuminated immediately in front of them, he knew he was passing far too quickly through one of the greatest wonders of the world. The priest seemed to know where he was going, and after several minutes at a deliberate pace, they reached a small opening between two massive rows of shelves. A reading table and several chairs sat in the opening.

"Wait here. Sit. Don't move," Parenti whispered. "It might take me a moment to find the book."

Bondurant sat in complete darkness next to the dog as he watched the bobbing flashlight make its way past a shelf several aisles from their spot. A few minutes later, the priest returned with a purposeful look on his face and a large book under his arm.

Bondurant peered at the massive tome Parenti held. He could tell it was ancient, but could make out little else in the darkness.

The priest's voice lowered to a whisper. "I have read every word of every interview with our Ravi since we last met. I'm convinced you are right. He wants to save mankind from misery and has turned to this beast Meyer and his Demanians for help. I am but a humble priest, but even I know that God cannot and will not come from man."

"Funny," Bondurant said, "I spent my entire life believing that man did not come from God, and that God *did* come from man. But I never imagined I would be a victim in someone's absurd experiment to prove it."

The two sat silently and stared at each other in the glow of the flashlight Parenti had set on the table between them.

"Are you ready for my tale, good Doctor? Would you like to hear my plan?" Parenti asked as he broke the silence.

"I came as you asked, didn't I?"

"Yes, you did. And when I finish, you will be glad of it. But first I must ask you to promise on your life that you will not reveal to anyone, not a soul, what I am about to tell you."

"That is a promise," Bondurant said as he leaned in to listen intently.

"Very well, then. Hear me carefully. I hold in my hand a book that is known to only a very few. It is second in importance to another book, one that I found here in the library many months ago and which I am not at liberty to discuss with you tonight. One day I will. It is safe in the hands of our Holy Father, and its discovery, interestingly enough, led us to you."

"I'm not following you, Father."

"No matter. It is this book, *this* book that I hold, that is of use to us tonight. I know you are familiar with religious relics, both real and imagined?"

"They have been a central part of my life's work, Father."

"Then you will be interested to know that the book I am holding is a catalog of sorts. A catalog of many Christian relics examined by special investigators of the Church and as commissioned by popes over the centuries. You might call them inquisitors of a sort. A truth squad. For many years, they have been on a journey for the truth. They have had but one purpose: a determination of the authenticity of our most holy relics."

"This is the same book you mentioned last night?" Bondurant asked.

"Indeed," the priest continued. "By design, there are only a handful of Church officials who are aware of this book and its contents. The book reveals that there are many, many relics throughout the Christian world that are venerated by millions of faithful but are of no interest to us. They are fabrications. Trinkets. They belong in the flea markets of Porta Portese here in Rome."

"I've written books on the subject," Bondurant said.

Parenti ran his tiny thumb across at least a hundred pages that contained lists of such examples and opened the book for Bondurant to see a page in the glow of the flashlight. Bondurant reached for the book to inspect it more closely, but the priest pushed his hand away.

"But there are some, a very few, that are beyond the shadow of a doubt authentic. They are listed plainly here. For those who believe, the very existence of these objects and the meaning they hold for the faithful stir the soul. They are divine."

Parenti paused for a long while and stared intently at Bondurant. Then he thumbed to a page he had marked when he first retrieved the book from the shelf.

"According to this book, there is one true relic in existence that may bear the blood of Jesus Christ. By the way, your work on the Shroud has confirmed for us a second."

Bondurant listened intently but shook his head. "And where do I find this 'true' relic? The Church has not exactly been forthcoming with them in the past, and I am sure I am the one person on earth it has no interest in sharing such relics with now."

"Very true. This is why we are going to have to steal it, Doctor."

"Are you really a priest, or do you just wear the collar?" Bondurant asked. "Thou shalt not steal, or am I wrong?"

"Yes, *and thou shalt not make for thyself any likeness of anything that is in heaven above* as well, sir. No false gods," Parenti replied. "Let me put it another way: no cloning."

The light from the flashlight he had set on the reading table began to flicker and fade and threatened to trap them both in the pitch darkness. They needed to find themselves back at the library's entry-way soon. Parenti stood up, shoved the book into his bag, and made haste to leave. As soon as he did, the faint sound of footsteps could be heard in the distance. Someone was heading in their direction. Aldo, who heard the noise, began to bark and jump and circle about Parenti in a frantic effort to leap back into his satchel. The priest looked astonished, as it was the first time he had ever heard the dog bark. He had thought him a mute.

"Can't you keep him quiet?" Bondurant said as the tiny creature continued to yap. "He's going to give us away."

"I'm afraid it's too late for that," the priest said. "I think I recognize the sound of those shoes, and if I'm right, God have mercy on us."

"Run or hide, Father?" Bondurant said. "Which is it?" The sound of the footsteps grew perilously close.

"He knows these shelves as well as I do. We have no choice," the priest said. Bondurant could tell he was calculating the best escape route. "Follow me, and run, run, run," the priest shouted.

With that, Parenti began to wind his way through the confusing maze of shelves as fast as his little legs would take him. Bondurant and the dog, who barked with every step, followed close behind. Bondurant couldn't see Parenti out ahead in the dark but could tell where he was from the occasional flicker of fading light that came from the dying flashlight. Parenti tried to be quick, but he moved too slowly, and Bondurant could hear the footsteps gaining on them.

They dashed down long corridors, turned right and left, and then right and right and left and left again. Bondurant was sure they had doubled back, and hoped the priest wasn't lost. Then, as he peered into the barely lit distance, he could tell they had finally emerged onto a central aisle. There was a faint light at its very end. Bondurant presumed it was the entryway, picked up speed, and urged on both Parenti and the dog along the way. When he reached the front entryway alone, he turned to look behind him and could make out the faint silhouette of a tall, lanky figure gaining ground on Parenti and the dog, now only fifty feet behind them.

"*Gobbo!*" the figure yelled out. "You'll burn in hell for this!"

Parenti, completely out of breath, struggled to make the last few steps to the door. Their pursuer, now only ten feet behind, stumbled slightly, dove for the little priest, and slid to a stop just feet away. His fall gave Parenti a chance to catch up to Bondurant, who had made it to the bottom of the first long flight of marble steps below the library landing. When the pursuer recovered and emerged into the light of the foyer, he stood atop the landing above them, his chest heaving from exhaustion. He glowered at the intruders.

"Not another step," Barsanti said. "I'll have the guards on you before you know it."

Bondurant, having gotten this far, was certain he could escape in a footrace, but hadn't a clue how to find his way out of the labyrinth that had brought them through the dozens of passages and doorways below. He was determined to snatch up Parenti and carry him as his guide to escape. But Parenti, scared for his life, was the first to ignore Barsanti's command. He made a dash toward the second flight of steps.

Outraged, the wraithlike figure leapt forward. Gaining ground on them with his long legs, he bound down the steps with apparent ease. But what he hadn't noticed when he planted his right foot to make a giant leap down the stairwell was the little dog by his ankle. Aldo sank his tiny but razor-sharp teeth deep into his skin. Barsanti yanked his foot away mid-leap and lost his balance when he landed hard on the opposing foot. His ankle broke instantly with a loud *snap* as he collapsed on the stairway. From there, he thumped his way down the remainder of the marble steps on his back. There were exactly twenty, by Parenti's count. He watched the back of Barsanti's balding head greeting each and every one. Barsanti lay unconscious at the foot of the stairs, his neck likely broken in the fall.

Bondurant, with Parenti behind him, bolted down five more

flights of stairs and stopped briefly at the bottom to listen for signs of other pursuers. Hearing no one, they stopped for a moment to catch their breath.

"Whoever that was, he must be dead," Bondurant whispered as he looked up the stairwell. "Did you see his head hit that landing?"

"He's Barsanti, the prefect," Parenti said. "Don't worry about him. The devil himself couldn't kill him."

"Prefect or not," Bondurant said. "Once we clear the Vatican walls, we'll call one-one-two for the police." He continued, "How about this relic? The one you said bears the true blood of Christ. What is it? Where is it? There are hundreds all over the world that are certain fakes."

"According to what I could tell from this book, you will find it in Bruges," Parenti said.

"Bruges? In Belgium?"

"Yes, in the Basilica of the Holy Blood. Do you know it?"

"Of course. Of course. The legend is well known. Joseph of Arimathea wipes the body of Christ after the Crucifixion. The bloodstained cloth is placed in a vial that has never been opened. It lies in the Chapel of Blood, where it's been for a thousand years. There's just one problem, Father."

"What is that?"

"You said 'steal it.' It can't be stolen. It's kept in a locked tabernacle of the Church under constant watch. It is one of the most guarded relics in Christianity."

"All true. But you are forgetting something."

"And what is that?"

"Once a year, in early spring, it is removed from that tabernacle and paraded by the Bishop of Bruges through the streets of that fair city. It is the Procession of the Holy Blood. It is really quite a colorful affair; one I have always longed to see. There are costumes and actors, revelry and confusion. No setting could be more perfect in which to steal the vial as it goes on parade."

"It's a huge long shot," Bondurant said. "If I remember, the Procession takes place—"

"Tomorrow, Doctor. We make haste for Bruges tonight."

CHAPTER 44

Mumbai, India
March 2015

Sehgal slammed his fist onto the heavy metal lab table so hard it toppled the centrifuge at the other end. He was angry enough with Laurent to kill him. At the same time, he was so despondent over what had happened the previous day that he was ready to kill himself.

"This did *not* have to happen, Laurent!" he shouted. "That boy was a son to me. I took him off the streets. I raised him. He was a good boy, *my* boy. And then, just like that, gone? In an instant? And that poor girl as well? You and Meyer will burn in hell for this. We will all burn in hell for this. And we should."

Crestfallen over the death of Kishan and his young companion, Sehgal was numb from head to toe. His legs had grown so weak that they'd been buckling underneath him since he heard the miserable news the night before. He hadn't slept. It was as if the once-radiant life force that was Kishan had been ripped from him, leaving him with nothing left inside.

"Ravi, it was Meyer's idea, but we are not at fault for this. It was an accident, and you know it," Laurent said.

Sehgal's hands began to tremble. He knew no amount of explaining would relieve the nausea he felt or bring the body he had just identified in the morgue back to life.

"We only meant to counsel him, you know, scare him a little to shut him up," Laurent said.

Sehgal could tell Laurent was still trying to convince himself that what he'd said was true.

Laurent tried again. "Who could have known he would flee from us like such a fool?"

Sehgal reached for a pair of scissors to cut tape for the boxes they were packing. For a moment, he imagined plunging them directly into Laurent's heart, twisting them slowly. And once he found Meyer, he would be next. But he also knew the pain was his body telling him something: that he was as much to blame as they were. Looking back, he wished he could eat every regrettable word he had hurled at Kishan when he last saw him on the rooftop several months before.

"Say what you want, Laurent. I count myself guilty in this. We have killed two young innocents, and believe me, for that you burn in hell."

"Were we supposed to let him wander around with what he knew? We were not supposed to pursue him?"

"You could have left him alone."

"After we heard him crying out to Bondurant for help?" Laurent said. "And he sent him the documents. Who knows who else he told?"

Sehgal said nothing.

"It's terrible, I know," Laurent said. "I lost a son to an accident as well. But your boy had to be stopped before he brought the entire project to a halt. We are just a few weeks from glory. You said that yourself."

Laurent turned his attention to the scale he had packed into the large wooden crate. The lab they had set up in the warehouse eight months earlier was no longer needed. It required only another hour of dismantling before their work was complete.

"Besides, Ravi," Laurent said, "Meyer's men gathered DNA from Kishan's remains before the police arrived. We can bring him back, I promise you that."

Sehgal stopped loading the box of reagents he had gathered. He was in no mood to be placated.

"To raise him all over again, this time as an infant in diapers? I don't think so," he said. "It would be twelve years before Kishan was the boy I first knew." Sehgal's mind began to drift to the day he had found him, grinning, standing happily atop a trash heap with a single shoe for sale in his hand.

"That was not an issue for Jacqueline or me," Laurent said consolingly. "We lost our Philippe when he was just minutes old. Now he's almost two. You have never seen such a child."

"What would it cost for me to see Kishan again?" Sehgal asked.

"How do you put a price on bringing back your only child, Ravi? Does it matter? I lost count. When it was over we had performed over a thousand cell transfers before it worked. Millions and millions of dollars. The hurdles were enormous. But we learned some things along the way with my son that helped us immeasurably with your Christ child soon to be born."

"Yes, the Christ child," Sehgal mused. In all the chaos, he'd almost forgotten what his quest was all about. The prospect of bringing to life a young soul that had the power to alleviate the suffering of so many was the only bright spot left in his life. "What price for him?"

They both stopped their packing. Laurent looked at him.

"You told me yourself, Ravi. 'What price salvation for us all?' That's what you said. I will tell you this. It involved over two thousand attempts from the DNA you rescued. Believe me, the money from your famous prize would not come close to covering what this cost Meyer."

Just the sound of Meyer's name made Sehgal's stomach churn.

"It's ironic, isn't it?" Laurent said. "You perfect a way to resurrect old genes, and the world rewards you with fame. I perfect a way to resurrect Jesus Christ to save the world and am on the run. Figure that."

Laurent's cell phone rang in three short bursts. Sehgal hoped it was the call they were expecting. Laurent listened for several seconds and nodded his head.

"Thank you," he said. "I'll be right there."

Sehgal looked at him anxiously. If this was the moment, he had to return home first to gather his things.

"No. Your Domenika's not in labor yet, but she's feeling some discomfort," Laurent said as he placed his hands on Sehgal's shoulders. "Patience, Ravi. It won't be much longer."

Sehgal put down the scissors and considered the forgone promise of the son he had lost forever. His only consolation now was the prospect of another very special son, the one he had been destined to create.

CHAPTER 45

Bruges, Belgium
March 2015

By the time their train slowly meandered into Bruges, the most preserved and beautiful of all the medieval towns of Northern Europe, they were late. They had taken the earliest plane possible from Rome that morning and spent the flight carefully rehearsing the plan they had hatched the previous night. Bondurant, usually the optimist, had tried to fight the forlorn feeling that had swallowed him on the last leg of their journey. He had slept little the night before, as he turned over in his mind one alternative scheme after another. By dawn he had discarded them all. He decided that even though Parenti's plan sounded ridiculous, it was probably the only realistic chance they had to steal the sacred relic purported to carry the true blood of Jesus Christ.

They hurriedly made their way from the restroom off the train platform in Bruges Station toward Mariastraat, the road that led toward the city center and the Basilica of the Holy Blood. As they walked out into a brilliant, sunlit day, step one of their plan was complete. They had donned the priest's vestments Parenti had "borrowed" from the Vatican's central sacristy during their escape the night before. Their bright-blue robes bore the unmistakable crossed keys emblem of St. Peter, the coat of arms of the Holy See worn by only the most venerated. As they angled across the medieval city, they sped down narrow, tree-lined walkways and across a series of footbridges that arched like swans' necks over the picturesque canals. The city was the most charming and inviting of all the ancient canaled towns of Europe.

In the distance, almost a mile farther on, they could hear the din of the parade already under way, the famous Procession of the Holy Blood. Each year since 1291, in the spring, the reliquary the Church professed to contain a cloth soaked in the blood of Christ was removed from the basilica on Burg Square and paraded through the center of Bruges. Normally locked inside the cathedral's splendid silver tabernacle beneath a life-sized portrait of the crucified Christ, its appearance before the tens of thousands of pilgrims that lined the cobblestone streets was eagerly anticipated each year. The rock-crystal vial holding the bloodstained cloth was originally a Byzantine perfume bottle from the eleventh century. Its neck was threaded in gold and held a stopper sealed in wax. It had traveled from Constantinople during the twelfth century as a gift to the count of Flanders in recognition for his service during the Second Crusade. For protection, the bottle sat encapsulated inside a small gold cylinder sealed with end caps in the shape of angels. Traditionally held aloft by the bishop of Bruges along a nearly two-mile route, the parade itself was fantastical. More than a thousand residents of the city trailed behind the bishop on foot and on floats and dressed in character to portray scenes from the Bible or in medieval garb to reenact the delivery of the sacred relic to Bruges centuries before.

Bondurant figured they had about half an hour before the parade would end at the basilica where it had begun. By then it would be too late. Once the vial was returned to its tabernacle atop the ancient marble altar in the upper chapel, it would be under guard and impossible to reach. He could see that as valiantly as Parenti tried, his short, childlike steps would never allow them to make it to the parade in time. Bondurant reached down beside him and hoisted the surprised priest, as well as the dog who bounced along in his satchel. He doubled their pace and covered almost a mile relatively quickly. They rounded a corner in a full sprint and entered Philip-stockstraat, the main thoroughfare for the parade. There, they joined the carnivalesque procession a quarter-mile from where Bishop van de Basil led the joyful revelers. Bondurant wound his way through costumed troupes and dodged past floats of Noah's Ark, Moses and the Ten Commandments, and the parting of the Red Sea. Dressed in Vatican vestments as he was, Bondurant's own costume helped to part the sea of actors and police officers keeping order along the way. All who looked on mistook Bondurant and Parenti for part of the official party that belonged at the front of the parade. Bondurant worked his way to within yards of the bishop, who was surrounded by a group of altar boys dressed in bright red and white. Then he lifted Parenti from his shoulders and set him gently down onto the cobblestone street.

He was nervous about their next move, but they had no other plan.

"You are certain, absolutely certain the relic is real?" Bondurant shouted to Parenti over the roar of the revelers. "Otherwise, we are risking our freedom for nothing."

"Have you learned yet how to pray, my son?" Parenti asked. "If not, now would be the time."

Parenti reached inside the small satchel he carried with him and quickly slipped a small, razorlike object up his sleeve. In his other hand, he held a large white envelope in plain view. He strode forward with confidence and broke into the ring of altar boys encircling the bishop. He began to skip along beside the towering figure to keep up with his long stride. Bondurant followed along, just outside the circle.

"A word with you, if I may, Bishop van de Basil!" Parenti shouted.

The bishop, a bearded giant with the girth of a large oak tree, festooned in full ceremonial regalia and a miter headdress, was briefly startled. Walking alongside him during the sacred Procession of the Holy Blood was a position of prominence offered only by specific invitation of the Church. He looked dismissively at the tiny priest, like a cat deserving of a kick. Meanwhile, he kept his pace and held the sacred vial heavenward with both hands as the throng of onlookers applauded from both sides of the street.

"You are . . . ?" the bishop bellowed.

"I am Father Antonio Barsanti, and I have a message for you, sir." Parenti displayed the sternest look he could muster.

Bondurant cringed at the pronouncement.

"Yes, and I am His Eminence Hans van de Basil, the Bishop of Bruges. I carry the blood of Jesus Christ. I must ask you to step aside," the bishop said, clearly annoyed.

Bondurant knew his cue.

"Hear me now!" Bondurant shouted in order to be heard among the musicians and revelers nearby. He stepped directly in front of the bishop and blocked his path. Then he spread his arms open wide to reveal the emblem of the Vatican in bright white and gold, a symbol worn on the vestments of few. "We are here under charge by Pope Augustine, and we will be heard!"

The bishop looked shocked and stopped dead in his tracks. With that, a massive chain reaction rippled through the entire mile-long procession behind them. Dozens of wheeled floats, marching bands, and over a thousand surprised actors were brought to an unexpected halt. An eerie silence fell over the crowd that surrounded the leading edge of the parade.

"Speak!" the bishop thundered so the entire crowd could hear.

"I bear a letter from his most Holy Father on this solemn and joyous occasion of the Procession of the Holy Blood," Parenti cried out. He glanced over at Bondurant as if to summon more courage. "It demands your consideration before this austere occasion is brought to a close." He held forth the large, ornate envelope.

The bishop looked surprised and impressed. "Shall I take the letter, Father Barsanti?" he asked.

"You shall. And for the moment, I should relieve you of the burden you have carried all morning." With that, the priest reached presumptuously out for the sacred vial to force an exchange for the papal message. The bishop was reluctant to make the momentary trade, but spying the gold seal of the pontiff clearly emblazoned across the envelope, he lowered his massive arms and placed the ancient vial delicately in Parenti's hand.

"Mind him," the bishop said as he glanced toward several of the taller altar boys. He carefully opened the envelope and pulled the tab gently away from the wax seal as though to preserve it for posterity.

Bondurant, having held his breath now for almost a minute, looked about them and marveled at the complete stillness of the enormous crowd transfixed by their every move. Then he watched as the priest's tiny hands receded slowly into his vestments and took the vial briefly from view while the bishop got his first full glance at the Papal letter.

The bishop read fragments of the communiqué aloud while Parenti fidgeted with the vial up his sleeve.

". . . It was with great anticipation . . . our yearlong search . . . your efforts in Belgium . . . am pleased to invite you to the Holy City . . . in service of His Name . . . The Holy Father, Augustine III."

A broad smile emerged through the bishop's thick, red beard, wide enough to put a smile on Parenti's face as well. He reached down for the little priest, lifted him off his feet like a doll and embraced him in a joyous bear hug. Bondurant thought he might squeeze the life from both Parenti and the tiny dog in his pocket. As he set Parenti down, the bishop threw his hands heavenward and proclaimed to the curious crowd: "By invitation of the Holy Father, I am called to Rome!"

The throng that surrounded them, clearly confused but happy to be caught up in the joyous moment, broke into a loud cheer at the bishop's good fortune and began to rush to his side. Parenti extended his hand once again toward the bishop, this time ready to return the sacred vial. He stepped forward and delivered it.

"Godspeed and peace be with you, Your Eminence," he said as he stepped aside and left the path clear for the bishop to continue the last few steps of the joyous procession.

Parenti worked his way outside the throng of altar boys and onlookers who congratulated the bishop and made his way toward Bondurant. As the bishop stepped forward and the parade resumed, Bondurant and Parenti drifted through the jubilant crowd as inconspicuously as possible and onto a side street that led away from the revelers. When they turned the first corner and were clearly out of sight of the celebration, they ducked into a small alley on the edge of a canal.

Parenti was effusive. "We had better lose these vestments," he said gleefully as he shed his and tossed them into the waters of the canal below. "That pompous bear. To think that the Vatican would summon *him*."

He carefully passed on the small piece of the bloodstained cloth he had taken from the vial. Bondurant could see Parenti had cut off but a tiny fragment of the ancient cloth and had left most of the original relic intact for the bishop and Church to keep. Parenti pressed it into Bondurant's palm and looked at him in deadly earnest.

"You hold a miracle. It possesses the blood of Jesus Christ, my son," he said. "Now run. Run like the devil."

CHAPTER 46

Mumbai, India
March 2015

Out of the corner of his eye, Sehgal saw Bondurant coming at him, but it was too late. Bondurant's flying tackle caught him off balance and knocked him to the driveway before he could make it to his car. The tip Bondurant had received from his old cabbie friend as to where Sehgal, his country's famous hero, lived was solid. For another thousand extra rupees, his cabbie had even driven him to the spot where Sehgal could be found at home. Sehgal's shoulder hurt from hitting the ground hard, but no one, including Bondurant, was going to stop him from witnessing what in just a few hours would be the second coming and the dawn of a new world.

His adrenaline pumping, he scrambled quickly to his feet away from Bondurant and made a run for it in the hope that he could lose him on the canyon trail just steps from his home. From there, he would figure out a way to make it to the convent of the Sisters of Mercy to witness the birth of the Christ child.

Sehgal wasn't thinking clearly. A few hundred yards down the footpath, with Bondurant in a full sprint only steps behind, he had begun to tire. Another diving leap by Bondurant when they came to a sharp turn in the trail sent the two of them tumbling down a steep ravine. Locked in each other's grasp, they somersaulted down a steep hillside together like a human boulder. Sehgal gripped Bondurant's jacket collar in both hands as he watched the sky and then the ground circle past his field of view over and over again. The journey downward was filled with countless painful rocks and branches. When they finally reached the bottom of the gorge a quarter mile below the spot where Bondurant had tackled Sehgal, they slammed to a stop in the dry creek bed and fell apart from each other, like a stone broken in two. They lay several feet apart, completely spent, and stared blankly at each other.

"You're a liar, Ravi!" Bondurant cried out.

Sehgal could see a trace of blood on the side of Bondurant's mouth. Otherwise, he looked to be in one piece. The same was not true for Sehgal. "If you're talking about my report on the Shroud, my friend," Sehgal said, holding on to his leg, which he feared was broken, "I won't deny it. I'm sorry. There was no helping it."

"Yes, there was, you liar," Bondurant fumed. He reached for a large rock to throw at Sehgal, but it was obvious he was too tired to lift it from his prone position. "You're a scientist. You've an obligation to seek the truth."

"Jon, I swear I meant no harm," Sehgal said. He could tell the fracture in his leg was severe, and the sharp pain in his side meant he had probably broken some ribs as well. "I needed to create a distraction. And you were prepared to believe the relic was a fake from the start. I gave you what you wanted to hear anyway."

He pushed himself up with his arms to rest his back against a log and tried to breathe deep to ease the pain. He sat across from Bondurant, who struggled to sit upright himself.

"No you don't. Don't put this on me," Bondurant objected. "I was willing to go where the evidence led. You obviously agreed to join the project because it's the blood you wanted all along. And now you've got some insane idea to . . . to . . ."

"To what, Jon? To what?"

"To raise Christ from the dead. You and that madman, Meyer."

Sehgal was afraid Bondurant had pieced together more of the puzzle than he'd suspected. He thought for a moment, rested his head against the log behind him, and stared upward toward the cloudless sky. He was angry at the spot he was in, but he felt sorry for himself as well. *He* was doing the world the magnificent service of a second coming, one that someone like Bondurant, a nonbeliever, would never be able to understand. *He* was the one who had lost his only son just weeks before. *He* was the one who had to contend with Bondurant, a self-righteous hero now clearly in the way. He decided to try to reason with Bondurant.

"What is so insane about wanting the living Christ among us once again, Jon? Have you looked around you lately? Have you seen the spiral of misery taking all of us with it? I have. And I vowed to use my gifts to do something about it."

"Ravi," Bondurant said with a scowl, "spare me. I find it hard to imagine that you actually believe it's possible to reconstitute a life lived two thousand years ago so that this same man can somehow change the world today. It's ridiculous."

"You say ridiculous," Sehgal said, shaking his head. "I say miraculous. God himself condoned human cloning in the Bible."

"You're losing it. You must have hit your head on the way down this hill," Bondurant said.

"Eve from Adam's rib. It's right there in Genesis."

"Oh, come on. Who are you kidding?"

"Who are *we* kidding?" Sehgal said. "You've been an atheist your entire life, Jon. Me? I was saved by Christ's hands before you were born. So let's agree to disagree, shall we? We're only copying what nature's already produced."

"Tell me this," Bondurant said. "Tell me you and Laurent hit a wall trying to do this. I stopped the thug you sent in Turin who was after more of the blood. Tell me you didn't have enough. Tell me I'm not too late."

Sehgal clenched his teeth from the pain that streaked through his leg as he tried to move it, but then he managed to break into a glorious smile.

"It's done, Jon. *It's done,"* he exalted. "It turned out I had all the blood I needed from the sample I took with me. It's just a matter of hours before the Christ child arrives. I was on my way to the birth. That's where I was headed before you jumped me."

Sehgal watched Bondurant grimace at the news and close his eyes.

"One lie brings another, Ravi," Bondurant said as he rubbed his shoulder. "Maybe you were able to reconstitute the DNA from the blood you had. That's what you do. But Laurent? He's—"

"You're right, he's no genius," Sehgal interrupted. "But he didn't have to be. It turns out it's just about numbers. Big numbers. The DNA, a batch of stem cells to get it going, a lot of enucleated eggs, and a lot of tries. And these Demanians, God bless them, were happy to oblige with the virgins and the eggs. I'm convinced they're led by the devil, but they have done the world a divine service."

"And this miracle child is to be born where? Where's the manger?" Bondurant asked.

"Not far from here. In a convent close by," Sehgal said as he tried to get up and hobble on one leg. It was no use, and he sat back down, unable to take the pain. "I can take you there if you will help me out of here. Obviously I am not going to make it out by myself." He had no intention of leading Bondurant to the birth, but he would promise anything to avoid dying in a canyon alone.

"And the mother?" Bondurant said with suspicion. "Who won the role of the Virgin Mary?" he said. The sarcasm in his voice grew thick.

Sehgal shifted uncomfortably against the log and avoided Bondurant's gaze. He could tell from the question that Bondurant had probably put the pieces together. There was a long silence as he considered how to respond. He reached deliberately into his jacket pocket for the object inside, ready to produce it if necessary.

"The mother?" Bondurant asked again.

Sehgal remained defiantly silent and refused to respond. He *knew* she had never fully consummated her relationship with Jon, as she believed. The evidence was there during the in vitro procedure. He turned away from Bondurant altogether.

"Ravi," Bondurant said. "If you want out of this canyon, then—"

Bondurant stopped midsentence, and a pall fell slowly over his face. Sehgal had extracted his gleaming pistol and was pointing it directly at him.

"I originally bought this for protection, wondering if I'd need it," Sehgal said. "Today I just might."

"Protection from what?" Bondurant said.

"From the likes of you, were you to find out," Sehgal said. He paused to gather his courage for what he would say next. "The first thing I want you to know is that she is fine."

"Who? The mother?"

"Yes, the mother." He gripped the pistol. "Domenika."

Anticipating that Bondurant's rage might give him the strength to charge, Sehgal placed his finger on the trigger, stretched both arms outward, and aimed the gun directly at Bondurant's chest. He didn't want to miss. But there was no need. Bondurant slumped against the rock behind him and stared blankly forward. A look of disappointment spread across his face.

"You're telling me Domenika is the mother. Is that what I heard?" Bondurant asked, expecting confirmation of the worst.

"You know her, Jon. Can you imagine finding someone more devout? She was perfect in every way. She knew it."

"She *volunteered* for this?" Bondurant asked. "She's been part of this all along?"

"Yes, of course," Sehgal said. "We tried dozens of virgins before her. None of them conceived."

Bondurant looked stricken.

"I have spent almost a year worried sick and combing the world for her. And she's been hiding here with *you*?" he yelled. "For what? To play the mother of *God*?" Bondurant began to tremble visibly at the reality of the notion that once had been only a wild suspicion. "Who else is in on this?"

"Jon, you have to understand. We needed a virgin. But also a truly devout one. You see—"

"No, *you* don't understand, Ravi. You, Meyer, Laurent, Domenika. You're all insane. Just insane. Did you ever stop to think that there is no proof the DNA you've resurrected is from the blood of Jesus Christ?"

Sehgal let out a sickening laugh. "Oh, I see, Jon. Now *you* are going to tell *me* it's from the blood of a goat. And we are back to where we started."

"No, Ravi, you fool," Bondurant said as he shook his head. "I am telling you there were at least *two* sources of blood on that Shroud. And that your miracle child, whoever it may be, stems from only one."

The claim was preposterous, but it shook Sehgal. He grew quiet and pointed the barrel of the gun squarely at Bondurant's head.

"Now you are the liar, Jon," he said, angry enough to fire.

"I wish I were, Ravi. The other blood sample, the one I held back from you for O'Neil. You remember that one, don't you?"

"Yes. It was for his tests. But he's long destroyed it by now for carbon dating."

"Not exactly."

"What do you mean, 'not exactly'?"

"I mean he can lie as well as you. It turns out he never needed it. He just didn't trust you. He used it to run DNA tests of his own later on. And, Ravi," Bondurant said as he stared intently at the gun barrel pointed directly at his face, "if these are my last words, they are ones you can believe. I have the DNA profile from your sample, and—"

"I know that," Sehgal said. He winced as an image of Kishan's broken body lying in the morgue came to mind.

"And I have O'Neil's."

"Yes?"

"And there is *not* a match. Did you hear me? Not a match. You won the Nobel. I know you're smart enough to understand what that means, Ravi."

Sehgal's face began to contort slightly from confusion. He lowered the gun to his side. The moment he did, Bondurant's cell phone vibrated twice, signaling a text had arrived. Bondurant pulled the phone from his pocket and stared down at the message. He shook his head slowly and tossed the phone to Sehgal to read it for himself:

JON: TESTS CONCLUDED. PERFECT MATCH. OUR SAMPLE IDENTICAL TO WHAT YOU'VE "BORROWED" FROM BRUGES. CONGRATULATIONS. YOU ARE THE PROUD OWNER OF THE TRUE BLOOD OF JESUS CHRIST. RAVI IS PLAYING WITH FIRE. FATHER, FORGIVE HIM, HE KNOWS NOT WHAT HE CLONES. ☺

Sehgal read the message several times. A feeling of dread crept over him. Soon he was paralyzed with fear.

"What did you 'borrow' in Bruges, Jon?" Sehgal asked.

"It's a long story, Ravi. But when one of the world's biggest religious skeptics—that's me—tells you he's held the blood of someone known as Jesus Christ, then believe me, he's held the blood of Jesus Christ. And Ravi, *now we know that you have not*."

"Jon, I don't know what to say," was all the despondent Sehgal could choke out.

The two of them sat quietly as Sehgal was left to the horror of his private thoughts and what he'd done. After a while, he began to shudder. He'd made a terrible mistake.

"Ravi, where is Domenika?" Bondurant demanded. "Exactly where is she giving birth?"

"Domenika? She's very close," he responded, distracted. His voice began to trail off from despair. He had no doubt that once the child was born, she'd be considered useless. Worse, she would know too much, just like the Sisters of Mercy in the convent, who would be disposed of. "Knowing Meyer, she's in real danger. I'm sure it's the child he wants, not her."

"Okay, then. No more lies, Ravi. No more secrets. What have you done with her?" Bondurant demanded.

Sehgal's guilt was overwhelming. For the lies he'd told. For the death of his son. For what he'd done to Domenika and the danger she now faced. And, finally, for the fate of the unknown soul of the Shroud about to be reborn.

"She's at the convent of the Sisters of Mercy, only a mile from here."

Sehgal paused for a long time. He couldn't look up. He was completely overcome with shame and guilt.

"She's innocent, Jon. We coaxed her here. We tricked her. We drugged her." Sehgal began to weep. "God forgive me, we raped her by in vitro. From the start, she's believed the child was her own by another man. We let her believe it all along." Sehgal covered his eyes with his hand.

Bondurant got to his feet and stood as motionless as a statue before Sehgal. "There's a place in hell for you. You know that, don't you, Ravi?" Bondurant said.

Sehgal opened his mouth to answer, but he was speechless. Bondurant watched as Sehgal struggled to respond several times but couldn't, as if the breeze that had begun to blow through the canyon had stolen his words away. Then suddenly, Bondurant watched as Sehgal sat upright and raised the gun again. In one quick motion, he inserted the barrel in his mouth, leaned his head back, and pulled the trigger. A single, loud shot rang out and killed him instantly.

CHAPTER 47

Outside Mumbai
March 2015

Bondurant peered from behind the tall hedge at the rear of the convent in the faint light of dusk, waiting impatiently for the dark of night to fall.

He'd stolen Sehgal's car from his driveway and parked it a hundred yards down the dirt service road, just out of sight of the sanctuary. Only darkness would give him the cover necessary to cross the thirty yards that separated him from the two-story structure where he hoped he'd find Domenika alive. A small motorcade of dark Mercedes 4x4s were parked bumper to bumper next to the convent, and just behind them was a pickup truck, last in line.

A wave of nausea had nearly overcome Bondurant as he crouched behind the hedge to look out. From his vantage point, he counted five black body bags zippered shut and stacked like logs along the length of the truck. Two tall men hoisted a sixth bag over the open tailgate and into the bed of the pickup. The guards were dressed all in black and had automatic weapons slung over their shoulders.

Inside, the convent was almost totally dark except for one window on the ground floor where a light was on. Bondurant could make out the profiles of two men sitting opposite each other at a table. He couldn't hear them but could see they were animated, as if in a heated argument. On the table between them, Bondurant could see a shotgun and what looked like a radio-sized box that one of the men continually adjusted. Standing guard beside the two men was another tall man who looked to be as well armed as the two who were loading bodies into the truck.

Bondurant knew that if he could make it into the convent undetected and find Domenika inside, only half his work would be done. Their chances of escape would increase dramatically if he could take a chase, whether by car or foot, out of the equation. He had to. He was alone, vastly outmatched and outgunned, and the body bags were a sure sign they were going to die if he failed. Armed with only the bloodstained handgun he'd pried from Sehgal's fingers an hour earlier and a long carving knife he'd grabbed from Sehgal's kitchen, Bondurant knew time was running out for him to make his move inside.

His plan was to sabotage the convoy in the driveway to prevent pursuit should he get away with Domenika alive. The motorcade was parked between a tall driveway wall and the convent. The line of cars could be rendered useless if he could somehow disable the lead car. He made his way on his hands and knees through thick brush along the hedgerow and ducked behind the wall that ran the length of the convent's driveway. He crawled along its length to the point where the lead car was and slowly raised his head to look over the wall. The guards he'd been watching before had moved back inside, and the driveway was deserted. If he could move quickly enough, it would be only a matter of getting under the hood of the lead car. Once there, he could reach the engine's critical distributor wire and disable it by slicing it in two.

He climbed over the wall and hoped he'd find the car unlocked. He knew the latch for the hood could be reached only from the inside. He slowly pulled the handle of the driver's side door and breathed a sigh of relief when it popped open.

As he swung the door halfway open and leaned in toward the floorboard to find the hood latch, his heart nearly stopped. He heard breathing. A major problem sat in the passenger seat a foot away. Another guard, a huge man with a set of double chins that seemed to form a pillow on his chest, was sound asleep beside him.

Bondurant knew there was no turning back. He slowly slipped the kitchen knife from his jacket pocket and held it firmly in his right hand. He positioned the tip of the knife blade only a few inches from the guard's throat, and with his left hand reached down to feel for the hood latch he sought. If the sound of the lever popping were to wake the guard, he was ready to drive the long steel blade through the man's trachea before he could let out a scream. Bondurant paused for a moment to look at the guard's eyes, still completely closed. Then he pulled on the latch as slowly as he could, hoping to dampen its sound. As he did, a *pop* that sprang the hood open echoed through the interior of the car. To Bondurant the sound seemed like a clap of thunder, loud enough to wake the guard as well as the neighbors next door. Bondurant had no choice. He quickly turned and placed both his hands on the knife handle, aimed the knife at the guard's throat, and prepared to plunge the blade as deep as he could.

The guard stirred, turned slowly on his side toward Bondurant, and started to open his eyes. Bondurant reared back and prepared to thrust every ounce of his body weight behind the knife and into the guard's gullet. He thought the blade would be just barely long enough to pin the man's massive head to the leather headrest behind him. But just as quickly as the guard's eyes had blinked momentarily open, they closed again. Bondurant held his breath for what seemed an eternity and waited for the guard to wake once more. The next sound Bondurant heard from the man was a welcome one—the beginning of a low, guttural snore.

Bondurant's heart was racing. He quietly slid from the front seat of the car out the driver's side door, leaving it slightly ajar, and worked his way to the front of the car. He delicately lifted the hood halfway open and strained his eyes to find the motor's distributor in the dark. It was no use. The engine compartment was shrouded in darkness, and, without a source of light, he hadn't a clue where the essential wire was. He quickly reached inside the compartment and frantically sliced as many wires as he could find, hoping to cut something vital enough to stop the car from starting. Then he turned, scrambled back over the wall, and retraced his steps toward the hedgerow where he'd begun.

Looking over, Bondurant could see a set of three lower-floor windows on the opposite end of the convent, one of them barely illuminated. The middle window was brightly lit and cast a small amount of light into each of the adjoining rooms. Now that he felt confident he'd likely disabled the convoy, he bolted from the hedgerow across the lawn and made his way to the wall with the dimly lit windows. As he looked in, he could see the light was from a bathroom in the middle with no one inside. Next door to it was a room lit by an object that glowed eerily in the dark. It radiated a faint orange hue. He knew what it was: an incubator with a tiny infant inside. Wrapped tightly in a newborn's blanket, the infant didn't stir. Alongside the incubator were several monitoring devices blinking on a rack, and in the corner of the room, Bondurant caught the outline of someone in the dark who sat in a rocking chair pointed toward the incubator. Bondurant leaned in more closely and realized he'd found another guard asleep on the job. This guard too seemed as wide as a wall. Bondurant pressed his hands against the brick and moved slowly away from the window to ensure he was out of sight. Then he gazed once more at the peaceful child, sure that he stared at the newborn, identity unknown, but remarkably cloned from the Shroud.

He had no time to waste. If Domenika was still alive, he knew she'd be very near. He quietly slid toward the window of the room on the other side of the bathroom and fixed his eyes on the dark space inside. There was just a trace amount of light, and as his eyes further adjusted to the dark, Bondurant could see the faint outline of a bed next to a large bay window on the opposite wall. A body lay on top of the bed. He couldn't tell if it was dead or alive.

He squinted and searched the window frame and glass for any sign of wires or magnets tied to an alarm. He saw none, and tried to pry the window open. It wouldn't budge. It was locked. But the window was old, and he could see the brass hook on the center of the sill needed only a nudge to pull it from its ringlet fastener. He inserted his knife blade between the sill and the frame and craned his neck so he could guide the tip of the blade against the hook. He turned the blade into position, and with a slight twist on the handle, the hook broke free.

He slid open the tall window and slowly stepped one leg through the opening. Then he straddled the sill and twisted the rest of his body into the room. He stood as still as a statue in the dark for almost a minute so his eyes could adjust to the light. He listened for the sound of anyone who might have detected him. He heard nothing. He walked over to the door and pushed the button on the knob to lock it. Beside the door was a heavy chair, one he quietly propped against the doorknob. Then he made his way across the room to the bed.

A woman was lying motionless, facedown. He was not sure yet whether it was Domenika. Bondurant grabbed a pillow from the bed and held it in his right hand. Whether it was Domenika or not, there was going to be a commotion if the woman was alive, and he needed to smother the sound. He reached down and gently grasped the woman's shoulder to turn her. As she turned over and he caught a glimpse of her face in the dark, he knew instantly it was Domenika. As she began to stir, he instinctively leaned in to kiss her.

Her eyes grew large, and she started to scream. Bondurant jammed the corner of the pillow into her mouth and smothered what little sound she could make.

"Domenika, don't say a word," Bondurant whispered. Her eyes grew wider as she pushed against the pillow. He could tell she thought she might suffocate. "I will remove this if you promise on your life to keep quiet. Will you do that for me?"

She shook her head no.

He pressed the pillow even more firmly against her mouth to signal how serious he was.

"I mean it, Domenika," he said. "We are both going to die if you scream."

She eventually nodded her head, and he slowly pulled the pillow back, uncertain whether she would keep the promise. Then she pushed herself into a sitting position and stared at him silently as though she were looking at a ghost.

"What's happened to you? Where have you been all this time?" she whispered. "Why didn't you answer my letters?"

"Letters? What letters?" Bondurant asked.

"And where is Christopher?" she said as she looked around in a panic. Her voice grew louder as she looked around them and flattened her back against the headboard. "Where is our son?"

Bondurant, completely taken aback by her first words to him in almost a year, recoiled. She wasn't making sense. He realized she hadn't fully regained her senses.

"What do you mean, *our* son?" he asked. He remembered Sehgal's last words and was trying to sort out the truth. "Domenika, did you willingly have this child?"

"Of course I did," she said, weak but exasperated. "We should have been more careful in Turin, I know. But he is ours now, and, Jon, you have never seen such a child."

"And you're certain *I'm* the father?" he asked.

Her reaction to his words was immediate. She swung her arm in a wide arc and slapped his face with enough force to nearly knock him off the bed. The stinging in his cheek had just begun to sink in when she reared back to strike him once more. He reached out and stopped her arm midswing.

"How dare you say something like that? It doesn't matter whether you want any part of him or not, he's ours. How dare you?" she cried out loud enough to give them away.

She struggled to free her arms from his grip to strike him again. He could tell by the look in her eyes and her growing outrage that she was absolutely convinced what she'd said was the truth. He also knew that if he didn't escape with her in the next few seconds, both of them would be dead.

"There's no time to argue," Bondurant said. "And it's too hard to explain. But the child is not ours. You've been tricked into bearing it. And if we don't get out of here now, we'll both die."

"I'm not leaving here without our baby," she cried out.

"I said, it's not ours," Bondurant insisted.

He grabbed her by the arms and yanked her from the bed. He heard a commotion starting several rooms away and knew they'd been discovered. As they struggled, her right arm broke free, and she swung her fist. She punched him squarely in the middle of his face. A bolt of pain shot toward both his temples, and he was certain she'd broken his nose.

Time had run out. He heard voices and footsteps rush down the hallway toward them. He had no choice if they were going to get out alive.

"Domenika, I love you," he said. Then, with one swift blow from his fist to the side of her head, he knocked her unconscious. He heaved her limp body over his shoulder and looked wildly about them for the best way out. The last sound he heard in the room was a deafening pounding as her captors struggled to get past the barricaded door. He leaned over with Domenika slung across his back and ran at full tilt toward the large bay glass window beside the bed. Then he ducked his head and burst through it at full speed, smashing it into a thousand pieces.

He was bloodied from head to toe, but still standing. He knew he needed to reach the hedgerow for cover, and beyond that it would be an all-out footrace to his car. But with his adrenaline now in full rush, he hesitated briefly, then turned back toward the convent and the first window he'd spied. He *had* to do it. He knew he'd never get this close to the child clone again, and he had no choice but to try to rescue it as well. Without hesitation, but with great fear for what waited inside, he kicked out the window of the nursery with two swift blows and shattered its glass across the room. Only a gaping hole lay between him and the incubator inside.

He struggled to draw his gun from his pocket with his left hand while his right hand clutched Domenika, draped from his shoulder on the other side. Miraculously, the infant still lay sound asleep in the incubator, and the giant of a man who once sat there to guard it was gone. Bondurant pressed his way through the shattered panes of the window and painfully gashed his side on the way in. He could see that Domenika had cuts of her own as small trickles of blood made their way from her exposed legs to drip on the floor below.

He was in, but the recognition of his next big problem came fast. He had only two hands, when it was clear he needed three. The only way to grasp the infant in such a rush was to either lose the gun, which was his ultimate protection, or Domenika, whom he could not leave behind. He lost precious time as he clumsily shoved the pistol back into his jacket only to lose it as it fell to the darkness of the floor below. Bondurant could hear that his pursuers, plenty of them, had smashed their way through Domenika's bedroom next door. He knew the nursery was next. He quickly flipped the cover from the incubator, grabbed the tightly wrapped infant, and cradled it like a football in the crook of his arm. Then he started to run.

Before he could make it cleanly back out the window, a piercing pain the likes of which he had never felt before shot through his shoulder, causing his entire body to shudder from the force of the thrust.

"No," a deep voice boomed forth in the darkness. "Give me the boy. Then I cut you to pieces."

Bondurant turned toward his attacker and could see behind him the towering behemoth who had once sat asleep in the rocker behind them. From the corner of his eye, he could also see the wooden handle of what he was sure was a large bowie knife, its blade buried deep in his side.

Bondurant cried out from the incredible pain that felt like a bolt of lightning had shot through him. With no sense of feeling in one arm, he dropped the baby to the floor.

"Yes, Jesus Christ. That's what *they* say," the giant man said. "This, I don't know." Inches before the clone child hit the ground, the assailant's massive hand, one that looked larger than the child itself, scooped the baby up. "I think we keep the girl too, hmmm?" he said as he started to tug at Domenika's leg.

As the behemoth stepped back slowly to claim his prize and set the child back into its incubator crib, Bondurant slumped against the window's ledge. While his heart raced, his body barely had the will. He saw but one way out. He used all the energy he had left to retrieve the long blade sunk through his shoulder, halfway into his chest. In one great heave, he slowly and painfully pulled the bloody knife from his body, inch by inch, until a thick and shiny blade eight inches long emerged. Then, as the attacker's back was turned, Bondurant raised his good arm high and planted the blade squarely in his enemy's back. The blade went only halfway in, as though it had plowed into stone. Bondurant heard a resultant roar, as if he had only temporarily angered a bear.

He had no time. His pursuer grunted and swung his giant arms around his back in order to reach and extract the blade. Bondurant knew if he were to escape with Domenika alive, he had to leave with only her. With his one good shoulder, he pressed his way through the window just in time to miss the onrush of more guards, who crushed their way into the room like linebackers on a blitz. Once outside, Bondurant never looked back.

He limped across the lawn and made it to the service road before his pursuers got through the door at the other end of the convent and got a fix on his direction. By then, Bondurant had reached Sehgal's car, hit the gas, and sped down the road.

CHAPTER 48

Rome, Italy
April 2015

The first thing Domenika saw when she woke up was Bondurant. He was leaning over her hospital bed, staring directly at her. He could tell she had no idea where she was or why she felt so drugged. He watched her as she struggled to focus, trying desperately to regain full consciousness. Bondurant, exhausted from his vigil at her bedside, waited anxiously for the powerful sedative to wear off. It had been a long journey from Mumbai to the papal suite in Rome's Gemelli Hospital. The doctor aboard the chartered jet had kept Domenika heavily sedated. She had been unconscious for nearly twenty-four hours.

Bondurant smiled at her and stroked the bandaged side of her head where he had struck her. Both of his eyes were slightly blackened from the punch he taken from her in the nose. His left hand, both arms, and his right side were bandaged from the cuts and stabs he'd received during their escape.

"You hit me," Domenika said quizzically.

"You hit me first," Bondurant said. He smiled and pointed to his raccoonlike eyes. He could tell from her voice that her throat was parched. He poured a glass of water from the pitcher and handed it to her. She gulped down a few mouthfuls, watching him warily.

"You *really* hit me," she said as she rubbed the side of her head and tried to sit up. He knew she had no idea where she was.

"Domenika, I want you to listen to me. The doctor said you will feel weak and a little confused for a few hours until the medication wears off. There is a lot to say, but I need you to trust me. What I'm about to tell you requires suspension of disbelief. And it's going to be difficult to accept. Do you feel clearheaded enough to proceed?"

"Yes, I think so," she said. She was still disoriented, but he could see that her eyes had started to focus. "Where am I?"

"Rome," Bondurant said. "Our friend Father Parenti was able to get to the pope when I reached him from Mumbai. He told them our story. It's the Vatican that brought us here."

"The pope? Why on earth? I'm in Rome?" She held her head in both hands as she struggled to comprehend his words. Then her eyes widened.

"Christopher! Where is he? Tell me he's here. Tell me we haven't lost him. Jon, I don't know where he is in this hospital, but go get him."

Bondurant cringed. He knew he had to answer her, and he had prepared for this moment. But he also knew the story would devastate her and rob her of everything she held dear. But he had no choice. He took both of her hands in his and leaned forward, locking his eyes with hers.

"He's safe," he said, hoping it was true. "I have spent the last year of my life searching for you and for the true source of blood on the Shroud. Your instincts were right—we should have listened to you from the start. Sehgal was lying about the Shroud. O'Neil and Father Parenti helped uncover the truth. We discovered there were *two* different sources of DNA from human blood to be found on the Shroud. No one had any idea that Sehgal was working with the Demanians in a crazed attempt to bring about a second coming of Christ. He deceived us all."

Domenika interrupted. "Jon, please stop," she said.

Bondurant watched as she tried to raise herself from the bed in order to get up and find the child on her own if necessary. "These are interesting stories, but I want our son."

More than a half dozen wires and tubes connected her body to machines around her, putting a stop to any search.

"What can you remember happened when you arrived in India?" Bondurant asked.

"Ravi begged me to come. He said it was all a mistake. That there was a problem with the results in his lab and he would fix it. I had no choice but to pursue it," she said.

Bondurant shook his head.

"Domenika, what could possibly have possessed you to stay there with him? I understand you had to know, but why did you remain with him?"

"I went to his home. He said an assistant had made a mistake in the tests. He told me he would correct it. We had tea, and then I'm told I fainted. The next thing I knew, I was with the Sisters of Mercy in their convent. I was told I fainted because I was pregnant. Now, Jon, please, if you love me, you will bring me our baby."

The pieces of the puzzle quickly began to take shape for

Bondurant. He now understood what Sehgal had told him with his dying words.

"Domenika, you didn't faint. You were drugged," he said. "Sehgal told me so himself. You became pregnant very soon after, but—"

"But what?" Domenika said.

"But the child wasn't ours. It couldn't be."

"Jon, what are you saying? Of course he's ours. You're the only one I— He is yours."

Bondurant closed his eyes.

"Domenika, as much as I wanted to make love to you that night, I couldn't bring myself to do it," he said. "I was not going to let it happen that way, not with you in that condition. I didn't want either of us to have regrets. I'm so sorry, but I'm absolutely certain you did not conceive that night."

Domenika looked at Bondurant in complete disbelief. She let go of his hands and said nothing for several minutes. She only stared blankly at the white hospital wall. Then she pulled her knees to her chest and wrapped the sheet around her body as if to protect herself. Bondurant was alarmed at how pale her face had become.

"Are you saying I became pregnant because I was raped as I slept?" she said as she shook her head over and over. "That I carried someone *else's* child?"

Bondurant watched as her entire body trembled. He was filled with anguish. "Not just any child. From what Sehgal confessed to me, you bore the child of the Shroud." He looked down, unable to look at her face.

Domenika's body instinctively began to convulse, and she looked as though she were going to vomit. But she was so weak and dehydrated that she only dry-heaved into her pillow, the spasms wracking her body.

"And Ravi is dead?" she choked out.

"Yes. He shot himself. But not before he told me where I could find you."

"And my complications? They were a lie as well?" she asked. She buried her face in the pillow.

"What complications?"

"Jon, do you really think I would stay in India, a million miles from my family, from you, from everything I know, when I found I was pregnant?" she said. He was heartened by the sound of anger creeping into her voice. He could see by her eyes that she too had started to put the pieces of the puzzle together.

"Why didn't you reach out? I was desperate to find you," he said.

"I tried. But I was deceived twice. Twice," she said as her voice began to trail off. Bondurant could see she was totally exhausted.

"What do you mean?" he asked.

"When I woke in the convent, there were the Sisters of Mercy. They were wonderful and tended to me so kindly. Always hovering nearby was Ravi. And then, there was Dr. Laurence."

"Doctor who?"

"Dr. Lau—" She stopped herself. "Oh my God," she cried out. "It was him, wasn't it? By another name." Her eyes began to well with tears. Bondurant tried to take her hands again, but she pushed him away.

"Jon, I was confined to my bed. The doctor told me I couldn't move. Not an inch. He said I had placenta previa and that my baby's life depended on complete immobility," she said. "It's why I stayed until you took me away."

"But not a word from you, ever?" Bondurant said.

"It was a convent, Jon. It was like a trip back in time to the Middle

Ages. There were no phones, television, computer, radio, visitors, or contact with the outside world. Nothing. The only way that I could reach you was through my letters. And you never answered a single one. You never—" She stopped midsentence. "You never got them, did you?"

"I'd have been there in a minute," Bondurant said. He knew he couldn't begin to imagine the shock she felt and that it would be a long time before she came to terms with what she'd learned. He searched his heart for something—anything—he could tell her, but the only words that came out were those he felt he'd waited a lifetime to say: "I love you, Domenika."

She looked at him, pulled him toward her by his collar, and wept as he enveloped her in his arms. He held her like that for a long time.

Eventually, she seemed to have cried herself out. She sighed and sat up. She wiped her eyes. Then she turned to him and took his face in her hands, looked into his eyes, and said, "Jon, I am absolutely, hopelessly in love with you."

At that moment, the door to her room swung open, and someone carrying an enormous arrangement of roses stumbled in. The arrangement was so tall that they could see only the legs of the visitor behind the stems. Nearly losing his balance, but then finding his way to a bedside table, the gift-bearer set down the massive vase. Parenti peered out from behind the arrangement and could see they were in each other's arms.

"You see," he said to Bondurant. "Just as I told you. It's in all the American movies. You say 'I love you.' She kisses you. And that is that." He stepped out from behind the roses.

"Father, I haven't kissed him yet," Domenika said, now smiling for the first time. "Besides, I—" She stopped, and it was obvious she couldn't believe her eyes. "My God in heaven, you've been cured! You must be—"

"Five feet tall," Parenti said, beaming.

"It was a miracle," Bondurant said. "I was there to see it."

"Correction. You were there to help," Parenti said. He came over, stood erect before them, and hugged Domenika. She pulled him in close to her and held him tight like the old friend he was.

"Jon Bondurant believing in miracles?" she asked. "That's a miracle in itself." She held them in both her arms. "Tell me all about it. I don't ever want to let go."

"It's a long story, angel," Bondurant said. He smiled. He couldn't remember being more happy in his entire life. "But something incredible happened while you were gone, and it changed my life forever."

"Tell me, tell me," she demanded. "But, please, Jon. Where is my baby? Where is he?"

"It's a long flight to Baltimore," Bondurant said. "I can tell you on the way there. For now, you should get some rest."

Domenika began to cry again and kissed him. He could tell she felt safe in his arms. But he knew that until they could rescue the child and put him in her arms, life was going to be a living hell.

"Baltimore? I just love adventures," Parenti said. "Do I have time to pack my things?"

"We'll leave tomorrow," Bondurant said. "Do you bring any news?"

"Of course. I almost forgot," Parenti said. "We checked the convent, as you asked. It's deserted. The sisters have vanished. Meyer, Laurent, they're not to be found. And the child is missing as well."

"Jon," Domenika said as she squeezed his hand tight. A troubled look crossed her face. "My child is missing? Jon, I have to know whose child I carried. Whose child was born?"

Bondurant hesitated before he responded. He wished he had the answer himself. "I don't know. But I know one thing for sure," he said. "Its DNA was unique, possibly even supernatural. But it was *not* from the blood of Jesus Christ."

An uneasy look settled on Parenti's face. He turned from them as if to avoid the conversation.

"Father, do you know something we don't?" Domenika asked.

Parenti walked toward the door to leave but knew he'd have to answer her. He turned. "No, I don't," he said. He looked at them with worried eyes. "But I know that Jesus was not the only supernatural being in the Scriptures, and—God help us—not all of them were heavenly."

ACKNOWLEDGMENTS

I have several friends who have written outstanding books that have sat atop the bestseller lists for weeks. I've noticed that the acknowledgments pages for their books almost always begin with a thank-you to their readers, and on this score, I am no different. Thanks for buying *The Shroud Conspiracy*, my first novel.

I think it's a book worthy of your time. I want to thank Beth Adams, senior editor at Howard Books, for making it so. She had the foresight and the courage to pull my manuscript from a slush pile, dust it off, and work with me to improve it so that others might have the chance to believe in me as well. Great thanks also go to Scott Lamb, my agent. Scott, a calm in the storm, has done for me in three weeks what others could not accomplish in three years. He is a risk taker who gave life to this book. There were others who, early on, prodded, urged, nudged, cajoled, advised, and enticed me to start, continue, and finish the book. Heroes of mine like Peggy Noonan for near-daily inspiration; Dorothea Halliday for excellent and early editing; Laura Hillenbrand for free, sound advice early on; Giovanni Navarria for his many helpful reads; Mark Levin for his guidance and expertise; Scott Edwards for all his valuable time and marketing genius; Gary Sinise for not tiring of hearing of each bump along the way; Craig Engle for his sharp eye and keen mind; Melissa Giller for her help and expertise; Tom Kelso for his caring and interest; Carolyn Magner-Mason for her constant good counsel on every page from the very start; Mark Jaffe for his always-helpful ideas; Dana Perino for setting the bar and providing smart people to talk to; Jimmy Wilkinson for his encouragement; Craig Shirley for his insight and experience; Linda Bond for her interest and reassurance; and Christian Pinkston, my topflight publicist, for his invaluable efforts for so long. Some of the aforementioned refused to grant me sleep or food or drink until this novel was complete. Shame on them. I won't soon forget their kindness.

And, most certainly, I want to acknowledge that I write to support those whom I love. Some, in particular, have sacrificed as I've practiced my craft. Here, praise goes to the love of my life—my wife, Marcella. She lifts me up, as a writer and otherwise, like no other. Always has. Always will. With her support and that of my remarkable children—Brock, Max, and Jordana—*The Shroud Conspiracy* became a reality. I hope you enjoy reading it as much as I loved writing it.

ABOUT THE AUTHOR

In a career that has spanned philanthropy, politics, public service, and the Fortune 500, John Heubusch served as the first president of the Waitt Institute, a nonprofit research organization dedicated to historic discovery and scientific exploration.

In 2007, working with a team of scientists and underwater-exploration experts, he spearheaded the organization's first deep-sea expedition to solve one of the last great American mysteries: the disappearance of Amelia Earhart during her famed global circumnavigation flight in 1937. Since then, successive efforts to locate Earhart and her airplane have failed, and the mystery remains.

Working with the National Geographic Society, John's efforts at the Institute also helped lead to the discovery, authentication, and preservation of the famed lost Gospel of Judas, the ancient text deemed to be heretical and ordered destroyed by the early Christian Church. The Gospel purports to document the last conversations between Judas Iscariot and Jesus Christ, as well as the true rationale for history's most famous betrayal.

John's involvement at the Waitt Institute also helped lead to National Geographic's launching of the Genographic Project, the largest-ever effort of its kind to chart the migratory history of mankind using DNA donated by hundreds of thousands of people worldwide. The project is informing the world about our ancient migratory history.

Cited often by the *New York Times*, the *Washington Post*, and the *Los Angeles Times*, John has also been a contributing writer for the *New York Times*, the *Wall Street Journal*, *Investor's Business Daily*, *Forbes*, the *San Diego Union Tribune*, and other leading publications. Currently the executive director of the Ronald Reagan Presidential Foundation, he oversees the activities of the largest and most visited of the nation's presidential libraries. He resides in Los Angeles, California, with his wife and two children.